WINKIES,TOILETS
—————AND—————
HOLY PLACES

What others are saying about *Winkies, Toilets and Holy Places*:

Timothy Merrill's engaging style, wide-ranging knowledge, "Far-Side" insight and loose grip on his internal censor make this a travel-narrative extraordinaire. Plus, if you're thinking about taking a sabbatical that includes your family, Merrill's book will convince you it can be done in a way that deepens family ties while keeping everybody sane ... more or less.

> —Stan Purdum, author of *Run Around Heaven All Day* and *Playing in Traffic*, books which recount his journeys by bicycle across America, both east and west and north and south.

Creativity requires rest. For pastors, creativity demands a sabbatical, as Timothy Merrill illustrates so vividly in this story of a five-month journey from Colorado to Israel and back. With honesty, humor, and a wonderful ability to leap faithfully into the unknown, Merrill and his family embark on a journey that both broadens their vision and strengthens their family bond. I hope their sabbatical adventure inspires others to hit the road, relish a time of rest and refreshment, and then return home with renewed creativity.

> —Henry G. Brinton, senior pastor of Fairfax Presbyterian Church in Virginia, co-author of *Ten Commandments of Faith and Fitness: A Practical Guide for Health and Wellness,* and frequent contributor to the religion columns of *The Washington Post* and *USA Today.*

Sabbatical is supposed to be a holy time for pastors, but often that holiness comes in unexpected forms. Timothy Merrill's travelogue/reflection is a wonderful journey into the idea of the holy rest and, sometimes, holy chaos, that is part of a time away from regular ministry.

> —Bob Kaylor, Senior Pastor, Park City Community Church (UMC), Park City, Utah, and Senior Writer for the clergy resource journal, *Homiletics.*

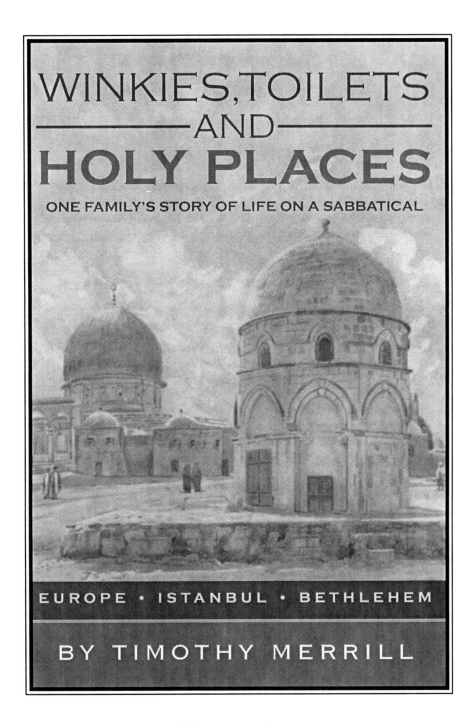

WINKIES, TOILETS
——AND——
HOLY PLACES

ONE FAMILY'S STORY OF LIFE ON A SABBATICAL

EUROPE • ISTANBUL • BETHLEHEM

BY TIMOTHY MERRILL

iUniverse, Inc.
New York   Bloomington

Winkies, Toilets and Holy Places

One Family's Story of Life on a Sabbatical

Europe ▪ Istanbul ▪ Bethlehem

iUniverse books may be ordered through booksellers or by contacting:

iUniverse
1663 Liberty Drive
Bloomington, IN 47403
www.iuniverse.com
1-800-Authors (1-800-288-4677)

ISBN: 978-1-4401-1431-1 (pbk)
ISBN: 978-1-4401-1432-8 (ebk)

Printed in the United States of America

iUniverse rev. date: 1/22/2009

For my children,
Danielle, Jonathan, Deborah,

and for
Jeanie

Table of Contents

Part One: Getting Our Act Together
  1: Money Problems. 2
  2: Pieces Fall into Place. 5
  3: What's a Sabbatical? 7

Part Two: Across America
  4: Packing Up to Ship Out 14
  5: We Say Goodbye. 20
  6: Trouble on the Road. 23
  7: School is in Session. 28
  8: At the Amsterdam in Manhattan 31

Part Three: First Tango in Paris
  9: Wheels Down 40
  10: The Esmeralda Hotel 44
  11: Wherein We Fall Asleep at Mass 49
  12: "Avez-vous un Ventilateur?". *52*
  13: What We Thought about the 'Thinker'. 58

Part Four: In Which We Travel by Car, Train, Boat, Bus and Plane
  14: The Naked Ladies of St. Malo. 67
  15: Why Travel?. 70
  16: Le Mont St Michel. 75
  17: On to Switzerland 79
  18: Our First Matterhorn Day 83
  19: We Convene a Family Meeting in Milan 91
  20: Vaperettos in Venice 95
  21: In Which We Explore Venice. 98
  22: The David's Winkie. 103
  23: Roma at Last 110
  24: In Which We Visit the Pantheon, the Basilica and the Coliseum. .117
  25: Alone in the Sistine Chapel 124
  26: The Chambers of the Dead. 126

27: We Board a Boat at Bari 130

28: We Travel by Bus into the Mountains of Greece 134

29: Hotel Kozani. 141

30: Change in Plans at Thessalonika 145

Part Five: Life on the Bosphorus

31: At Home in Üsküdar 152

32: The Lay of the Land. 161

33: What Friends Are For. 165

34: We Find a Church. 174

35: The Case of the Mascot Murder 179

36: The Cappadocian Caper. 188

37: Fairy Chimneys and an Underground Hittite City 195

38: Wherein Someone Gets Groped 201

39: Spenser Has a Birthday. 208

40: Grandmother Comes to the Bosphorus 218

41: Taxi Terror. 221

42: Goodbye to Grandmother 226

43: Midnight on the Pammukele Express 231

44: Belly-dancing on the Bosphorus 239

45: We Sing for Our Supper. 242

Part Six: O Little Town of Bethlehem

46: Tantur Ecumenical Institute. 247

47: Is the Holy Land Holy? 251

48: Via Dolorosa. 254

49: The Mount of Olives 258

50: Into the West Bank 263

51: The Two Seas 269

52: Hezekiah's Tunnel. 278

53: Bedlam in Bethlehem 281

Epilogue. 288

Appendix I—The Best and the Worst Of 292

Appendix II—The Church of the Holy Sepulchre. 294

Appendix III—Yad Vashem. 298

Appendix IV—Torrance of Tiberius. 301

I F YOU THINK THIS IS A BOOK ABOUT TRAVELING WITH children, well, of course, you're right.

But that's only part of what this book is about. More than simply a "travel" guide, this is a book about relationships.

It's the story of a new family, a family brought together by a recent marriage: the step-father, the mom/wife and the step-children, two young boys. It's about being together 24/7 in this new arrangement for more than five months.

It's a family that's been cobbled together for only twenty-four months and this adventure will be a test. It's a journey that will take them from Colorado in August to Bethlehem on Christmas Eve, just a day after the city of Christ's birth was released by the Israeli government to the Palestinian National Authority.

This little tribe is what family therapist and sociologist Barbara Carnal calls a "patch-work" family—four separate, unique individuals with different life experiences, not necessarily connected by blood bonds, but stitched together by love, conversation, respect, and a good sense of humor.

We would be tested not only by the sheer demands of traveling and living together, but by the need to home-school the boys. Taken out of school for an entire year, the boys became our students. In an odd way, we also became *their* students; we learned much about children, about learning and about how children learn. Still, it was now our responsibility to educate them so that they could fall into their next grade level without tripping over their multiplication tables.

This story happened long ago. The world was different then, in the late 20th century, less than three years into the Clinton administration. Looking back on it now is like arriving, finally, on a high mountain pass and turning to assess from whence you came. The valley you've crossed is in the hazy distance shrouded by cloud or fog and details which once had been vivid and bright are now simply too indistinct to make out. The road you've traveled is a string-like ribbon that also dissolves in the mist of the far plain. You recall the trip fondly, and if you're like me, you stop, and start to walk back down the road to revisit some of the memories you most cherish. But even so, they're faded and fragile and fall apart like ashes to the touch.

So much has changed since then. In a pre-9/11 world, although we were aware of terrorists, we didn't think too much about them, we knew little of the World Wide Web and the Internet bubble of the late 90s was only beginning to percolate. Only tech-savvy gearheads had electronic mail and laptops, and mobile phones still looked like Velvetta cheese boxes only black and with an antenna. No Euros. No iPods. The fashion revolution inaugaurated by Michael Jordon that would soon have virile young men wearing bloomers for pants, or gravity-defying trousers that sagged impossibly, or cargo-pocketed knickers that came to the knee, had just begun. Monica Lewinsky had not yet begun her tour of service in the White House. Taking pictures required the use of film, and we had no choice but to allot considerable and precious space in our backpacks to scores of film cannisters in order to adequately—we thought—record our trip. And the trial of the century had just come to an uproarious conclusion: O.J. Simpson's lawyers won him a controversial acquittal, a verdict which shocked the nation. "If the glove doesn't fit, you must acquit."

So how did we do on this trip?

I have my own answer to that question, but perhaps as the reader, that's a question for you to think about. Without doubt, you'll find yourself second-guessing some of our decisions; had you been in our North Face hiking boots, you would have done differently.

Maybe. But perhaps you'll also see that we were all doing the best we could.

There's no villain or hero in this story. We're not an extraordinary family.

Just a family on a journey.

In *Walden Pond*, the 19th-century transcendentalist, Henry David Thoreau, has some great lines about people who can't escape the mundane. They're people who live "lives of quiet desperation," he said. They're people who, when they come to die, discover too late that they have not lived.

Jeanie and I do not want to live this way. I suppose we want to suck out "the marrow of life," as Thoreau put it. Perhaps our generation would call this "going for the gusto," or "living life to the fullest."

As people of faith, however, even this is not enough. Until we find a connection, a relationship with That-Which-Is-Beyond-Ourselves, we're oddly alone.

This trip, then, was a journey deeper into relationships and intimacy—parent/child, wife/husband, stepparent/stepchildren, as well as our relationship with God. As one family among many families of the world, visiting other families, we learned a lot and tried to lived faithfully with each other and before God as best we knew how.

The book is divided into several parts. Parts One through Four focus on the journey from Colorado to Istanbul. In Part Five we're situated in a beautiful flat on the Bosphorus. The final section takes us to Bethlehem.

The Epilogue briefly describes what has happened with the children in the fourteen years since this adventure took place and provides some other notes about people in this story as well.

Some, but not all, of the names of people have been changed for reasons of respect and privacy.

So, see what you think. This book is written for people who enjoy travel and traveling with children. But it's also for those who are curious about how human beings manage to stay connected and in harmony with each other.

It's really a love story.

—Timothy F. Merrill
Shanghai,
P.R. China
21 November 2008

"The original 'Thinker' can't be both in New York and Paris. It's either here or there. And I happen to know for a fact that the original is there — in New York."
—p. 61.

SHE WASN'T BAWLING.
    IT WAS A QUIET WEEPING.

My wife.

We were standing apart—she on the sidewalk, and me in the street, the Rue de Leopold Belland in Paris—so that we were almost eye level.

We were only fifteen days into Our Great Journey, and now it was all collapsing.

After two years of planning, the idea that our trip might fail seemed impossible, like the Eiffel Tour clattering into a heap of twisted scrap metal.

And no one in the Second Arrondissement seemed to care. The flower vendors were doing a brisk business, and in the late afternoon, the espresso bars were full, and perfumed madams were walking their perfumed poodles.

Nearby, I hear one of the children speaking to the innkeeper of La Marmotte: "Cle numero sept, s'il vous plait," and then they clambered up five stories to our viewless room in Paris.

But the long-suffering wife was crying. Her arms were gathered about her waist as though to tighten a knot. "I don't think we can do this," she whispered.

To tell you the truth, I wasn't sure either.

But I knew one thing: If this Venture failed, it was my doing.

And if *that* was true, maybe there was something yet I could do to save it.

Part One
Getting Our Act Together

"If you limit your choices to what seems possible or reasonable, you disconnect yourself from what you truly want, and all that is left is a compromise."
—Robert Fritz

1

Money Problems

A WHITE GUY.

He was with a woman with a weary face who lingered a few yards away, her hair pulled back and up, held by a clip. She was holding a diapered infant who sat on her hips hugging his momma like a bear cub on a pine tree. A noisy little boy about 4 years old, he ran around our yard playing in the wood pile, checking out the aluminum shed, and climbing aboard the swing which was tethered to an old, gnarly cottonwood branch twenty-five feet up.

The man was working on a five day beard, holding a roll of cash, and flipping through Ben Franklins until he had thirty of them in his hand. Stuffing the rest into his ratty jeans, he handed the $3,000 to me.

"Okay, thanks," he said without emotion.

We signed some paperwork, and he took possession of our red, 1988 Mazda RX-7. We needed all the money we could get, and I wasn't about to quibble as to the source of the cash now in my hands.

The woman strapped the clinging child into a car seat in the back of a Ford station wagon, and then climbed into the driver's side. "Come over here!" she yelled at the urchin who had started to climb a cherry tree. "Right now!"

They pulled out of the driveway on to 20th Avenue. Her husband positioned himself behind the wheel of the RX-7 and ripped out of the yard right after her and they were gone. Never saw them again. But I had $3,000. Cash.

Jeanie was standing by the doorway, hand on hip in a relaxed way, eyebrows slightly arched. I shrugged and held out a fistful of cash. "Three thousand dollars," I said.

"Yeah, and that will get us from New York about halfway across the Atlantic." Hand was still on hip. "We're going to need a lot more money than that if we're going to be gone five months." She turned and went inside.

My wife was thirty-four years old. Sometimes when I looked at her I just stared, as though by staring I could see beyond her lightly-freckled oval face and above the gentle slope of high cheekbones and through her languid brown eyes into the vastness of her geneaological terrain where, mixed with ancestors from Scandia were unmistakeable hints of liasons with Oriental and Indian blood. Her hair was black and shoulder-length. I thought she was beautiful. And any reasonable person with 20/20 vision would say the same thing. So she can say in that certain tone, "We're going to need a lot more money than that," all she wants and I don't complain.

"I know, I know," I said, following her.

I found her in the cramped, two-step kitchen of our 1940s house. Two steps in any direction took you to the fridge, or the sink or the stove. She stood in front of the stainless steel sink on a checkerboard floor of black and white linoleum tiles. This old house was falling apart. The windows were double-hung/single pane, the insulation in the attic was sparse, the pipes were of galvanized steel, the wiring was hopelessly out of code, and the plumbing medieval. The wood siding was splintered in many places, and the nails had been weathered out by fifty years of harsh winters and summer storms so that you stick the claw end of a hammer around the heads and yank all the siding off in thirty minutes if you had to. We were thinking that soon we might have to, and had spent some time exploring ways to remodel the house.

But it was home. The boys slept in bunk beds in one of two bedrooms. Our bedroom was no master bedroom—more like servant's quarters. One tiny closet with one shelf above a pole that stretched four feet from wall to wall. That's it. No built-ins. No master bath. That was out the door and down the hallway.

We all shared that bathroom, a very special room because it was the first and last room Jeanie and I attempted to remodel and decorate together. She had rolled out some clay tiles, dried, glazed and fired them. For weeks we had tiles laid out on the sun room floor with sheets of plywood on them to keep them from curling. Later, when they were ready, we prepared the bathroom floor, an area about four by six feet, and began to slop adhesive on the floor, lay down the tile and finish with the grout, and we tried to do this together—in this small, tight space—because we were in love, because it was fun to do stuff together and because we were complete idiots. It wasn't long before an argument flared up, and soon the project was left for one of us to finish. I think I finished the floor work, and Jeanie painted the walls and hung a horizontal stripe of very lovely wallpaper for an accent.

I made an observation later: "We *were* working together, sweetie."

She said, "Well it didn't feel like it."

3

"No, because when we were in the same space, we were actually working *against* each other not with each other. Finally we realized that to work together we had to parcel out the responsibilities. So the project was finished *because* we learned how to work together. See?" I think she saw, but I'm not sure.

Jeanie had stalks of rhubarb in the sink and cookie dough in the mixer. We were going to get pie and chocolate chip cookies. "So where are we going to get the money, hon?" she asked.

I stuck a finger in the cookie dough. She slapped my hand. I pretended not to notice. "I don't know," I said, "we'll figure it out. But we've got three thousand dollars. It's a start."

She turned on the cold water over the rhubarb.

I gave her my speech: "Sweetie, we can do this. Like the college thing. A year and a half ago you didn't have a college education. You're 33, and you want to start on your dream. So you go to Metro, you take full loads each semester, you go to summer school and get straight A's except for one B in professor Butthead's class, and you still take care of us three guys at home. You're amazing! You and I *together* will figure this out!"

The truth is, I relied on Jeanie more than she realized. She was, and is, completely remarkable—and determined. So, if she bought into this idea of a sabbatical, I knew she had the true grit to help make it happen.

2

Pieces Fall into Place

B UT MONEY ISN'T OUR ONLY PROBLEM. THERE ARE OTHER VARIABLES as well. Jeanie and I have been married two years. She had, at the time of our marriage, two children, 5 and 8. That makes me a stepdad at the very point in my life in which my parenting days were thought to be over. My kids are out of the house and on their own: Danielle, 24, a single mom with a preschooler and soon to be married; Jon, married, but no kids yet; and Debbie, 18, working for Mesa Airlines, a regional outfit based in Denver.

What was I thinking?

That's what my kids were wondering when Jeanie and I exchanged vows by the lagoon in Belmar Park. The larger question was how this new relationship would fare under the stress of traveling for five months, and being together 24/7. Too much sun can take the bloom off the rose real quick.

"We'll be fine," I said. See, that's me. Can't ever see any negatives.

Others were not so sure.

Dick Kaufmann, a World War 2 vet who had married Edie, an Austrian girl, after the war, told me one Sunday after church that we'd have a few of "those days." Meaning certain emotional contretemps and disagreements.

"No problem," I said.

Of that I was certain. We could handle it.

What I was less certain of was how I'd manage as a stepparent. Talk about stress. My "scorched earth" parenting style tended to be firm—take no prisoners. Jeanie is a *mother*, a phenomenal mother, and she actually *listens* to what the boys have to say before reacting to any situation.

Not me. *Assess, assert, and expect results.*

Jeanie would ask questions: "Would you like to go out and do your chores now?"

I would say, "Time to feed the rabbits. No Game Boy until it's done."

Still, I thought we'd be just fine.

The money problem was a concrete problem, formidable but solvable. So this is what we worked on. On relationship issues, we figured we'd do what we needed to do if and when any conflicts came up.

The money came in from unexpected sources. A branch from the neighbor's dying cottonwood fell off during a wind storm and landed square on our dilapidated metal shed. Four hundred dollars from the insurance company.

A hail storm blew through Jefferson county causing considerable damage. I inspected the roof and didn't think we had a claim.

"You should at least call the insurance people," Jeanie said.

They gave us $2,000 for damage I couldn't even see.

We also had savings which amounted to about $4,000 by the time we left.

I didn't think we'd be able to rent out our house for just five months.

"You should at least put an ad in the paper," Jeanie said.

The Turicos family answered our ad. They were a Hispanic family in transition, looking for a place to buy. They couldn't speak much English, and I was nervous as to whether they understood—clearly—that they would need to vacate the house in five months.

"Si, si," Oscar Turicos said. They gladly accepted the conditions and agreed to pay $1,000 a month, which more than covered our mortgage payment. I put my son, Jon, in charge of collecting rent and monitoring the situation and gave him the names of handymen who could repair this or that if an emergency arose.

We actually were going to charge them more than $1,000, but we asked them to do us a favor by taking care of our two dogs while we were gone. Kirby was a young black lab with lots of energy. Sandy was four years old and a Chesapeake Retriever/Golden Lab mix. Two male dogs: one hyper, and one very relaxed. We had a large fenced-off area for the dogs, and with the Turicos in the house, it made sense for them to feed the dogs and take care of them, if they were willing.

They were willing. So another piece fell into place.

It's a good thing, because the plan was ambitious.

3

What's a Sabbatical?

THE CONCEPT OF "SABBATICAL" HAS ITS ROOTS IN THE OLD Testament. The "Sabbath" was the seventh day of the week, and was supposed to be a day of rest, when all labors ceased so that people could worship their God and be renewed for the work of the week ahead.

Leviticus 25:1-7 extends the concept even further by proposing a sabbatical year in which every seven years the land lay fallow so that the soil could be reborn, become fertile again.

In the academic community, sabbaticals have a long history, and are usually granted so that the scholar can devote his or her time to research without the distractions of teaching, tutorials and lectures.

As the clergy left the halls of the academy, they felt the need for a break from ministerial obligations so that they could retreat in search of renewal and a fresh vision. Congregations saw the advantages, too, when they realized that they could retain their pastor for longer terms of service if they gave the pastor some time off.

Most churches don't stipulate how the pastor is to spend his time during the sabbatical. Usually they require that a sabbatical proposal be presented which must be then approved by the governing body of the church.

My interest in Istanbul, and the reason for my first visit in 1990, was rooted in my Ph.D. dissertation relating to the first crusade, 1096-1099 A.D. Turkey is of enormous interest to all biblical students, however, particularly New Testament scholars, because of the apostle Paul's travels through what was then known as Asia Minor. A return trip to Istanbul would give me another opportunity to pursue this interest and to explore sites previously unexplored.

Sometimes, a church board will ask to see a reading list. My colleagues, upon hearing my plans, also wanted to know what theologians or philosophers

I would be reading while I was gone.

"Barth?"

"I got enough of Barth at Princeton."

"Then, Bultmann, Moltmann, Heidegger, Kung, Kaseman, Tillich?"

I laughed. I'm interested in theology, of course, but I am suspicious of theologians primarily because their interests seem to be so far removed from parish life. I did have a reading plan, however.

"I'm going to read the works of most of the major British novelists of the 19ᵗʰ century," I told my friend Ken Williams, Senior Minister of a large church in my community. "Austen, the Brontë sisters, Thackeray, Trollope, not Dickens, but George Eliot, and especially Hardy. And probably Henry James, if he counts as a British novelist."

When I was asked to explain myself, I simply said, "I can learn more about the human condition and our feeble attempts to comprehend an ineffable God by reading Thomas Hardy than by reading Paul Tillich any day."

So when the church where I was the pastor included the offer of a sabbatical, I jumped at the chance. The church board gave me a couple of options. I could take off for three months at full salary, or six months at half salary

I opted for three months at full salary, and one month of accrued vacation time, and one month of accrued study leave. Five months at full salary. It was a sweet deal. I admit it.

Now, if we could just pull it off.

ॐॐॐ

Jeanie and I sat down at the kitchen table made of planks from a Scottish malt mill. Paper and sharpened pencils were at the ready.

"Basically, we have to be able to live on thirteen hundred a month," Jeanie said.

"And if we don't have a mortgage payment to worry about, with the Turicos renting the house, then we simply have to figure out the cost of food and lodging," I added.

The round trip air fare was going on Visa. We would pay that off when we returned.

We had about $9,400 cash in savings, thanks to the sale of the car and the hail storm.

"I'm going to have a pottery sale," Jeanie said, "and we can do a couple of garage sales, too."

Jeanie's pottery had always sold well. She had her own wheel and kiln, mixed her own glazes.

She had another idea. "Why don't I make a little pot, maybe in the shape of a beehive, with a small hole at the top. Then whenever we have loose change, or a dollar or two, we can put it in the beehive pot, and when we leave, we'll take a hammer to it, and all the money we've saved we will spend on just 'fun' things, like ice cream or a movie, or a boat ride."

So she did. Even the boys put some of their allowance money in the beehive pot, and it wasn't long before it began to feel really heavy.

"We're going to be fine," I said, and I believed it.

Our plan was to leave Denver in mid-August, 1995, and return in early January, 1996. We would arrive in Istanbul on October 1, and spend the six weeks prior to that traipsing through Europe.

"The first six weeks are going to be the hardest financially because it's not going to be easy living in hotels for six weeks and eating out all the time. When we get to Istanbul we'll at least know what we're paying and the per-night cost will be reasonable," Jeanie said.

She was right. For our stay in Istanbul, we made arrangements to stay with the Near East Mission operated by the United Church of Christ. Alan (Mic) and Sally McCain were the senior "missionaries" there. I wrote to them about staying at their facility for three months—October, November and December—laying out the whole trip for them, and hoping that they'd treat my request favorably.

They were hesitant. And who wouldn't be? Why would anyone want to commit to allowing a family of four, whom they had never met, to stay with them for three months? Especially when that family included two boys aged 7 and 10? I imagined them discussing the possible horrors of children running around screaming and getting into mischief and generally misbehaving and creating unpleasantness for the other guests who might be dropping by.

We would not be staying with Mic and Sally in their home per se. They lived in a downstairs apartment; we would occupy the upstairs apartment that had three bedrooms with bunk beds and single beds. It was used for missionaries passing through or other guests related to their mission in Istanbul and Turkey.

They agreed to take us for the month of October for $500 and go from there. Meaning, if the arrangement worked, we could stay longer. But no promises.

I could live with that. I knew they would love the boys and that as a family we would be very accommodating of other guests who would be staying with us, in the same apartment, from time to time.

But there was yet the question of where we'd stay while in Europe.

So during the year before we left, we made reservations for lodging at certain points throughout the trip. For our three weeks in Paris, we made no reservations. Not one. We felt that we'd have no trouble in a city that size finding something when we arrived. But we reserved space in hostels in New York, St. Malo, the Loire River Valley (chateau country), Zermatt, Florence and Rome and Bethlehem. That's it.

No reservations for Paris, Chambery, Venice, Greece or Cappodocia. We'd take our chances.

Hostels would be a new experience for the family. Many people think that hostels are primarily "youth" hostels, a place where young people with little cash and few concerns about amenities can crash while wandering around the world. In fact, people of all ages now stay at hostels and many hostels offer an alternative to the bunk bed dormitory style. We had no trouble reserving a private room set aside for families. Of course, in most cases we had to share a common bathroom, kitchen and lounge with the other guests.

For the cost, these inconveniences were minor. The cost, compared to hotel living, was extremely reasonable.

So we applied for membership in the International Hostel Association in order to get better rates. The cost of a membership then was a mere $25, well worth the investment. We then began the process of securing lodging. We were able to secure some reservations through e-mail, but electronic communication was still a relatively novel thing in 1995. So we used mail, fax and phone to make our reservations when we had to.

🙟🙟🙟

The boys, of course, were scarcely aware of all these goings-on. Spenser was in first grade. He was playing with Power Ranger action figures. Taylor was in third grade and he was the one we were worried about. He valued comfort and security. He worried about things only adults should worry about. He wasn't comfortable with change. The C in Spenser's middle name was for Christian, but it could have been for Change. Not Taylor.

So we tried to keep them in the loop as much as possible to avoid the surprise factor. To do this, we posted a map of the world in the sun room and traced our itinerary with a red felt tip marker. We got books about Turkey; we posted pictures of the Eiffel Tower and the Coliseum and the Matterhorn. We put up a calendar six months out in which we crossed off the days. We read stories to them of Hodja, the Turkish wise man.

They knew we were going on a long trip.

桾桾桾

As the time for departure approached, we had only one more problem: Since the renters were taking over on August 1, where would we stay until August 13—D day?

We couldn't leave earlier because Jeanie's summer school class didn't end until the second week in August.

Homeless for two weeks.

And we didn't have a plan.

Part Two
Across America

"If everything's under control, you're going too slow."
—Mario Andretti

4

Packing Up to Ship Out

P AQUITA COUCH CAN'T BE AN INCH OVER FIVE FEET SHORT, but she stands tall when she wants to, and that's most of the time.

Paquita was on the Search Committee when the church hired me back in 1990. The interview was held in her home which was because she was renown for the food she'd spread out on the dining room table whenever a committee meeting convened at her house. So the Search Committee routinely did their searching at chez Paquita.

Paquita isn't one to suffer fools gladly; she lets her opinions be known. She calls 'em as she sees 'em. She's got a bigger "no spin" zone than Bill O'Reilly. In her politics, she's a Republican but she'd be an opinionated Democrat if knee-jerk liberalism was her cup of tea. She wasn't outspoken about her politics, but one visit to her home and you'd understand. She collects elephants. Elephant figurines, stuffed animals, posters, hats, tee shirts—elephants everywhere. Her late husband, Don, was a leader in Republican politics in Jefferson County. He passed away suddenly in the late 1980s, and Paquita now in 1995 still doesn't seem to have gotten over it. There's a sadness about her.

But we were good friends. She could laugh easily. And I could take criticism from her. She once told me after church, that "that was the worst sermon I've ever heard in my entire life."

"Your entire life?" I repeated.

"My entire life," she said, smiling. "I mean it. That was terrible." I think I had been too political for her taste. Usually, I prefer to lift up the biblical text, try to relate it to life, but not to use the pulpit to champion personal causes on which good people can easily and defensibly disagree.

My relationship with the church was an uneasy one from the beginning once it became clear that there was a strong and vocal constituency that was far more liberal in theology and politics than I; soon it was well-known that I could identify better with those whose leanings were less strident than many of the self-absorbed baby-boomer Democrats in the congregation. I often wondered why the Search Committee recommended me to the congregation. Perhaps it was because I was a good pulpiteer. My communication style is lucid, quick and persuasive, even if some complained that I could take a well-reasoned argument to the wrong conclusion. Perhaps they thought that anyone so verbally articulate must be a *reasonable* person, and all reasonable persons are liberals, feminists and theologically generous, to borrow a term from Brian McLaren.

I was none of those things.

It wasn't too long before Arbutus Castor approached me as I was standing in the church office, and handed me a book.

"Here," she said, "this might help." It was a copy of the Inclusive Language Lectionary with Scripture readings paraphrased to reflect a feminist perspective. I accepted it graciously, I thought, and later threw it on the floor by the study door. It would make a good doorstop.

I suppose it would have been worse if I had used the pulpit to argue for my own point of view on certain social and cultural issues. I didn't, although as early as 1993 I was calling Milosevic a butcher and I publicly ridiculed Warren Christopher's totally inept foreign policy as it was applied to Serbia, and Bosnia-Herzegovina.

One Sunday in the early 90s, I stood in the pulpit with a large picture of Sinéad O'Connor, an Irish singer who was hot at the time. She'd made the cover of *Rolling Stones* and I retrieved a copy and took it into the pulpit with me. Only days before, O'Connor had publicly taken a photograph of Pope John Paul II on *Saturday Night Live* and tore it to pieces in a rant against the Church and "institutional" religion. I took umbrage. In the pulpit that Sunday I tore her photo into confetti as I preached.

Those kinds of public tantrums were rare. I usually confined my sharper comments to the written page. Once, when Dan Quayle was being remarkably misunderstood by the press (and this was before the days of Fox News, before we knew that *The New York Times* and *The Washington Post* and *The Boston Globe* had reporters who were making up their stories, before Dan Rather was insisting that bogus memos were authentic), I wrote that Quayle did, in fact, have a point. His point was not that single moms cannot raise their children, or that they do a bad job of it. His point was, supported by a growing number of studies, that—all other factors being equal—children do better when there are two parents in the home, Murphy Brown notwithstanding. Liberals didn't really hear what he actually said. They saw red.

There were several single moms in the congregation, all of whom were doing a fabulous job raising their kids—in spite of having to do it alone, work two jobs, trundle the children off to day care and so on. Yet, when they read my defense of Quayle, they took it in the gut and marched like squawking penguins to the Pastor's Study to give me an earful.

That said, most of the congregation appreciated my ministry, and found me to be open, approachable and of good humor. Most, but not all.

Paquita was a kindred soul. In late June, Paquita got wind of our plans, and began to interrogate us about the details, and it soon came out that we had a two week gap during which we were homeless.

"Well, you'll come live at my house," she announced, as though there would be no further discussion. "I've got two empty bedrooms upstairs, and a bedroom downstairs."

"No, no, Paquita, we couldn't," I said.

"Of course you could," she insisted. "Besides, my grandson, Gregory, will be spending the month with me visiting from New York—

"No, really, it's too much—"

"—He's 11, and he'd love to have some company to play with, and there's the swimming pool…" And she went on.

The idea intrigued us. She did have a nice pool which would be a great relief in the hot August weather. Plus the boys would have a playmate and their own bedroom. Why not?

And then there was the food. Paquita's reputation as a cook was impressive. We'd be eating her famous cheese-covered nachos, and casseroles of every description, and the freezer was always full of ice cream. We'd have a room, a home base for two weeks, and a swimming pool. Why not? Of course, she wouldn't take any money from us.

By the end of July the house was ready for the renters. The major items remained, like furniture. But personal stuff we put in the downstairs den and locked the door.

We took some extra clothes with us to Paquita's so that we didn't have to actually live out of our packs for two weeks. We'd be doing enough of that.

Being at her house gave us a taste of being away from home without really being away from home. An abrupt departure from 8657 West 20th Avenue in Lakewood, Colorado, was possible. But this mini-move was ideal; it helped us reinvent what "home" was all about. Like most Americans, we defined home as something called a "house" with a mailbox outside and a telephone inside. Home was an apartment in the city, or a ranch house in the suburbs. Home was the "familiar," and it would take a strong attitude adjustment in order for us to understand that the truly "familiar" was *family*. The trip was in this sense going to be revealing: If we were already "familiar" to each other, if we had heretofore created and forged strong relationships, then these bonds would continue to hold the family and the sense of "home" together. But if we had been too individualistic, too independent, too selfish, too wrapped up in the tangible, the material and the toys in our life, then the trip would be a disaster.

Living at Paquita's gave us the first sense of how we could function as a mobile, in-transit "home" and would reveal to what extent it would be enough.

The two weeks at Paquita's were wonderful. Wonderful—what a weak word to describe the great time we had. Paquita was a super hostess—gracious, accommodating and enthusiastic. The boys called her place Club Paquita. And why not? They had the time of their lives watching *American Gladiator* in the morning, playing *Sega Genesis*, and snacking on Rice Krispy bars whenever they wanted, splashing about in the swimming pool and living a life totally bereft of any responsibilities.

During those two weeks we packed our packs. The packing wasn't the hard part; it was the unpacking, or de-packing that was hard. The kids would put stuff in their packs, and we'd take it out of their packs. One pack per person. That's all we were taking. For five months, one pack each, and we each carried our own. And they were red! We wouldn't have too much trouble spotting each other in a crowd.[1]

The boys although young were not close enough in age or size to be able to wear their clothes interchangeably. They took a couple pair of shorts, one pair of tennis shoes each, and of course socks and underwear. Other items included a toothbrush, floss, Game Boy and games, a journal book, and a reading book which we'd discard once it was read. Then we'd pick up something else to read.

The packs were most critical for the six weeks we would be tramping through Europe. Once in Istanbul, we'd be able to settle in and the packs would not play a role until we were ready to return to the States. That's why we didn't pack long pants or light jackets for the boys. We could pick these up inexpensively in Istanbul when the cold weather set in.

Our guidelines for packing were simple: We made a list of what we needed. Then we went down the list and crossed off most of what we'd written. For example: Did we need two or three pairs of shoes? No. We each were allotted one pair. Period. In fact, we wore the shoes, and did not carry an extra pair.

Then we made a list of what we wanted. Our packs left little room for anything but the "necessaries."

Jeanie and I took two pairs of long pants each, and two tops, so that we could get four outfits by interchanging tops and bottoms. We also each took one pair of shorts each and socks and underwear. Jeanie insisted on packing one skirt. In addition, we had the passports, credit cards, travel info and maps, toothpaste, brushes.

Jeanie was going to take a hair dryer along, but decided against it. Instead, she used some free time while at Paquita's to have her hair cut and get a perm. On the trip she'd just wash her hair and let it dry. It was what it was.

I needed to be able to write. So I packed a slim Sharp electric word processor with a window where you could see about two lines of text before it was printed on the page which was scrolled just like a normal typewriter. This is what I would use to keep a journal of the trip. The plan called for me to write for a week or so, and then send off the pages to Jeanie's mother, Barbara, who would then copy the pages and send them out to a pre-selected list of recipients, primarily relatives on both sides who might be interested in what we were doing. This little proto-laptop required four double D batteries to work. And since the ribbons would be virtually impossible to get overseas, I ordered a dozen packs before we left and these went in the packs as well.

In spite of our best efforts, however, the packs were heavy. We also had to carry some textbooks for the boys' schooling.

> *"I worried about things I wouldn't be able to get overseas. So I wanted to make sure I had things for the kids we would need, like medicines, for example."* —Jeanie

The boys are enrolled in a public school, but it is a chartered school that emphasizes strong academic performance. It's not for everyone. You won't find the "open room" philosophy at Dennison Elementary School. Dr. Carlton, the founder of the school, didn't believe in low expectations. Students in his school would learn the "elementary" or fundamental skills needed to succeed at higher levels. He also didn't believe that getting an education was the same thing as getting high self-esteem. Strong performance leads to healthy esteem. How can you feel good about yourself when you're always getting stars and stickers for turning in crap? Kindergarten students in Mrs. Winter's class sat at desks. They would need to sit in desks in first grade. He firmly believed that 5-year olds could learn to sit and get on task.

Critics were suspicious of the highly structured environment. They felt it inevitably led to stifled creativity. When he heard a comment like that, he frequently would march his guests out into the hallways where the artwork was posted. The work of the students at every grade level was impressive.

"Does that look like the work of students who aren't creative, or can't think for themselves?" he would ask. His theory was that you can't break the rules, whether in art or writing, until you first learn the rules and learn to work well within them. Then, and only then, is an artist equipped to expand the boundaries and see what happens. He understood—and in this he seemed to be before his time—that structure and creativity are not mutually exclusive.

Students get in on a lottery system. Taylor didn't get in until the third grade, and now we were pulling him out for fourth grade, and we worried that he wouldn't have a spot in his fifth grade class when we returned. Spenser was in from the get go, and because of the vagaries of the registration process and class sizes, he was virtually assured a spot in third grade when we got back. Taylor's re-entry depended upon a student not returning; if that happened, he was at the top of the list. Since someone always dropped out either because of a family move or academic difficulties, we were certain that he could rejoin his classmates for fifth grade.

We also notified his teachers of our plans and made arrangements with them for the boys to periodically send a report of what they saw and what they were doing. Their teachers eagerly supported this idea because it would be a tool for them to use to teach their students about geography and other cultures.

So for an entire academic year which included the winter and spring quarters of 1996 when we returned, we would be home-schooling the boys.

This meant we needed to lug along some textbooks. And it fell to me to carry the heavy stuff: the books and typewriter and anything else that could be stuffed in. To ease the load, we cut the hardback covers off the textbooks; this also made it easier to wedge them into an already full pack.

---

[1] The packs were a loan from Keith and Norma Daly, also church members, who had spent a year abroad with their children, Jane and Curt—who were in their early teens at the time. They took a huge interest in what we were doing and had a lot of good advice for us.

5

We Say Goodbye

As much as we enjoyed our stay at Club Paquita, we were anxious to get started. I was bored. Jeanie's classes were finishing up. She had finals, so she was still somewhat distracted. And although I had final details to wrap up, time passed slower than a snail on sedatives these penultimate days. There wasn't much to do except mark off the last remaining days on the calendar. After eighteen months of X-ing out dates, the empty calendar boxes were now very few!

In the immediate days before our departure we convened two "going-away" soirees. The first was actually at the behest of Paquita and was held at her house. She invited a number of her own family members who were also good friends to come over for a backyard barbecue and swimming party. Some close friends from the church showed up as well. Among others these were Keith and Norma Daly and Loretta Trane, a single mom who had not appreciated my remarks about Dan Quayle and with whom I had had a famous, although friendly, disagreement over the meta-message of *Thelma and Louise* (I saw it as a movie with more testosterone than *Rocky I* through *V* put together, a movie depicting two women who essentially adopted typically male methods for solving their problems; she totally bought into the feminist hype).

The highlight of the evening for the boys was the opportunity to crack open the beehive pot Jeanie had made and into which we had been stuffing fun money for almost two years. This was money we'd spend only on extra things to have some fun.

Jeanie brought the pot out on the deck and set it on a picnic table. Taylor and Spenser each had a small hammer and took turns taking a whack at it. Once the pot was in pieces and the coins and bills exposed the next task was to count it. This responsibility fell to Taylor who spent the next half hour counting it up. The total came to $934 and change! To a 10-year-old, that was a lot of money!

The second gathering was an outdoor picnic at Panorama Park near our house for my family. Jeanie's mother, Barbara, and her grandmother, Marie, came. All of my children were there. Danielle was there with her husband-to-be, Scott, and her little boy, Alex, 4. She was back in Colorado after getting her degree in Communications from Oregon State University in 1993. Jon and Marah, married now for a little over a year, lived nearby and he was on the 6-year plan at Metropolitan State College majoring in business. And my baby, Debbie, 18, was there with her boyfriend, Chris. She graduated from high school at age 17, and went to work a few weeks later for Mesa Airlines, driving a shuttle bus from Concourse B to the Mesa gates at Stapleton International Airport. Now she worked at the ticket counter and in operations. Sometimes I could get a free flight on America West if I was going to Phoenix or some other destination served by Mesa. Once Jeanie and I went to Jackson, Wyoming, on some passes she provided.

I would miss my children. I knew that. But my travels in the past had taught me a hard lesson: they were quite able to live their lives now without me. I would miss them more than they would miss me. They would leave this picnic, go to their respective homes and life would go on. Of course, that's the way we want it, as parents, to be. But it can be disconcerting.

Once, I was in Paris—it was in June 1990—and I decided to call my youngest daughter, Debbie. She must have been about 14 at the time. So I inserted my card in the phone and rang her up.

"Debbie? Debbie?"

"Huh?"

"It's Dad."

"Hi."

"I'm calling from Paris, from the Champs Elysees!"

"Where?"

"The Champs Elysees. In Paris."

"Okay."

"Did I wake you up?" It was about 11 a.m. on a Saturday morning in Denver.

"Yeah."

And that was about it.

I told her later that if I ever called again from overseas I wanted her to respond differently. I wanted her to say: "Dad? Dad! I'm so glad you called. I miss you, and can't wait until you get back. When are you coming back? Please don't stay away for so long! I love you!" That's what I want to hear. It's a joke with us now.

But I knew my kids were fine. Grown up. A life of their own. They would do well, and of course they'd hear from us while we were gone, and when we got back it would be awfully good to see them again, and I knew they loved me and would be glad to see me, too, when we returned.

It was a quiet affair. We had hamburgers, potato salad, watermelon, corn on the cob. Didn't do too much but enjoy each other and express how we'd miss everyone.

The next day after church, we left. The 1990 Chevy Lumina was packed. We drove to church. I preached a sermon, shook hands with parishioners at the door. We drove out of the parking lot, got on I-70 headed east with Denver, Colorado, and the Rocky Mountains in our rear view mirror. The digital clock in the van read: 12:00. We were on schedule!

6

Trouble on the Road

NEW YORK SEEMED FAR AWAY. AS EXCITED AS WE WERE there was a slight sense of foreboding. We now felt the enormity of the responsibility we had embraced. Perhaps it was the heat: temperatures were nearing 100° and the air was heavy. We didn't have air conditioning, so we gave spray bottles to the boys which they used liberally. Perhaps it was because we were leaving on the 13th. Nah. Perhaps it was simply the vast unknown that stretched out before us as endless as the highway that shot straight across the plains of eastern Colorado toward Kansas.

We voiced none of this however. We didn't have far to travel; we were headed for Beaver City, Nebraska, only 300 miles east, where we would spend the night with our friends Harvey and Peggy Knott. No worries, then.

We left on the day that Mickey Mantle, the "Mick," died. I'd seen the Mick play center field for the Yankees many times although never at Yankee Stadium. When the Yankees came to Chicago, living on the NW side, the Cub side of town, I'd nevertheless get out to Comiskey Park to see the White Sox and was fortunate to see them play the last year they won the American League pennant, 1959. The Yankees were winning everything then. The Mick played with Moose Skowron, Enos Slaughter, Yogi Berra, Whitey Ford, Hank Bauer and others. But in 1959, the White Sox took it all with players like pitcher Billy Pierce, Sherm Lollar behind the plate, and the best double play combination in baseball: Hall of Famers, Luis Aparicio and Nelli Fox. Fox was creating a record at the time for the most consecutive years leading the league in singles, 1954-1960, and was the league's MVP in their pennant year. Beating the Yankees and winning the pennant galvanized the city.

Alas, the White Sox lost the World Series to the Dodgers. In those days there were no divisions or divisional playoffs. Just two leagues, eight teams each.

So the Mick was dead. Jerry Garcia had also died, gratefully one presumes,

"Jeanie stripped the shirts off us three boys, sat us in chairs and slung a towel around our shoulders and took a hair clipper to our heads, shaving us virtually bald and giving us a faintly alien appearance." —p. 30.

and I gave a passing thought to the notion that now, perhaps, the Sixties were dead. People were always saying the Sixties were dead. Maybe the Sixties died long ago with Jimi Hendricks, or Janis, or Abbie, or Jim Morrison. Funny the way the Sixties were about death: the death of God, the death of absolutes, the deaths of Kennedy, King and Kennedy. Vietnam. And within a year of our departure, the high priest of the Sixties sanctorum, who had reportedly left instructions that he did not want to be brought back during a Republican administration, was himself dead: Timothy Leary. The ex-Harvard guru, who said that if he ever got bored it was a simple matter to pick up the needle and move it to another groove (baby), was most famous for his advice: turn on, tune in, and drop out. Soon, he'd drop dead.

They said the Sixties were dead when Nixon died in 1994. I wasn't sure the Sixties would ever really die; they had changed the country so profoundly, and like a mutation in the gene pool, the postmodern effects would last for generations.

I was thinking about this when I hear a thump and a flapping sound. The car started pulling slightly to the right. I knew immediately what this meant and pulled over to the shoulder.

Forty-five miles out of town, 98° and getting hotter and we have a flat tire! I'm still attired in my Sunday church clothes—suit pants, white shirt and tie, long since loosened at the collar. I was in no mood to change a flat. We'd never had a flat tire! And now? Why now? Unbelievable!

The boys were of a different mind. They fell out of the car enthusiastically, Jeanie being careful to shoo them a safe distance from the road.

"And I was worried about gas!" Spenser declared. Indeed, Spenser had become the Purser in Charge of Gas Requisitions for the trip. He continually monitored fuel levels. He told us whenever we needed to stop at a station, "if not to get gas," he said, "to release gas." Funny.

A Colorado State Patrol officer soon pulled up to see what was going on. This further elevated the excitement for the boys. By then, I had the little spare out and was preparing to put apply the lug nuts. So he didn't stay long, but before he left he gave the boys a packet of Colorado Rockies baseball cards.

We limped into Byers on this doughnut of a spare tire. Every tire establishment was closed. It was Sunday. So now, we had arrived in less than sixty minutes of a trip that was to last over five months, to our first Change In Plans. We had intended to take Highway 36 from Byers on in to Kansas. It was the shortest and quickest route to our stop in Beaver City, Nebraska. But if we did that, nothing would be open in the small towns along the way. Our best chance to get a new tire was to continue on I-70 and head for the truck stops of Limon.

When we pulled into Limon we were relieved to find the Firestone tire center open and doing business. But the fellow who was going to perform the operation couldn't find the right plug with which to do the job. He suggested Wheeler's, "just a piece on down the road here."

At Wheelers, a store newly opened, a young man was listlessly assembling a wheel barrow and was glad to do something more interesting. He sold us a brand new tire on account of the nail had drilled a hole on the side wall and a plug wouldn't last 200 miles let alone 2,000 miles. A patch would give out within the hour.

So our route and our schedule were skewed, and now our bank account had been unexpectedly tapped, too. We grimaced and shrugged. What could we do?

When we pulled away from Wheelers, we were about ninety minutes behind schedule. Taking a longer route and getting the tires changed would make us considerably late to our destination. We had told Harvey and Peggy we'd be there about 6 p.m.

But we had also forgotten that there was a time change between Denver and Beaver City. Leaving the Mountain Time Zone and entering the Central Time Zone would cost us an hour. So when we showed up in Beaver City, Harvey and Peggy were sitting on the front porch of their 1903 Victorian house sipping margaritas and wondering what had become of us.

I don't know what she was thinking, but Peggy had fussed over a hot gas/ wood stove on a humid, scorcher of a day preparing ribs, whole red potatoes, beans and corn on the cob—and it had been ready to eat two hours ago!

Both she and Harvey were totally gracious. No matter that they had made a significant foray into their garden to retrieve the corn, beans, and potatoes for the evening meal. The wine was home made. We marveled! And we enjoyed every morsel!

Harvey and Peggy have been married for six months—second marriages both. In May they came into Denver and stayed with us for three days and then flew to Germany, taking with them an entire room full of suitcases! But my friendship with Harvey had begun several years earlier when he lived across the street in a Victorian house which he restored, and in which he had reassembled a pipe organ in the basement and remodeled the house so that the bass pipes extended up through the main floor into the second.

Now he works for the state government in Kansas, just 30 miles south, but his passion is the restoration of Victorian houses. This house, in Beaver City, looked more like a museum than a house. He has an incredible knowledge of

Victorian residential architecture, and had a bloodhound's instinct for finding period pieces. Their house was awash with tapestries and antiques, including a square grand piano.

That night we slept in a four poster bed grateful that we had safely navigated through our first day away from home.

"Tomorrow will be a better day," I whispered to Jeanie before we fell asleep.

"Today was a good day," she said. "A very good day." And I was grateful. What a woman!

I snuggled closer. She pushed me away. "This is an antique bed. It'll smash to pieces!"

Okay, then.

"And the kids are in the next room."

The pillows were big and fluffy. I don't like big and fluffy pillows. I pounded mine a couple of times to flatten it out.

7

School Is in Session

IN FACT, THE NEXT TWO DAYS WERE RELATIVELY UNEVENTFUL.

Monday morning we set out from Beaver City early under a lowering, gray sky. The air was fresh and cool and smelled of fresh cut alfalfa. Our route took us up to I-80, across the fruited plain through Lincoln ("The highest state capitol building in the United States, boys") to Omaha, across the Missouri into Iowa, on to Des Moines and Davenport. The boys learned that Iowa was bordered on the east and the west by rivers that begin with the letter M.

That night, after driving about 700 miles, we stopped at Morris, near Joliet, Illinois. We hoped to get up early and avoid the rush hour traffic on the south side of Chicago.

This evening we began what would become a ritual: journal writing. The boys had no trouble spelling Mississippi. Evidently teachers don't bother too much with Missouri. When we drove across the Mississippi, Taylor's comment was that "it looks like a lake." Yes, a long, skinny lake. These two rivers, the Missouri and the Mississippi thwarted a plan we had, namely to take a picture at every state border. We had done so at the Kansas and Nebraska borders, but the borders at Iowa and Illinois were mid-bridge. Stopping to take a picture would not have been a wise or safe option.

Jeanie also opened school at the Super 8 motel where we were staying. We made quite an affair out of it. I had been designated the Assistant Principal in charge of discipline, and I introduced them to their new teacher, Mrs. Jeanie Merrill. And they better not talk or do anything stupid or silly.

Their new teacher, with whom they immediately and shamelessly began to flirt, instructed them to take out their journals. They were to write about three things: *What I Saw*, *What I Learned*, and *What I Thought About What I Saw and Learned*. These three ideas would—throughout the trip—form the rhetorical rubric for their written scholarly endeavors.

She wrote down some key words for Spenser to use in his journal since

Spenser routinely turned a fifteen minute writing exercise into a sixty minute marathon of exasperation.

I supervised the second session, opening a map of the USA and helping them trace with a pink highlighter the path which we had already trod through the heartland of America.

ॐ ॐ ॐ

We rousted the boys at 4:45 a.m. Tuesday morning, August 15, and when we pulled out of the parking lot, the digital clock in the dash read 5 a.m. We were on schedule!

We agreed to leave early because: First, it was the only way we could ensure beating the rush hour traffic, and second, we thought it would be a hot day and we wanted to get in as many miles during the morning as possible.

I closed the door to our motel room and stepped into the morning. The air was warm and moist. Semi-tractor trucks were gearing up and pulling on to the freeway. Traffic was heavy as we moved toward Indiana, and the sun rose like a giant red gong announcing our arrival in the Hoosier state at 5:45 a.m. The boys were asleep and slept soundly for the next couple of hours completely missing Indiana. Spenser slept across most of Ohio as well.

> **August 14, 1995**
> *I saw the Mississippi and Missouri Rivers. We had a flat tire 10 miles away, it was very hot. I learned that the Mississippi River is the biggest river in the USA. I learned that Lincoln Nebraska has the biggest capitol bilding in the USA. I learned it's hard getting ready to go to Europe.* —Taylor, 10

In spite of traveling on interstate highways, the trip so far, while not being exciting, had been interesting. We'd journeyed across a quiet America, being observers of small and silent communities one never hears of or reads about. We passed through eastern European and German villages in northeastern Kansas, like Leoville, for example. Must have been named for a slew of popes who bore that name. It's a small town that's surrounded by corn fields and in the center of town rising as so many do in Europe is the village church, an incongruously large structure with twin, onion-topped towers which shadow the village square.

We crossed rivers of infinite variety both in size and nomenclature.

Sacrament Creek must have an intriguing history. Republican Creek was narrow but deep; we expected to cross Democrat Creek, presumably wide but shallow, but it never appeared.

Morris, Illinois, to East Stroudsburg, Pennsylvania is 730 miles. We stopped. We were only miles from New Jersey. Tomorrow we'd be in New York! In two days, we'd traveled from Beaver City to New York; the one with a population of 900, the other a huddled mass of nine million!

That evening, after we had written in our journals and applied the highlighter to the USA map, Jeanie stripped the shirts off us three boys, sat us in chairs and slung a towel around our shoulders and took a hair clipper to our heads, shaving us virtually bald and giving us a faintly alien appearance. We would have no worries about hair for some time to come, although it had been a lot of years since I'd had much hair to worry about.

We left East Stroudsburg at 7:30 a.m. and descended into Jersey through the beautiful Delaware River Gap and within ninety minutes of our departure we were on the doorstep of Mrs. Anne Parker's Mine Street home in Bernardsville.

Mrs. Parker was an elderly lady and the mother of a colleague of mine in Colorado. He had volunteered his mother's house as a place where we could leave our car for five months while we were abroad. Of course, he had cleared this with his mother first, and we had been in conversations with her as well. So she was expecting us on this clear, bright morning, and was quite interested in the details of our adventure. She had a place around the back of the house where the car could be parked and where it would be out of the way.

We left her a set of keys as well as some financial remuneration, and pulled our backpacks out of the rear hatch door of the van. From now on, or at least for the next six weeks, we'd be living with whatever we could carry on our backs. Mrs. Parker's sister, Mary, generously offered to take us to the train station in the heart of town.

When she pulled out of the parking lot at the station, Jeanie and I just stood there watching her leave until the car turned right and disappeared. Even when she was gone, we didn't move. We were like statues in the Main Street park. Pigeons could've roosted on our shoulders. We didn't have Denver anymore, we didn't have Club Paquita anymore. We didn't even have the freakin' van anymore.

What we had were these red packs and two kids who were like: "Okay, what's next?"

And we're thinking, "What now?"

8

At the Amsterdam in Manhattan

GETTING FROM BERNARDSVILLE TO MANHATTAN WAS NOT WITHOUT ITS DIFFICULTIES. We boarded the New Jersey Transit Authority train in Bernardsville and an hour later we were in Hoboken where we dashed across the platform—if a family of two adults and two children can ever truly be said to be "dashing" anywhere—to catch a PATH train to lower Manhattan. We caught it, and the boys thought it was novel that the train could travel under a river, in this case, the Hudson river. It did, and when it made a first stop, we hastily got off, but soon repented of it because when we emerged above ground like moles in the light, we had no idea where we were. I thought we'd be getting off beneath the World Trade Towers. I could navigate from there.

I was wrong, and it wouldn't be the last time.

We stood mute on a street corner, like visitors from a distant planet, in a swirling vortex of human commerce in a city of the world, a city of nations. Street vendors crowded upon each other selling American hotdogs or Polish sausages, while above in air-conditioned offices stockbrockers, bankers, accountants, architects and publishers worked their deals. Young Jamaicans tapped on a tin drum, and an old black man with a salt-and-pepper beard blew on a dented alto sax coaxing a jazz tune from the gulf city of New Orleans. The avenues teemed with cosmopolitans flowing to unknown destinations with the speed of a rip tide; shoulder-to-shoulder in cross currents, an undulating sea of bobble-heads. The women promenaded in high heels, and smart-collared outfits, hemlines unfailingly above the knee, while the men, traveling in fraternal packs of two or three, wore the starched, cuffed uniform of Wall Street. Scattered among these sophisticates like floating flotsam were a younger pale-skinned sub-class of rebels attired in baggy gravity-defying jeans that brushed and swept the grey sidewalks. This generation had recently taken to mutilating their bodies with the most outlandish piercings, driving multiple

31

pins through ear lobes, and spikes through cheeks, eyebrows, nasal bridges, lips and tongues. Over this package they wrapped themselves in Draculan trench coats of black, and the girls painted their lips black and highlighted their eyes in black and starely at you blackly and blankly. Their heads might be full of colored hair, or shorn to the scalp. One young man's hair was moussed into pink and green spikes like those on the Statue of Liberty. Jeanie and I looked at each other: We weren't in Kansas anymore. We were facing a fiery leviathan with pungent urban breath and the prospect filled us romantically with an acrid mixture of delight and apprehension as the beast pressed in upon us and then wrapped us in its sweaty embrace.

We insisted that the boys always walk in front of us. They were not allowed to fall behind us, and they were scolded if they did.

We walked a couple of blocks to the Hudson, caught a bus that took us across town to Broadway. There we caught an N subway uptown, transferred at the 42nd Street/Times Square station to a Broadway Local #9 and took it up to 103rd Street.

Stop reading for a moment to consider the snappy conversations that took place between Jeanie and me to make all of that happen!

We got off at 103rd and walked one block east to Amsterdam and shortly thereafter arrived at the Amsterdam Hostel, our destination for the night.

Jeanie noticed in the subway that the city was evidently trying to persuade New Yorkers to adjust their attitude. Motivational signs are posted which read, for example: "Turn your back on a tourist, and tourists will turn their backs on New York." Another: "Instead of a wise crack, crack a smile."

The campaign must be working because when we stepped out of the subway, a gray-haired lady whose blood-red lipstick was smeared slightly above the lip-line accosted us and inquired sweetly, "Looking for the youth hostel?"

In fact, we knew exactly where it was—now—but we enjoyed the conversation anyway.

"You should avoid 103rd Street," she advised gravely, "especially late at night because there's a liquor store on the corner."

When we got back at 9 p.m. from cruising around Times Square, we took 103rd anyway; we were too tired to walk the extra distance taking 104th would've required.

The red brick Amsterdam Hostel, a recently rennovated century-old landmark building, is a very active place. It was, in fact, the largest such hostel in the United States at the time with 480 beds in both dormitory and private-style rooms. In the lobby area, six clocks on the walls above the reception counter noted the current time in London, Paris, Frankfurt, Rome and Beijing. Maps of Manhattan, Queens, Brooklyn and the subway system plastered the walls, and young people milled around the room, some sprawled out in corners resting against their backpacks on the floor. Others may have been doing laundry, passing time in the TV lounge, relaxing in the game room, or meditating in a one acre garden.

We had a reservation for our two night stay here. Everything was in order, and soon we were in our room. We were extremely pleased. The boys had bunk beds and there was a double bed for Jeanie and me. We also had a bath and shower in our room, an accommodation we knew we wouldn't have too often on our travels.

The boys quickly left to ride the elevator up and down and explore other areas of the hostel. Jeanie and I sat down on the bed, took a breath, and then thought about how we might spend the next twenty-four hours. We definitely wanted to take a lunch over to Central Park and spend some time there.

The next morning, we set out to face the leviathan known as New York City. Since we were not too far from the Cathedral of St. John the Divine, we hiked up there to take a look. The largest gothic cathedral in the United States, St. John's is still under construction even though work on the site began in the nineteenth century. The work today centers on the towers and the church has trained and hired kids from Harlem as stonecutters, masons, and laborers. It's slow work. But the cathedral is impressive. The interior is dark and solemn as a crypt. The nave and the altar cover two football fields. I heard John Denver give a concert there once. Just him—before his breakup with Annie, and his music went into the toilet. Alone, he came out in the darkness. No backup band or backup singers. A narrow spotlight illuminated a wooden stool. He sat on it, and played his guitar and sang and talked. Great stuff.

From the cathedral, we went to lower Manhattan and walked up Canal Street where vendors offered us deals on watches, radios, Walkman's, shirts and shoes. We perambulated through Chinatown with its fish markets, and then stopped in Little Italy for a gelato. We sat at little round tables.

"This is great, eh," I said, for no particular reason.

"We don't even need to go to Europe," Jeanie said. "Europe is right here—the Italians, Germans, French. The world. The United Nations. The Chinese, Japanese, Koreans, Ethiopians, Vietnamese. There was an Afghan restaurant we went by."

"And a Greek place."

"Wish I could see it all, or pay more attention to everything." She was eating a pistachio gelato in a cup. It was almost gone. The boys were across the narrow street looking into a toy store window.

"What do you mean?"

"The boys. You just walk on," she said with a wave of her hand, "not worrying about anything but I can't just walk and enjoy myself—I mean I enjoy myself—but I also have to watch out for the boys. Know what I mean?"

I nodded. I knew what she meant. Jeanie walked up and down the New York streets and avenues with a sort of radar that whirled constantly about her and that continually picked up the two boys as blips on her maternal screen. And when a blip was missing, she's stop and say, "Wait! Where's Spenser?"

It was usually Spenser about whom she inquired. Taylor was not as likely to simply wander off. Spenser lived in an alternative universe, a universe which we had to visit often in order to find him and keep track of him.

August 16, 1995

"Two scenarios: I'm walking through New York City by myself, and I'm not thinking about anything other than where I'm going, what I'm seeing. Or, I'm with my children, and I'm not just thinking about where I'm going, or what I'm seeing. There's always this concern overlaid on everything I was doing that involved the kids. We were in some really crowded places. Where are they? It's a different kind of travel. And then a husband who has an agenda..."

—Jeanie.

"He's over there," Taylor said. This could be another responsibility for Taylor: helping us keep Spenser within our jurisdiction.

So Jeanie could not enjoy traveling as though she was just on her own and had no one else to worry about. But she loved it; she was thrilled by the sights and sounds of what she saw. Still, it was tempered by that maternal instinct to always be aware of where her children were.

To help us know where the boys were when we were walking in crowded squares or plazas, or moving up busy streets and avenues, we insisted that the boys always walk in front of us. They were not allowed to fall behind us, and they were scolded if they did.

From Little Italy, we migrated to mid-town and Times Square again where we had some SBarro pizza and then used some of our beehive fun money to see *Babe*, a movie about a talking pig.

Back at the hostel, we prepared for bed. We wanted to be rested for the flight to Paris, even though it didn't leave until 6 p.m. But there was one more thing we needed to do: Taylor had to make his call.

Before we left Denver, Jeanie had agreed with her ex-husband that the boys would place a call back to Denver at least once a week. A pre-arranged time was set to avoid confusion. Now it was time for that first call. Our room in the hostel did not come with a telephone, so Taylor and his mom left in search of a phone elsewhere in the building, perhaps in the lobby.

About ten minutes later, there was a soft rap on the door. It was no doubt Jeanie and Taylor who had not taken a room key. I opened the door, and for a moment the two of them just stood motionless. Jeanie was pale and haggard, as though she'd just donated five quarts of blood to the American Red Cross. Taylor's eyes were red and swollen. The phone conversation had not gone well.

Here let me say a word about the boys' dad—all good. I like Donnie. He's certainly not my next best friend, and we don't hang together, but he's a likeable fellow. He works hard with his construction business, spending his days framing houses. He gave Jeanie a support check for the boys from day one and has continued to do so faithfully on the first of the month ever since.

There was a period of wrangling between he and Jeanie when she shared our sabbatical plans with him. She certainly was not going to leave the boys for five months with their father, not because he could not have taken care of them—although he wasn't really situated to do so—but because she didn't want to leave them. They would go with her on this trip or there would be no trip.

Donnie engaged an attorney and took us to court to prevent us from leaving the country. But the judge ruled that the trip would be a great experience for the boys, even at their young age, and it appeared that the mother had made all the necessary arrangements for their education, and therefore she, the judge, could see not an impediment to our leaving.

Once that ruling was handed down, to his credit, Donnie threw in his support. And a call back to Denver once a week certainly was not unreasonable. And, looking back on this, were I in his shoes, I'm not sure that I wouldn't have done the same thing.

For Spenser, 7, such a call posed no problems. This child lived in the moment, in the present. Not the past or the future. He chattered on the phone, got off, and was on to other things.

A phone conversation for Taylor, 10, however, was a major emotional event. Taylor valued comfort and safety, he appreciated the familiar and the known. And his dad didn't really understand how to help Taylor with this problem.

I stepped aside and motioned for them to come in. Jeanie gave me a distress-signal look that let me know we had a problem.

"Hey, kid, what's the matter?" I said, sitting down on the edge of the bed with him. Jeanie sat on the other side and stroked his hairless head.

"Nothing." His chubby hands were folded in his lap and he sat slightly slouched, his lips pouty and his eyes almost closed. Tears were forming around his eyes like a slow leak on a faucet.

"Was it hard talking to your dad? Did it make you miss him?"

"No."

"What did you talk about?"

"Nothing."

"Nothing? You didn't tell him about Chinatown, or the subways?"

"No." He started to cry.

"What did he say to you?"

Jeanie spoke up. "He wanted to know if our hotel had a swimming pool, and whether there was a game room, and whether there was a television, and then he said that he was going up to the mountains for some dirt-biking tomorrow and that he wished Taylor was with him—old buddy!"

August 16, 1995

"I remember being surprised that a child would be homesick when he was with his family—with his mother! But I realized then that it has to do with personality, that this would either really open up a world for Taylor and he would lose this fear of leaving the familiar, or—he would never, ever want to leave again! This could be for Taylor, even at his young age, a defining experience in his life!"

—Jeanie.

Ah! I have no doubt in my mind that his dad meant no harm by this. He just didn't understand how hard that was for Taylor to assimilate. The child was already prone to homesickness and everything his dad said exacerbated the problem. We had hoped that he would've spent the time inviting Taylor to talk to him about *his* life, rather than his dad talking about his own life—a life that Taylor was no longer a part of, and from which he now seemed so alienated.

The key for us would be to keep Taylor busy and give him responsibility. A classic oldest child, Taylor was eager to help and assist and took his jobs seriously. We would need to give him duties for which he alone was responsible.

We would also need to prepare him better for his next conversation by having him write out a list of things he wanted to tell his dad—things he could talk to him about rather than simply sticking the phone in his ear and hearing about life in Denver—when, right now, he didn't have a life in Denver. His life was wherever we happened to be at the moment.

I gave him a hug and wiped some tears out of his eyes. The crying had stopped.

But we continued to worry about how Taylor would adapt. We were only three days out of Denver and Taylor was seriously homesick, and nothing seemed to cheer him up.

The next morning we all got up excited.

We had several reasons to be excited. We were going to take a ferry; we were going to the Statue of Liberty; we were going to climb up the statue inside; we were also going to go to the airport; we were going to board a 747 Air France jetliner; we were going to leave the United States!

August 16, 1995
I saw New York. We wint to China Town. Thay eat fish. I learned how to ride the Subway. I learned that George Washington crossed the Delaware river.

—Spenser, 7

We caught a Broadway local and took it to Battery Park where Jeanie purchased tickets for our trip to Liberty Island. While we were waiting to board the ferry, we were entertained by three young men who sang and performed and passed the hat. They were the same kids who worked the crowd when Jeanie and I were in New York in 1993. We arrived early to avoid the long lines later in the day and thus were able to get in to the Statue of Liberty rather quickly and begin the ascent to the top.

"This is scary," said the boys repeatedly as we ascended the narrow, circular staircase, painted industrial green, to the top. We were only in the crown a few minutes, but the boys managed to peer out the small windows to view the New York skyline from every possible angle.

Later. "I learned that the Statue of Liberty is located in New Jersey."

"I learned that the Statue of Liberty was a gift from France to the United States."

We got off the ferry at Battery Park, and returned to the hostel to get our things. We loaded up our red packs, took the Broadway local for the last time and went down to the Port Authority Terminal building where we caught a bus for Newark International Airport. We thought we might as well kill time there as anywhere. Once at the airport, we bought some postcards and wrote notes to loved ones and mailed them stateside before leaving.

As we waited to board the Air France Boeing 747, Jeanie and I sat together, holding hands, hardly able to believe we were doing this. So far on this trip there had been several defining moments, no-turning-back moments. One was when we pulled out of the church parking lot at noon on Sunday, August 13, only four days ago. Another was when we left the van at Mrs. Parker's house in Bernardsville. This was now another one. We would board that plane, and ready or not, we were going to be—within hours—separated by a huge expanse of ocean and by cultures foreign to us and by thousands of miles and a number of time zones, from all that we knew and loved.

I squeezed her hand. "This is it, babe!"

She squeezed back and smiled. Spenser ran to the window and pressed his nose against the glass. Taylor sat quietly nearby, playing with his Game Boy.

The gate agent started the boarding process at 5:15 p.m. We settled into the center section in Row 51, Seats D,E,F, and G.

We were all buckled in, tray tables in the upright, locked position, when Spenser claimed he need to go to the bathroom. I didn't believe him for one minute. He must have visited every toilet on the plane before the crew insisted that everyone be seated and strapped in.

Taylor was faring quite well. The process of boarding and being in a superjet distracted him. Unfortunately, a man passed out in the aisle right beside him after we were in flight, sending his stomach into a nervous tailspin. But Jeanie calmed him down and he soon went to sleep.

I thought ahead. Once again, we were headed into the unknown. We had no reservations in Paris. No place to stay. A wife and two children were my responsibility.

But we would find a place.

I was sure of it.

Part Three
First Tango in Paris

"The difference between stumbling blocks and stepping stones ... is how you use them."
—Anonymous

9

Wheels Down

ORLY, FRANCE. WHEELS DOWN AT 1 A.M. NEW YORK TIME, 8 a.m. Paris time. We were very tired, but the adrenalin rush overrode the exhaustion for the moment at least. It was a goofy combination this exhaustion and excitement, like drinking Coke mixed with NyQuil.

I tried to get some sleep, but it just didn't happen. The flight itself was great. The Air France flight attendants served a number of different snacks, as well as a delicious dinner—I'm serious—which included a salmon fumé appetizer, fillet of red snapper with Dugléré sauce, rice with almonds, a fresh garden salad, cheese, pastry, and "café de Colombia." The wine was complimentary; Jeanie and I made a toast with a Bordeaux sauvignon. This is *coach* we're talking about here. We're packed in the back of this 747; even sardines have more breathing room. But the food and service were excellent. Didn't matter; I couldn't sleep even though the cabin lights were dimmed and everyone else was sleeping.

Those who did get some rest didn't get much. It was only a six hour flight. So once off the plane, we wearied ourselves through customs, and then found some seats where the family could sit while I went off to secure a place to stay.

I had marked off some lodging possibilities in our Frommer's travel book, so when I got to the yellow France Télécom phone booth, I started with these.

"Avez-vous une chambre pour quatre personnes?" I tried to speak fast so the hotel clerk would have no idea at all that I was an American passing himself off as a Parisien. I was aware of all the stories about how the French, especially the French in Paris, hate Americans. Perhaps it's not hate, just contempt—it's the emotion some Americans have for say, welfare moms, or that Yankee fans have for Red Sox fans, or New Yorkers vis-à-vis anyone west of the Hudson, that the monied have toward the un-monied. It's the curl of the lip and the flare of the nostril that we have toward those beneath our station in life. I had heard that the French regard Americans as not only beneath their station in life, but not even close to the station.

But I hadn't had that experience. Of course you can't expect everyone to be having a good day; you'll always run into someone who's got her knickers in a twist, but by and large, I thought that the French were very considerate and friendly.

The familiar refrain is that "if you at least attempt to speak their language, they will appreciate the effort." Perhaps. Maybe they will. Maybe they won't. The reason so many Americans have experienced hostility in Paris and elsewhere is that Americans can be total jerks, most of the time.

I grew up having no doubts about the superiority of the American way of life, and knowing that there was no country in the world that did anything better than the good old U.S. of A. This is an arrogant *weltanshauung* which unfortunately too many Americans don't leave at the gate when they step on foreign soil. Fortunately, when I began to travel (my first trip out of the country was to Ecuador in 1968—although I was a foreigner from the get-go, being Canadian by birth and living in Canada the first ten years of my life) I was so eager to learn about other cultures and experience new things, that the issue of whether the "American way of life" was superior was moot. Who cares?

Too many Americans are snobby, demanding, irritating gadabouts, and I don't even like them myself. No wonder the French don't.

So I had no beef with the French, nor they with me—as far as I knew.

The first hotel was full. I tried another and it was booked full as well. Then I tried the Esmeralda Hotel. Bingo!

It was a forty-five minute ride by buses, trains and automobiles to the Esmeralda. We left Orly on a "JetBus," ("Le trajet le plus sûr pour être à l'heure!"). We knew exactly where we were going because the hotel was located on the Left Bank caddywampus to Notre Dame—it was a small white-washed, red-roofed hotel situated across a cobbledstoned lane, rue St. Julian l'Pauvre, from a small park, Place Rene-Viviani. When we stumbled through a narrow, low doorway into a modest sitting room of dark wood paneling, rich deep carpeting, ancient stone walls and oiled antique furniture, we thought we'd stepped into the anteroom of Hogworts, and that Harry and Hermione were in the vaulted library through the door, past Dumbledore, the clerk at a small lamp-lit desk in the corner. Our room, on the fourth floor, was up a steep circular staircase of eighty-one steps, according to Spenser. It came with a bath and shower and was a room with a view because when we threw the shutters open we looked out on the small park below and to our left we had a magnificent view of the Seine and Notre Dame Cathedral. Oh, now we were in Paris!

After settling in, this "Now what?" feeling swept over us. Often, our bodies gave us a clue when we didn't know what to do next. In this case, we wanted nothing more to do than to sleep—no matter that an unexplored city lay just beyond the window. Our bodies said, "You're not going anywhere until you get some rest." So we curled up on our beds and snoozed for three hours right there in the middle of the day.

In the later afternoon we went down to the park and sat for a while as the boys played nearby. I had my book—Eliot's *Mill on the Floss*. Jeanie pulled out a sketch pad.

"What are you doing?" I asked, leaning over. I saw she had a little set of colored pencils.

"I thought I'd sketch you," she said, tucking a wisp of hair behind her ear.

"Sketch me?" Then I went British: "You kawn't be serious, darling."

"Sure. Sit still."

"So how would you describe me?"

She had started with a large oval for my big head. "Well, your head is a little large—"

"Size 7 plus. I can never find hats to fit my head," I said. "Is it really noticeable? I mean I hate to think that people are gawking at the bloke with the oversized head on a skinny neck."

"No of course not, honey, your head's fine. It's not a small head, that's all, it's just right."

I don't know why but I don't like the thought of having a big head; it makes me think I'm some sort of curiosity.

"Your perfect head is roundish—no not round, a very nicely shaped oval—with a dimple at the bottom of the chin, very pleasant and rounded features; your nose, it's not sharp or angular like some people, and it doesn't stick up or turn up, it's just there, nicely … blue eyes, and receding forehead, well, your forehead sort of just continues on back to your neck—" She laughed out loud and shoved me in a friendly sort of way.

"But you like it, right?"

"Of course I do, and I like your beard which gets whiter by the year and which you keep trimmed very short—thank you very much—and you used to have long hair from the back and sides of your head, but now it's gone, thanks to me. Do you want me to sketch with the long hair back in, or leave it out?"

"Back in." I didn't like my hair short; it made me seem balder and made my head look bigger.

"Okay then," she said. "And you're always wearing a baseball cap—"

"Everyone's going to think I have cancer," I said glumly.

Jeanie giggled. "No they won't. Why are you being such a doofus?"

And for the record I'm 6 feet 1 inch, pushing 190 pounds.

That evening, Jeanie and I strolled hand-in-hand down rue St. Andres des Arts toward the Place St. Michel while the boys scampered like puppies in front of us.

"This is where the bombs went off, isn't it?" Jeanie asked.

"Right here," I said.

"But it's okay," she said.

"It's okay."

The bombs exploded about a month before we arrived. They'd been hidden in some trash cans in Place St. Michel. The police thought it was the work of Algerian nationalists. Now, of course, every trash can in Paris had been sealed tight with a cover and screws. Even in the Metro.

These thoughts, however, could not dampen even in the slightest our merry mood as we walked the streets of the Left Bank. Here they're narrow and crowded with little restaurants trying to be noticed, offering everything from hot dogs, to pizza, to gyros. Some restaurants were clearly beyond our budget. The boys had hot dogs "avec frommage," while Jeanie and I had gyros in a pita for a simple meal.

When we got back to the hotel, the boys wrote in their journals and prepared to take baths and I sat in the open window facing Notre Dame, and literally placed the typewriter on the sill of the window and began to write. With my pipe lit and smoking, it was the only place Jeanie would let me work.

10

The Esmeralda Hotel

OUR ROOM WAS INDEED A ROOM WITH A VIEW, BUT it was also a room with a lot of noise and the noise came from the street below as crowds of late night revelers decamped from bars and restaurants, cars raced along the river and motorcycles revved their engines at the stop light nearby.

We couldn't close the windows because of the stifling heat, yet leaving them open exposed us to the continual clatter of city life. The drumming was the worst. A group of loud youths had camped along the Seine on the quay below the bridge on the left bank across from Notre Dame and they had drums to help them pass away the night. For the life of me, I could not then, nor can I now, understand the appeal of sitting among a group of strung-out wayfarers, tapping a beat on a bongo that was as boring as it was irritating. It was like listening to an orchestra of jackhammers. You want contempt? That's contempt, to provide another example. Drums—in my mind—are not solo instruments.

About 3 a.m., in despair, I suggested that we all get up and play card games for a while. It wasn't just the drums. Our bio-rhythmic clocks were still in the process of re-setting and it would no doubt take a couple of days to regain some kind of internal equilibrium. The boys heartily agreed, so we did, and had great fun. About 4:30 a.m. we crawled back into bed to give it another go. We hoped the noise would abate and we could get some rest.

It did and we did, sleeping until 10 a.m. But Jeanie and I knew that we would not be spending another night in the Hogworts Hotel even if the location was *tres romantique* and so close to the Latin Quarter and many of the sights we wanted to explore.

"Want to hear a little history about Paris?" I asked. It was Sunday afternoon, the next day. We were sitting on a bench in the *Jardin du Luxembourg*, or Luxembourg Gardens, and Jeanie was fumbling for change so that the boys could play in a fenced playground which cost 11fr each to enter.

"Sure," Jeanie said. "But I'm out of francs. Can you get some more?" She continued to paw around in her bag. "I bought two carnets of Metro tickets, and had to use the bathroom, cost 2.5fr. Maybe I have enough. Boys!" She left me on the bench and approached the attendant on duty at the playground entrance. There was a conversation. Jeanie peered into her hand to count coins, and bills. This went on for several minutes. Then, she gestured helplessly like a mother might do if her child was being left to die on the operating table. The attendant's dour demeanor said it all.

"She won't let us in. We're 2.70 short."

She sat down. The boys raced around some trees. "Can you go get some francs?"

"Sure, let me just read some of this to you. Let's see, in its early, early history, Paris was just a small fishing village on the Île de la Cité—"

"What's that?" she asked. "We really need some francs."

"It's the boat-shaped island in the middle of the Seine where Notre Dame is now, and Saint Chapelle. Here—" I pulled out a map to show her. Then I continued: "Small fishing village on the Île de la Cité that was conquered by Julius Caesar in 52 B.C. The Romans expanded the city to the left bank and the catacombs continue to remind us of the Roman presence. Much, much later—I'm summarizing here—St. Denis is said to have been martyred on Montmartre (hence the name—Mountain of the Martyr), and—do you know who's the patron saint of Paris?"

"Geneviève," she said.

"St. Geneviève, who's said to have protected Paris from the Huns and other invaders. Clovis I and several other Merovingian kings made Paris their capital; under Charlemagne it became a center of learning. In 987, Hugh Capet, count of Paris, became king of France. The Capetians firmly established Paris as the French capital. During the reign of Philip Augustus (1180-1223) the streets were paved and the city walls enlarged; the first Louvre (a fortress) and several churches, including Notre-Dame, were constructed or begun; and the schools on the left bank were organized into the University of Paris. One of them, the Sorbonne, became a fountainhead of theological learning with Albertus Magnus and St. Thomas Aquinas among its scholars. Are you listening?" She had turned to scout for the boys. For Spenser.

"I'm listening," she said.

"Just a little more. In the 17th century, Cardinal Richelieu, Louis XIII's minister, established the French Academy and built the Palais Royale and the Luxembourg Palace—right behind us, over there." We had passed the palace on our way to the playground.

"Paris frequently had an uneasy relationship with royalty, and Louis XIV, distrustful of the Parisians, transferred his court to Versailles 1682. Then we have the enlightenment period, and the French Revolution and the events of 1789—this is happening at roughly the same time as our American Revolution— in which the peasants or the common folk overthrew the aristocracy, stormed the Bastille on July 14th and later ratified the Declaration on the Rights of Man and Citizen, which is similar to our Declaration of Independence. Then Napoleon—"

"Skip to the modern era," she said. "Spenser, don't do that!"

"I was going to say he started the construction of the Arc d'Triomphe. Okay, the modern era. The Georges Pompidou National Center for Art and Culture—that's the building with all the tubes on the outside, remember?—was built in 1977 and includes the National Museum of Modern Art. The Louvre underwent extensive renovation, and EuroDisney opened in the Parisian suburbs in 1992."

"The boys want to go there."

"And go they shall," I said. "A number of major projects in the city were initiated by Mitterrand, the current President. They include the new Bibliothèque Nationale, the glass pyramid at the Louvre, Grande Arche de la Défense, Arab Institute, Bastille Opera, and Cité de la Musique. There you go." I stuffed the travel book back into my pack.

"I need you to get me some money, some francs," Jeanie said matter-of-factly.

"Okay, I'm on it," I said. "You'll be here, right?"

"Right here."

So I headed toward the edge of the 55-acre park admiring the abundant flowers, walking pathways colonnaded by trees, and watching children in rented boats paddling on a glassy pond. I strolled past the *Verger du Luxembourg*, an orchard of a thousand espaliered trees and two hundred species of apple and pear trees, still hand-tended as it has for almost two centuries by the Carthusian Order. Oldsters in berets were playing chess, too. This is sooooo French, I thought. Reaching Rue de Fleurus, I strode confidently forward expecting to find an ATM within minutes. Up Rue d'Assas, down Boulevard Rasspail. I walked past espresso bars and cafés, Tabac shops, boutiques, and chemists. But after twenty minutes of walking, found nothing. Finding an ATM in Paris is harder than finding a Bible in the house of Madalyn Murray O'Hair.

Surely there's a Credit Lyonnais, or Soceite Generale somewhere. So I inquired of an old couple shuffling by, and they said there was an ATM just a block away! When I arrived, the ATM was inside the bank building which was locked. It was Sunday. In the States, the ATM would have been located in an outer room available 24/7 throughout the weekend. Not here.

I was beginning to chafe. Not just an internal chaffing—impatience—but real, raw, burning chaffing from which I suffer intermittently when I'm on a long hike or playing eighteen holes of golf. Usually before setting out for the links, I apply a liberal application of Desenex powder to my crotch area that prevents the chaffing I've come to expect. But today, I hadn't planned to be gone long, and in any event couldn't have applied the powder in the park—at least not too easily, and I didn't have a franc to pay for a toilette in which to do it in any case. And, the Desenex was in the hotel.

The problem was exacerbated by the fact that I wasn't wearing any underwear—which I thought was a very Parisien thing to do. We had not yet found a *lavagogo* to do laundry. We went shopping for underwear in Montmartre where some souvenir shops had boxers fluttering in the breeze like flags at a porn convention. Jeanie found a pair with a huge Eiffel Tower plastered on front that she wanted me to buy, but I said no.

I was also developing a blister on my foot.

> *I had total faith in Timothy's ability to make this trip come off. So I never worried about that. I never worried about where we were going, what we were doing, would everything be okay. I never worried about that at all. My only concerns centered on keeping the boys healthy: Did they eat enough? Did they drink enough? Did they do their homework? Are they wandering off? —That sort of thing. Not being caught by surprise.*
>
> *So when we were in the Luxembourg Gardens—we had only been in Paris a couple of days—we went there and realized we needed money. So Timothy went off to get some money from an ATM and I stayed in the park with the kids. And that's when I realized that I didn't know where we were, I didn't know the name of our hotel, I didn't have any money, no passport, and I realized right then I needed to be a little more responsible for knowing where I was and not turning all of that over to Timothy.*
>
> —Jeanie

The fire in my loins intensified. I started to walk with a limp like a cowboy who's been in the saddle too long. I'd been gone over an hour, and Jeanie was no doubt wondering where I was, thinking perhaps I had gotten lost or mugged. I don't get lost. I knew how to get back to the Gardens. I didn't know whether I would find an ATM.

And then, voilà! I turned a corner and there it was! Quickly, I pulled

400 fr from the machine and began a fifteen minute limp back to Jeanie in the Gardens.

She was still there. Indeed, where could she have gone? She had no money, no passport, no idea where the hotel was located. Indeed, had I abandoned her and the family that afternoon, she'd still be sitting on that park bench in the *Jardins du Luxembourg* with pigeons resting on her shoulders.

Jeanie approached the attendant like Antonio to Shylock, clutching a fistful of cash and gave the woman her pound of francs. The boys then were unloosed like bear cubs into a trash pile and they played for a full two hours while Jeanie and I sat under some eucalyptus trees and kept them on our radar. There was a breeze. It was pleasant. Jeanie started reading *Pride and Prejudice*. I was still laboring through *Mill on the Floss*.

11

Wherein We Fall Asleep at Mass

OUR NEW HOTEL, *LA MARMOTTE*, IS SITUATED IN A QUIET neighborhood in the Second Arrondissement. We're on the fourth floor. Spenser didn't count the steps. The ground level, which doesn't count as a "floor," or stage, has an espresso bar, and wine and liquor is served too. The room has a toilet and shower and a TV! This counts for a lot. The TV. Even if the boys can't understand a word, it's a TV.

I paid for three days. I didn't want to commit to more than three days. We'd wait and see how we liked it at the Marmotte.

We returned now to the Marmotte to relax before going to mass at Notre Dame which was at 6:30 p.m.

Our grand plan, which had all the strategic brilliance of the Bay of Pigs invasion, was to at all costs keep the boys up until about 9 p.m. so that they would then get a full and normal night of rest, and be ready to rock and roll at 7 or 8 a.m.—and we'd have, for the first time a normal day.

What better way to keep anyone awake than to go to a Roman Catholic mass said or sung in a strange language?

"You have the water bottles?"

I checked my pack. "Yup." We found that we were drinking a lot of water. Walking will dehydrate a person real quick, and the Paris weather right now was hot, hot, hot.

We found a pew, a hard, straight-back bench of varnished oak as severe as the catechism itself. It was on the right side of the nave which smelled of candles and incense. The boys had been inside St. John the Divine in New York, as well as St. Patrick's. Here, it wasn't as dark as St. John's, or as bright as St. Patrick's. I left Jeanie in the pew, and took the boys on a little tour down the side aisles, around the apse of the church, visiting the Treasury and pointing out the stained glass windows of the clerestories and so on. They

"The mass began. I had Spenser on my left and Taylor on my right. ... We sang the responses in French. The matron seated next to Jeanie, an old lady with filo face skin, pouty red lips and whose head was crowned with a pillbox hat with a feather sticking out, was keeping a wary eye on us." —p. 51.

were interested in this stuff! Our plan could work.

The mass began. I had Spenser on my left and Taylor on my right. I helped Taylor follow the liturgy and Jeanie helped Spenser. We sung the responses in French. The matron seated next to Jeanie, an old lady with filo face skin, pouty red lips and whose head was crowned with a pillbox hat with a feather sticking out, was keeping a wary eye on us.

When the homily began, in French, we started to lose the boys. Taylor's head fell with a thud to his chest. I gave him a stiff elbow in the side, startling him and causing the missal to crash to the slate, dusty floor with a resounding twack! Madame Matron stiffened and peered our way with an arched eyebrow. I picked up the book. "Sit up and stay awake and pay attention!" I hissed in Taylor's ear.

What were we *thinking?*

August 22, 1995
I saw Luxemburg park. I played there. You have to pay to go potty. I learned that the Mona Lisa is famous. —Spenser, 7

This little dance and variations on the theme occurred several times in the next fifteen minutes. Once, I thought I was listening to the priest, and the next moment there was a sharp pain in my side. "Sit up and stay awake and pay attention," Taylor whispered. I glared at him. He smiled.

When the sermon was over and the congregation was standing, we ushered the boys outside to some fresh air. There was no way they would make it through the Eucharist.

It was a wacky plan, but Spenser was in bed at 9:30 and slept soundly until 8:30 a.m. the next morning—as did his brother. From then on, we were on Paris time!

51

12

"Avez-vous un Ventilateur?"

WE ARE OFTEN ASKED WHY WE STAYED IN PARIS FOR three weeks. Good question.

My answer is: "How long do you stay in Paris? Two days? Four days? A week?" You can't "do" Paris in one or two days. We had six weeks allocated for travel through Europe. We could've started in Oslo and made our way south, hitting Stockholm, London, Copenhagen, Amsterdam, Brussels, Frankfurt, Cologne, Paris, Vienna, Budapest, Geneva, Milan, Venice, Florence, and Rome. I mean, come on. Get serious. We were *not* going to have the kind of trip where we're running around with guidebooks in hand and cameras mounted permanently to our eyes like typical touristic cyborgs, seeing nothing. Wasn't going to happen.

Three Principles to Observe When Traveling As a Family
- *Take time for routine stuff.*
- *Make time for fun stuff.*
- *Don't sweat the small stuff.*

I did *not* want to hit the ground running. I wanted hit the ground walking, observing, listening, stopping to smell the espresso. I want to land in Europe, stop, regroup, and re-establish our home as mobile, living organism. Three weeks in Paris would give us a chance to do that as well as to explore the inexhaustible treasures of this city.

That's precisely the effect we achieved. We landed in Paris. And we weren't off and rushing about. We had plenty of time. We relaxed. We enjoyed.

And we saw tons—and took our time about it. Sacre Coeur, the Picasso museum, the Paris sewers, the Louvre, Musee d'Orsay, cafés and bridges, Notre Dame (climbed the North Tower, saw the Bourbon bell), Saint Chappelle, the Eiffel Tower, the Arch of Triumph, open air markets, Saint Eustache, Versailles, La Defense, a boat trip by night on the Seine—and much more.

But *taking time for routine stuff* was the key. We were going to be together 24/7 for five months. I mean together 24/7! We needed to establish a rhythm, a beat, a routine. Without it, we'd all wake up some morning screaming bloody murder.

We decided to stay at the Marmotte. This decision was greeted with rejoicing by the boys. See? They didn't want to be bouncing around. "You mean we don't have to carry our packs to another hotel?" Taylor said brightly.

"That's what I mean, buddy."

So I grabbed the laundry and taking Taylor with me—he put in the coins—we left a load running in the *lavagogo*, and went to see the hotel manager. "Nous partons Paris quatre Septembre, nous voudirons rester ici." He reached below the counter, and retrieved a big book, and flipped through some pages. He said that not only could we stay, but there would be a reduction in the rate because of the length of our stay. The bill came to 5,780fr, or about $1,230USD for a 16-day stay, or roughly $76 a night.

It was a good decision. There is a *lavagogo* next door. The street, rue Leopold Belland is small and quiet. The neighborhood is full of shops and markets. Here we could maintain more easily a comfortable rhythm for living.

Our routine was as follows: We arose and cleaned up somewhere between 7 and 8 a.m. Then the four of us went out for breakfast. It was far too expensive to eat breakfast at a restaurant or café, so we walked a short block to the *boulangerie* where we got a croissant. I always took the *pain de chocolat*. We then went to the *grocerie* and bought a yogurt each, and some fruit, usually bananas, and some juice or coffee. Then we walked with our breakfast to a park at the end of the street, right by St. Eustache. We called it the "head park" because there was a huge egg-shaped sculpture of a human head, sort of on its side with a large hand cupped to the ear. It was the work of a Henri Miller. Nearby there was an enormous open area for the boys to run about, steps to climb, fountains to watch, as well as gardens to enjoy. This was our routine every morning we were in Paris: breakfast in the head park. Often, on our way back, we stopped in the flower shop or the spice shop. Always interested, always curious.

Back at the hotel, having left the key at the front desk, we needed to retrieve the key. This was the responsibility of the boys. They took turns asking for the key in French.

Spenser went first, after we had rehearsed him thoroughly, because Taylor was too shy: "Cle numero sept, si'l vous plait." And the moustachioed manager handed him the key to room number 7. Taylor came through the next time, and indeed, even if we were in a rush because we needed to use the bathroom, the manager soon refused to give us the key unless one of the boys asked him for it in French. He was a nice man. He liked the boys.

Once we were back upstairs, it was time for school. The morning hours were reserved for instruction. In the afternoon we would play. Jeanie and I could accomplish more in two to three hours of solid teaching than a typical teacher could manage back home in six-seven hours. That's no knock on the school system. The reality is that if you have a 1-1 teacher-pupil ratio and no other activity except an instructional activity, cognitive development is going be fast and significant.

Not that all the school work was done in the hotel room. Often, we'd take our work with us to the head park, and after breakfast, get right to it.

I wasn't always involved in the instruction. My involvement depended on two things: What Jeanie had planned for the morning curriculum, and whether there were family or travel matters that needed attention.

For example, we were having trouble sleeping at night. It was so hot, and add some humidity, 90° seemed like 100°. At night, it didn't cool off that much. We flopped on our beds, throwing off the sheets and thrashed and turned hoping that the night air would cool. In the morning the sheets would be wet. We were sweating more than O.J. Simpson on trial. So, the family thought that if we could purchase a circulating fan, it would help considerably in the sleep department.

After Taylor and I made arrangements to extend our stay at the Marmotte, he went to school with Spenser and I went off in search of a fan.

The clerk at the first store smiled when I asked, "Avez-vous un ventilateur?" I don't know whether he was chuckling at my French or the very idea that after a summer of super hot weather there would be any *ventilateurs* left in Paris.

I went to several stores and the results were the same: no fans. So we decided to accept the heat and the difficulty of sleeping as part of the adventure. To that end, we adjusted our schedule so that we stayed up later, and slept in later, too. And we reminded ourselves frequently, that the heat would break, and in any case, we would soon be setting off for the coast of Normandy!

Back to routines and comfort zones. We have the hotel, we have breakfast, we have shopping for breakfast, we have eating breakfast, we have school in the morning—the routine was developing. We also tried *to make time for fun stuff*.

Like going to a cool bookstore, or *librairie*, for example. Our favorite was Shakespeare and Company, on the left bank within eyeshot of Notre Dame.

This bookshop is how bookshops should be: cramped with wooden shelving, two or three stories high, circular staircases, low ceilings, boxes and crates, posters, classical music, and eccentric clerks who look like they've just flown in from a meeting of the coven.

Once, while Jeanie and the boys were inside, I sat down on a bench on the cobblestone in front of the shop. I noticed a chalkboard where several personal ads had been written. One read: *Paris bookstore owner looking for outdoor girl to build cabin in north woods. If she will cook him trout for breakfast every morning, he will tell her dog stories every night.* Here's another: *Modest expatriate wishes to correspond with girl who has a tragic sense of life and magical sensibility to people. Box 20.*

Another fun thing to do was visit Pere-LaChaise Cemetery. For this trip we packed a lunch and took one backpack with us. We'd need the Metro for this trip, and the closest Metro station was only a block away.

The boys quickly learned how to use the Metro system. After only a week, we were confident that, if there were an emergency and Taylor needed to get back to the hotel on his own via the Metro, he could do it. He understood *sortie, correspondence*; he knew how to check the *direction* of the train by spotting the *destination* of the train.

September 1, 1995
I saw the Eiffel Tower. We went on a boat ride. I saw the grave yard.
I thought the boat ride was fun. —Spenser, 7.

So we went to the nearby Sentier Metro stop, each putting our ticket in the machine so that we could get out to the platform. There we boarded the green line, Gallieni destination which had a Pere-LaChaise stop. This trip, we were on the first car and seated close to the engineer's cabin. Built into the door to the cockpit—as it were—was what looked like a two-way mirror. When Spenser saw it, he jumped up, approached it, and spent some time admiring his beautiful self.

Taylor spoke up: "Spense, you can see the track ahead in the tunnel if you look through it."

Spenser looked again in the mirror and saw nothing but himself. "Where? I don't see anything."

His mother spoke up: "Spenser! Look beyond yourself, and you'll see what's coming ahead."

Spenser then refocused his eyes to look *through* the glass rather than *at* the glass, and instead of seeing himself, he saw the train rushing through a spectacular tunnel on its way to the next station.

And if you don't see a moral in that story, you might as well put this book down, turn on the TV and watch the Jerry Springer Show.

We got off the Metro at the Pere-LaChaise stop, and walked up three flights of stairs to street level. The area was teeming with traffic, pedestrians, newspaper kiosks. We began to walk in the direction of the cemetery. I noticed that Jeanie was hustling the children past the kiosks with uncharacteristic zeal.

And here's where—when traveling with a family—*you can't sweat the small stuff.* "What's the matter?" I whispered.

"They don't need to see all those girlie magazines," she muttered.

Indeed! I hadn't noticed.

But there's no way you're going to walk a couple of boys, three boys, I suppose, through the neighborhoods of Paris, and they're not going to see women's breasts on magazine covers, or women in provocative poses. Once, in a flea market, Spenser quickly discovered a stash of very interesting Parisien postcards, and Taylor was found giggling over a deck of playing cards. There's no point in freakin' out. You just accept it, and move on.

> **September 1, 1995**
> *I saw Chopin's grave. I went on a boat ride down the Seine river. I learned Rodin made the Thinker. I learned Chopin is buried in Pairs. I learned France gave the Statue of Liberty to the U.S.A. I thought Picasso had some crazy pictures.*
> —Taylor, 10

In the Louvre, we walked down a hall featuring rows of statues of male figures. Spenser noticed something immediately.

"Why are all their winkies broke off?" he asked. Jeanie shot me a glance as though to tell me that it was my turn.

"Hey, these statues are really old, like thousands of years old. So the winkies got knocked off. Look at their noses. Not many noses left either."

The answer sufficed, and we moved on. You can't sweat the small stuff.

We found Pere-LaChaise and as soon as we were within the gates, I handed the boys a map of the cemetery with the graves of Chopin, Oscar Wilde and Delacroix marked. The game was to see if they could successfully find these graves by following the map.

It was great fun. Pere-LaChaise is not just a cemetery, it's a cemetery right out of *Nightmare on Elm Street*, or an old black-and-white movie with Bela

Lugosi. Situated on rolling hills, there are graves with huge headstones, and mausoleums both big and small, some looking like outhouses that have been tipped over. Stone slabs rise up from the ground, some groaning skyward over centuries of winters and springs, rain, snow and frost. You can walk freely among them, and be lost to the sight of others, and then peek and say "Boo" at the people you love most in life. The boys played "peek-and-boo" a lot, but they also found the graves we were looking for.

At Chopin's tomb, we posed for pictures so that the boys could give a copy to their piano teacher, Mrs. Orrick, back home. We ate lunch by Delacroix, Oscar Wilde nearby. While venturing on my own a little, I found Jim Morrison's grave, a search made easier by the scent of marijuana floating over the headstones, because around his grave were a half dozen youths sitting silently, passing around joints, honoring a man who, were he alive, would be older than I was then. Go figure.

Jeanie and I leaned back against Delecroix (Jeanie loves his work), and ate our sandwiches and watched the boys play. Everything had turned out so well. The boys were happy. We were happy. We were living a dream, sharing an experience that we'd treasure to the very end of days.

And we were in love. This is what it's all about: entwining our lives together, looking down a path in the same direction, hand in hand, and our hearts interlocked. It couldn't get better than this.

I was right. It couldn't get better. The bubbles in our champagne were about to go flat!

13

What We Thought about the 'Thinker'

I PUT PRESSURE ON JEANIE TO VISIT CHARTRES CATHEDRAL. IT WAS a forty minute train ride out of Paris. I would tend to the kids; she needed a break. I'd seen the cathedral at least three times. She would enjoy it on her own and at her leisure.

"No way," Jeanie said.

"Yes way," I said. "You took the kids to EuroDisney for the day, and I stayed here by myself, had a whole day to goof around on my own. Now you need a day to yourself—you know you want to see Chartres. Just do it!" I didn't understand why she was pushing back so hard on this. "Are you afraid you'll get lost or something."

"No, I won't get lost—don't treat me like a child."

"I'm not, I'm not. I'm just trying to understand what's going on here."

"There's nothing 'going on' here, I just don't want to go by myself."

"You mean you just don't want to go without the boys." This was the heart of the matter, I suspected. "You don't trust me with the boys."

"Yes, I do. Don't be silly."

"No, no, you think I'll be charging ahead on a mission, and I'll leave the boys in the Metro somewhere. They'll be riding the Metro all day not knowing where to get off."

She fell into silence. "I don't want to go."

She went. The boys and I spent the day at the Bois de Boulogne park, which is huge, and with its playgrounds, paths and open fields, we had plenty to do. Taylor elected to wear his goofy Goofy hat he'd bought at EuroDisney. But the good news is that I didn't lose them, not even for a moment.

It was a case where, for once, I knew what Jeanie needed and what she'd enjoy. And she later thanked me for it. But this little spat was only a harbinger of things to come.

The next day was supposed to be a rather full day. It was a Saturday and I had planned a heavy day of activities. We weren't going to the Louvre or the Georges Pompidu Centre, because we could get in those places for free on Sunday. Since this was a Saturday, school was out, and we were going to be busy.

First order of business: The boys needed to make their weekly call to the States. So we rehearsed with Taylor. We sat with him and helped him draw up a list of everything he wanted to tell his dad that he'd seen. It was a lengthy list. If we could get him to talk about his list, he might be okay.

But we were running late. Jeanie was in the bathroom forever. She was moving slower than molasses uphill. Later I learned that Aunt Flo had arrived and she had a serious case of the cramps. And she felt bloated and ugly. I should've cancelled the day then and there.

The boys were fussing. Taylor was getting melodramatic about his call. His eyes were already puffing up and getting red. "I don't want to cry," he said.

"I know you don't" I said. "You'll be fine."

We finally tramped down the stairs, left the key with the manager, and headed for a phone booth near the Sentier Metro stop. We couldn't get the call to go through. So we tried La Poste where there were usually some pay phones. But before we could get there, Jeanie needed a bathroom, and was forced to use a sidewalk kiosk bathroom. You insert 2fr and a door slides open, you go in, do your business, and the door closes behind you when you leave. The boys were all over this, because there's nothing like it in the States.

Finally we got to La Poste. The connection was made and we handed the phone to Spenser, who rattled off a series of very cool and exciting stuff he'd seen ("I saw some postcards with boobies on them!") and then we handed the phone to Taylor. I took Spenser outside.

Ten minutes later Taylor and his mother emerged from La Poste. Taylor's eyes were red, but his face was dry; he was wearing a glorious smile! What a relief! So now we could get going.

Our first destination was the Paris sewers. After that, the tomb of Napoleon and then the Rodin Museum, and if we had time, the Musee D'Orsay.

Visiting the sewers of Paris, of course, seemed like a very cool idea to the boys. But in fact we were interested as well. The sewers date back to 1850 when Baron Haussmann and engineer Eugene Belgrand began a system that would provide both potable water for Paris and a means of disposing of waste—other than dumping it in the Seine. In the 150 years since it was first began, the sewers have been modified and enlarged making it almost a "wonder of the world." There's no system anywhere quite like it.

It was also a place where the French Underground met during World War 2.

This was an historical fact we tried to play up with the boys: Resistance Fighters plotting their strategy in the sewers of Paris!

We were glad to get back above ground—the "Eau de Waste" had become a trifle strong. The experience hadn't worn out the boys, however, and as we recouped briefly at the above-ground exit right on the banks of the Seine, Spenser took to cavorting on a series of steps.

Then he fell. He had been skipping along the steps, tripped over his own foot, and went down like a sack of bricks, tumbling headlong to the bottom.

The trip down from the top to the bottom was about eight steps. He fell silently, but at the bottom the silence ended. Both he and his mother started wailing.

Taylor stood by and just shook his head. "Spense," he said.

There was nothing for me to do either, although I, too, rushed to his aid. The kid was complaining about his chest. Jeanie ripped off his shirt, and we could see diagonal abrasion across his upper chest. But the wound hadn't drawn blood. It looked like someone had drawn a piece of #9 sandpaper across his ribs.

That, of course, was a relief to both Jeanie and I. The child would be fine. No broken bones, no wound that required stitches. No doctors, no hospitals. So, let's get our packs, and head down to the Tomb of Napoleon.

But Spenser would not stop crying. Maternal ministrations and encouragement were of no avail. I thought the injury was less physical and more psychological: the child was embarrassed. One moment he's leaping gaily over the steps; the next, he's tumbling like a rag doll out of control.

This wailing went on for at least ten minutes. My irritation was increasing by the second. I wanted to revisit our agenda and get going. Jeanie thought a couple band aids might help.

"He's not bleeding," I pointed out clinically.

"I know that," she whispered. "But it might help him think he's going to be okay."

"He *is* going to be okay," I said. Jeanie glared at me, and I backed off and sat down on a step to see how long Spenser was going to drag this out.

After what seemed like an interminable delay, she got him to wobble to a standing position and take a few steps. He stood there like a new born foal.

Now we could be off. "Just wait a few minutes," Jeanie said. "What's the hurry?"

We started walking to the Rodin museum, deciding to postpone a visit to the Tomb of Napoleon for another time. It was about a twenty minute walk, and Spenser sniffled the whole time.

"What's the matter with him?" I complained.

"For Pete's sake, he's got a laceration across his chest, Timothy."

"No, he doesn't. A laceration is when your skin is flayed open and viscera is hanging out or something."

"What's viscera?" Taylor asked.

"It's guts," I said. "Blood and guts."

Jeanie still wasn't feeling her best, either. Only Taylor and I were physically and emotionally healthy and ready to see some new stuff. I patted him on the head.

The Rodin museum is beautiful. Behind the two-story chateau, a large garden is laid out in the French style. The museum was for a time his home and where the German writer, Rainer Maria Rilke, lived as well when he was Rodin's secretary. Inside, I was intrigued by the pieces, "The Hand of God," and "The Hand of the Devil." They are much alike, suggesting perhaps, that one cannot know in the circumstances of life whether you're in the hand of God or his adversary. The pressures can seem similar.

As we walked to the entrance of the museum, we noticed "The Thinker" in a small area to the right.

"Ah, there's 'The Thinker'" I said. I have this habit of stating the obvious. "Interesting to see it in two places, New York and Paris. The original's in New York."

"No," Jeanie countered, "this is the original. The *copy's* in New York."

"No it's not."

"Yes it is."

"I remember distinctly reading about it. New York has the original," I said emphatically.

"Nope," she said.

"Wait a minute," I grabbed her arm so that she'd stop walking and we could have at it. "I didn't just imagine this. I read about it. The original is in at the Metropolitan Museum of Art on Fifth Avenue in the Rodin hall."

"That's a copy of what you see here."

I was hot. I felt like a grenade with the pin pulled. "You think that I don't know squat about art, don't you? That's it, isn't it? I know that's it."

"Don't be ridiculous."

"You think that on all things pertaining to art, that you're the big expert, and I'm a complete idiot."

"I do not think you're a complete idiot." Pause. "You're only half an idiot."

"You don't respect me."

"Timothy, what in the world has got into you? Let's just drop it. Who cares?"

"I care. The original 'Thinker' can't be both in New York and Paris. It's either here or there. And I happen to know for a fact that the original is there—in New York."

"Whatever."

We entered the museum and didn't say another word to each other. We moved from piece to piece in separate arcs. I was fuming like a pack of Camels at an AA meeting. This was not over by any means.

We moved out into the gardens and found an arbor under which to sit and enjoy the spectacular view. But we said nothing to each other except to mumble something about how it might be best to head back for the hotel.

"Fine."

"Fine."

So we did.

Arriving at La Marmotte, the boys got the keys from the manager ("Cle numero sept, s'il vous plaît") and Jeanie sent the boys upstairs. "We'll be up in a minute. Watch some TV."

We stepped out into the rue de Leopold Belland, crossed the street and stood on the sidewalk. I knew I was in for it—big time. I felt like a bandit in front of a firing squad; all I needed was a blindfold and a cigarette.

She turned to face me and the face I saw was a face streaked with tears. And more were coming. And when she spoke, her voice quavered and her lips trembled.

"I don't know if we can go on this way," she said softly.

I was stunned and had absolutely nothing to say. What I needed was about three hours to frame a response. For one thing, the fact that she was crying, totally changed the emotional landscape. Why is it that guys hate it when their women cry, but it's only when they *do* cry that somehow everything seems to come back into focus? It's because we have the emotional intelligence of a turnip. When she cried, it was like I was able for the first time all day, to see through her own tears and understand what a complete cad I'd been. So I said:

"Don't know if we can go on *what* way?"

"This way. I don't know how we can live for a hundred and fifty days this way. Five months. I just can't do it." She put one arm across her waist and leaned the other elbow on it and put a hand to her face to cover her mouth.

We stood apart in silence, a gulf the size of the Grand Canyon yawning between us.

I shuffled toward her and wrapped her up in my arms. "I'm sorry," I murmured. And I was. Really, really sorry. I clearly needed to change my ways. I pulled away, and looked into her eyes, and wiped her tears away.

"Look, here's what we need to do."

"What?" she said, sniffling.

"We need to go up to the room, and tell the boys that we're going to be gone for forty-five minutes. Show them a watch, and let Taylor know exactly what time we'll be back, and that they're to stay in their room, watch TV, play Game Boy or read while we're gone. And we need to go to the café at the end of the block and have a glass of white wine."

Remarkably, she agreed.

We sat at a sidewalk table and for the next forty-five minutes nursed a couple glasses of Chardonnays. I won't go into the details of that conversation, except to say that we realized then that if this trip were to work, Jeanie and I had to schedule time for ourselves—just the two of us, and that such time was an *investment*, not only in our relationship, but in the adventure itself.

Truth was, we'd been mangled in Paris, when we'd hoped to tango in Paris. We hadn't done the tango or any other dance since we left Denver, and there was no telling when we'd ever dance again. If you get my drift.

"Dick Kaufmann said we'd have a few of these days," I said. She smiled and reached into her handbag to retrieve a piece of paper. "Here," she said, sliding it across the table. "I wrote this for you."

It was written on a lined page ripped from her journal and dated "Paris, August 28, 1995." It read:

> *My darling,*
>
> > *You are so good, caring and loving to me. I apologize for the fuss I made about the Chartres trip. As I rode on the train, I realized that the "not wanting to go alone" was fear mixed with weaning myself from the boys and a little PMS thrown in.*
>
> > *I want to always be honest with myself, and you, when I react to situations, rather than allowing my ego to mask what I'm feeling.*
>
> > *You are my best and dearest friend and I know that in order to maintain the closeness we have, I have to open myself up to you.*
>
> > *Thank you for your patience, tenderness, and your love.*
>
> *Always,*
> *J.*
> *Your loving wife.*

I folded it slowly and put it in my shirt pocket. Then we leaned forward toward each other and I kissed my wife.

"I'm crazy about you," I said.

Part Four
In Which We Travel
By Car, Train, Boat,
Bus and Plane

"Nothing happens unless there is first a dream."
—Carl Sandburg

"It's absolutely stunning and romantic; the narrow streets and quaint shops exude the air of a bygone age. ... It was a pleasure just to saunter through the *ville ancien*, admire the cathedral of St. Vincent, or buy an ice cream from a vendor." —p. 68

14

The Naked Ladies of St. Malo

W E LEFT PARIS ON MONDAY, SEPTEMBER 4, 1995, AT PRECISELY 10 a.m. I picked up the flaming red Renault *Clio* at the local AVIS rental agency, promising to return it to their Chambéry location in seven days on the 11th.

Before we left, however, there was one thing we wanted to do: Go to the Place de l'Étoile in the middle of which sits the Arch of Triumph and do a few laps around the Arch.

We got on the Champs Elysée and drove up the boulevard watching the Arch getting closer. "Buckle up, folks!" I shouted. "Tray tables in the upright position!" I put the pedal to the metal and swung into the flow of traffic zipping around the arch.

"Yippee!" Spenser cried.

"Honey," Jeanie said, "Honey, not so fast! Not so fast!" What we have here is perhaps the world's most famous roundabout; we burned three laps around the Arch like we were doing the Indy 500 before whizzing off at the Avenue de la Grande Armée in the direction of La Defense.

"Want to do that again?" I yelled.

"Yeeeeaaaaah," the boys sang out.

"Did you get that out of your system?" Jeanie asked. "Could we please slow down now?"

We slowed down, if for no other reason that we promptly got misdirected in a maze of cone zones on the way out of Paris. It took us a good ninety minutes before we could truly say that we'd left the City of Lights.

"We're lost, aren't we?" Taylor suggested nervously.

"No, Taylor," I said, "we aren't lost because we know that where we are is not where we want to be. All we need to do is to find out how to get to where we want to be from where we are now. Okay?"

Silence. "Could you repeat that?"

"No."

Jeanie intervened, ever the peacemaker: "It's okay. We all have each other and chocolate. We'll be okay."

We took the N 12 out of Paris to Alençon and from there the D 33 to Fougères and from there the D 155 to St. Malo. Sounds easy, but in some towns, notably Lassay and Fougères we were quite frankly driving like rats in a maze.

St. Malo is a beautiful, medieval walled city on the Normandy coast and for our stay there, I wanted to stay *intra muros* (within the walls). As a fortified city, the area in its past was home to monks, merchants and marauders and its influence extended not only to the estuary of the Rance river, but also to the open sea.

It's absolutely stunning and romantic; the narrow streets and quaint shops exude the air of a bygone age. It was a welcome change, too, from the grating noise and busy-ness of Paris. It was a pleasure just to saunter through the *ville ancien*, admire the cathedral of St. Vincent, or buy an ice cream from a vendor.

The city also played to the imagination of the boys because we'd just gone to the cinema and seen *First Knight* with Sean Connery and Richard Gere, the story of King Arthur, Lancelot and Guinevere. Now we were staying in a town that looked every bit the Camelot of the movie!

We stayed at a little inn with restaurant called *Les Chiens du Guet*, or, "The Watch Dogs." Doesn't sound like much, but its location at the base of the fortifications was just perfect. We clambered out of the Clio, gathered our packs and walked into the reception area. The desk clerk looked up and said, "Ah, Merrill's?"

"Yes," we said.

"This is for you," and he handed us an envelope. It was a letter from my mother, 77. How cool was that! We also received the first of many letters from the noun fairy. We had no idea who the noun fairy was, but in each of her letters, she gave the boys a list of nouns and then a fairy story without any nouns. They had to supply a noun that they thought would work best with the context. Epistolary visits from the noun fairy throughout the trip were exciting for the children, and since the noun fairy was kind enough to write to us, we made certain that the kids obeyed everything the noun fairy told them.

He showed us to our room, first floor, only thirteen steps, Taylor noted, compared to the seventy-six at La Marmotte. Later, we grabbed some sandwiches and climbed ancient steps to the top of the walls and took a long walk around much of the city, peering through the *machicoulis* where medieval defenders poured Greek fire on their attackers. We stopped to munch a lunch on the ramparts while watching ships far out on the ocean.

It was at St. Malo that we took another step as a family: we arranged for two rooms. This was actually out of necessity because the hotel rooms were quite small, and none would accommodate a family of four. For the first time, then, the boys would spend the night without us in a room of their own.

The corollary reality was that we, too, would be spending the night in a room of our own without the boys.

At first they resisted. But their protests were half-hearted. In fact, they found it exciting to be "on their own," knowing full well, of course, that we were only two doors down the hall.

The next day, cultural matters once again intruded. We were down on the beach outside the walls enjoying a beautiful day. The beach was almost deserted, but a few sun bathers had laid down towels, including a couple of women who had laid down a lot more than their beach towels: they were enjoying the sun topless.

I had spotted them long before Jeanie did, but when she did, she wondered how the boys would react. It's one thing to find dirty postcards in a flea market in Paris, it's quite another to get a gander at a woman of real flesh in real time—and to do so for the first time.

Spenser didn't notice. He was busy having a life of his own. Taylor noticed and his beach program and activities required frequent trips past the women to the ocean's edge.

Had Spenser noticed, we'd have heard about it instantly. Taylor never said anything. It was only months later in a conversation on an unrelated matter that he admitted that he had very much noticed the bare naked ladies. And since he said nothing at the time, neither did we—although Jeanie had a few words for me.

You don't sweat the small stuff.

15

Why Travel?

W E INTERRUPT THIS NARRATIVE TO DISCUSS WHY WE'RE DOING WHAT we're doing. Why do people travel? Where does the itch to travel come from and why does that itch need to be scratched?

Before we left on this adventure, Jeanie and I sat down at Chili's over a platter of supreme nachos and presidente margaritas to talk about it. We knew that we didn't need to justify what we were doing, but we wanted to be clear about what exactly we expected to happen on this journey so that we could measure its success against the original objectives.

As we talked about it, the reasons for traveling started to tumble out like water over Niagara Falls. Here's what we decided: We travel—

The Eight-Fold Path to Enlightenment on the Journey
- Gain understanding
- Learn
- Experience
- Make connections with the past
- Create memories
- Escape the banal
- Seek renewal
- Have fun

To gain understanding

Wherever you live, you tend to adopt the perspective and values that are embraced by the local culture and community. This isn't a bad thing. It's a part of being integrated and assimilated into a neighborhood and being a part of that experience. In our case, it means rooting for the Denver Broncos, the Nuggets, or the Colorado Rockies. It means appreciating the benefits of living in the Rocky Mountains. We take an interest in the political life of our city and our state, and as Americans, we naturally and understandably appreciate our life in the United States; some level of nationalism lives in all of us.

Just as it takes others to help us assess our personal strengths and weaknesses and to give us insight into ourselves that we cannot gain ourselves, it also takes our neighbors around the world to help us see things that we might not otherwise see. Canadians have a perspective that we, south of the border, do not. The French have a worldview different from our own. The Brits often find Yanks incomprehensible. The world is quite a different place in Nablus, or in Singapore, than it is in Denver, Colorado.

Many people travel in order to broaden their understanding of themselves and of others. No wonder then that we support exchange programs between countries, especially between countries that have traditionally been antagonistic. This was the impulse behind Ted Turner's venture with the Goodwill Games, back in the Eighties—athletic contests between what was then the U.S.S.R and the U.S.A.

There are earnest efforts underway to encourage exchanges between Israeli and Palestinian school children, and some Palestinian/Israeli drama and musical troupes have toured the United States to emphasize the commonalities that unite us, since the world apparently has no problem focusing on the differences that divide us.

Many cities in the United States have "sister city" arrangements with other cities around the world. Our own community, Lakewood, has a sister city agreement with Stade, Germany, as well as other cities. Students of Stade, as well as civic leaders, have visited Lakewood, and vice versa. Why? To promote understanding which in itself bears the fruit of peace and cooperation.

Jeanie and I believe that travel in other parts of the world helps us to place ourselves in a global community, and to understand ourselves as citizens of the world, not just of Denver, or Colorado, or the United States.

To learn

Being curious has always gotten me into a lot of trouble. Being quick with words has usually gotten me out of trouble. Curiosity is just another way of saying "thirst for knowledge." Without curiosity, there's no desire to explore, discover, or learn.

Travelers usually are eager to learn. They're even willing to learn at the cost of comfort and safety. The objects of learning might be works of art, buildings, customs, nature, people, or literature. Often to increase the store of knowledge, travel becomes a part of the agenda.

To experience

Of course, you can go to the local library and study the customs of the

Maori peoples in New Zealand. Travelers, however, are not willing simply to travel in the imagination. They must also travel in real time and space. They've got to see it or do it for themselves. They want to sit at a sidewalk cafe on the rue de Flore in Paris, or paddle in a dugout canoe down a tributary of the Amazon, or explore the underground Hittite cities of Cappadocia. Experience is the drug that keeps them high and excited.

Travel junkies get out there because they've got to see and do something that's beyond the realm of their normal experiential life.

To make connections with the past

We enjoy traveling because much of the traveling we do is a journey backward in time. We enjoy learning how people in the past experienced life, and what they left behind of their lives. In stopping by the Sistine Chapel, or the Uffizzi Museum, or the Coliseum, the temples of Luxor, the headwaters of the Congo, we get flashbacks into a varied human experience. We learn more about ourselves, we're able to place ourselves into the story of human existence and understand why we today are who we are, or aren't who we aren't.

To create memories

This is huge for us. We knew that our journey was the trip of a lifetime. We knew that the experiences we'd share would stay with us forever. We even evaluated the difficulty of our trip, or the harshness of some of the circumstances by the "memory quotient." Would this experience pass the memory test? Strong memory material? Weak memory material?

To ensure that some of the weaker memories would survive, we of course carried a camera. We also wrote letters and kept daily journals. These exercises were the trowels we used to throw the mortar on the experiences we had to create the structure of a memory that would be lasting.

To intentionally work at creating memories means that you ensure that your experience, your pilgrimage, is one that can be relived time and time again. The enjoyment can be multiplied, and indeed, intensified. We experience the same memory differently as time goes by. With the passage of time, the memory gains a level of poignancy that isn't present at first. The memory also softens the edges of some of the difficulties endured to make the memory possible.

To escape the banal

Traveling is pleasant because it immediately lifts you out of the ordinary and puts you down in the different and often the extraordinary.

Jeanie and I are often distressed by the banality of our American culture, the Walmartization, the McDonaldization, the Starbuckization of the landscape, the ubiquitous presence of chain stores, movie-plexes and restaurants. The malls and shopping centers are architecturally and stylistically the same. They have a lifespan of about 30 years—tops. Then they're torn down to make way for a new banality. Inside a mall, you could be in Denver, Colorado, or Grand Rapids, Michigan, or Tampa Bay, Florida. That's why the great cities of our country try to retain their cultural distinctives. Some of the great travel destinations in this country in my opinion are Savannah, New Orleans, New York, Boston, San Francisco, Seattle. Those are the cities. And of course everyone has their own list. But in Ohio and Pennsylvania you can experience the rolling hills of Amish country, in Iowa the vast fields of corn, and in Wyoming you can still catch a sense of the desolation of the old West, and appreciate the mountains of the Wind River range.

You can still get out of town to flee the banality of the mundane world and find the unusual, the culturally unique in our own country. But traveling abroad enhances the possibility of discovering cultural, architectural, and social differences. Of course, it's difficult to get away from the McDonald's or the Burger Kings or Wendy's (there's a *Wendy's* in Venice—what were they thinking?).

To find renewal

The search for peace and spiritual renewal is frequently the motivation for travel. To get out of the environment that is associated with the level of life at which we're living, and be jolted into a new consciousness by confrontation with a different culture can often be refreshing. A person, too, can get lost in a strange environment and can welcome the anonymity that comes by disappearing into a vortex of strange and intriguing sights and sounds. One of my most profound and moving spiritual experiences as a Christian was when I stood inside the Blue Mosque in Istanbul. Even in the presence of a religious tradition alien to my own, the majesty of the human experience, the longing and thirst for God was so powerful that my spiritual thirst was slaked in a way it hadn't been for a long time.

To have fun

You can lie down on a bed of nails and experience enlightenment. That's not what travel is all about. Jeanie and I had no doubt that the four of us were going to have wagonloads of fun along the way. We're a laughing family mostly. Every day was full of smiles, and at the end of the trip were we able to count all the smiles they would have outnumbered the sand on the seashores of the world. We had fun.

These, then, became what we called our eight-step program to sobriety, the eight-fold path to enlightenment on the journey. We never expected Nirvana, but frequent periods of bliss were welcome!

16

Le Mont St Michel

L E MONT S^T MICHEL IS NO DOUBT THE MOST WIDELY photographed monastery in the world. Situated a mere quarter of a mile off the coast, at high tide the island was inaccessible to visitors. Today, a causeway keeps the monastery open year round.

Actually, it's not really a monastery anymore. A community of monks do live there, and have since 1969, but it has ceased to function as a monastery for centuries. Tradition has it that Mont St Michel was founded in the early 8th century by St. Aubert of Avranches, but it wasn't until around the turn of the millennium that the first pre-Romanesque church was built, followed in the 11th century by a Romanesque church built smack on top of the island and over a number of crypts. Monastery buildings were also constructed at this time into the south and west sides of the island.

It was Philip Augustus in the 13th century who donated the funds after conquering Normandy that enabled the Benedictine abbey to expand the monastery by building two, three storey buildings topped by a refectory and cloister. During the 100 Years' War, Mont St Michel managed to defend itself for over thirty years. During the French Revolution, the abbey became a prison and was so once again in the mid-19th century.

Mont St Michel is really a small town. It has a main street that wraps around the island in ever smaller circles to the peak. The street is lined at the base with shops and eateries. Walk further up the "mont" and you'll come across museums, and the abbey itself.

We were visiting the mountain of Saint Michael in September. The crush of tourists had abated somewhat. We decided, however, to wait until about 5 p.m. to visit. The crowds wouldn't be too bad, and the light at that time of day could make for some spectacular photographs.

We were right on both counts. There were only three tourist buses in a

"After shooting a roll of film on the sheep and the mont, we all headed into the main entrance and began a leisurely walk to the top."   —p. 77

parking lot clearly designed to hold fifty. In fact, the lot was virtually empty. The sun, low in the sky was creating a sepia effect, although brighter. Sheep grazed in the pasture nearby. Whether the curators of the museum kept a flock there for artistic and photographic reasons is unknown. But the ovine creatures added to the effect.

After shooting a roll of film on the sheep and the mont, we all headed into the main entrance and began a leisurely walk to the top, where we found to our disappointment that the Abbey chapel was closed. We had to be satisfied with a close up glimpse of the archangel Michael perched upon the chapel spire.

꙳꙳꙳

On the night before our departure from St. Malo, Jeanie and I brought two *verres du vin blanc* to our room to relax. The boys were in bed, if not asleep, in their room down the hall. We read them "goodnight" stories, and tucked them in.

Jeanie had a Jane Austen book, and I prepared to do some writing. Her reading, however, reminded me of my own reading list. I finished *Mill on the Floss*. Dreadful. Dreadful ending. I was exasperated that I'd spent so much time reading it, although the story itself was compelling. I'd also finished *Portrait of a Lady* by Henry James. His heroine (as he himself called her), Isabel Archer, had a difficult time of it and James never lets her have any satisfaction. The conflict is wrapped around her marriage to a boorish husband—a plot typical of the 19th-century British novelists. The writers of the first half of the century are always trying to get their females into a happy marriage. In the second half, the Victorian half, they're trying to get their females out of an unhappy one.

For James, it won't do to simply have the heroine marry and live happily ever after. Instead, James asks the question: "What condition can I thrust upon my heroine that can reasonably promise a story replete with hopelessness, despair, humiliation and loss?" Marriage—a hopeless marriage—is of course the answer. Perhaps, as one who never married himself, it was his personal view of marriage. William, his famous and frequently depressed older brother, did not enter marriage quickly, and when he did, it wasn't an oasis of happiness. His sister, Alice, was a "career invalid," as one biographer has noted. His mother, Mary Walsh James, whose pragmatism and skill at household management, held the family together, had a marriage which by today's standards would have been suffocating.

In the middle and last half of the nineteenth century, many women were increasingly embracing home and hearth as their proper sphere, but others were drifting away from traditional Victorian moorings. A nascent women's movement was already afoot, and it was during this time that the "Harvard Annex," later to become Radcliffee adjunct was established, and other schools—Wellesly, Smith, Vassar, to name a few—devoted to the elevation and education of women, were also founded.

Isabel Archer was not so fortunate. It was not an uncommon theme. Ibsen would be publishing *The Doll House* soon.

The next morning was glorious and fair. We took our *pétit dejeuner* on a small island a few hundred yards off the rocky point of St. Malo and accessible by foot only at low tide. Inattentive tourists have frequently been stranded on the island for up to ten hours waiting for the tide to go out. It's here that the French writer, Chateaubriand (born in St. Malo, 1768, and died 1848 on the fourth of July), is buried in a grave marked by a cross and surrounded by stone pillars each connected by iron poles.

We climbed up to a promontory that has a magnificent view of the ocean. There we sat and ate our croissants, bananas and yogurts.

We were at our western-most point of the trip. From here, within minutes, we'd leave and head east—ultimately arriving, we hoped, in Bethlehem "of Judea, the city of David," in time for Christmas Eve.

17

On to Switzerland

THE AUTOROUTE WAS BUSY. WE WERE IN THE LEFT LANE on the A5 headed to Orléans, and I had a big, black Mercedes in my rear view mirror, so close I couldn't see the license plate. There was no doubt about the driver's intentions; he wanted to get past, and the sooner the better.

I was in no mood to argue. It was raining, we were in a little Clio, and we simply wanted to get around the 18-wheeler we were passing, and then I'd pull over.

Driving through the Loire valley is like driving through Amish country in Ohio or Pennsylvania. The topography is marked by rolling hills, woods and forests, apple orchards and vineyards. It's only when you spot a chateau on a hill, or dwellings carved out of cliffs that you remember how incredibly old this region is. They've discovered pre-historic remains of *homo sapiens* around here.

The plan was to get to Orléans and then take the N60 over to the A10 and from there head south, southeast to Lausanne, Switzerland, although the A10 would certainly not get us that far. But it would get us to Besançon, and from there the N57 would take us into Lausanne. And from there? Well, we'd head further east and stop somewhere to position ourselves for a quick trip in the morning to Zermatt. We had a reservation in Zermatt. We did not have a reservation for tonight.

I pulled over into the right lane, and the Mercedes flew by and splayed water into our windshield temporarily causing us to fly blind. The boys were quiet. So I asked them, "What was your favorite thing we did in the past two days?"

"The farmhouse," they shouted in unison.

"The farmhouse?" I said. "What did you like about the farmhouse?"

"The horses," Taylor said. "Can we have a horse when we get home,

Mom?"

"The ducks," Spenser said.

I had to agree with them. The old stone farmhouse had been a great experience. Over one hundred years old, *La Ferme de l'Epeigne* in the Loire valley near Tours was a working farm populated by horses, chickens, ducks, geese, and cattle. The separation from city life was now complete; St. Malo had been an intermediary step. Here there was solitude and tranquility; the contrast was appreciated by all of us.

Martine, our host, was very gracious and seemed to express a bemused air when she spent time with us. This was becoming a common reaction to us as people learned our story—the family from America, two small boys. The upside was that everyone, so far, was eager to help us, and extended every possible kindness and courtesy.

We had two rooms in the farmhouse; *petit dejeuner*, breakfast, was served in a large room with overhead oak beams, and a fireplace. We were joined by six other guests—not one of them spoke English, even Martine was without English. Martine brought out Kellogg's Corn Flakes, a basket with bread varieties and grape and rhubarb *confiture*, and milk and hot chocolate which the boys had requested.

Jeanie noticed that one woman had poured her coffee into her cereal bowl, a deep porcelain bowl about four inches across. The other followed her lead. In the mean time, we put cereal, not coffee, in *our* bowls. Long story short: in the country, they apparently drink their coffee in large mugs, rather than the espresso thimbles they use in cities like Paris. Martine brought out some more "cups" so that we, too, could have coffee.

"I think my favorite thing was the visit to the chateau at Chambord," Jeanie said. This didn't surprise me. Visiting the chateaus in the so-called "chateau region" of France was something to which Jeanie had been looking forward. Chambord was the biggest of them all: over 400 rooms and 365 fireplaces. We explored every room—it seemed.

"What did you like about it?" I asked.

"Well, first, it's in this big forest, surrounded by forests and woods—"

"—Where the king went hunting for stag and wild boar," Taylor put in.

"And it's so easy to visualize the movement of French high society when you walk on the grounds, or step into the ball rooms, or climb the staircases."

"That's what I found interesting," I said. "Here's a guy, Francis the First, who, when he's building his chateau, builds it as a place where he can romance his women. So he builds a double-helix staircase so that his mistress can flee down the stairs while his wife is going up the stairs, and they never meet or see each other. Now that's cunning."

"Oh, puleeeze," Jeanie said.

"What?"

"Nevermind."

"I like the beds, they were like for short people," Taylor said. He was right. People were a lot smaller in those days.

I continued: "But *my* favorite chateau was Chenonceax, the jewel of the French renaissance. It's cool the way it extends over the Cher river—do you remember the walk we took along the Cher river?—and it has a more colorful history than Chambord—"

"You mean like during the world wars?"

"Yeah, during World War I those rooms above the river were used as a hospital. Can you imagine? And during World War II, the chateau was a bridge between France and Vichy France. But I was thinking of Henry the Second."

"What about him?"

"Well he gets the chateau when Thomas Bonier the owner and the one who built it dies, because Bonier owed him money. Then, he deeds it over to Diane de Poitiers, his mistress who designs the gardens and expands the chateau out over the Cher, but when *he*, Henry dies, his wife, Catherine de Medici, kicks the mistress out on the streets, and adds the two gallery levels above the bridge. What an interesting story!"

"Wasn't cheap, either." Jeanie added. Chenonceaux is privately owned which perhaps accounts for the fact that it's in better condition than some of the other chateaus. But it cost 130f to get in. "But I like the gardens, Catherine's garden, Diane's garden."

"So pull out your journals, boys. What did you write? What did you learn?"

While they were pulling out their books, I turned to Jeanie: "Are you getting hungry? I could use a sandwich." As budget travelers, we've become true professionals. To the bakery for a bagette. To the fruit market for fruit. To the grocery for salami and cheese and puddings. We always have water in the water bottles. Jeanie pulled out a jack knife and began to stab through the bagette like she was fileting a trout to make some salami sandwiches. I had bought some Dijon mustard to add flavor.

"Ready, boys?" I asked.

"I learned that chateaux are big houses," Spenser read.

"I learned that the symbol of Francis I is the salamander," Taylor said.

"Anything else?"

Taylor added more: "I learned that Chambord is the biggest chateau and was built by Francis I."

"Excellent!" I said. "Now let's eat and hope we can find our way to the N60 so that we can get to the A10 and to Switzerland! Yeah!"

Taylor processed this for a few minutes. "Are we lost, Timothy?"

"No"

"We're not?"

"We are not lost because we know where we are. We are here. We know we are here. We could not be lost because the moment one realizes one is lost, he is found and no longer lost. However, a person may wish to stay lost by not asking for directions."

"Are we going to ask for directions, Timothy?"

"No." Silence.

"Could you repeat that?"

"No." Then I added, "We're going through Orléans. Does that name ring a bell?"

Taylor ventured: "It's like New Orleans."

"Right, and what nationality were the original settlers in New Orleans, do you think?"

"French?"

"Exactly! So whenever you see a city or a state in the United States that has 'New' as part of its name, chances are that the town was settled by people who wanted to remember the town or country that they came from."

"Like New York," Taylor said.

"Right! What nationality?"

"I don't know,"

"Chinese," Spenser said, laughing.

"Dutch—isn't it?" I said, asking Jeanie.

"New Mexico," Taylor shouted, getting into the game. "Mexico."

"Right again."

"New Jersey," he continued. I hadn't thought about that. Where was Jersey?

Jeanie spoke: "I have a treat for you," and she pulled a Diet Coke from her bag. "This cost me five francs," she said.

"I love you, I love you, I love you," I said, flipping the pull tab.

"I want one," Spenser said.

And I learned that there is an infinite variety of ways in which one can put bread, salami, mayo, mustard and cheese together to make a sandwich.

18

Our First Matterhorn Day

TALK ABOUT THE FRENCH, SWISS AND ITALIAN ALPS, AND THE conversation always comes around to the one peak that more than all the rest symbolizes the rugged, the majestic, the breath-taking—and all the other trite expressions that come to mind—beauty of these mountains: The Matterhorn.

At a little less that 15,000 feet, this peak is certainly not the highest peak in the world, not even in the Alps themselves. But it rises like a craggy, granite thumb into the sky daring mere mortals to take its measure. One of the last of the Alps to scaled, today thousands reach the summit every year and in every season, and regrettably, fixed ropes on all routes make things easier for even the non-experienced mountaineer.

When our trip was only in the planning stages, Jeanie and I wanted to see this incredible mountain with our own wondering eyes. But to do so would mean a significant side trip off our primary route, and we'd only be able to allow for one day. We'd have to hope the weather cooperated because if a storm front moved in bringing clouds into the valley, we'd be out of luck. We were hoping for the best.

We motored on toward Switzerland, and as we did, the skies broke open, and the sun dried the water spots on our red Clio.

"Get the passports out, hon," I said. "We're at the Swiss border." Jeanie began to fumble around in her pack.

"I can't find them," she said.

"They're in my pouch," I said. I slowed down as we approached the border guards at the crossing. The white-gloved officers were dressed in natty blue uniforms cinched about the waist with a thick white belt from which hung semi-automatic pistols. A white belt-sash ran from shoulder to waist diagonally, making them look like an animated cartoon for the universal "forbidden activity" sign. They were chatting and laughing. They took one look at us and waved us through without so much as a bonjour, wie gehts or a yodel. I was disappointed. I thought that at the very least we'd get our passports stamped.

"We're in Switzerland boys!"

From Lausanne, we veered sharply east and headed up a long valley toward Visp. Although we didn't have reservations, we hoped to be able to find something for the night. The next day, we'd either see the Matterhorn, or we wouldn't, but in any case we had a reservation at the *Jugendherberge*, youth hostel, where we'd spend the night and then leave the following morning.

The drive up to Visp was great, just what we had expected we'd see in Switzerland. Vineyards latticed steep mountain sides, and villages clung to the cliffs above us like Tibetan monasteries in Lhasa.

By the time we got to Visp, however, we were as tired and hungry as feral street cats. We'd traveled over 800km, which by U.S. standards wasn't that much—as accustomed to freeway travel as we are when you can easily do 600-800 miles in a day, like we did from Beaver City to Morris, Illinois, and from Morris to East Stroudsburg, Pennsylvania. But when you're traveling in a country where the signage is different, and you're on a route you've never been on before, it slows you down.

Arriving in Visp in the late afternoon, we quickly found accommodations in Hotel Adler for about $100. That was more than we wanted to spend, but we thought we could afford it. We noticed immediately that Switzerland was more expensive than France, but we'd been very frugal in France, and we were very much "on budget." Our French francs, of which we now had very few, were as useless as Monopoly money in Switzerland, so we pulled some Swiss francs out of the ATM and set out for dinner.

We had eaten out only once since arriving in Europe, and that was our second night in Paris. After getting the bill for that dinner, we decided that we'd have to forego the pleasure of dining in French restaurants. Tonight, however, we treated ourselves to dinner.

We found a *Bahnhofbuffet*, a station café, at the *Gare de Pontarlier*, and after using the toilettes, were seated at a cloth-covered table near the train tracks! The boys ordered spaghetti, while I tried the *lasagna al forno*, and Jeanie the *agnoltti al ragu* and we insisted, to the chagrin of the waiter, that tap water, rather than bottled water, would be just fine for us. The bill, with gratuity, came to $68 USD!

When we awoke the next morning, we discovered to our profound disappointment that the sky was as dark as a January day in Seattle. The whole valley was pillowed and tucked with clouds. We had hoped that we would catch a clear day, because the success of this particular day of travel, more than any other, depended on good weather.

We started the day with spelling tests. Not practice quizzes. Tests! Score of 100% would be rewarded with a surprise treat! Last week, both of the boys scored 100%. But today, Taylor missed both *exposed* and *until*. Spenser missed *alongside* spelling it *elongside*. There was much groaning and wailing.

We were excited and anxious to head up to Täsch. So we checked out of the Adler, packed, and piled into the car. Because we were headed for Täsch, Spenser had an idea.

"I think we should call our car, Tush, because we're going to Täsch," he announced.

Even with clouds overhead, the drive from Visp up the divide toward Zermatt was spectacular. When we arrived in Täsch, we parked our Tush in a huge parking lot and fell out of the car like sailors on shore leave. Church bells were caroling the mass. Vehicular traffic isn't allowed in Zermatt, so visitors must take a train the last twenty minutes up to the village. We purchased tickets and were on the train to Zermatt within minutes.

Two young fellows across from us were conversing in German, but Jeanie noticed that one was wearing a Denver Broncos hat. So we spoke to them. It was another rule we had: Talk to the people! Don't be shy!

The young man was an avid Broncos fan. He buys a *USA Today* every Tuesday for the Sunday scores, and he told us that the Broncos had won their first game under new head coach Mike Shanahan, 35 to something over the Buffalo Bills.

We stepped off the train at Zermatt, and into a village that reminded both Jeanie and I of Vail, Colorado. Chalets with multi-tiered balconies from which hung baskets and boxes of daisies and geraniums lined the streets. The walk to the hostel was an uphill climb that, according to the street map I produced from my pack, required us to walk a few blocks due north from the bahnhof to the ChristKirchen, then left on kirchestrasse, cross the river and walk north again to the hostel. Wasn't quite that easy, and did I mention it was all uphill?

We settled into our third floor room, with a great view of—clouds and more clouds! With the sky still overcast, and it still being only mid-morning, we weren't quite sure what to do.

When we checked in at reception, a couple sitting at a desk noticed us. This wasn't unusual; what's not to notice about Americans with two boys, one who's carrying a Pooh bear, and the other hugging a large version of Goofy? This couple, about sixtysomething, started a conversation with Jeanie. As it happens, they were from Louisville, Colorado, which sits on the turnpike between Boulder and Broomfield. They, like us, were on their way to Istanbul!

They were to be there the entire month of October. So we exchanged phone numbers for both Istanbul and Colorado. We ran into them several times during the day.

We moped upstairs to continue unpacking. The boys argued about who got the top bunk. Jeanie went to the bathroom down the hall. I threw open the shutters again. But now, what I saw caught my attention like a neon sign in Times Square! High in the clouds, there was a hole, and through the hole I could see the snow-sprayed granite walls of a mountain—not the mountain—but the cliffs of the mountain!

It had to be the Matterhorn!

"Taylor, come here!" I yelled. Taylor jumped to my side. "Look at that!"

"What?"

"Over there in the clouds! Do you see that hole in the clouds?"

"Yeah."

"We're outta here. Get your mother!"

Within thirty minutes, the clouds had lifted like a velvet curtain at the Met and there, framed by our third story shuttered window was the Matterhorn in full glory, the crown jewel of the Valasian Swiss Alps!

We could scarcely believe our good fortune. For three days, nothing but drizzle and drab. Zermatt, we later learned, had likewise sweated under a blanket of thick, wet clouds for days. But now, we had glorious sun!

I gathered the family quickly and we made for Winkelmatten where we caught a tram for the Klein Matterhorn (Little Matterhorn). The tram is the highest in Europe with two incredible spans across glacier and rock. The views were beyond words; what we saw was primal, raw, and sterling.

> **September 8. 1995**
> *I learned this is how to say thankyou in German dankenshoen. I learned this is how to say please in German bitte.*   —Taylor, 10

This day was what I called a "Matterhorn Day." You don't get them often. It was one of those days when the stars are aligned, when you hit all six numbers in the Powerball drawing, when you find out the newborn child is healthy. It's what Sheldon Van Auken calls in *A Severe Mercy*, an "eternal moment,"—something so grand and exquisite that it cannot be erased or deleted from memory. If you're of a cheery disposition, you're likely to enjoy most of your days. But to mention—later—our "Matterhorn Day" or to suggest we'd experienced a Matterhorn Moment, became for us a signal that we'd experienced something uniquely special. This had not been the first, and it wouldn't be the last. And one thing about Matterhorn days—you're entirely aware of their value, their rarity. You stand there like a post in cement knowing that what you're seeing and doing will never come your way again. We were completely aware of how fortunate we were.

But not Taylor. We should've known that the tram ride would push him way beyond his comfort zone. We could've prepared him by showing him brochures, and talking about it in anticipation, rather than springing it on him at the last moment.

We arrived at Winkelmatten. The poppy-red tram car, which looks like a boxcar with an iron arm extruding from the top to grasp the cable, holds about thirty people. From the platform, we could see the cables swaying in the wind as they stretched upward and onward, disappearing in the atmosphere like railroad tracks to heaven.

We stood in line, not yet aware that Taylor was sinking. The line seemed long, and people jostled for position as though it made any difference who got in first, or last.

On board, we all got a window view, and within moments, the tram was lurching forward and upward while at the same time Taylor's gastro-intestinal tract was lurching every which way but loose—and "loose" would happen soon enough.

Soon we were over a thousand feet above the rocky and glacier-dotted terrain below. Taylor's symptoms were now quite visible—pale face, droopy eyes and the inability to laugh or even smile when Spenser did something stupid. The boy was in trouble. The swaying, the lurching, the altitude, the uncertainly—for Taylor, it was a recipe for disaster. Jeanie grabbed him and together they shuffled through the crowd to the center of the tram where the child held a pole—white-knuckled—while his mother hovered over him so that, encircled by the crowd of people, he couldn't see anything.

September 9, 1995
We went 12,000 feet. I got hot chocklet on the mouten. I fell down at the top of a mounten, and it hurt. —Spenser, 7

"Just look down at the floor, Taylor," his mother said, "You'll be okay."

When we stepped off the tram into the thin, oxygen-deprived air near the top of the Klein, he was dragging. "I've got to go to the bathroom."

Jeanie looked alarmed. "You have to throw up?"

"No, I just don't feel good."

"Timothy, you go with him."

"No, I can do it," he said.

"I'll go with him," Spenser chimed.

"You'll need some money," I said, handing him a couple of Swiss francs. "We'll wait right here."

They left and Jeanie waited near an elevator that would take us to the top. Five minutes later they emerged from the toilette and the visit seemed to have revived them both.

"Mom, mom!" Spenser said, wide-eyed. "You should see that toilet!"

"What about it?"

Taylor was smiling and giggling. But Spenser did the talking. "You sit down on this silver bowl—"

"It's metal, aluminum, Spense." Taylor was always one for being precise.

"And you poop, and your poop like goes into this plastic bag, and when you flush, the bag is like tied shut and dropped into the hole."

"Isn't that *wonderful!*" Jeanie exclaimed.

"Don't use the word *like*," I said sourly.

The toilet on the Klein was yet another cultural experience for the boys. This toilet employed technology that was environmentally friendly so that when your waste went into the toilet and you flushed, it actually went into a plastic bag that then was automatically clipped and the little package dropped into a larger container—just as Spenser described.

The tram station on the Klein is bored into the rock. We got off and walked through a shaft to the other side where skiers took off or climbers began their ascent of the nearby Breithorn. Halfway through the shaft is an elevator which took us to the penultimate summit. From there, we climbed several more flights of stairs to the top. Taylor stayed below on some steps feeling miserable.

September 9, 1995
This morning we woke up early and went to the train station and went to Zermatt. We went on cable cars to the top. I got mountain sick. Then we hiked down and saw cows and a remote control helicopter. We ate dinner at our hotel. We had soup, salade, rice and chicken and fruit. —Taylor, 10

At the top there's a large crucifix, perhaps fifteen feet high, The Frozen

Christ, so-called I suppose because the cross, as well as the Christ, is encrusted in snow and ice. We posed for pictures, and then turned to survey the 360° view of the Swiss Alps, including the Matterhorn.

Of course, from this vantage, the Matterhorn doesn't look like the Matterhorn at all. Didn't matter. We loved it.

We didn't linger too long. We were anxious to get Taylor down to a lower elevation. So when the next tram arrived, we got on.

The tram trip actually involved two legs, a short span from Winkelmatten to an upper stop, and from there, the serious ascent to the top of the Klein. At the transfer point there is a café and shop. So on our way down we stopped for a *Caotina* hot chocolate for the boys and coffee for us. Taylor was beginning to revive.

"Why don't we walk the rest of the way?" Jeanie suggested. "It's a beautiful time of day, we have the time, it would be good for Taylor, and it'd be fun."

I immediately agreed. So we set off joyously on a path marked with arrows pointing toward Zermatt. All we lacked were feathered caps, alpenstocks and lederhosen. The path meandered through verdant forest and golden meadows where big-eyed bovines waddled about filling the air with the sound of cow bells. It was *so Swiss*. Inspired, Jeanie began to sing the entire score from *The Sound of Music*. Once, when we rested, the boys and I sat on a bench while Jeanie took a movie of us, and I spoke fake German to the boys: "Zegundenmeit mit der weltanshauung verboten ein dast bahnhof fur die dumbkopt shonen mit Gott in himmel geshunheit—" and so on. The boys got a kick out of that. Taylor laughed. He was back.

Arriving at the hostel, the boys unwound by playing chess on a huge outdoor layout. Then we ate our evening meal, family style with the other guests. The boys said it was the best meal they'd had on the entire trip. We were given a huge bowl of salad from which we could spoon out greens to our individual bowls, and that was followed by whole wheat bread and a main entrée of something that was like chicken stroganoff with curry flavor over rice. For dessert, fruit. Ice tea for beverage.

After reading stories to the boys, we turned out the lights.

"Goodnight, Taylor-boy!"

"Goodnight, Mom."

"Goodnight, Timothy."

"Goodnight, Spenser-boy."

"I hope you don't snore, Timothy," Taylor said.

"At the top there's a large crucifix, perhaps fifteen feet high, The Frozen Christ, so-called, I suppose, because the cross, as well as the Christ, is encrusted in snow and ice."   —p. 88.

19

We Convene a Family Meeting in Milan

SPENSER DISCOVERED A NEW TOILET.

"TIMOTHY, YOU SHOULD SEE THE toilet!"

"Let's not talk about toilets again, Spenser, come on!" Jeanie said.

"Why not?"

"Because it's not something you talk about."

"Well, can't I for one more time?"

"What?"

Spenser has this habit of twisting his fingers and popping them while he talks. His fingers were active now. "Well, when you flush, you can see the train tracks, the ground, going by through the hole in the potty!"

"Fine," Jeanie said. "Did you wash your hands?"

"Yes."

"With soap?" She grabbed his little paws, palms up, and looked them over like a Jewish mother-in-law in a goyim kitchen. "These you call clean?" she asked, dropping his hands like they had plague. "Go back and use soap."

"I'll go with you, Spense," I said. I thought watching the train tracks through the toilet hole would be sort of cool.

It was great to be on the train, my favorite mode of transportation. For speed, airplanes are best, of course, but not exactly comfortable. Cars provide flexibility—you can turn left or right or take a side trip if you want. But you're saddled with the responsibility of figuring out where you are and how best to get to where you want to go. Buses are the worst: all the discomfort of a plane, and it takes you forever to get anywhere.

But trains are cool. You can walk from car to car, grab something outrageously expensive to eat in the café, stretch when you need to, and on some trains, book a sleeper and spend the night on the rails, arriving at your destination in the morning. And in Europe, unlike the pathetic rail system in the States, they're fast and ubiquitous.

The morning after our Matterhorn Moment, we packed up, took the little red train back to Täsch to pick up Tush, and from there backtracked and drove over some mountain passes, traversing the foot of Mont Blanc and on to Chambéry, the historic capital of the Savoie and the *cœur alpin de l'Europe*.

We spent the night in Chambéry and returned the Clio the next morning. I dropped the family of at the *Gare de SNCF Chambéry* and returned the car and then hied back to the station, bought tickets to Torino for 338fr and boarded the train with 10 minutes to spare.

At Torino, we got off. Jeanie pulled some Italian lira out of an ATM. I studied our options for train travel in Italy. We found that a *kilometric* pass was the best deal for the four of us. For 200,000 lira (about $135USD), we could travel 3,000 km, about 1,850 miles, the mileage being divided by the number of travelers, in this case four. But children travel for half price, so the mileage was in effect divided by three. And you could pay a supplement and add miles as needed.

Our destination is Milan, but when we pulled into Milan at 2:30 p.m. we called a Family Meeting.

"Here's the deal," I began, after we all had detrained. We were sitting against a marble wall in the station, away from the pedestrian traffic, but not the noise. Trains were arriving and leaving. Announcements of departures alerted travelers as to track number and time of departure. The huge information board was within sight, and its little flash card technology kept the numbers constantly whirling as trains left for Rome, Venice, Florence, and Paris.

"We have no reservations for tonight, but if we stay here we'll certainly be able to find something."

"What are we going to do here?" Taylor asked.

"Good question," I said. "We might be able to do some shopping in Milan's mega mall—I think there's even a McDonald's there!"

"That's what I want to do!" Spenser shouted.

"Shssssssssh, Spense," his mother said. "Inside voice, please."

"This mall is huge, called the *Galleria Vittorio Emanuele*. But we also might be able to go to the Santa Maria delle Grazie church to see Leonardo da Vinci's *Last Supper*, and or visit the La Scala Opera House, and or see the cathedral which is spectacular. What do you think?"

"If we don't stop here, as planned, then we continue on to Venice?" Jeanie asked. "I'm just thinking that it's 2:45 now, and by the time we find a *pensione* or hostel and get settled in, the afternoon's going to be shot, and I don't know how much we'll be able to take in for the rest of the day, although we could stay longer tomorrow."

"If we continue to Venice, we won't have to travel tomorrow," I added.

"What time would we get into Venice?"

"About 6:15 p.m."

"What do you think, boys?" Jeanie asked.

"Venice," Taylor said.

"Milano," Spenser said, drawing out the word with his impression of an Italian accent.

Spenser was voted down. Taylor and Jeanie headed for the toilettes and Spense and I in full pack regalia raced to the ticket office on the lower level to have our kilometric pass validated for the trip to Venice.

Completing that transaction, we ran back, darting through the madding crowds, headed for the escalators up to the main track. I got ahead of Spense a bit, but was keeping an eye on him.

Jeanie and Taylor were waiting as I rounded the corner to the train platform.

"Where's Spenser?" Jeanie asked, alarmed.

"Spense?" I looked behind me, but he hadn't yet made it up the escalator. "I thought he was with you!"

"No! What do you mean? He's not with me! He went with you! Where is he?" Jeanie went from peace to panic in less than a nanosecond. I realized I had made another colossal mistake—but it was too late. I was swimming in the toilet and Jeanie was about to flush.

Spenser appeared huffing and puffing, and Jeanie relaxed momentarily and then her panic morphed into a frozen stare—the *Look* : "Don't you *ever*—ever do that again!" she said. Grabbing Spenser's hand, she marched off without me—or Taylor.

She had no clue. Perversely, I waited a couple of seconds. Then I hollered: "This way, honey," pointing in the opposite direction to Track Nine where our train was about to pull out.

"I was just kidding around," I whispered as we race-walked to the track. I was pretty stupid if I thought that would make everything okay.

But then, I'm pretty stupid a lot of the time.

September 14, 1995
I saw a gondola traffic jam. I learned they don't have houses in Venice. I saw the Rialto bridge. We went on a gondola across the grand canal. We're leaving Venice on a train tommrow. I think Venice is old.

September 14, 1995.
I saw the Rialto Bridge. I saw lots of Gondolas. I went to San Marco Square. I chased lots and lots of pigeons. I thought there were 2000 pigeons.

chased Gondolas

there

Awesome!

20

Vaparettos in Venice

WE WERE LATE GETTING ON THE TRAIN FOR VENICE. ALL of the compartments appeared to have people in them. We were hoping to find an empty one.

Like many trains, this one featured a narrow aisle that ran down the length of the car on one side or the other, with small doors opening to compartments that seated six, three on one padded bench facing the other three. Tiny linen curtains on the door windows could be pulled for privacy. We found a berth occupied by two Japanese students and encamped with them. I'm sure they were thrilled.

"Taylor," I said, motioning to him, "come on." We left Jeanie and Spenser and went off in search of the entire train to see if we could find an empty berth. We succeeded!

"Do you want to stay here and save at least four places for us, or do you want me to stay and you go back and get Mom and Spense?" I asked.

"I'll go get Mom," he said gravely. And off he went.

Having this cabin to ourselves was a unique and happy experience for us, and it was great fun! We spent the time talking, enjoying the window views as we whirred through Lombardy to Venezia very conscious of the blessing of *being* together.

The boys shifted into full electronic mode: headphones or earpieces in. Check. Batteries. Check. Game cards. Check. Game Boy. Check.

When we weren't peering through the window, Jeanie and I returned to our reading. "When are you going to be done with Austen?" I asked. By now, Jeanie was speaking to me again.

"Well, I'll probably have it done by the time we leave Venice."

"Oh good, then I'll start."

"You're done with Cather?"

"Just finished it."

"And you liked it?"

"Well, she's no Henry James, but the problem—well it's not a problem—with James is that he writes so well that you find yourself admiring the writing. With Cather, the story's the thing, like in *Oh! Pioneers*, it's a sad story but you don't really think about the writing because she tells the story so well."

"Cather's all about local setting," Jeanie said. "With James it's about cultural or class setting. Oh, look! I think we're pulling in to Venice!" The train had slowed, and it would no doubt take another ten minutes to crawl into the *Santa Lucia* station.

The four of us emerged from Santa Lucia at 6:30 p.m. and encamped on the steps of the Grand Canal, marvelling at the beauty of the Venetian tapestry spread before us—the canal bridges, the plaster-encrusted homes, the grand palaces of the doges, the street vendors and sputtering *vaparettos* and silent *traghettos*. Someone was playing an accordian nearby. The day by now was almost spent, the sky, a watercolor mauve, and the evening was cool, like the fruit cellar in Grandpa's house. We sat down on the *fundamenta* to consider our next move.

"What're those boats, Timothy?" Spenser asked.

"They're called *vaporettos*," I said. "They're sort of like water taxis."

We could take a freshly varnished vaporetto and get off the other side of the island and take our chances. Or, we could start walking, proceed over Ponte degli Scalzi and see what we could find. Or, we could get something close to the station in this neighborhood.

The problem with taking a *pensione* or hostel near any train station is that it's likely to be noisy. On the plus side, you don't have to haul your packs too far if you take a place nearby. I didn't think the family was in the mood to hike through Venice looking for a place to stay. If we had reservations, it would be a different story.

"Spenser, Taylor, you stay here on these steps with Mom. I'm going to get us a room. We're going to stay here for five days, so it's got to be nice. Be good, okay?"

"Can I go on the *vaporetto*?" Spenser asked.

"No."

Twenty minutes later, I returned. "Let's go," I said.

"You found something?" Jeanie asked—rhetorically, I think.

"Yup, but you'll have to trust me on this one," I said.

"Why? Now what?" Her voice was filled with suspicion twinged with alarm.

"Just follow me."

We walked away from Santa Lucia, past the Ponte defli Scalzi and down the Rio Terra Lista de Spagna, past *trattorias*, a post office, and the Adriatico Hotel until we reached a narrow alley.

"Here," I said. The alley, between tall plastered buildings, was about three feet wide and led away from the street about thirty feet. But twenty feet in, we saw a small door on the right.

"Here," I said.

"Where are we going?" Spenser asked.

September 12, 1995

I saw water streets. I saw boats under breidghes. I rod on ε traines. I woced in the ochen. [After making required corrections]: *I saw water streets. I saw boats under bridges. I rode in 3 trains. I walked in the ocean.* —Spenser, 7

"Follow me," I said. I led them into a room that looked like it had been decorated by Sanford and Son. Tail pipes, mufflers, tools, ladders, paint cans, electrical cables and drop cloths littered the area. Across the room were some stairs.

"Let's take the stairs." Up we went, to a door at the top of the landing. Through the door, and into a hallway. Now, I led my family, following me like ducklings, to the end of the hall, inserting a key into a door with the number 6 on it.

"Voila!" I exclaimed triumphantly.

Jeanie peered into the room, fearing what she might find. The boys twisted and strained to see around her. But when she stepped into the room, she said: "How did you find this, Timothy?"

"Did I do good?" I asked, my lips pursed in expectation of a gratitude kiss.

"You did good!" she said, walking right by me. "Looks like it's been remodeled. Two beds, a sink, lots of room. Where's the bathroom?"

"Down the hall, and it's very nice," I said. "We're right above the street, but I asked Lucia, the owner, about it, and she said they'd just put in double-paned windows, and that you could also close the shutters to keep out noise and sunlight, and there's a fan overhead if it gets too stuffy. I told her we'd take it for one night and let her know tomorrow if we wanted it for all four nights."

After cleaning up, we set out for the heart of Venice, and found a small restaurant with a reasonable menu for supper. There, the boys had the first of God-knows-how-many marguerita pizzas they would consume over the next three weeks.

Jeanie and I? We sampled some Italian wine.

21

In Which We Explore Venice

I T'S NO FUN TRAVELING IF YOU ALWAYS HAVE TO FOLLOW someone who's telling you what to do, when to do it, where to do it, and how to do it.

That's why I don't travel with groups. It'd just kill me to be wandering like mindless sheep following a shepherd who's waving a little red flag and telling us to "gather over here, now." You won't find me spending my retirement padding around with an elder-hostel group learning about Paleolithic dentistry or something.

"That's because you have control issues," my wife would say—which is the most exasperating thing she can say and which, I've noticed, is the favorite putdown women use about men in general. Men, they say, have control issues. Well, duh. We're men. So women don't have control issues? They just have issues. I don't have *control* issues, I have *freedom* issues. I need to be free, to be flexible, to be able to dash off on a whim. Some dogs will walk nicely and heel when told. Other dogs never learn to walk; they're straining at the leash, even if a choke collar is about to squeeze the last vapor of life out of their bodies. They've caught a scent to die for, and they just about do. I'm the lunging dog. I'm always catching a fresh scent.

I say that because, clearly, I carried a lot of the responsibility for this adventure, and the family looked to me for guidance, protection, and direction. But sometimes, you've got to cede that role to someone else—even the kids.

Many times, we set aside our agenda and asked the boys how they'd like to spend the day, and then we tried to accommodate their interests.

But this morning, Jeanie held the reins, and she yanked them hard and cracked the whip. We'd slept until 8:30 a.m. The shutters had kept the interior dark. We thought it was about 6 a.m.

"Line up," she ordered. "Come on, out of bed!" It took about five minutes but we were finally all out of the sack and standing in our underwear before

Madame SourPuss.

"Today is Laundry Day," she announced. "You will get out of your underwear, you will not wear underwear today, you will not wear socks today, you will only wear shorts and a T-shirt. You will gather all clothing items except the shorts and the T-shirts you are wearing and you will put them in a pile on this bed. Is that clear?"

"Okay, sure, fine," we mumbled, rubbing the sleep out of our eyes.

"I can't heaaarrrr you!" she barked.

"Ma'am, in a pile on the bed, ma'am," I shouted. I turned to the boys. "Come on, boys!"

"Ma'am, in a pile on the bed, MA'AM," we shouted.

"That's better," she said. "School starts at 0900 hours."

ช่ช่ช่

She had us over a barrel, because we all wanted to get out and see Venice—the canals, the markets, St. Mark's, the shops, the narrow streets. But she wouldn't let us do anything until we'd taken care of the laundry and done our homework. "First things first," she said. After getting the boys started on their school work, she went down to the laundry which was only three minutes away from Hotel Adua where we were staying and she left it with the attendant who told us to pick it up around 4 p.m. When she came back, she had some croissants, yogurt, fruit and juice. "The French have it all over the Italians as far as bakeries go," she said.

I grabbed a croissant and a yogurt and began to read *Pride and Prejudice* while the boys tried to master long division and cursive writing.

"It is a truth universally acknowledged that a single man in possession of a good fortune must be in want of a wife." What a great opening line! In one sentence, Austen captures the essence of the plot of a rather lengthy novel.

ช่ช่ช่

Finally, we were allowed to leave our rooms and explore the city. We set out for Ponte Rialto and the Piazza San Marco. We gave Taylor a map of the city and turned over to him the responsibility of leading us through the urban labyrinth, ultimate destination: San Marco.

It wasn't long until he was able to use the yellow direction signs embedded in the brick or stone of buildings along the way. Taylor got us to Piazza San Marco, or St. Mark's Plaza—which has got to be one of my favorite places in the world! The plaza itself is the size of a couple football fields—I'm guessing here—and is essentially the center of the city as it was of the Venetian republic, surrounded as it is by major public and administrative buildings. The square is bordered on three sides by cloistered shops and restaurants. But the fourth side is dominated by St. Mark's Basilica so-called because in 828 A.D., zealots made off with the body of the apostle Mark which had been resting in Alexandria. His body was laid to rest in a new church that didn't survive for long.

The present basilica was built in the 11th century and thus is about a thousand years old! When I was here last, in 1990, scaffolding covered much of the exterior. Now it has disappeared except for a small section on the north side. The mosaics date from the 12th to the 19th centuries.

Near the basilica stands the *campanile*, or bell tower, which is also more than a thousand years old, or a hundred years old, depending on how you reckon such things. The original suddenly collapsed in a heap of rubble in the early 20th century, but an exact replica was rebuilt, and christened on April 25, 1912, precisely a thousand years after the foundations of the original structure had been laid. Views from the top are awesome. It is here that Galileo showed the Doge his famous telescope in 1609. Emperor Frederick the Third is said to have ridden his horse to the top of the tower in 1452.

"Mom, look at all the pigeons!" Spenser cried.

"Come on," she said. "Maybe you can feed them."

We moved to the center of the plaza and approached a vendor who was selling pigeon feed. He charged 1,000 lira, about 75 cents, for one bag. So we got both of the boys a bag each.

Soon, the boys had those birds eating out of their hands, and one paused momentarily on Taylor's head. Fortunately, the fowl didn't leave anything foul behind.

> **September 10, 1995**
> *I saw Venice way of a taxi, a boat. I went on a train to Venice, Italy. I learned how to say hello in Italian bon journo. I learned good by in Italian ciao. I learned there are no cars in Venice.* —Taylor, 10

We entered St. Mark's, laid out in the shape of a Greek cross, where our movement was restricted by cordoned walkways. We didn't see any bones or bodies, but we were able to admire the magnificent gold leaf mosaics dating from the 12th to 19th centuries.

Leaving the basilica, we wandered along the *fundamentum* near the plaza, passing the Bridge of Sighs, a bridge across which prisoners shuffled on the way to meet their fate. Gondoliers here plied the waterways, carrying tourists and lovers in red-cushioned seats, sometimes jostling for position as they passed each other in the narrow canal.

"Are you going to take me for a gondola ride?" Jeanie asked in that certain tone that leaves no doubt as to what the answer should be.

"Of course," I said, "but we're not going to spend sixty dollars to do it."

"Okay," she said, good-naturedly.

"We will," I said. "Just wait and see."

We continued to the home of Antonio Vivaldi and then returned to the *fundamentum* where we caught a vaporetto which took us up and around the Grand Canal. We really didn't need to get anywhere; it was just an inexpensive way to see the Canal and the sights of the city.

We headed back to our hotel, a twenty minute walk, via a different route than the one we had taken to get to the plaza. This was by design. Soon we were on the Grand Canal and I spotted what I had been looking for.

"There! Let's take the traghetto!" I said. A *traghetto* is really just a ferry that takes passengers across the Grand Canal when a bridge is not close by. It's a passenger gondola and the price for a trip across the Canal is 50 cents!

We climbed on board. "I told you I'd take you for a gondola ride," I said to Jeanie.

"You did!" she exclaimed. "I love it!" Then, fearlessly, she stood up in the gondola and filmed us as we crossed. I was sure she was going to fall into the drink, and we'd have to fish her out wetter than a duck's bottom. But I said nothing—didn't want to treat her like a child.

We would use the *traghetto* many times during our stay in Venice.

That night, we set out to find the pizzeria at which we had dined the night before. Getting from Point A to Point B is always a circuitous affair.

"Are we lost, Timothy?" Taylor asked.

"No, we are not lost. We're on an island. How can you get lost on an island? We simply have not yet determined the relationship between our destination and our present location. Discovering the relationship is called *navigation*. We're not lost, we're navigating."

"Are you sure?"

"Yes."

"Really sure?"

"Ferme le bouche."

We found our restaurant and ordered the usual. I lifted a glass of wine to Jeanie and said, "Do you know what day this is?"

"Hmmmm, no."

"September 13," I said. "We've been gone—on the road—for a month now!"

"Really?! It seems longer than that, but in some ways shorter than that," she said.

"In about two and a half weeks, we'll be able to stop wandering. We'll settle in for a while."

"That's going to be really nice," she said. "But so far, this has been great. We're still on budget, we're all safe—it's been fabulous."

Then she leaned over to give me a kiss. The boys looked away.

"Thank you," she whispered.

And I felt like a knight in shining armor.

22

The David's Winkie

MY WIFE WAS NOT HAPPY. AND WHEN THE WIFE IS not happy ...
We had just pulled out of the station at Bologna and were on
a train for Florence. Since all the seats and berths were occupied, we were
standing in the aisle.

The "aisle" is not a center aisle, such as you might find on an Amtrak train
in the States or the fast trains in France. It's a narrow passage along the side of
the carriage which houses a number of berths.

We did not have a berth. Therefore, we were standing.

We were not the only ones. It might've been more pleasant if we were.
Instead, the train was crammed with passengers—grandmothers with
shopping bags and grandchildren, mothers with fussy infants, and old men
leaning against the windows for balance. It was more crowded than the New
York green line to Yankee Stadium with the Red Sox in town.

We had arisen in Venice on this morning at 7 a.m. and were packed and
ready to go within thirty minutes. We donned our backpacks, waved a cheery
goodbye to Hotel Adua, and hiked to the Santa Lucia to await the 8:25 a.m.
departure to Bologna.

No problems. The train was slow and made numerous stops. But that was
a minor annoyance.

At Bologna, we had to switch trains, and at first we couldn't find the train
for Florence. And yes, we knew that in Italy the board would read *Firenze* for
Florence. Soon we realized that the Italians don't list intermediate destinations,
only *final* ones. At least this board in Bologna didn't. The train we wanted was
bound for Roma.

Unfortunately, none of the trains to Rome were of a class that accepted
our kilometric pass without paying a supplement. So I paid it, but it wasn't
enough for the conductor who charged us another 26,000L on the train itself.

This train, which had originated in Milan, was full.

"Where are we going to sit?" Jeanie asked. There was an edge in her voice, the sort of grim steeliness that only a husband can recognize.

I think it was a rhetorical question. It was obvious that we weren't going to sit. "The boys can sit on the floor. Boys, take your packs off and you can sit on them, here," I said as I started to help Spenser get his pack off.

Jeanie turned away, visibly upset.

I'm not sure why she was irritated. She's a darn good traveler. It was no doubt connected to the "mother" thing, and perhaps there was a hint that I should've made reservations.

"I could've gotten reservations," I barked, "but it'd have put us way over budget."

"You had to pay a supplement—twice," she said, her gorgeous brown eyes boring a hole through my empty head.

I said nothing, and tried to help the boys get comfortable.

"It's only an hour," I said, deciding to say something after all. Then I had a thought. "Remember when we were on the train from Milan to Venice? Remember the people who were standing on that train while we enjoyed a nice cabin?"

Jeanie said nothing.

"This sort of thing happens. It's part of the experience."

Another factor that might have played into her frustration is the heat. Had to have been 90°. The heat, the children, the people jostling against her, the standing, the weariness—it was all just a bit over the top for her.

Me. I was thankful. We were moving and in sixty minutes we would be in Florence.

She? She was irritated. That's okay. She's allowed.

We arrived in Florence at the Stazione Santa Maria Novella and happily decamped outside to get our bearings.

After checking our maps, and looking for cross streets to locate the Insituto Gould operated by Casa Evangelica Valdese (as is our hostel in Rome), we headed for the Arno river. The hostel was within walking distance. "Walking distance" is defined as anything we can get to on foot within thirty minutes.

We found the Institute without too much difficulty, but the office was closed and it wouldn't be open until 3 p.m. and it was now 1:40 p.m.

"Boys, are you hungry?" Jeanie asked, which was like asking a pride of lions if they'd like some red meat.

Spenser and I went out for some lunch and came back with slices of pepperoni pizza and diet Pepsis and gelati for everyone.

The office opened at 3 p.m. as advertised. They had our reservations. We were given a set of keys and we trudged happily up several flights of stairs to our accommodations on the fifth—the top—floor. Again.

Moving into new digs is always exciting for the boys. In this case, our room featured a cathedral ceiling and a loft where there is one bed. An argument immediately ensued as to who would get to sleep in the loft. A large, shuttered window opens to a courtyard below and a nice view of clay-tiled homes beyond.

The room had its own bathroom and shower. A definite plus!

Here's the deal: Seasoned travelers, as we were now becoming, are grateful for the smallest blessings. This is one of the benefits of travel: learning gratitude. It's true of all travelers, whether from Europe, Asia, South America or the United States. When you travel, you learn gratitude. If you don't, you're miserable, and you stop traveling. Simple as that.

> Seasoned travelers, as we were now becoming, are grateful for the smallest blessings.

Gratitude is an attitude that's harder to develop when you're at home. You become accustomed to the comforts of custom and language, to familiar surroundings that are seldom appreciated.

In Denver, you scarcely notice the snow-capped mountains that tower in the distance. In Newport, Oregon, you drive by the ocean that churns relentlessly only yards away with scarcely a glance. In New York City, you grow impatient with the untiring energy of the city.

Affluence—and if you live in the United States, you're affluent compared to the inhabitants of 85% of the rest of the world—tends to breed contempt, indifference and arrogance. Moving out of our circle of convenience positioned us in unfamiliar territory so that it became easier to recognize the blessings that fell our way, blessings undeserved, unmerited and therefore all the more appreciated.

Moreover, traveling enhances our sense of gratitude once we return home. We notice the mountains and appreciate the view, we stop by an oceanside rest area to watch the sun sink beyond the horizon, and to smell the salt air. We listen to the sounds of the city, appreciating its diversity and energy.

So when we arrived at Insituto Gould, we were immediately taken by its gracious courtyard, the atrium in the reception area, and the ferns and foliage in planters and large pots. We enjoyed the pictures on the whitewashed walls, the large common area with magazines to read and tables at which to write and do homework.

Even the children catch this attitude of gratitude. They immediately made comparisons to the other places in which we'd lodged. This hostel fared quite well. Our accommodations had more room than our smaller space at the Hotel Adua in Venice. There was a loft, as well as more windows which were larger and opened up to a view of the horticulture and courtyard below.

And when our accommodations weren't as commodious as the previous stay, we still experienced gratitude, what you might call "retrospective gratitude." We were grateful for the blessing of the previous arrangement, and the present, more inconvenient experience would only sharpen our sense of gratitude, not dull it, as we moved forward to our next location.

The Gould Institute is a non-profit organization founded in 1871 to help disadvantaged children. They operate three boarding-houses for these children and this hostel—a commercial venture—helps support this endeavor.

We had a list of places we wanted to visit while in the city of Savonarola and the Medicis. Our time was limited, so we had to carefully draw up what exactly we wanted to do and then stick with the plan.

The *duomo*, or the Basilica di Santa Maria del Fiore cathedral, of course, is a must, along with the Baptistery across the street. Ponte Vecchio, the bridge, is fascinating, and we had already crossed it en route to the hostel. It was about ten minutes away; the cathedral fifteen minutes. Michelangelo's *David* was a must-see item on the list. The markets. The Ufizzi museum. And the church of Santa Croce.

So, having settled in, we were anxious to begin immediately. We set out for Ponte Vecchio, lingering now to examine the goods in the shops that line the bridge: jewelry, hats, scarves, purses and souvenirs.

The bridge has existed since the time of the Romans and is built over the narrowest part of the Arno river. It was the only bridge in Florence until about the 12th century. When the Germans were in retreat in 1944, the commander didn't have the heart to blow it up, so he spared it, destroying instead some nearby towers to make the bridge impassable.

The cathedral is magnificent, quite different from the cathedrals in France which we had visited. Jeanie, especially, enjoyed it immensely. Brunelleschi's dome always evokes wonder, the engineering marvel that it is. The church, begun in 1296, is about 700 years old. We saw the panels on the bronze doors of the Baptistery which included scenes that Jeanie recognized from her art history class. Taylor was even able to identify some Bible stories that the panels depicted.

After snapping innumerable pictures and wandering in and out of both the cathedral, the Baptistery, and the campanile or bell tower, we had dinner at a restaurant in the shadow of the dome and rehearsed where we had been and what we'd seen.

಄಄಄

The next morning it was raining and raining hard! We dodged the showers as best we could, stopping to get some rolls and coffee at a bar.

Soon we were at the Ufizzi museum. We had planned to arrive at 8:30 a.m. to avoid long lines which were sure to develop during the day. But a serpentine queue had already formed! We got in at 9:45 a.m. waiting in the damp and the cold for about seventy-five minutes. The boys, not sure why it was so important to get into this museum, were good-natured about it, and we let them scamper hither and yon as long as they didn't venture beyond eye-shot.

When we finally shuffled up to the ticket booth, the matron behind the glass window seemed so typical of many Italians we'd met who serve—and I use that word generously—the public. She acted as though her work was a terrible tribulation and that our mere presence was a particularly aggravating circumstance. We thought this air of self-imposed martyrdom might be directed only toward all tourists in general, but no, it was simply her way. We had a good laugh as we lurched with the crowd into the museum.

September 15, 1995

I saw the bridge Ponte Vecchio. I learned Ponte Vecchio was built in roman time. I learned ambulances are boats in Venice. I learned Michleangelo made the David. I think this trip is fun.   —Taylor, 10

The Ufizzi is a museum of primarily renaissance art, and Florentine art to be specific, much of it donated by the Medici family, the last surviving member of which died in the 17th century. Bottecelli owns the Uffizi; four rooms are devoted to his work. Jeanie had a fabulous time here as well. It was a pleasure to watch her enjoy these treasures, including Bottecelli's *Birth of Venus*.

We saw a number of annunciations, including Da Vinci's. They are rather typical: two figures in the foreground, an angel (Gabriel) to the left, and a maiden (Mary) to the right. The background looks suspiciously Florentine: gentle hills, fir trees, flowing rivers or lakes. In any case, I pointed out these particulars to Taylor and soon he was spotting "annunciations" before even seeing the little card denoting the author and title of the work.

"There's an annunciation," he would proclaim, pointing proudly. And of course he was right.

But there were also German (Dürer) and Dutch artists. But Florentine art predominates. (I saw Dürer's *Martin Luther and Katie von Bora* again, remembering them from my visit in 1990, and also Dürer's *Luther and Melancthon*, both Protestant reformers.)

When we left the Ufizzi, the clouds had broken and the rest of the day was beautiful. We wandered in the direction of the San Lorenzzo church where the outdoor markets are located and ambled about smelling the fresh leather of jackets, belts and purses. From there we entered a large hall where meat vendors and fishmongers were selling their goods: calf brains, tripe, goat heads, tongue, squid, chicken feet and more. The boys were both fascinated and "grossed out." It was an amazing scene for eyes that had never seen such a display, and although it was the lunch hour, they weren't quite ready to eat.

We decided to walk in the direction of the *Galleria Accademia* where Michelangelo's *David* is kept. We wanted to know where the Galleria was located so that we could get there early on the next day. But when we found it, we discovered the line to get in was only about fifteen minutes long, so we decided to visit now. Jeanie and the boys went for lunch while I held a place in line.

The admission prices to these museums have not been cheap. For the Ufizzi and the Galleria we spent over $50. Of course, it was worth every penny, but it was also a considerable chunk of change. We would assess the budget again that night.

> **September 16, 1995**
> *I saw the Ufizzi Museum. In side I saw the David We are staying in a hostel. We made paper airplanes. I saw goat brains. We waited in line for one hour. We had breakfast at a café. We past the construction. We went to the meat and fish market. I saw the statues called the prisoners.*   —Spenser, 7

We entered the *accademia*, walked through several halls and then rounded a corner to another, wider hall. Immediately we saw the *David* at the end of the hall, standing under a sky-lit dome—an absolutely breath-taking sight even for someone like me who doesn't know too much about art. This magnificent sculpture, thirteen feet high, is crafted out of a single block of marble. The effect is stunning.

This visit turned out to be a major event, a highlight, especially for Jeanie, of the entire trip so far.

Jeanie spent a good twenty minutes circling the statue and chatting about it—to the consternation of the boys who, when we go to museums, are always in school and must learn and remember stuff and be on good behavior.

The boys, 7 and 10, were fascinated by *David's* winkie. Jeanie didn't have any commentary about it, however. And no comparisons—to other statuary—were forthcoming.

In summary, this day was a "Matterhorn" day for Jeanie: the Ufizzi and the *David.* It had been a good day indeed.

We returned to the hostel. We had laundry to do and we needed to rest.

Later, I supervised the journal writing for the boys in the common room while Jeanie spent some time in the room reading.

Taylor must write his journals in cursive and is doing very well. Spenser—well, Spenser's Spenser.

This chore completed, we returned to the Arno river, crossed Ponte Vecchio and walked to the Piazza dello Signoria, the very square where Savonarola was burned at the stake five hundred years ago. There we had dinner, sitting at a table outdoors on the piazza. Jeanie and I shared a half liter of wine.

I absolutely forbade any discussion whatsoever of mosquito bites, Power Rangers, movies or television, pooh bears, Goofys or cartoons.

"But what will we talk about?" Spenser complained.

"Exactly," I said.

The evening was *tres romanique* and again we rehearsed what we had seen and what we had done.

23

Roma At Last

"Prayer is fun," said Jane Vennard. Jane is a spiritual director, retreat and workshop leader and lecturer, and an adjunct faculty member at the Iliff School of Theology (United Methodist).

I was chatting with her on a sunny summer afternoon in 2006 in a spare but quietly elegant dining room in her Cherry Creek home in Denver. I asked her what she meant, because I had usually experienced prayer as a chore or a burden; something one did because it was expected of a person of faith, even if sometimes there seemed to be little faith.

"It's fun," she insisted. She went on to explain that she's in prayer when she's gardening, or when she's out running.

"But not everyone who pulls ragwort is in prayer," I insisted.

"Of course not," she said. "It's a matter of intention. One person may be pulling up weeds, and the other doing precisely the same thing but has offered up this experience as a form of worship and gratitude to the Creator. It's fun."

I understand what she means.

She expresses what I was feeling when we got to Rome. I was very conscious of the prayerful nature of what we'd been experiencing, being grateful for everything that had come our way—everything! The discomforts, the delays, the art, our health, the children, the wife, the breadth of the human experience we'd seen in so many different media—on the canvas, in sculptured marble, in architecture, in the natural world, in the people of the lands and nations through which we'd passed. In everything—the good, the bad and the ugly—I gave thanks.

It was a journey into prayer and into a closer relationship with God.

Perhaps it's not surprising that I recognized this first as we came in to Rome, a city that is so central to much of Christianity's history. I thought about this as I sat at a patio table atop the five story Casa Valdese which was our hotel while in Rome. The air at 6 p.m. was September cool, and the sky was the kind of blue you might see through shaded glasses and was a-tumble with cottony clouds as though they'd just been freshly pulled from the stock. I had lit my pipe with fresh Drum *milde shag* tobacco which had been purchased earlier in the day from a vendor along the Via Giuseppi Belli. It has the texture of moss, not the wider shredded variety one gets from South Carolina. Jeanie was nearby with the boys who were "in school" (having received another missive from the noun fairy) and she was also in possession of a half liter bottle of San Marco Frascati white wine. Being a schoolteacher does that to one, I suppose. You're drinking by five in the afternoon. "Prayer in fun," Vennard said.

Jeanie and I felt our relationship was getting stronger. I was still the "new" husband, as the judge had put it when she ruled in our favor in the court case about this trip. We'd been married for two years. We were still learning and unlearning a ton of stuff about ourselves and about relationships, and a lot of it was confusing. But when we got to Rome, there was a sense that pieces were coming together in a way that they hadn't been before.

It had helped to have had a few days with Enrico and Deanna Formiani in La Spezia after we left Florence. Deanna is Jeanie's cousin. She had married an Italian man, educated in England, and they weren't far from Florence.

Our last day in Florence was a memorable one because of our visit to the Basilica of Santa Croce. We walked our usual route to the Arno river, over the Ponte Vecchio, through the Piazza del Signoria, and on to the church. We arrived about 1 p.m. and learned that the church would not be open until 3 p.m.

If we're going to travel, we have to be ready for delays like this. What do we do when we're with two children and we have to wait, wait and wait? We have to be ready, that's what, and we can't convey to the children that this is any particular problem! We're traveling! We're in an interesting and strange place! We can't be bored! We amuse ourselves by having lunch, reading, writing post cards to folks back home, watching people, and—by letting the boys romp to their hearts content in the square in front of the church.

Once inside Santa Croce we were impressed by the Egyptian cross layout of the church in the shape of a T with three interior naves, and frescoes galore by Giotti. Jeanie commented on how impressive the Duomo was for its exterior beauty, but Santa Croce, unimpressive from the outside, was stunning inside. Huge frescoes, the brilliantly decorated chancel transept and chapels, not to speak of all the tombs!

Michelangelo's tomb is very large and ornate, while a few tombs away in less ornate circumstances we found Machiavelli. The most interesting, especially to the boys, was the tomb of Galileo. Above the stone box, there was a statue of the man holding a telescope. It was of particular interest because Galileo had been, up to only a few years ago, under the condemnation of the Church as a heretic. The tomb of Dante is empty: because of a dispute, his remains remain in Ravenna. There are other tombs, too, in the first cloister, beneath the loggia by the church, and in an underground hallway.

The next day we left Florence and headed for La Spezia to visit Enrico and Deanna Formiani, La Spezia being the place where Catherine de Medici and her entourage had stopped after leaving Florence in the 16th century on her way to Marseilles and her marriage as a 14-year-old girl to the 14-year-old Henry II of France. We stopped at Pisa and took off from the train station on a thirty minute walk to the Leaning Tower where we took pictures and left. An entrance fee was required for both the church and the baptistery so we decided to forego it.

Enrico, whom we had not met, greeted us at the station in La Spezia and rushed us off to their home which had a balcony that opened up to a view of the Apinga range of mountains to the northeast.

It was fabulous to be with family! Enrico and Deanna warmly received us, welcomed me, and extended to us every convenience they could think of. Deanna was not feeling well. They had just had their second child, and their first was a little girl, two years old. Nevertheless, they had places for us to sleep, they had a television—on which the boys could watch cartoons—and they provided home cooking!

Our first night, Enrico prepared *gnocchi*, a potato dumpling of sorts with butter and a fabulous pesto. In his kitchen, attired in a cotton apron wrapped around a slightly expansive waist, Enrico was in his element. He stands about five feet eight, and appears portly—an impression that's not quite fair, but probably comes to one because of thinning hair, a round, affable face, and a girth that suggests the gourmand. His eyes are bright and inviting and his manners as gracious as his heart is big.

He speaks excellent English—of the British variety—because his parents moved to England when he was a child and his grammar school and secondary education was completed in London. His parents had been in the restaurant business, and Enrico's love of food no doubt was nurtured in the kitchens of England, not necessarily a recommendation.

Enrico, however, was an excellent cook. We never had the opportunity to sample Deanna's cooking; she was too busy throwing up. The *gnocchi* was fabulous, and it was followed by *Pepperonala* and pork chops and a tomato dish.

Earlier in the day he'd prepared tea, and beginning our meal we had a sweet wine, and during the meal a dry white wine, and we finished with coffee and a little cake. It was all delicious and over these courses we talked of past personal histories, of Italy, customs, food, traveling and cultural curiosities.

We spent a couple of days there. It was a welcome respite from the traveling, even though by most standards our traveling had not been rushed; five days in Venice, three days in Florence. We were not sprinting through Europe by any means. Yet, this sojourn with a family member was as refreshing as sleeping on a posturepedic mattress instead of plywood. We sank into it, we groaned with pleasure. We loved it. We were refreshed.

So, sitting in the evening atop Casa Valdese in Rome, I could reflect on our experiences thus far, and for the first time, I recognized the gratitude, the amazement, the joy as a lengthy and continuous prayer, a soulful communication with my Creator in which I was quite conscious of the awesome presence of the Divine. I knew we were walking and living in the presence of God every moment of this trip. I was convinced of it.

We stayed two nights with the Formiani's. On the morning of September 20, Enrico rose early to make sandwiches for us to enjoy on the train to Rome. He then took us to *la stazione* in La Spezia where we found an ATM machine for Jeanie.

This was no small matter. One of the major decisions before we left Denver was how we were going to get cash along the way. A generation ago, travelers cheques were popular and safe. By now, however, travelers cheques were antiquated and little used. I had used a bank card on my trips to Europe in late 1989 and 1990 and had no need to carry large amounts of cash with me.

So, the decision was not difficult: we would carry our debit cards and use ATMs to get cash when we needed it, and take out large sums when we did to avoid fees on every transaction were we to withdraw smaller sums. Moreover, the exchange rate was quite good. It was an excellent way to travel.

However, in Italy, the ATM's were not so cooperative. On this morning, when Jeanie attempted to withdraw cash the ATM wouldn't accept her card. Enrico thought the problem had something to do with the national bank system which wouldn't recognize just any card. In any event, he and Jeanie dashed off in search of other ATMs and banks hoping to find one that would take her card.

Time, of course, was an issue too, because our train would be arriving and departing soon. Enrico's stress level rose as available time diminished. An ATM was found that took her card, but the receipt indicated that now we were out of cash!

Long story short: We had cash, but we found the Italian ATMs weird and of all the countries we visited, including the back country in Greece and Turkey, Italy made it most difficult for us to get cash when we needed it.

Enrico also made certain arrangements for our trip to Rome, and checked the schedule for Bari, ensuring that we had the proper tickets and supplements. His help was invaluable.

He—always the gentleman—then waited with us on the platform until our train arrived from Torino. Other passengers crowded the staging area, some reading either *La Nazione*, or the *Corriere della Sera*, others—young people with colorful North Face backpacks—were plugged into their Sony Walkmans. Children fussed with their mothers, and old men smoked cigarettes. We all looked down the track toward the green mountains where the track and the electrical lines converged and curved. That's where the train would appear, disgorge a few passengers, pick up those who like us were waiting, and then speed southward down a track that would hug the Mediterranean coast before swerving inland near the end for the *Termini* in Rome.

When it arrvied, we hugged, shook hands, said, "Ciao, arrivederci!"

By 2 p.m. we were in Roma, the Eternal City, the Holy See and the World's Spaghetti and Pizza capital.

❧❧❧

Our first order of business followed the pattern we'd adopted everywhere we went: we confirmed travel arrangements to the next stop and beyond.

We'd learned that it is best to take care of this chore immediately, rather than wait until the day of departure or within hours of departure.

September 21, 1995
I learned the Colosseum's side was brocken off in the 13ᵗʰ and 14ᵗʰ centry's by a earth quake. I learned Pantheon means "all of the gods." I road on a Roman subway. I walked through the biggest Basilica in the worled, St. Peter. —Taylor, 10.

Enrico had assured us that we could get a train for Bari from Rome, and reminded us that in Rome we'd need to pay a supplement when we actually purchased the tickets. So, before we left the station, we checked and double-checked the train schedules to see when the train would depart for Bari on Monday, September 25. The departure times we saw were a five hour tour leaving at 7:15 a.m. putting us in at 12:30 p.m. or a six hour journey leaving at 9:15 a.m. and getting us there at 3:15 p.m.

We had a Family Council and voted for the former, even though it meant that we'd be getting up early on Monday morning. We didn't like getting up early, but we did like having plenty of time to search for options for an overnight ferry to Greece.

After purchasing the necessary supplement, we looked about for the Metro, and found it and Linea A and within 30 minutes we were checking into Casa Valdese.

ȡȡȡ

The boys are becoming travelers. The visit with the relatives was fun. But traveling was funner. We checked into rooms 301 and 302, each with bath facilities and a shower, but we didn't linger. The boys wanted to get out on to the street.

So we left and headed by foot in the direction of St. Peter's. Within 20 minutes we were standing like ants on a tennis court in the middle of the vast St. Peter's Square staring at the looming Basilica before us. We stood near the Egyptian obelisk that had been brought to Rome by Caligula in 38 A.D. from Heliopolis. Two massive colonnades circled around us, each with a roof that's supported by four rows of Doric columns at least sixty feet high. These "arms" of St. Peter are symbolic of the Church's embrace of the entire world.

We didn't stay too long. The boys romped for a while in the colonnade, darting in and out and around the columns—a single column is so huge that only Jeanie and I *together* could encircle its girth—playing a version of "Hide-n-seek." We passed through an arch in the walls of Vatican City and soon were at Piazza Risorgimento. We stopped to eat at a sidewalk table on the Via Vespasiano. Spenser had *tortelli al ragu* and loved it.

> **September 22, 1995**
> *I saw the Sistine Chapel. I saw the pyramid. I ate at the hotel. I ate a banane milkshak.*   —Spenser, 7

By now it was dark. The sun set at 7:15 p.m. in Rome on this September day. Our walk back to Casa Valdese took us through narrow streets still alive with commerce, bar hoppers, drinkers and idle youths. The boys ran on ahead of us, jumping and leaping, laughing and playing, happy to be in a new place.

They seem seasoned now, experienced and knowledgeable. Jeanie and I looked at each other. We thought we'd taken a major step here. Sights that fazed them and sent them to their mother's skirts in Paris, leave them unfazed now, scarcely worthy of mention.

There was a lot of traveling yet ahead of us before we reached "home" in Istanbul. We hoped that this new enthusiasm was a sign that they had relaxed and were ready to be present—with us—wherever in the world that might be. If they were unaware of it before, they certainly are aware now that the world is a tapestry of many colors and patterns. Perhaps they will be less inclined in the future to think they must weave their own tapestry in only one approved way.

24

In Which We Visit the Pantheon, the Basilica and the Coliseum

THE NEXT DAY WE TOOK OUR BREAKFAST IN THE HOTEL. It was included in the price of our room. We dined on croissants, salami, cheese, ham, soft-boiled eggs, yogurts, cereal and milk, juice and coffee. No reason to leave the table hungry.

This is a typical European breakfast. The salami, I think, is a particularly curious variation.

We were eating with others, of course, including an older American couple who struck up a conversation with us. They were from Nebraska, and had lived for a time in Denver. I'm not one for idle chatter, but it was always nice to chat with speakers of English, and it was also surprising to meet so many during the course of the trip who were from regions close to home.

But we couldn't linger too long over breakfast. We had a big day ahead of us, perhaps one of the most ambitious sightseeing days of the entire trip: The Basilica of St. Peter, the Coliseum and the Forum.

And we were going on foot!

Looking back, I don't know if Jeanie would have done it differently. She didn't complain. We were used to walking. We did it all the time. It was the rule, not the exception. Probably, we didn't think about whether we should walk or take a subway or taxi. We operated on the assumption that we would walk, unless it was transparently obvious that walking was not an option.

So we walked, returning to St. Peter's Square and entering the basilica itself.

It's hard to comprehend the vastness of the Basilica di San Pietro in Vaticano simply by *writing* about it. If you've ever walked into a domed baseball or football stadium, you might have a sense of the enormity of this structure built centuries before domed athletic arenas were even contemplated. From the enormous doors at the entrance to the apse dominated by the baldachin is the approximate length of two football fields and the length of its transepts are a football field and a half again. It covers, all told, almost six acres and can accommodate over 50,000 people.

The basilica is arguably one of the most holy sites of the Christian faith, second perhaps to the Church of the Holy Sepulcher in Jerusalem and home to over 100 tombs, including, it is said, that of St. Peter himself, although the head of St. Peter, we told the boys, is in a reliquary at the church of San Giovanni in Laterano which we promised we would see later.

Its vastness together with its architecture, and the statuary, all combine to evoke a sense of the holy. We passed the statue of St. Peter Enthroned which dates, according to some scholars, back to the 5th century, and ran our hands over the feet of St. Peter, now worn smooth by millions of pilgrims who've kissed it. We didn't.

We stood at the crossing and looked upward into the magnificent dome, designed by Michelangelo, an engineering marvel for any time period, but all the more remarkable considering it was constructed five hundred years ago. It's almost 140 feet in diameter, just a skoosh smaller than the dome of the Pantheon—which we would see later in the day—and some say that Michelangelo did this deliberately so as not to diminish the glory of that most ancient of monuments on which so many domes, including the Jefferson Memorial in Washington, D.C., had been patterned.

As for the height, you can stand the Statue of Liberty including the pedestal under the dome with about fifty feet to spare.

We paused by Michelangelo's *Pietà*, which was particularly moving for Jeanie: A mother cradling her dying son. My comments about the oddity of a mother who looks to be 17 years of age, holding a grown man who is her son, weren't appreciated, nor was the issue of proportion of any concern to her either: Mary is too small, the Christ figure too large, although some have speculated that the statue was originally elevated and Michelangelo distorted the figures to compensate for the optical disadvantage. Nevermind, it was impressive.

❦❦❦

We left St. Peter's and now headed for the Pantheon, after making sure the boys had taken some water. We always carried two large water bottles that had a protective covering that helped to keep it somewhat cool. Although it was September, it could still get hot walking under the Roman sun, and today was

118

no exception.

The Pantheon was on a fairly direct line from the Basilica to the Coliseum/ Forum, located about equal distance between the two points. To get there, we had to cross the Tiber river which once again offered an opportunity to quiz the boys about the cities we'd visited and the major rivers associated with them: Denver (the Platte), New York (the Hudson), Paris (the Seine), Florence (the Arno), and now Rome. "This is the Tiber river, boys. The Tiber, almost like Tiger, but Tiber!"

We found the Pantheon in a common neighborhood, crowded by shops, cafés, pensiones, and small office buildings. There's a small square in front of its porticoed entrance. But it all seemed shabby to me.

The Pantheon itself is dark on the exterior; it looked dirty and uncared for. Litter floated about in the breeze, the detritus of milling tourists flowing in and out of the entrance. We decided not to rush into the interior but, having arrived on the scene, take a break, and relax.

Since it was about noon, we needed to eat. We found a Burghy hamburger joint on the far edge of the square and sat down at a table that gave us a clear view of the Pantheon itself. The Burghy is a burger chain seen often in Italy and the boys took to it immediately. It felt good after walking to the Basilica and touring inside the Basilica and walking now to the Pantheon, to simply rest. We had learned to listen to our bodies and to listen to each other. Although we were still seeing some incredible things, in the larger picture we were having a great day with each other—as a family. And perhaps that—really—is what it was all about.

So the boys relaxed, ate their cheeseburgers, sloshed down Cokes, and either sat in the shade jabbering at us, or ran around in the square within eyeshot. Our bill came to 36,000 lira, including a small charge for ketchup. We were sitting outside on white plastic chairs under an umbrella at a round, white plastic table emblazoned with the Burghy logo. I took a swig of water and crossed my legs to get comfortable as I watched the boys. I looked at my trousers, the same tan corduroys I'd been wearing for over a month. Of course, I could've worn my black slacks, but I thought it would be too hot for black. My trousers have cuffs. It's funny how cuffs come and go depending on the fashion. *There's dirt in my cuffs*—more debris than in my roof gutters in October. I leaned forward to shake out the rubble that had accumulated up in my cuffs—dirt, small pebbles, a paper clip and the nub end of a French fry. I had to unfold the cuffs to get the stuff all out.

"What on earth are you doing?" Jeanie asked.

"I'm doing a bit of personal tidy-ing up," I said. "I just noticed all the junk in my cuffs here."

We were quiet again. I looked past my trousers to my boots. I'd worn these lace-up, ankle-high gray boots since August 13. These were a great pair of boots. My dad gave them to me back in 1964, on my 18th birthday. And the miles they'd covered! They took me over every trail in the Grand Teton National Park, and the Kings Canyon Wilderness Area, and Indian Peaks in Colorado, and the Rocky Mountain National Park. They'd gone to Ecuador, been to eastern Europe as well as France and Rome prior to this trip, to Israel and the Palestinian West Bank. These boots were *travelers!* I thought I'd retire them after this trip.

"Hello!"

"Huh?"

"Where you off to now?"

"Oh, I was thinking about my boots." I kicked a foot in the air to give her a better look.

"What about them?"

"I don't know. I've just had them forever, like for more than thirty years. They're almost as old as you are."

"You've stayed with your boots for thirty years. Can you stay with me for thirty years?"

"I had to re-sole them once."

Jeanie wiggled her own boots. They were also ankle high, but not trail boots like I was wearing. Sturdy nonetheless. And comfortable.

I looked again at Jeanie. Same frizzy hairdo. She hadn't blow-dried her hair since we left Denver. She was cute. Her face was now deeply tanned, and had a sun-dried and wind-blown appearance. She was wearing her sunglasses, and had selected the white blouse with short, shoulder-sleeves over which she wore a full-length dress.

"Nice outfit," I said.

"You like it?"

"I do. Have I seen it before?"

She laughed. It was one of two blouses she had on this trip, so, yeah, I'd seen it before. "It's just something I pulled off the rack, thought you'd like it."

I kissed her right there at Burghy's.

❧❧❧

The Pantheon, this dirty, shabby building, not particularly large, is just the oldest, continuously used building in the world, dating from the ancient period, and is almost 2,000 years old. It was originally built, in fact, around 25

B.C. but destroyed in 80 A.D. Emperor Hadrian rebuilt it, keeping the original inscription that refers to Marcus Agrippa. Like the dome of the basilica and Brunelleschi's dome in Florence, the Pantheon's dome is an engineering marvel. Unlike the others, however, there is an opening at the top of it, an *oculus*, or eye, and if the expansive dome suggests the heavens, the *oculus* suggests the sun.

ॐॐॐ

We stepped into the interior about 1 p.m. and the sunlight pouring through the *oculus* bathed the interior in a stunning light; at certain angles the sunbeams, picking up the dust in the air perhaps, appeared as a giant spotlight that, as the sun moved across the sky, moved likewise in the interior.

The opening also provides great ventilation since, as the wind passes above the dome, the low pressure it creates sucks the air from the open entrance at the portico and the interior of the Pantheon up and through the *oculus*. Sometimes, as we stood inside, there was almost a "rushing" sensation we felt as the breeze swept through the open doors behind us, swirled about in the interior, and then exited through the *oculus* above.

It's been a Christian church since the 7th century and it contains a number of tombs, including that of Raphael and some Italian kings like Vittorio Emanuele II and Umberto I. Masses continued to be celebrated there, although on an irregular basis.

We moved on. Next stop: The Roman Coliseum. We went through a quick check for backpack (we carried one, taking turns) and water bottles. Check! "Let's go!"

The boys really enjoyed the Coliseum. We were able successfully to play to their imagination. They were familiar, of course, with the concept of a "stadium" because the Denver Broncos play in Mile High Stadium, and they even knew the word "coliseum" because, in fact, in Denver we have a sports venue known as the Denver Coliseum where the circus performs when it comes to town. They'd been to the coliseum on a number of occasions to see the circus and when they did, they saw the lions and the tigers and dancing bears, and lumbering elephants.

This was the Roman, not the Denver, Coliseum. Visually, they were immediately able to understand the function of the building. We showed them where the people sat, the arena itself, and the subterranean areas where the gladiators had their "locker rooms," where slaves and Christians were kept in shackles until taken to the blood-stained field above, and where the lions were

121

kept, pacing and prowling, until unleashed into the arena itself to face fearless gladiators, or terrified Christians.

Since I was last here, the city has planted a square of grass near the Coliseum, making it possible to photograph it in a way that creates the illusion that the stadium rises above a grassy lawn as part of a garden or park system. The reality is that buses, cars and scooters swirl about the Coliseum constantly.

The Coliseum was the largest amphitheater in the ancient Roman world and could seat about 45, 000 people, roughly the size of most modern baseball stadiums today. When necessary, the arena could be flooded to allow the staging of "naval" battles. It was built about the same time as the Pantheon was being rebuilt, give or take a few years, construction beginning in 72 A.D. and finishing about 80 A.D. under emperor Titus. So the apostle Paul, executed by the Romans in the sixties, never saw the Coliseum, but the apostle Peter surely did. And, as the Christian faith was now in a period of rapid expansion, and since there was already a strong Christian population in Rome itself, it wouldn't be long before Christian blood stained the sand in the arena (the word "arena" comes from a Latin word meaning "sand") satisfying the bloodlust of the crowds who were still largely emperor worshippers or devotees of the pagan gods in whose honor the Pantheon—not too far from the Coliseum—had been built.

The building had eighty ground level entrances, and a number of levels, and of course then like now, the first level, or *podium* level, consisted of box seats reserved for senators and the wealthy. The nosebleed section in the highest tiers were for the women and the poor.

ॐॐॐ

The Coliseum was an active venue for centuries, but unfortunately suffered periodically from lightning strikes, fires, and especially earthquakes. Some of the popes used the Coliseum as quarry for marble, and indeed, some of the marble in St. Peter's Basilica came from the venerable arena. A 19th-century pope put a stop to the practice.

It was an 8th-century Englishman, however, the Venerable Bede, who put into words the sentiment of many Italians:

Quandiu stabit coliseus, stabit et Roma
Quando cadit coliseus, cadet et Roma
Quando cadet Roma, cadet et mundus

As long as the Coliseum stands, so shall Rome;
When the Coliseum falls, so shall Rome;

122

When Rome falls, so shall the world.

From the Coliseum we wandered to the nearby Roman Forum. I have been in the Forum on other occasions and have always been able to get into the Forum. But the Italian government must be expressing some sort of pique at our government because they're charging Americans for everything.

At Florence, we expected to get the boys in to see *The David* for at least a reduced fee (in France they always got in free). But, no! The clerk asked us where we were from, and when we said the United States, we were told they would have to pay full fare.

The same was true here as well. The idea of charging to get inside the Forum itself seems strange. But the boys were required to pay a full fee as well. So we said, "Forget it."

Instead, we walked around the Forum, peering through the wrought iron fence at the area below, roughly about ten acres—although that's just a guess.

The Forum was the city center of Ancient Rome. Think of it as "downtown." Here, everything took place, including cultic worship and prostitution. The area featured a number of temples, as well as shops, restaurants, office buildings, parks and squares for social gatherings and arches erected to celebrate military victories. It wasn't the only such area in the city; other "malls" existed elsewhere, but this one in the heart of the city, was the most important.

I did manage to get a photograph of the Arch of Titus which was erected to celebrate the emperor's victory over the Jews in 70 A.D. and the destruction of Jerusalem, when the city was leveled to the ground, not "one stone on top of another." It was also the period when 900 Jews committed suicide during the three year siege of Masada. This arch at the Forum, celebrated those events.

But of all the things we saw that day, it was at the Forum where we saw something that stuck in our memory the most: the cats.

If Paris is a city of dogs, Rome is a city of cats. The Forum and the ruins throughout the city are so lousy with feral cats that they now number about 300,000, living in about 2,000 colonies. They lay around everywhere, and they don't look particularly healthy. They gave us the willies.

The government is in no mood to remove them, and have even passed legislation to protect them as part of their "bio-heritage," since the cats have evidently been around since antiquity, feeding on pigeons, lizards, mice and other rodents. Some have argued that had the authorities not attempted to exterminate the cats in the 14th century along with heretics, the Black Plague might never have occurred.

Perhaps.

We found the cats of Rome to be spooky.

25

Alone in the Sistine Chapel

THE NEXT DAY WE SET OUR SIGHTS ON THE VATICAN, the Sistine Chapel, in particular.

We ate a quick breakfast and hiked rapidly to the Vatican Museums to get there *early* to stand in a line at the entrance.

We were certain that we'd be competing with hordes of *touristica*. Large, modern Mercedes touring buses had already arrived and continued to arrive, disgorging old people—balding men with thick glasses wearing short-sleeved shirts and a Nikon camera slung around their necks and stooped, thin-haired women in print dresses with handbags and a husband—on to the cobblestone parking area outside the walls of Vatican City.

We had expected it and were resigned to it. We'd battled crowds everywhere we went: Mont St. Michel, the Louvre, the Ufizzi, *The David*, the Duomo. Nothing we could do about it.

Except—we did have a strategy.

The problem with large tours is that a group can move only as fast as its slowest person. Moreover, the tour group follows the agenda of the tour leader.

The Vatican Museum is full of countless treasures. But the jewel is the Chapel of Michelangelo, the Sistine Chapel. Therefore, as soon as we were inside, we would march directly to the chapel, and perhaps be able to bypass the groups that were ahead of us.

This is precisely what happened. The doors opened at 9 a.m. and the line moved with remarkable speed and soon we were in one of the long hallways that reeked of opulence—ceilings overlaid with gold leaf and Renaissance art, and to our right, statues of multi-breasted fertility goddesses and to our left the bust of a senator from the Republican era of Ancient Rome. And so on.

As we tripped down the hallway, we passed several groups who had paused to listen to their tour leader discourse on an arcane matter related to thirteenth-century incunabula or pre-Republican statuary. When we walked into the Sistine Chapel, it was virtually empty!

Jeanie was thrilled. We stayed about thirty minutes in the chapel, much of it sitting on benches and looking up at the ceiling where Michelangelo had labored over five hundred years ago. I had a perspective that Jeanie didn't in that I had been in the chapel before the restoration of the chapel had begun. I was now looking at the fruit of those labors and the results were stunning. The colors, which had been drab and shadowy, were now bright and vibrant. There was a huge difference. The contrast was most pronounced with *The Last Judgment*, and we spent some time with the boys talking about the meaning of the work, and also discussing other panels which told stories they recognized from works we had seen elsewhere. Taylor took pride, for example, in being able to identify the hand of God touching the finger of Adam in the central panel of *The Last Judgment*.

As we sat on the benches, Jeanie shed more light on the technique involved in painting frescoes; how Michelangelo would get the plaster wet and sometimes blow pigment through a straw upon the plaster rather than using a brush. Such details brought more meaning to what we were seeing.

Having seen the Sistine Chapel, we left to enjoy the rest of the Vatican museums: the ancient papyri, the 14th- and 15th-century illuminated manuscripts, codices, breviaries and incunabula. We saw many gifts that had been given to the popes by a variety of foreign governments or heads of state. We examined fragile pottery and delicate pots, reliquaries and crosses, canes, staffs and crosiers, frescoes and mosaics—all wonderful and overwhelming.

Our tour of the museums was cut a bit short by our need of a *toilette*. We found one, and each made a stop, and then, since we were near the cafeteria, we stopped to have a banana milkshake, and then we left Vatican City.

26

The Chambers of the Dead

THE SISTINE CHAPEL WAS PERHAPS THE HIGHLIGHT OF OUR VISIT to Rome. For us.

Not the boys.

Not even close.

They had been promised a trip to the catacombs and it was the catacombs that would be the highlight of this visit.

They'd already been disappointed once when, in Paris, the catacombs there were closed. This was a small matter, however, if they could visit the catacombs in Rome! Once in the catacombs they'd see thousands of Christian skulls lined up in racks like bowling balls, or stacked atop each other cranium upon cranium, with bones—tibia, femurs, ulnae, and more—scattered about, too. This is what they thought.

Today was the day. We set out on the Metro and from this point on the day quickly unraveled. We simply could not—despite our best efforts—locate the right bus that would take us to the catacombs outside the city. We walked here, we walked there, we asked questions, we consulted an extremely unhelpful travel book, we looked at maps and schedules, and still we could not find the stop until it was almost noon, and by then it was too late to get to the catacombs on time. They closed at noon.

I felt this failure keenly of course. You hate to disappoint the people you most want to please, and I felt bad that I hadn't been able to deliver for the boys.

So we made the best of it. The bus stop where we were to catch a bus for the catacombs was located near San Giovanni in Laterano, so we went inside San Giovanni and saw the golden reliquaries atop the *baldacchino* that contain, it is said, the heads of saints Peter and Paul. This was a fascinating assertion for the boys to contemplate even if the actual heads themselves were not visible.

Still, it was a letdown for them, compounded by the fact that we now had to do laundry. So we took the Metro to the termini where we knew there was a Laundromat, did the laundry, had something to eat and then returned to Casa Valdese where we spent the afternoon relaxing, doing homework and reading.

That evening, we headed out again. This time it was for the Fontana di Trevi, always spectacular at night. These evening excursions were always fun, because Rome, like most cities, is a different city at night. The evening before we had trekked over to the Piazza del Popolo where the Blessed Virgin is represented by three churches: Santa Maria del Popolo, Santa Maria di Montesanto, and Santa Maria dei Miracoli. We visited all three, but the real reason we'd taken that walk was to see two Caravaggio paintings: the Conversion of St. Paul and the Crucifixion of St. Peter. Jeanie had some knowledge of Caravaggio (the realism and naturalism of his work as a departure from conventional approaches, she said—although she said more, but nothing that I really understood), so seeing these Caravaggios made the visit to the Piazza both important and very special.

But on this night, after the disappointment of not seeing the catacombs, and of having to do laundry, and having to do homework, it was fun to step out into the night life of the city and visit the world-famous Trevi fountain. The fountain itself is beautifully illuminated at night, and considering that it's eighty-five feet high and sixty-five feet wide, it's like the mother of all fountains. Finished in 1762, the Roman god of the sea, a nearly-naked Neptune himself, stands as the center piece of the fountain, astride a shell chariot with horses and tritons aplenty, navigating cascading waters that tumble over marble and stone into a large pool, into which we all cast a few coins.

The next morning, we tried again to reach the catacombs.

After breakfast at Casa Valdese, we boarded the Metro for San Giovanni in Laterano. There, we knew, we could catch a #218 bus for the catacombs.

Indeed, the #218 bus appeared, we got on, paid our fare, and took the bus to within a fifteen minute walk of the San Sebastiano catacombs on the ancient Appian Way.

But once again, the travel book we'd been using failed us as it had failed us the day before. There were no bones, and no skulls to be seen as the travel book had suggested. Not a one.

The boys were disappointed—again.

Scores of catacombs exist in Rome and I'm sure we might have been able to find one with some bones still lying around, but all the reading I'd done on the subject suggested this one as the one most worth visiting. It is certainly the most famous of the catacombs of Rome. But these travel books are clearly not written by children or for children.

But it was very interesting, as the visit did take us to a subterranean network of tunnels and rooms and we could see where the bones and skulls used to be piled up. After all, this used to be a burial site for thousands of first to fifth century Christians and Christians thereafter visited San Sebastiano regularly to pay their respects to the early Christian martyrs.

To get into the catacombs we had to walk through a doorway in a walled forecourt of a little Baroque church, the Church of San Sebastiano. Although on this September day the temperature outside was very warm, as we descended into the underground passages, the air quickly became cool, even chilly.

Our guide was an Indian woman who spoke to us in accented English, and who took her job seriously but joyfully. She was, for the next hour, our teacher, and she looked the part as she stood before us in a dark, patterned dress, arms bent and hands folded together making her presentation. Glistening black hair was pulled back away from her face, and she gazed down upon the boys through framed glasses that rested on her pointy nose.

"These rooms," she announced, "are the chambers of the dead!" It was her most memorable line of the experience, spoken like a bad quote from *A Nightmare on Elm Street.* The words, uttered in her particular accent, and with her idiosyncratic emphasis, stuck with us for the rest of the trip. Often, when we would step into a mysterious room or chamber in our future travels, one of the boys would mimic her: "This room is the chamber of the dead!"

The first chamber to which we were led by our enthusiastic guide was the tomb of St. Sebastian himself. The room functions as a chapel and there's still an annual pilgrimage on St. Sebastian's feast day, January 20.

Leaving this room, we were led into the "real" catacombs where we discovered row upon row of shelf-like niches carved out of the porous *tufa* rock. The bodies of the dead were wrapped in shrouds and then placed in the niche which was then sealed with a slab of marble if the family had the resources to afford marble. If not, bricks were used. Since Roman tax laws required brickmakers to stamp their bricks with a symbol bearing the emperor's name, the graves can be easily dated. This is why we knew that the San Sebastiano cemetery was in use from the first to the fifth century A.D.

As more bodies arrived, we told the boys, the grave diggers simply dug deeper into the tufa, which is why the catacombs are filled with miles of passages, and of course we didn't travel through all of them. Perhaps, if we had, we'd have found some bones.

"I thought we were going to see some skulls and stuff," Taylor said glumly.

"Me, too," I said, trying to sound as disappointed as he was. "I promise you, you are going to see some bones before this trip is over."

As one of the most well known of the catacombs in Rome, the San Sebastiano catacombs were vulnerable to vandalism, and the scoundrels over the centuries unfortunately carted off all the skulls and bones.

To their credit, the boys took this crushing disappointment in stride. Truth is, I was disappointed, too. I wanted to see some skulls and stuff too. Don't ask me why. I just did.

From the catacombs we journeyed to San Paolo Basilica (or, St. Paul Outside the Walls) where the body of St. Paul is said to be buried—without the head, of course, which is in San Giovanni as we had learned the day before. A mass was in progress so we didn't explore too much. After St. Peter's, this basilica is the largest in Rome. Although it was first built in about 325 A.D., it was destroyed by fire in the 19th century and then rebuilt. The exterior façade, featuring gold overlay on mosaics, faces a beautiful courtyard of tall marble columns. Inside, there are no side chapels as in most cathedrals or basilicas; just a huge open nave interrupted by columns.

After our visit to St. Paul's we headed back to Casa Valdese. Rome wasn't built in a day, and you can't see Rome in a day either.

When we returned from our visit to the Trevi Fountain the night before, we'd learned that in Rome the time was going to change and we would need to set our clocks back an hour. This gave us an extra hour of sleep, and tonight we went to bed early so that we would be rested when we caught our 7:15 a.m. train to Bari.

From Bari, we'd be off to *Graecia,* the land of philosophers and mathematicians, I told Taylor. We'd have to emphasize math while in Greece. This prospect did not amuse him.

Leaving for Greece we would once again be stepping back farther into ancient civilization, even as Rome took us deeper and farther from the European medieval period, so too we would now be traveling from A.D. to B.C., to a still more ancient civilization, the civilization of Plato and Aristotle!

27

We Board a Boat at Bari

WHEN WE ARRIVED IN BARI, IT WAS RAINING. WE WONDERED how we would get from the train station to the port. The staff at a tourist office nearby furnished us with a map which showed the location of the port. We thought we could walk it.

But first, I had a postal chore to take care of. I had a package for home, including a chapter of my journals, that needed to get off. There was an office of LA POSTE across the street. I had forgotten that Enrico had warned me about mailing packages from Italy. It would involve an incredible amount of paperwork, he said. He was right.

The clerk didn't like the way the box was wrapped. Indeed, it wasn't wrapped at all. It was just a box with lettering all over it and so forth, a box, actually, which I had retrieved from the garbage on a street in Rome (In France, I was able to purchase cardboard boxes—you fold it up—but in Italy they are not available from the post office). He instructed me to go next door to an office supply store and get the box properly wrapped and taped.

I did so. The staff there wrapped it in brown paper, taped it, and then strung twine around it, all neat and tidy. For this service, they refused payment, to my utter astonishment.

I returned meekly to the clerk at LA POSTE, trusting that the box was now wrapped, taped, and twined correctly.

It was.

He then moved me to another window and turned me over to a matron whose countenance forewarned that she would brook no impertinence from a customer, especially an illiterate American such as myself. Twenty-five minutes later, I had completed six forms, signed my name four times, and she had wielded a rubber stamp at least five or six times. I fully expected her to require my passport or to produce other signatories to the treaty we were about to conclude. To pour salt in the wounds of my impatience, the bill came to over $20.

The package sent off, I returned to Jeanie and we headed for the harbor; the rain had tapered off. We checked our bearings once by asking a police officer for directions. He sent us on the longer way of the two paths that lay before us. We're finding that one cannot always take the advice of locals; they're often as confused as you are. In this case, it wasn't simply a language problem; we had the map, we pointed out the possibilities, and we were directed to take the longer route.

Perhaps something was lost in translation.

In any event, we arrived at the *Statione Marittima* to purchase our tickets for the ferry. For the four of us, passage cost $140. For this, we got a cabin where we could sleep, and of course we got transport across the Adriatic. By combining transportation with our lodging needs, we saved ourselves some money.

❧❧❧

We can't do everything together.

We couldn't board the ferry until 6 p.m. The kids were tired and in no mood to explore the old city of Bari nearby. They'd walked from the train station on a long, circuitous route along the harbor bay to the ferry station, packs on their backs. Now they were only interested in taking off their packs, getting an ice cream and running around post and pier. It was play time.

I offered to sit and keep an eye on them so that Jeanie could meander on her own. But she preferred to stay with the boys and I—seeing no reason why two adults were needed to supervise the children—elected to wander off to see what I could see.

"Go ahead," Jeanie said. She had her book which she already had opened. "We leave at 6 o'clock," she said. "Don't get lost."

"I won't get lost."

"Don't lose track of time."

She's the wife. She's supposed to say things like that.

So I headed out. I was interested in Bari because of its connection to medieval crusading history. During the First Crusade, almost 900 years ago, the French nobility had gathered at Bari to board ships for the Adriatic crossing to Greece, and from there they had planned to proceed to Constantinople— much as we were planning to do.

They loaded the ships with grain, oil, wine, ropes, tools, weapons, food and supplies for the long overland journey to the second most important city in the world behind Rome. The *Nova Roma* it was often called. But their ships had scarcely been loaded and boarded when, to their horror, three ships snapped in two—broke in half—tossing their contents into the sea and 600 lives were lost.

This is where it happened.

So these were the thoughts that filled my mind as I strolled through the old city, a city of narrow streets, whitewashed houses in the Mediterranean style, immaculate stoops, no motorized traffic. Washing hung from balconies overhead, and children swept and cleaned the street in front of their houses, homes marked by Romanesque arches and courtyards. Flowers bloomed in boxes beneath their oiled wood-framed windows. It was all very appealing and wonderful.

I soon came upon the Church of St. Nicholas, the *real* St. Nicholas, the *real* Santa Claus, the patron saint of children. The church is a beautiful Romanesque building, with an elaborately decorated wooden ceiling in gold overleaf, and in the crypt below lie the mortal remains of the man who saved the children from slaughter and performed other miracles. I snapped a picture, and later bought a small block of wood on which was affixed a picture of St. Nicholas portrayed in the Byzantine style. It was a Christmas tree ornament. Jeanie would like it. She had been collecting ornaments from every country and various cities throughout our travels. It would be another way to remember our trip in years to come when we celebrated Advent.

On my way back to the harbor I stopped in a bar, an espresso bar and ordered something for myself, and then watched as others in the bar had a glass of tonic water which they drank, followed by the espresso. I hadn't seen this particular habit, and I wondered about it.

ॐॐॐ

Taylor and Spenser were excited about the adventure that awaited us. They were 10 and 7 years old. They were about to board a ship! The Athens Express was not a cruise ship. Built in Australia in 1969, it was a working ferry and amenities were not the top priority. Moving people from Bari to Igoumenitsa was its mission. So when the 6 o'clock hour arrived, the chatter and hyper-activity increased.

We trudged up a long ramp that put us in the hold of the ship—the same ramp that was used for cars and trucks to get on board—and then ascended several flights of steel, grated steps painted green arriving after some huffing and puffing on the main deck, We were given a key to our cabin (#205) and soon we were settled into our accommodations.

The boys loved this ship! There were so many places to explore, and Spenser immediately visited the bathrooms. Of course. We could hardly wait to "set sail."

The ship pulled away from its moorings twenty minutes late at 8:50 p.m. Soon we were out in open water. It was now dark, but it was beautifully romantic to stand at the rail with my wife and the boys and watch the lights of the ancient city of Bari slowly recede from sight.

Although I am prone to motion sickness, I had no doubt that traveling on this boat, so large, would pose any problems for me. Indeed, throughout the evening I thought little about it.

After having a bite to eat in the cafeteria, we retired to our cabin below and made arrangements for the night. The room was small, equipped with four bunk beds. Taylor said what we all were thinking: "I want to go to bed." He was tired. We all were. They took the top bunks, Jeanie and I took the lowers. It felt good to crawl into bed, knowing that we would awaken in a few hours in Greece!

28

We Travel by Bus into the Mountains of Greece

THE FAMILY QUICKLY DRIFTED INTO SLEEP. JEANIE HAD ROLLED ON her side with her face to the wall, and I knew she would be in that position for the next seven hours. When she sleeps, her nervous system shuts down. Her muscles go into a hibernation mode in which she never stirs. Spenser was breathing with a light whistle, and I could see by the dim light of a port lamp that Taylor, too, was sound asleep.

What helped them to sleep, however, was the very thing that kept me awake. I was not ready to rock and roll. The pitch and yaw of the ship, however gentle it was to most, was disturbing to me. But in the late evening hours, it was something I could put up with, and I went in and out of a fitful sleep always aware, even vaguely, of the rock-a-by baby motion of The Athens Express.

But after midnight, the swells and rolls of the boat became more pronounced. I braced myself atop the swells, and hung on to the sides of the bunk as this creaky vessel raced to the bottom and lurched forward and upward over yet another Adriatic crest. My stomach grew weary of the repetitive forces pushing and pulling against it. The motion of the boat seemed to toss me about, even though the others continued to sleep. I experienced—I imagined at least—G-forces every time the ship plunged down and surged upward. I felt a thickness in my throat and a fog in my head. My stomach seemed like a limpid pool of gastric juices ready, if I would give the slightest signal, to power upward and outward.

My greater fear, however, was that the ship itself must be in peril, given its dramatic motion. I had heard no alarm, heard no siren, heard no hands on deck attempting to stave off trouble. Yet, clearly, something was not right.

Reluctantly, I clambered out of my bunk, and grabbing a blanket and a book, staggered out the cabin door, and made for the main deck to see just what kind of peril we were in. I stepped out into the cool sea air, expecting to find the deck awash in sea water, and I braced myself to catch the salt spray of the ocean in my face. I wished then that I had the faith of the apostle Paul who, when shipwrecked somewhere in the Mediterranean had shouted to the crew, "Be of good cheer, not a man shall be lost."

Emerging on deck, I was as a lost man myself. To my utter wonderment, the deck was as dry as whale bone and as I peered into the darkness of the Adriatic night, what water I could see by starlight and ship-light as I leaned over the railing was placid. Not a white cap to be seen.

I sunk into a deck chair and wondered how I would survive if the ship actually ran into a patch of rough weather. I'd want to die. This has happened before. Before moving from Oregon to Colorado back in the late 70s, I thought that I should try deep-sea fishing at least once. Alone, I drove from the Willamette Valley over the coast range to Lincoln City, and down to Depoe Bay which bills itself as the Worldest Smallest harbor. Boats returning to safe haven must thread through a narrow channel defined by high dark cliffs of slabbed rock on both sides, like ancient ships passing by Sybill and Carbibdis. There I fell in with about a dozen souls who likewise wished to spend the morning fishing on the ocean, including a three young couples, three men in their thirties, two grandmother-types, and myself.

On a pleasant summer morning, we pushed away from dock, and motored under the high bridge that conveys traffic on the Pacific Coast highway, and went out to sea. I hadn't been asea fifteen minutes when waves of nausea hit me. I emptied the contents of my stomach over the side rail, and then continued to heave at intervals for the duration. To this day I have no memory of how long I was on the water or how I got back. I only remember asking the Lord to take me home to gloryland. I didn't care if I saw the faces of my children again. It was brutal.

No wonder that in literature, especially the Bible, the sea is a symbol of chaos and disaster. The Bible begins with the "Spirit" brooding over the face of the water when, according to the Scriptural account, the planet was without form and "void." Later, in an act of fury, God sends the waters back up over the earth in a great flood as a punishment for the wickedness of the earth's current inhabitants. The disciples of Jesus found themselves once in a storm of such magnitude on the Sea of Gennesaret that they feared for their lives. Their fear was mixed with irritation that while they were up manning the sails and the oars, Jesus was asleep in the hold, unaware of the raging tempest without. Of course, they woke him up and he famously said to the sea, "Peace, be still," and the wind ceased, the waves shrunk and the hearts of the disciples became calm.

The Bible ends with the sea—or it's absence. The writer of the *Revelation of St. John the Divine* makes a pointed observation that the "sea was no more." All sickness, tears, suffering and pain are gone.

That's the promise of an eschatological future. It was of no comfort to me on this night. Jesus was not asleep in the hold, and in any event, the Adriatic was calm. I was simply cursed with a defect in my ailimentary canal that made me susceptible to motion.

I decided to read for a while there on the deck in the post-midnight hours of the early morning, the lone passenger up and about, the only one—of the several scores of souls on board—who couldn't stomach the journey. But, after an hour, I returned to the cabin, and was able to relax and let the boat work with my body to help me sleep.

When I awoke, we were off the coast of Greece within ninety minutes of Igoumenitsa, a small port village in northwestern coastline of Greece that spills upward on the flank of the northern mountains in the Epirus district. The last sixty minutes of our voyage were truly scenic as the boat sailed quietly through the inter-island coastal waters, gliding on the glassy sea toward the harbor.

As we debarked, we showed our passports to the police, and then set out in full pack regalia for the bus station—wherever that was.

As we walked we saw a Greek Orthodox priest with a thick white beard and a head topped with a *klobuk,* a stove-pipe sort of black hat, and dressed in full length black cassock. The boys stared.

We asked a few questions, and soon were buying tickets for a bus that would leave for Ioannia in fifteen minutes! Timing is everything!

We boarded the bus. The only seats available to us as a family were seats along the very back of the bus. There was a reason these seats alone were not taken by anyone else. We found that every bump in the road was multiplied to the fourth power because we were sitting on the fender of the bus.

Even more exciting was the view we had of the road as we looked down the aisle and out the front windshield. At the wheel was Mad Nikos whose firm belief in the afterlife gives him license to pass trucks and cars on blind curves and short straightaways, barreling down the valleys full throttle and up the mountainsides like Blue Thunder at Six Flags. Traveling by bus in Greece was by far the most dangerous portion of our journey to this point. I felt like singing, *Nearer My God to Thee, Nearer to Thee.* A trip that—according to the official time table—was supposed to take a full 150 minutes, instead took only 110 minutes.

It was a shock to travel this way after enjoying the ship, and the trains of Italy and France, and the rented car. This bus driver was nuts. Watching the road flash by us, we felt like we were in an IMAX theatre—a thrill a minute.

We arrived at Ioannia, the provincial capital, and got off the bus and tested our legs. I found a small hotel near the station called Hotel Paris. And so here we were for the rest of the day.

We found that in Greece, unlike Italy, ATMs were plentiful and easy to use. Accessing our account was never a problem in Ioannia or in any town in Greece.

That night, after eating in a lousy restaurant and doing some sightseeing and curio shopping, we prepared for bed.

Jeanie says, "Time to brush your teeth, boys."

"Ohhhhhhhhhhhhhh."

"And wash your face and hands."

"Ohhhhhhhhhhhh."

This has been the routine every night whether in hotel or ferry. The routine has been important not only for hygienic reasons but for emotional ones. The boys knew that we live in a morally-structured universe. They wouldn't have said it that way. For them, morally-structured universe is another way of saying "rules."

Nevertheless, the teeth must be brushed whether in Denver, New York, Paris, Rome, or Ioannia. Nothing is different tonight from last night and the night before it. This is what we do, this is what we are expected to do, this is the way it has always been and always will be—is now and forever shall be, world without end. Amen.

The cosmos, or moral universe, beyond our family may not be so well-ordered but in our family it was. It's a subject particularly apropos during our stay in Greece which, of course, is the land that gave the world Plato and Aristotle and eminent mathematicians for whom an interest in the order and structure of the cosmos (a Greek word) was so important.

This meaning is even carried over into our word *cosmetics*. What are cosmetics if not ointments, powders, unguents, et cetera, that restore order and structure to a face which, during the night hours, has become disordered and unstructured and which, in the light of the morning, needs to be restored and re-structured?

Our bus for Konitsa left at 10:30 a.m. the next morning. This time Crazy Cyril was driving. *Nearer My God*, verse two.

Konitsa is a small village that's perched on the side of a mountain about sixty-five kilometers to the north of Ioannia. It's only a few kilometers from Albania and we could see mountains not far away clearly in one of the last communist states of the old eastern communist bloc.

The bus chugged up the twisted streets of Konitsa past gnarled olive trees—some of the 137 million olive trees in Greece—and beyond the Orthodox church built into the side of the hill, picturesque with its onion perched on top of a tower and the cleric in *kolbuk* and black cassock standing at the door. Soon it pulled into the village square ringed with fruit trees and firs and we got off and secured our bags.

The hotel-hunting ritual then began. This time, however, Taylor went with me while Spenser and his mother sat on our bags under a shady plane tree.

There's only one hotel in Konitsa, a village of 2,800 souls, and it was adjacent to the bus station. The old innkeeper, bent over a ledger, just stared at us with a blank expression on his leathery face. The effort to accommodate us, given the language barrier, must have been too great a burden to bear. We decided to go elsewhere. After some walking around, we spied a sign that said, "Rooms to Rent." So we investigated. A middle-aged lady in a floral print dress and an apron sashed around her waist met us and showed us the rooms: two single beds in each, a nice toilet and shower with tile floors down the hall. The price was 5,000 drachmas for each room. Taylor thought they were "nice."

Good.

We take.

Yes, it is fine.

I grabbed Taylor's chubby little hand and opened his palm and laid out the money. He stared at me speechless. I gave him a subtle head-motion for him to give the money to the lady and then faked a movement away as though I was going to take another look at the rooms. He was on his own. So he placed two 5,000 drachma notes in her hand and she gave him the keys and the deal was struck.

Moments later, four Americans trudged up the hill from the village square, turned left and walked into the compound to our rooms, happy to find a place we could call "home" for twenty-four hours.

It was in Greece, traveling these back mountain roads and visiting these remote villages, that we had language problems. The innkeeper at the hotel clearly didn't understand a word we were saying. You would have thought, however, our intention was clear. For what other purpose other than to rent a room might an American family show up in the lobby of your hotel?

We were always respectful of the local language wherever we traveled. In France, I used as much French as I could. Elsewhere, we never showed exasperation because our hosts had difficulty understanding English. Why would we expect people in other countries to understand us? So we didn't.

Generally, however, we found that people had a smattering of English and usually we could communicate what we wanted.

But not in Konitsa, and especially not when we had dinner that evening at an outdoor table in the village square.

A kindly, old gentleman waited on us, appearing from the little dilapidated restaurant on the edge of the square. His face was round and cheeky, and his full mustache was draped over his mouth like a walrus. He wore a dark, food-stained vest over a blousy white shirt. With a little pad in one hand and a pencil poised in the other, he was ready to take our order.

The menu was in Greek. And we didn't have a handy-dandy guidebook to explain a thing. We decided on Greek salads, but we wanted only two. We thought the boys could share one, and Jeanie and I could share the other. We didn't want four plates of something we didn't like.

He beamed and nodded his head. "Yes, yes," and off he went.

A few minutes later he reappeared with two plates, and we saw that he had prepared tasty little hamburgers with fries. Perhaps he thought this is all that Americans eat. In any case, we were delighted at our good fortune and appreciated the fact that we had not been given minnows on a skewer or something with the eyes still in it. And the fact that we appeared pleased with the food, also pleased him very much.

So we asked him to bring us two more such plates.

And this is where the trouble began.

The poor man who moments ago had been beaming, now was frowning and concerned. We held up two fingers. Then four fingers, pointing to the boys and ourselves.

Then I intervened: "WE-WANT-TWO PLATES—HAMBURGERS!"

The old man stared at me.

"Honey, why are you shouting?"

I turned to Jeanie. "Huh?"

"You're shouting. He can hear you."

I tried again: "We like food. Two more this." And I pointed to the plates.

"Honey."

"Whaaaat?"

"Now you're talking in a stupid accent. *I* don't even understand you."

"I'm just trying to keep it simple. We like. Two plates. Yum-yum. More." Spenser started to imitate the Greek accent. I told him to hush.

"You can't expect him to understand English that's not even English." She turned to the proprietor and said, "Thank you for the food. We would like two more of the same."

I said, "Like he understood what *you* said."

"Probably not, but at least I didn't yell and I spoke good English. Let's see what happens."

The old man turned and went back to his kitchen.

We saw him pick up a phone. About ten minutes later, a young girl appeared in the kitchen and the two of them conversed in a highly animated manner, heads bobbing and hands waving, and an occasional look in our direction.

The girl walked out to meet us.

"My father," she began nervously in halting English, "does not know if you want two more plates, or four more plates." Jeanie explained carefully and pleasantly that we had ordered two plates and wanted two more. Initially she seemed as confused as her father, but then she said: "You ate two plates. Now you want two more."

Indeed, the boys had consumed everything. We smiled broadly and said, "Yes, that is correct."

Five minutes later, the chef delivered two more plates of hamburgers and fries to our table.

29

Hotel Kozani

THE NEXT MORNING WE CAUGHT A BUS FOR KOZANI AT 10:30 a.m. When the bus arrived it was already full of passengers, but the back row of seats was available. As we were boarding, three young Brits appeared with mountain bikes which they wanted to stow in the cargo bay beneath the bus. There was considerable—and agitated—conversation about how this would be accomplished as the cargo bay appeared full. The passengers took the delay good naturedly and laughed about the apparent dilemma.

I got off the bus to chat with the chaps. They had been touring all over Greece, but in this mountainous area had become fatigued and wanted to get down to the plains of western Macedonia where we ourselves were headed. So they decided to take the "coach" to the next stop, rather than bike it. While this conversation was taking place, the driver was transferring some of the luggage to another compartment on the other side of the bus, and the Brits were breaking down their bloody bikes. One bike ended up in the aisle inside the bus. Once we were all on board, we continued to share our stories, and they were as fascinated by our account as we were by their's.

Once we were moving, however, my interest in the conversation waned. Blind Basil was behind the wheel. *Nearer My God*, verse three. The trip from Konitsa to Kozani was the most mountainous section of our journey. The passes were long and grinding going up and horrifying going down, bad enough in good weather, but now it was raining furiously. The water came down in torrents, flung at us as though there was a cosmic pail above us that the gods had just tipped over. Even the Greeks had stopped talking.

Still, that wasn't the end of it. In places the cloud ceiling was *below* us, and we were essentially flying blind in the rain through the mountains.

I couldn't look. I started to think about my life. Seriously. I started to think about my life. I thought of my children back home. Debbie was about to turn 19 on Saturday and she was working hard for the airline, and oh, how

I missed her. And then Jon and Marah—Jon working on the ten-year plan at the college and in his fourth year with the bank, and Marah a senior in college and what did Jon think of the Broncos and Shanahan and would the Rockies win the division and why can't they get some good pitching? And Danielle and Scott planning on a marriage next summer and here I am in this Volvo bus zooming downhill in the northern mountains of Greece so far away, and grandson Alex, 4 years old in preschool and his "papa" not going to see him until January—assuming Basil can get us to the bottom of this mountain, and Danielle running her Small Sprouts licensed daycare program.

And Taylor and Spenser: they are sitting here without a care in the world playing Game Boy. Taylor even read a chapter of *Swiss Family Robinson.* How on earth is that possible?

When I wasn't fearing for my life, I wondered about the wisdom of taking this excursion through the backcountry of Greece. It was supposed to be a shortcut in a way. Bari to Igoumenitsa was quicker and less expensive than a ship from Bari to Athens farther to the south. Then we would cut across northern Greece by bus, taking our time to see the towns along the way and arrive at Thessalonika, a city rich in biblical history. From there, we'd take the train on in to Istanbul.

We gave serious consideration to going to Athens and then taking a ship from Athens to Istanbul. But it would cost us more money, the stay in Athens would be expensive, and we reasoned that if our money held out, we could always find time to make a side trip to Athens later on. So we elected to take the road less traveled.

"And that has made all the difference." Yes, and for a while I wished we'd taken another road.

Kozani is a city of about 45,000 with its own airport. Although a major city situated in western Macedonia it is by no means a part of a typical tourist agenda. It's not even mentioned in our travel books. For us, it was simply a stop on the road to Thessalonika. When we got off the bus, therefore, we had no information about hotels. There was no tourist office to help us either.

Our experience here proved to be the nadir of our travels so far. I have no one to blame but myself. It was another reminder for me—how many times do I need to learn this lesson?—that what might be acceptable for me is not necessarily acceptable or agreeable for others. Had I been thinking about the comfort of others, the amenities they might prefer, the concerns they might have, the ambiance they desired, I would have made a different decision.

I looked at the peeling wallpaper, the drab hallways, the dinghy lobby, the squawking pipes, the dark stairwells, and said, "Oh, how quaint and bohemian."

Jeanie looks at the same things with her children huddled about her waist, and said, "What a dump!"

It was our version of the Hotel California: "What a lovely place/ what a lovely place." It might not have been hell, but we were certain it wasn't heaven, either.

Kozani became a catchword for "Never again," or "We'll pass and look for something else." To this day, we compare accommodations to "Kozani." Jeanie will say, "We don't want another Kozani."

We found a small park not far from the bus station where we were able to unload our packs, rest, munch on some food. I set off by myself to look for a hotel. The only hotel I found in the area was the cheesiest place we've stayed on our journey since we left Denver. I should have hailed a cab and told the driver, "YOU TAKE TO NICE HOTEL!" But I was always thinking about the money. Our money had to last. Our resources were not infinite.

So this was not good. Making matters worse, Jeanie had caught a cold which was getting worse and the very sight of this place made her nauseous. Taylor was getting over a cold. The only people who were happy with this arrangement were myself and Spenser (who was particularly delighted by the five story climb up a circular staircase from which he could spit and watch his spit fall all the way to the bottom). Spenser and I were fine with this.

I hope I'm being fair to Jeanie. Some wives would have refused to step across the threshold of that room. She really was good-natured about it—to a point. I tried to make nice-nice.

"Well, when you said 'whither thou goest, I will go; where thou lodgest I will lodge,' I'll bet you never thought you'd be in Kozani," I said, smiling.

She coughed and blew her nose into a tissue, and then wiped at it. Her eyes were half closed, and her nose had reddened and her face was puffy. She looked at me: "Actually, I never made that vow and besides, why do they even say that at weddings? It was spoken by a young widow to her mother-in-law for pete's sake."

She was right on both counts. We didn't use the language of Ruth at our wedding, and that quote was spoken by Ruth to Naomi. But I wasn't going for literalness here, just the idea that when you make a mutual commitment to each other, you might end up in places you'd rather not be.

"Well, tell you what. From now on, *you* arrange for the accommodations."

"Okay," she said, sniffling again into a Kleenex. She was in no mood to argue.

That night we had gyros for supper and when we came across a video arcade, we gave the boys some change to play for a while. I pulled out Austen's *Persuasion* as I was about to finish it. It's a shorter version of *Pride and Prejudice*, it seems to me. Did she find a formula with P&P and decide to stick with it? Since the only book left in our traveling library is *Northhanger Abbey*, I planned to start on it the next day.

30

Change in Plans at Thessalonika

FRIDAY, OCTOBER 1, 1995. BUSES LEAVE FROM KOZANI FOR THESSALONIKA on the hour. We boarded the 9 a.m. bus and were on our way. No need for hymn singing on this leg of the trip. The highway was generally straight and wide as it traversed the Macedonian plain. Nearing Thessalonika, we were even on a six-lane expressway!

With nearly a million inhabitants, this city is huge, and as the capital of Macedonia, it's second only to Athens in size and economic importance. When we got off the bus, there was no trouble hailing a cab. We directed the driver to take us to the gulf where we were sure we could find a hotel.

When we'd spotted a hotel we—Jeanie—thought we might like, my wife went into the reception and conversed briefly. Then the two of them left so that Jeanie could have a look at the room before we spent any money. Jeanie accepted the accommodations and a cot was moved in so that all four of us could be in the same room.

The room was spacious, featuring a large table at which the boys could do homework, and I could write. There was also a bathroom, and unfortunately, a balcony that opened up to the noisy street below.

Our first order of business, once we'd settled in the room, was to leave it, and head for a ticket office to purchase our fare for the train ride to Istanbul. Once we had bought the tickets and had made our plans, we would call Alan McCain at the Near East Mission to let him know what was happening.

We were in for a major, major surprise. Our plans, according to the lady behind the window, would not include traveling by train.

Yes, we could take the train from Thessalonika, but we would have to get off at the Turkish border because the trains in Turkey are on strike! It might be possible to get a bus from the border and take it to Istanbul, but she wasn't sure.

There was, yes, a bus from Thessalonika to Istanbul and it left at 3 a.m. every day; it was a 12-hour trip. Why it left at such an ungodly hour the clerk could neither explain nor did she have the inclination to do so.

Jeanie and I turned away from the ticket agent, yelled at the boys, and we all went outside to Aristotle's Square and found a park bench on which to sit and have a Family Council near a statue of the famed philosopher.

❧❧❧

Jeanie started: "I don't want to take the bus."

"I second that motion," I said.

"Well, motion is what gives you a problem," she said. "I can't imagine you'd want to spend twelve hours on a bus. And I'm still not feeling great."

"And I don't want to get up at 3 o'clock in the morning," Taylor said, piping up. Taylor stayed close. He generally enjoyed getting in on adult conversations, especially any that concerned him directly or indirectly. And besides, this was a Family Council—although Spenser had left the decision-making to us and was climbing up onto Aristotle's lap.

"It'd be more like 2 a.m.," I said. "We'd have to get up at least an hour early to get there on time."

Before leaving the ticket office, we had gathered some additional information. We considered the possibility of flying. At first, we'd rejected the idea out of hand because we assumed that purchasing tickets for the four of us two days before departure would cost an arm and a leg. But when we asked, we discovered that we could get to Istanbul on Olympic Airlines for $600.

We left Aristotle's Square after retrieving Spenser, and went for some lunch. Over the lunch table the Family Council continued. The boys were enthusiastically in favor of taking the plane. Our other options were to take the train to the Turkish frontier, get off and hope for the best. Or to take the 3 a.m. bus and endure a 12-hour trip. And of course, the bus fare itself was a factor. Subtract the bus fare as the minimum cost to get us to Istanbul from the air fare, and the additional expense to fly made flying a very attractive option. Flying would have the additional benefit of getting us to Istanbul in about two hours with a minimum of discomfort.

Moreover, we had saved on transportation costs elsewhere and we were actually ahead of where we thought we'd be at this stage with our budget. The $600 expense would surely be worth it, we thought. And, we told each other, this is precisely why we've been so careful with our money, so that should an emergency arise, or something unexpected, we would be able to deal with it.

The family was ready for a vote. There was never any doubt as to the outcome. We would fly out on Sunday, and arrive in Istanbul's Ataturk International Airport at 3:50 p.m.

We had booked a room with the hotel for Friday night; would they extend it for one more night?

They would.

I called Alan McCain and told him what had happened. He said that he could meet us at the airport on Sunday and take us to our much anticipated "permanent" lodging in Istanbul. No problem.

We were pleased. We would arrive in Istanbul on schedule. Except for this little hiccup, everything had gone exceedingly well. We really didn't know how it could have gone any better.

శకాశకాశా

We had planned on a full day of travel Saturday with an arrival in Istanbul on either Saturday evening or sometime Sunday. Now, however, our new plans gave us an entire day in the ancient city of Thessalonika. This, too, was another bonus, and added value for the $600 we were spending on air fare.

Saturday was a beautiful fall day in this Macedonian city of the apostle Paul. We walked along the gulf which is rimmed by a four-lane, tree-lined avenue and five story office and apartment buildings. In the distance we could see the White Tower, a medieval structure which was now a museum which houses artifacts from the early Christian era (the city was founded about 2,300 years ago) as well as from historic eras of the city. We saw coins, lamps, vases, and tombs with frescoes still visible. We climbed the stairwell to the top for a magnificent view of the gulf and the city, and in the far distance, we could see Mount Olympus, home of the gods!

From the White Tower, we walked to the Hagia Sophia, a Greek Orthodox church modeled after the great Aya Sophia in Istanbul. It is quite small, but the 9th-century mosaic of the Ascension in the dome is an exquisite example of Byzantine art.

Yet, something more startling awaited us in this church.

The boys, who had wandered off, rushed back to us excited by a fresh discovery! They had found a small chapel which was home to the mortal remains of a past—long past—metropolitan or patriarch. The body, actually the skull and complete skeleton, had been carefully laid out under glass and draped with ecclesiastical garments. Still, the bony hands and feet and skull were quite visible, and the boys were completely ecstatic. They would now have something important to write about in their journals! For them, this was the highlight of the trip. Taylor said he wanted to change his vote for best church to this church in Thessalonica.

After lingering for a while, we stopped for lunch. Wonder of wonders, the boys spotted a McDonald's, the first since France. Soon we were up to our elbows in Happy Meals, Big Macs and French fries!

కళకళకళ

That evening, after rest time and school, we left for a walk to the old city. This involved climbing the hills that ring the Gulf of Thessalonika. Evidently the old harbor was no doubt set farther inland than it is now, and the town was built on a hill with the markets below. This was confirmed when we came across a large area where archaeologists were digging the ruins of a Roman marketplace including amphitheater.

When we returned to our hotel room, I read to the family from Acts 17:1-10 where the first visits of Paul, Silas, and Timothy to Thessalonika are described. It mentions the "marketplace" (v.5) and says that the city was in an uproar over Paul's teachings and that they grabbed Paul's local host, Jason, and hauled him into the "assembly." Paul and his cohorts are described by their accusers as "people who have been turning the world upside down…"

Paul left soon for another town, but when I read from his first letter to the Thessalonian Christians, it is obvious that the seeds of Christianity took root there: "In spite of persecution, you received the word with joy … so that you became an example to all the believers in Macedonia … In every place your faith in God has become known." It's interesting to speculate that the amphitheater and the Roman marketplace that we saw are probably the very sites at which much of this uproar took place 2,000 years ago!

All of this was ancient history. We were more concerned about recent history. We'd heard that Denver had just experienced a freak summer storm and eighty percent of the city's 250,000 trees had been damaged. Our newly planted aspens probably didn't make it.

But although it was cold in Denver, elsewhere in the world things were heating up. The jurors in the O.J. Simpson trial were now getting their instructions from Judge Ito. The people of Bosnia-Herzegovina were bravely resisting the Serb rebels and experiencing some success in spite of the utterly inept ministrations of Secretary of State Warren Christopher. In the mideast Israel was moving forward with its plans to complete the transfer of six West Bank cities by the end of the year (Jenin, Nablus, Tulkarem, Qalqilya, Ramallah

148

and Bethlehem) but Prime Minister Yitzhak Rabin warned that this could only happen if two bypass roads could be completed by the end of December. If the Bethlehem bypass could not be finished, we wondered whether it would affect our plans to be in Bethlehem over Christmas.

The next morning, we caught a taxi to the airport. Our six week journey through Europe had been fascinating and rewarding, but it has been only prologue. We'd journeyed from post-modernity backward in time to the Renaissance and the medieval periods in time, and now to the ancient and classical world.

We were ready now to return to a sense of "home," to settle down, to open ourselves to a fresh experience and a strange culture. We were leaving a world that had been dominated by Christianity to live in a culture thoroughly Islamic.

We could hardly wait!

Part Five
Life on the Bosphorus

"Life is either a daring adventure or nothing.
Security does not exist in nature, nor do the children of men as a whole experience it.
Avoiding danger is no safer in the long run than exposure."

—Helen Keller

31

At Home in Üsküdar

O
UR FLIGHT LEFT THESSALONIKA UNDER CLEAR SKIES. WE LANDED EIGHTY minutes later under overcast skies. The two engine jet propeller aircraft was full; we were fortunate to have found seats at the last minute to make the flight at all.

Although it was a short flight, there was a smoking section on the small plane and we were right in the middle of it. They were lighting up like bank tellers on a fifteen minute break. We were glad to touch down at Ataturk International Airport where Turkish passport control immediately slapped a $20 visa charge on us, $80 total. The surcharge was for Americans only, and was not in place when I traveled to Istanbul in 1990. The United States was making it difficult for Turks to travel to America, there being some concerns about Turkey's alleged human rights violations. The *Turkish Daily News* carried an article about Senator Bob Kerrey of Nebraska who had been bloviating in the Senate about Turkey and its geo-political position, arguing that we shouldn't allow Turkey's strategic importance to blind us to its record on human rights.

So we paid our $80 to support political awareness, got our visas and proceeded through customs without difficulty. It was Sunday, October 1, 1995.

Our luggage arrived promptly and soon we were out among the crowd who were greeting arrivals. The Reverend Alan McCain spotted us right away. How could you miss four Americans toting red packs who have been traveling for six weeks? He said later that he had talked to Carol Garn who teaches in one of the schools in Istanbul and had asked her to describe us. We had met her a year earlier when she was on leave in the States. She said that she remembered my beard and that I wasn't the three-piece suit type and that I was rather casual and "flamboyant."

We had a good introductory chat, and were on our way to Üsküdar. Alan pointed things out along the way. He had hoped to catch the "car" ferry, but we just missed it, so we had to drive further north to the Fatih Sultan Mehmet bridge (also known as the Second Bosphorus Bridge) and then back down the "Asian" side of the city. He reminded the boys that we landed in Europe, but we would be living in Asia.

We were shown to our apartment. When Alan turned on the lights, it was like switching on the Wow Factor. Ah, this is sooooo great! We were more excited than squirrels in a peanut warehouse. We scurried about quickly exploring our new home: three bedrooms (we would use two), two baths, and a fully equipped kitchen including dishwasher and a washer/dryer. The living room was huge and the walls on two sides consisted of floor-to-ceiling windows that allowed natural light to filter in, and offered expansive views of a walled patio outside and the Bosphorus and the ancient European city beyond.

So through our windows, we face west and can watch the sun setting behind the Hagia Sophia and the Blue Mosque on the European side of Istanbul. The patio sits directly above the Bosphorus.

We were very happy to be able to call this home for at least a month—and if they liked us, we could stay for three months!

The building itself consisted of four stories, and the Near East Mission owned the first two floors. It was notched into the side of the bluff that followed the Bosphorus. Our second floor apartment was actually the ground level apartment. Mic and Sally took an outside set of stairs to the lower level, while tenants above us had to climb up one or two floors. From Mic and Sally's level, a steep set of concrete steps—which actually were three-foot cement slabs with a landing area of about six inches—plunged down the bluff to a road far below which ran along the Bosphorus. These slabs—Spenser said there were eighty-two—had been tucked into the earth one below the other, so that over time, they'd settled and now heaved in any which way, making a journey down to the busy street below an adventure to which you gave your full attention, especially since they were laid through thick woods and undergrowth making the road virtually invisible from the top. We occasionally used this route, but although there was a bus station within walking distance, few businesses were open, so we generally walked out to the street behind us to get to the ferries, the bakeries, grocery store or barber.

After we had been shown our apartment, and put down our things, Alan, who said that people call him Mic for McCain, said that they were having dinner below (they called their apartment the Lower Room, and ours the Upper Room) in about thirty minutes. They were expecting some German friends and we were invited, too.

The dinner was fabulous. The Germans were theological students from Hamburg. The conversation as well as the food was wonderful. We had wine, salad, a meat dish, bread and more. We were a very happy, excited family that night!

❧ ❧ ❧

The next day we got better acquainted with Sally.

Mic's wife is fifty-ish, short and stout, roundish face with cheeks that reddened when the temperatures dipped to freezing. Her small eyes were inset below strong black eyebrows and above her smile was a button nose. She had a congenial disposition. And she was very capable.

Their children were stateside, but Mic and Sally had no inclination to return to the States although they'd had many chances. Indeed, they could leave whenever they chose. But Istanbul was their home. They visited their children annually, and then returned. But still, our boys inspired Sally, and the mothering instinct arose.

Shortly after lunch, she appeared at our door and announced that she would take us on an orientation tour.

We began with a walking tour of the neighborhood. Just a block away was a small corner store with no more than one hundred square feet. Eggs were stacked in crates four feet tall. Candy, and toys and cigarettes and much more were for sale. Sally introduced us and explained who we were, telling the shopkeepers we'd be around for a while. We were taken to other places where we met the clerks, stopped by the bakery and pastry shop where we could get the best baklava, visited the fishmongers and vegetable markets, the butcher, flower stalls, and fruit markets.

She introduced us to the *dolmus*. "You see all those people over there?" she said, pointing. We nodded. She had drawn our attention to an old yellow Chevrolet. It was full of people in both the front and back, and more people were crowding in, like women at the doors of Macys the day after Christmas. The dolmus stopped whenever someone wanted on, and stopped whenever someone wanted off. It cost about 40 cents as did a ferry across the Bosphorus.

After our walking tour, we climbed into her Toyota and lurched through hot traffic congested with taxis, dolmus, buses, and bicycles to the Capitol Mall about fifteen minutes away. This mall was only three years old and appears both inside and out just as any American mall might appear. Inside are clothes shops, electronics stores, toy stores, office supply, bookstores, restaurants and a food court with McDonalds, Pizza Hut and KFC. How depressing! But for the boys, how uplifting! And movie theaters! The movies here are in English; it's considered a good thing here to know English or be able to speak it. In France, it's unpatriotic to consider English as a language one might want to speak.

Shopping for food was a learning experience. We discovered that the shopping went much better when we wrote on a piece of paper the Turkish word for the food we wanted and showed it to the grocer. We also took pen and paper to the store with us so we could write down words and figures. Most shopkeepers had a little calculator; they would punch in some numbers and show us a price in Turkish lira.

We had dinner with the McCains our first night in Istanbul as I mentioned. But after Sally's tour the next day, Jeanie immediately went shopping for grocery items to stock up the kitchen and the refrigerator. We were going to have a home-cooked meal.

She and the boys returned from their venture in the late afternoon. Jeanie had spent 1,200,000 TL, about $25, on food. The Turkish lira was presently at 43,500 TL to $1. Inflation was awful and a serious problem.

Getting the shopping bags set up on the kitchen table, she began to unload the provisions.

"And I got us a couple of pounds of hamburger so we can have Swedish meatballs tonight," she said.

This was indeed good news. She withdrew the hamburger from the shopping bag.

"That's a lot of hamburger, honey."

She held the package in both hands. "Yeah, I thought so too."

"Two pounds?" I asked.

"Two pounds."

"But don't they do kilos here? Like kilos. The metric system."

She stared at me blankly.

"I think you got two *kilos* — like five pounds — of hamburger," I said gently, sensing the eggshells cracking slightly underfoot. Pause. "That's a whole lot of hamburger there."

She looked at the package again.

"I think you're right," she said gamely.

"But we can always use two kilos of hamburger, honey. It's *not* a problem. No, no, no, no. Hamburger is good. Hamburger is a *good* thing."

It was not a problem, not with three carnivores in the family. But the incident was a reminder that we had to be careful about weights and measurements.

That night Jeanie made her meatballs loaded with fresh ground spices and diced onion, as well as fried potatoes and vegetables; the next night it was Cajun-style chicken and carrots in angel-hair pasta, plus French baguette and for dessert, Turkish baklava from the bakery down the street.

"Turkish baklava is the best," a Turkish friend later told us. "The baklava you get in Greece — it's not good. It's okay, but it's not Turkish baklava."

Not long after our arrival in Istanbul, the doorbell rang at 7 a.m. I ran through the apartment, and jumped up the two steps to the small ante-room where the door was located and swung it open, expecting to see Mic.

Before me stood a wide little Turkish man, about 5'3" short. He might've been shorter, but he was wearing a turban that sat on his head like a large curled dinner roll. His heavy, long coat was buttoned securely across his chest, and his neck was wrapped in an Arabic scarf. His face was large and weathered but swathed in a bushy, six-inch white beard stained with tobacco juice. His eyes were black and gleaming, and his nose was prominent and strong.

"Merhaba," he said, his lips parted in a friendly smile that revealed missing teeth, and yellowed, rotting teeth that sank into his gums at odd angles like tombstones in a New England cemetery. In his arms, he held a brown bag with several loaves of golden French bread extruding from the top.

"Merhaba," I said. Then he started speaking in Turkish, and of course it was incomprehensible to us. By now Jeanie and the boys were gathered around me, staring at this novel sight.

"I think we should get Mic," I said to Jeanie.

"Taylor, go down and get Mr. or Mrs. McCain," she said.

"I'm in my pajamas, Mom."

"It doesn't matter," she said, waving him out the door. "Tell them we need some help up here."

Sally came up and introduced us to our "bread" man. We never learned his name. To us he was always the Merhaba Man, "merhaba" meaning "hello." We learned that he would be here every morning and that a loaf of bread, a baguette, cost 25 cents and if we had some shopping to do, he would do it for us. He's paid by the mission to do this. It's what is done here in Turkey and the mission does their part. He also sweeps around the building some.

One night after we'd finished dinner, Jeanie raised a question about the bread.

"What are we going to do with all this bread?"

It was a good question. We got baguettes every morning. Two feet long (actually that would be about a half meter long, and 60-70 centimeters around).

That's a lot of bread. We simply couldn't eat all the bread the Merhaba Man was bringing. Spenser had two round crusty pieces on one finger of each hand and was twirling them creatively. I pretended to ignore him and came up with a suggestion: "Two words," I said.

"Two words?" Jeanie asked. "And what would those two words be?" Spenser stopped goofing around in mid-twirl.

"Bread pudding."

"Bread pudding?" she echoed.

"Yes, bread pudding. I love bread pudding. You can use the crusts and it doesn't matter if the bread is dried out. So as we accumulate a bowl full of extra bread and heels and crusts, we'll toss in some eggs, sugar, cinnamon and raisins and have bread pudding."

"Except no raisins," Taylor suggested.

"Yes, raisins," I said firmly, countermanding his idea. "You can't have bread pudding without raisins. It's the *raison d'etre* for bread pudding in the first place."

The family was quiet.

"Get it?" I asked. They looked at me like I was speaking another language. "You learned this when we were in Paris. *Raison. D'etre.* Reason for being. A little play on words. We need raisins in our pudding because they're the *raison d'etre* of pudding."

They got up from the table and left me there counting the "raisins" why I even bother trying to expand the canon of knowledge and enlightenment in this family. I didn't come up with many.

So, while we lived in Istanbul, there was always, *always,* bread pudding in the fridge, and I enjoyed Jeanie's raisin-less version very much. Not to be out-maneuvered, I often prepared on the sly a strong rum sauce and slathered it over my portion. There's more than one *raison* for eating bread pudding. The boys were none the wiser, and after a while, the sauce being so good and all, I just stopped eating the bread pudding, and enjoyed the sauce.

Kidding.

Not only were these meals very good, they were very cheap compared to the way we had been living.

So we settled into a routine. Jeanie cooked meals for us at home. We'd not experienced this sort of routine since back in July! We loved it.

There was a water problem. We had been able to drink the tap water wherever we have traveled so far. But not here.

We woke up Monday morning after our fabulous dinner with the McCains, went to the bathroom, turned on the tap. The sink filled with red muddy water that looked like it had been piped in from the Rio Grande. It didn't change throughout the day. It was either red water, or no water at all. And there was very little warm water and no hot water.

When we inquired about it of some of the neighbors, they would say with a shrug of the shoulders, "They are working on the pipes today." We learned that this is a euphemism for "We're looking into the situation, but aren't sure what's wrong."

It's part of the experience. Jeanie took this all in stride and the boys thought of it as an adventure. The McCains had prepared us, so we knew what to do.

"Let's go, Taylor," I said.

"Where are we going?" he asked, suspicious.

"We're going to get water for the family, and I need someone big and strong to help." So off we went each of us carrying a large white plastic container. We knew where to get water. The water station was about five minutes away, near the Dogancilar Parci. What looked like a gas pump was located in an open-doored shop. The pump was of the same design as a typical gasoline pump; same sort of pump handle. But it was not a gas pump. It was a *water* dispenser. The attendant stuck the nozzle of the pump into our five gallon containers; water swooshed out and within seconds both were full. The dial on the pump showed the amount of water in liters and the price per liter, and the total for this purchase came to 35 cents, about 15,000, TL.

> **October 3, 1995**
> *I saw a yacht on the Bosphorus. I saw the AyaSophia. I saw the Blue Mosque. We took a bus from Kozani to Thessalonika. We're living in Asia. We flew to Turkey. I think the Bosphorus is big.* —Taylor, 10.

From now on, this became Taylor and Spenser's daily job. Even more important, Mic and Sally were impressed. Maybe they'd let us stay in the Upper Room after all. We were only promised and we had only paid for October.

The water problem continued for some time. We'd been in Istanbul for a week and hadn't taken a shower. Finally Jeanie had had enough. She was determined the children should have a bath. So she sent the three of us out for 30 liters of water, no small task. We did it and she poured some of the water in pots on two stove burners, mixed in cooler water and then gave the boys their baths. Later Jeanie and I both had baths in bathwater that was about an inch and a half deep.

We learned that the water problem we were having was unique to our building. We were told it would be corrected soon.

✿ ✿ ✿

A sure sign that we had settled in was the arrival of mail, which we treated with a reverence akin to that accorded sacred Scripture. Letters were handled carefully like holy relics, and then laid upon the dining room table where we'd pass by them in wonderment. We'd examine the envelope itself, lingering over the postmark, hefting the weight of the letter in our hands, pondering its possible contents. Only after a suitable period of adoration did we then take a letter opener, and slice the flap and retrieve the contents.

We received a letter from Mom Merrill six days after it was postmarked in Salem, Oregon. She had written three times while we were in Europe: St. Malo, Zermatt, and Rome, although the Rome letter never arrived.

We also got a letter from Grandma Martin, Jeanie's maternal grandmother. She gave us news about the big snowstorm the previous week in Denver, said that she was going to have surgery on her hand, and that she had to cut her letter-writing short because she needed to get to church for a lecture on the subject: "Morality for Women in the 90s." We found it amusing that a person as saintly as was the white-haired Grandmother Martin, now about 85 years old, would be interested in a discussion of moral issues for women in the 90s.

"The Noun Fairy" continued to send mail. These exercises for the boys contained stories with missing nouns. The boys had to read the story and insert nouns from a list provided. It was great fun.

Our connection with home was further cemented by the occasional phone call. We got a call from Danielle, my daughter, who was using a Sprint access number. We talked for forty-five minutes. It was a free call for her, but she said she had to dial, like, thirty-five numbers to get through!

One night when we had Mic and Sally up for dinner — Jeanie was serving up her famous krautburgers — Mic brought a manila envelop full of mail for us. We whooped and hollered. We had letters from Jeanie's dad, Lee Dalberg, Dick Martin (Jeanie's uncle) and more. It had all come in an envelope from Barbara, Jeanie's mother.

The steady arrival of mail helped as we recalibrated our understanding of home. Yes, we had a "home" in Denver, but, as we had continually preached and modeled by our behavior, home was "ourselves-being-together," wherever that was.

Best of all, the water crisis began to abate. One morning while the boys were on recess outside playing, Jeanie discovered that there was water pressure. The pressure was good, the water was clean, and the hot water was working. She immediately jumped in the shower for the first time in days.

I had gone to the market for some detergent. When I got back, she yelled at me: "We've got hot water." I could hear the shower running. I dropped my pants and jumped in the shower with her before the Water Gods changed their minds. It had happened before. We thought we had water, we'd stripped, jumped into the tub and got just a few drops of warm water. That was it.

This time, the water was plentiful and hot!

Of course, the drain in the bathroom floor inexplicably backed up and we had to mop up and clean afterwards.

It was a small matter.

32
The Lay of the Land

O NE DAY ABOUT TWO WEEKS AFTER OUR ARRIVAL IN ISTANBUL, I came back from the bookstore in Karacöy with a fistful of maps.

I love maps. I love everything about maps. When my dad took me hiking as a kid to the Grand Teton National Park, he always got us topographical maps of the area. He taught me about lines and legends. He showed me how to interpret the angel-thin wavy brown lines, so that I could compute the elevation gain or loss on the trail up Paintbrush Canyon, over the divide and on to Lake Solitude. He explained the function of the legends so that I could quickly tell where a creek ran through the canyon, or a forest camp was located.

Maps are my friends. I don't need to ask for directions. I have the map. I know where I'm going.

But in Istanbul, I *didn't* know where I was going. When I was in a taxi, I wasn't able to communicate where I wanted to go, so I got some maps of both Turkey and the city of Istanbul.

I love laying a map out on a table and smoothing out the folds. Then I lean over the map to take a look. My head hovers over it like a space agency satellite, my eyes like a Hubble camera taking and capturing images of foreign nebula. I lean closer for a better look. "There!" I say, standing back erect and turning to my entourage, "That's where we live." They lean forward uncomprehending. I point to a spot on the map. To them, it's just a spot on the map.

Men love maps. Women hate maps. This is just a general observation from my many years of experience studying the way men and women *communicate*. In 1995, communication styles were on everyone's mind. The Clarence Thomas hearings were a recent memory. Just four years before we left Denver, linguistics professor, Deborah Tanner, had published a ground-breaking discussion of gender differences in communication in her book, *You Just Don't Understand:*

Women and Men in Conversation. Even more recently, John Gray was selling millions of his *Men Are from Mars, Women Are from Venus: A Practical Guide for Improving Communication and Getting What You Want in Your Relationships.* We spent a lot of emotional energy in the 90s worrying about our communication skills with the opposite sex. In 1995, the conversation was simmering; soon White House shenanigans would bring it to a full boil.

Tanner has a great chapter on men's use of *report* language, and women's preference for *rapport* language. Men are good at one and lousy at the other; same goes for women. Tanner doesn't argue that one dialect is better than the other. It is what it is, boys and girls. We just need to understand it. Report language works well when reading maps and getting one's bearing on site. That's why I prefer to get directions from males. Men give me reports. They give me distance, direction, and data. "Stay on County Line Road for 3.2 miles, turn left and continue to Wellington Drive. Go two blocks, and you'll find 3454 to be the third house on the left." Women give me verbal photographs: "Go down this road with all the trees, and you'll pass a McDonalds, but don't turn yet, so when you get to Home Depot, turn there and go up the hill past the cemetery till you see a large billboard for the Colorado Lottery, that's where you'll want to turn again and just keep going until you see a red Ford pickup in the driveway."

I thought it was important that Jeanie and the boys have a general understanding of our host city, and where we lived, and why we had to cross a body of water almost every time we wanted to do anything. Spenser, only 7, was not too interested, him still not sure what state of the union we lived in back home. The only state that concerned him was his own state of mind, and most of the time no one else in the family quite knew what that was. Taylor, however, was always interested in maps, so in this matter, he was my only ally.

It's not too hard to get the lay of the land in Istanbul.

The city is huge, no doubt about it, numbering a good seven million inhabitants. But those residents are spread out over two continents separated by a body of water.

Sitting right above (north) of Istanbul is the massive Black Sea. The city itself is perched close to the Marmara Sea, and the channel that links these two bodies of water is the deep blue Bosphorus. The channel that links the Marmara Sea to the Ionian Sea is a twenty-eight mile strait known as the Dardanelles, and the Ionian Sea farther south opens up broadly to the Mediterranean.

The Bosphorus is a crucial shipping lane for ports in Georgia, Russia, the Ukraine, Romania and Bulgaria, not to speak of Turkish ports on the Black Sea. Ocean-going vessels and double-hulled barges, oil tankers, flat decks, floaters, and front end motor barges ply these waters at all times.

The word Bosphorus means "Ford of the Cow," which evokes the Greek legend of Zeus and Io (hence Ionian Sea). Zeus and Io were lovers, but once in danger of being discovered by Hera, Io was changed into a cow so that when Hera came upon them, she found Zeus with this lovely cow grazing nearby. But Io as a cow was chased from the mountains and desperate to get away, swam across the waters separating Greece from Asia, and the waters came to be known as the Bosphorus, or "Ford of the Cow." Something like that.

There are two suspension bridges over the Bosphorus. The first, the Bosphorus Bridge with six lanes of traffic, connecting Beylerbeyi and Ortaköy, opened in 1973. The second, the Fatih Sultan Mehmet Bridge with eight lanes, opened in 1988. If you want to get from the Asian side to the European side by car, you must take one of these two bridges. There are no tunnels beneath the Bosphorus.

If, however, you can't take the bridge, you then take advantage of the ferries which have a criss-crossing transportation pattern making it quite easy to get relatively close to where you want to be on the other side.

The Bosphorus, then splits the city, but splits the continents as well.

However another body of water divides even the European part of the city, and two bridges span this "river" as well in an area known as the Golden Horn. The bridge with the most fascinating history, and considered to be one of the distinctive landmarks of Istanbul, is the Galata Bridge, a bridge that has existed in a number of incarnations since the fifteenth century. Both Leonardo da Vinci and Michelangelo submitted designs for the construction of the bridge. In 1990, the bridge then in use when I was visiting Istanbul had been operational since built by a German firm in 1912. It was built on pontoons. Driving across the four lane bridge one could see and feel the undulations of the road beneath the tires as pontoon sections heaved and ho-ed in the ebb and flow of surging and relentless traffic. After a fire in 1992, the bridge was reconstructed, the pontoons removed, but the shops and merchant stalls below the bridge remained in place.

The Galata Bridge links the commercial and financial districts of Galata and Taksim to the north, with the site of the ancient city to the south. The core of the old city juts like a thumb out into the Bosphorus, and it is this area that was the Byzantine and Ottoman fortress known for centuries as Constantinople.

It's here that one can wander narrow and winding streets, shop in its markets, enjoy the intimate cafes, and explore much of the city's vast store of historical and cultural treasures.

You can climb one of the seven hills of old Constantinople and visit the Mosque of Suleiman the Magnificent, the sultan under whose leadership the Ottoman Empire reached its zenith in the sixteenth century. While Henry VIII and Elizabeth I were casting Renaissance England in their image, and Martin Luther had the Roman Catholic Church in turmoil, and while Michelangelo was flat on his back painting the Sistine ceiling, Suleiman was ruler over half the then-known world. His empire extended west to the gates of Vienna and east to Persia and south into the continent of Africa. The Michelangelo of this civilization was Sinan the Architect whose work still dominates the landscape in Istanbul. The city in that era was the center of the Ottoman Renaissance as Rome (you could argue Florence) was of the western version. The two cities, in fact, parallel each other in curious ways. When Emperor Constantine (fourth century) moved the capital of the empire from Rome to Constantinople, he called it the *nova Roma*. As Rome had seven hills, so did his own city. The emperor could rename the city, but the Roman influence was pervasive and even today one can visit, indeed drive beneath one of the city's busiest thoroughfares, the Aqueduct of Valens which dates to the era of Roman imperial dominance. Eighty-six of its arches still remain. For centuries it brought water to this isolated and arid peninsula, securing the future of one of the great ancient cities of the world.

It was this peninsula and its hills and mosques and minarets that we could see from our perch on the bluffs across the Bosphorus in Üsküdar. Our home in Üsküdar was really the only point of reference we needed for the Asian side of the city. When we went to the city, we always crossed the Bosphorus by ferry, map in hand, and referenced where we were going by referring to certain landmarks or locations which, on any given day could be the Dutch Chapel, Taksim, the Tunel, the Galata Bridge, Eminönü, the Hagia Sophia, the Grand Bazaar, or Topkapi Palace. Usually, any place we wanted to go, was in the vicinity of one of these locations.

We couldn't get lost. No one could get lost.

No way.

33

What Friends Are For

WE HAD A FEW FRIENDS IN ISTANBUL BECAUSE OF MY prior visit to Istanbul in 1990. I had traveled to Istanbul to see one friend, but came home with several others with whom I have been able to maintain a relationship over these many years.

We'd only been in Istanbul a week when one of these friends, a teacher of English, Göksel Goçer, gave me a call. We made arrangements for him to have dinner with us. I was to meet him at the fountain near the Bosphorus on a particular Wednesday night.

I found Göksel to be a very likeable fellow when I first met him back in 1990. He taught English at the same school as my friend, Megan, and he shared an apartment with three other teachers including Megan, an apartment provided by the school.

"Come on," he said to me one night. "We will go have party." He took me with some other friends to the Chik Passage, or Flower Passage, where we dined in a second floor room. Calf brains on a bed of lettuce and other Turkish delights were spread out before me. He laughed when he saw me staring at this incomprehensible food. Turkish music was piped in through speakers.

"It is okay," he said, nodding. He had a Mediterranean complexion, and thick black hair. He was a gentle soul; warm, compassionate and eager to be service. Later, he and others danced to loud, traditional folk songs. In fact, he loved to dance, and even off the dance floor he carried himself with grace.

When I arrived at the Bosphorus on foot, it was already dusk. The large open square was a central area where ferries and small boats docked, people visited a mosque nearby, vendors sold their goods, shoeshine boys plied their trade, and commuters from the other side of the Bosphorus disembarked from the ferries and small boats. It was a bustling scene.

Göksel did not appear. I waited an hour. Then I returned home.

He called. He, too, had been waiting, but in a different location. The confusion was mine, because I misunderstood what he meant by "fountain." I was looking for something where flowing water was involved. He was referring to the "fountain" or water taps by the mosque where one washes before going in for prayers.

So we rescheduled for Thursday night. I waited by the mosque, and we made our connection.

When he arrived he was accompanied by Zacherias, a friend I had met here before as well. He was then engaged to Turkan and later married her. They went to New York where he worked on a M.A. degree in Albany. But he didn't finish, and they returned to Istanbul where he was now Director of Studies at Best Institute, which is a school that provides instruction in English to adults and the business community. Zacherias was wearing a heavy gray wool coat and a worsted mosaic scarf in deep-blues was wrapped around his neck and thrown over his shoulder. He was wearing his trademark horn-rimmed spectacles, which sat on a prominent nose which was in turn planted in a triangular face accented by a Jay Leno jaw. Even when he shaved, it appeared he had a beard of at least three days' growth.

Zacherias is a naturally friendly and ebullient fellow and he was glad to see me as I was to see him, and he was surprised that I remembered his name. I assumed he was joining us for dinner, but no, he was going home. He didn't live too far away.

Göksel and I clawed our way into a crowded dolmus, taking it to Dogancilar Parci. We stopped at a small market for wine, and then walked home. I introduced him to Mic and Sally and then brought him upstairs to the Upper Room. Jeanie had shopped for the ingredients of a wonderful dinner and it was delicious. Göksel was very glad to have some speakers of English to talk to. Actually, he was happy to have *anyone* to talk to. He stays so busy he sometimes feels isolated.

After dinner, we took coffee out on the patio where he smoked three Marlboro's and I lit up some Captain Black in my pipe, made by Tom the Pipe Carver in Princeton and we talked for another hour before repairing indoors for more conversation. Everyone who knows Göksel enjoys his company. Lean and fit, he seems relaxed and comfortable, at home "in his own skin," as the expression goes. He was a handsome young man by any standards, now in his late twenties, and not involved with any particular girlfriend as he was when I first met him in 1990. Then, when I bunked with him and a couple of other teachers in the school-provided apartment, he was the only one who shared a bedroom with another teacher, a fiery Irish lass, Bridgette, ten years his senior. He was her whipping boy; he never seemed to please her, and we all wondered why he put up with it. The answer lay, no doubt, in his easy-going compliant nature. Even now, as we talked, he sat back in the deck chair, languidly, almost indolently, and you had the feeling that only the most alarming emergency would startle him into action. He was above all charming, with a quick smile and easy compliments. When he smiled his white teeth blazed in contrast with his sepia skin and wavy, coal black hair. He was highly conversant on local politics and was quite aware of Turkish internal affairs as well as the country's position in the geo-political cosmos. Although his birth certificate said "Muslim," he was, in fact, a "secular" Muslim and seldom went to mosque, although respected those who did, and there was never the slightest argument over religious issues—he knew we were Christians— and thought religious wars were folly. He was highly supportive of Turkey's unique political approach in the Islamic world: his country was thoroughly Islamic, but equally a thoroughly secular state. So, the conversation ranged far

> Having someone in Istanbul whom we knew, however slightly, was important to us who were living as aliens in a strange land. It gave us a connection, a sense of belonging, however faint that sense was right now.

and wide equally over weighty as well as petty matters. I walked him back to Dogancilar Parci and we agreed to meet again Saturday night in Taksim in front of the Marmara Hotel.

Having someone in Istanbul whom we knew, however so slightly, was important to us who were living as aliens in a strange land. It gave us a connection, a sense of belonging, however faint that sense was right now. Still it was a connection. Friends keep us connected. That's what friends are for.

Mic and Sally provided that connection as well. We had never met them before of course. But there were connections. They were Americans. They spoke English. They had devoted their lives to ministry, there were theological commonalities which we all shared. On a certain level, we shared cultural interests as well.

The next evening, Friday, we were out for dinner with different friends: Megan and Bulent Eryigit. Megan was a friend of mine from the Reagan years back in Denver. We met when we were taking some English classes at Metropolitan State College of Denver back in the 1980s. I was taking English classes to qualify for certification to teach Secondary English, thinking that I couldn't make a living at preaching, and in any case was tired of pastoral work. Teaching at the high school level seemed to be a more attractive option. I don't know what I was thinking.

There were four of us students who became close friends: Megan, Carol, Kevin and myself. We studied together, worked on group projects, and often, in the summer, attended the outdoor Shakespeare Festival at the Mary Rippon Theatre at the University of Colorado at Boulder. We spread out a blanket, opened a bottle of chardonnay, snacked on wafers and white cheese and grapes, and munched on pastrami sandwiches. Always, there was great conversation prior to Act I which never began until dark — about 9 p.m.

The interesting aspect of this group of friends — since we're talking about friends and friendship — is that there was not the slightest romantic entanglement among us whatsoever. We were all single at the time, except for Carol, whose husband was a well-heeled professional in Denver. Truth be told, had Kevin showed a romantic interest in Megan, she probably would have responded. But, fact is, this was not about romance; this was about being friends. We were friends before there was *Friends*, before there was Ross, Monica, Joey, Chandler, Rachel and Phoebe. I was still about three years away from meeting my Jeanie, the Great Love of My Life.

After we finished our course work at Metro, we sort of split up. Carol took an English position at West High School in Denver where she continues to teach to this day. Kevin took a position in Avon, Colorado, just outside of Vail, and married. And Megan took a teaching job in El Paso, Texas, and then grabbed a job teaching English in Istanbul in the fall of 1989. She had been fearful of going and in fact was in tears the night before she left Denver. So I told her that after she'd been there a while, I'd travel over and see her. I was single, unattached, and had a sabbatical coming and had never been to the region where the Apostle Paul had preached and traveled. I could see her on a stopover on my journey.

When I arrived in late December, 1989, however, she was faring quite well, and even had a Turkish boyfriend, Bulent Eryigit.

One day I asked her about him. We took a walk down to the Bosporus near the Dolmabahce Sarayi. We found a park bench and sat for a while and watched the ships plying the waterway. Less than forty years earlier, Khrushchev had sent missiles on boats through the Bosporus on their way to Cuba. On this particular day, the green water was churning with barges chugging through from the Black Sea, and fishing boats and ferries crossing to and fro between the European and Asian sides of the city. Nearby vendors were selling simits, borek, chestnuts, fish sandwiches, corn kebab, doner kebab, water by the glass and yogurt. By the water's edge fishmongers were cleaning and selling the day's catch: blue-fish, bonito, turbot, anchovy, scad, red mullet, gray mullet and sardines.

"You can't be serious," I said. "What are your parents going to think?"

"I'm not serious," she said, laughing, and tugging on her head scarf.

"Bulent is," I said.

"No, not really."

"He phones and pesters you all the time!"

"He's Turkish, what can I say?"

"What does your family think about this — your brother the priest, your sister the sister?"

"They don't know. Did you talk to my mum?" she asked, changing the subject.

"I called her before I left. She said to say she loves you." Then I asked, "Do you go to mass?"

"Not much," she said, giggling.

"Should I give you some reading material — Teresa of Avila, or Hildegaard von Bingen?"

"Don't worry about me, really, I'll be fine, Timothy."

I couldn't imagine her becoming a Turkish woman, the wife of a Turkish man, and possibly converting to Islam. Maybe she'd at least insist that the fruit of their union be Catholic. But at this point there was no talk of marriage.

In the intervening years, I at long last found my Jeanie and we married under a hot, July sun by a small lake in Belmar Park, Lakewood, Colorado. But even sooner, Megan married Bulent in a quick ceremony when both were in Denver. Now he picked us up at Dogancilar Parci and delivered us to their third story apartment in Acibadem about fifteen minutes away. They have a beautiful little home there. The flat is divided into separate rooms, nothing "opens" up to anything else. Every room has a door. They went to a great deal of trouble for us. They have two children, and Megan was nine months pregnant, due any time and she had a table full of dishes for our meal.

She tried to get us all to drink a concoction of yogurt and water called *aryan*, but it was too unique for most of us, although I think I could develop a taste for it. There was also *yaprak doma* (vine leaves with rice inside) and *zeytinyagli patlican* (an olive oil eggplant dish) served cold, and *zeytin sebzeler* (olive oil vegetables) and *kuru sasuliye* (a bean dish) and of course baklava. It was all very tasty and we enjoyed the experience very much, although I thought at the time that eating food cold might take some getting used to.

Megan had a nice room in which she taught her private students and seemed very happy with her work. They appeared to be doing very well. Bulent would soon start teaching a full load at the university.

After the dinner was over, we pestered Bulent into taking his lute off the wall to play it for us. He complained that the only time he plays the lute is when Americans visit and force him to. But, he is very, very good. No frets on a lute and his fingers jump about on the neck of the instrument so adroitly that it's obvious he's a master of the instrument and with more practice—well, it's hard to imagine how he could be more accomplished than he is. We enjoyed listening to him, and the songs he sang as well.

It was an important evening for us, because, although we and the Eryigets saw little of each other in the following months, we felt at ease in our new surroundings. We had friends who'd help us if we needed help, and with that sort of a safety net, the worry factor had been completely eliminated.

Our friends — they were all so eager to help us. Isn't that what friends do? Megan and Bulent offered to take the boys and let them watch TV and hang out if Jeanie and I ever wanted to get out alone. Göksel and his roommate offered some help with lodging in the event that Mic and Sally thought it necessary for us to move out of the Upper Room.

The next day, we took a ferry at the Üsküdar docks and caught a boat across the Bosphorus to Beşkitaş on the other side. From there we took a dolmus to Taksim Square where we were to meet Göksel at 4 p.m. We did, and he showed up with a friend, Nerendim who, although born in Turkey, had lived his young life in Albany, and thus spoke English very well. He has a M.A. in teaching English as a second language and had been in Istanbul since August and was teaching in a private middle school here. His apartment is provided by the school, so his expenses are minimal. We all went to a nearby park. The others thought it a bit chilly, so we sat at a café in the park, outdoors, and had çay (tea) before going further.

This ritual completed, we walked down the most famous street in Istanbul, the street where Istanbul lives and works. The Istiklal Caddessi (caddessi means "street") is to Istanbul as Seventh Avenue is to New York, what Nanjing Lu is to Shanghai. The Istiklal Caddessi is like Broadway in New York without the traffic. In 1990 when I was here, it was full of motorized traffic. Now it has been closed to vehicles from the Tünel at one end and Taksim at the other. Only pedestrians fill the street although there is a single trolley car that ferries pedestrians on a single track. Sometimes, the conductor let Taylor ring the bell. On this particular night, the street was full of heads bobbing like apples on a sluice line.

After some window shopping, Göksel took us to the Hajic Abdullah restaurant. I had a dumping with lamb meat and Jeanie had a chicken dish and eggplant.

What are friends for?

To make sure you don't go hungry.

Friends can also be a royal pain.

One evening — it was a Saturday — there was a dinner party to which we were invited. It was, in fact, in "our" apartment. The Near East Mission, of which Mic and Sally are Directors, uses the Upper Room with its spacious living room and dining area for large entertaining projects and this was one of them.

Two Americans were coming in, and the wife of the director of the American school in Izmir would be with them, and the director and wife of the school here in Üsküdar would be here as well, and one other American who has been here twelve years.

They all arrived about 5 p.m. and we ate around a huge table and chattered about a variety of matters. We struck up a conversation with Shirley Stendahl from Izmir who boasts of having the nicest house in the city, located next to the home of the regional governor. She heard that we might be traveling down her way and insisted that if we do, that we stop by to see them and spend the night or nights with them.

After dinner, and after the guests had departed, Shirley and her two American friends, Joan from Downer's Grove, Illinois, and Flo from Cleveland, staked out their beds in the other bedroom which we had not occupied. We learned that we would be sharing space with these ladies for the next three days. I thought it would be fine. And the ladies loved the boys—thought they were well-mannered. As a person who needs a certain amount of space to be comfortable, I was remarkably sanguine about the prospects for the next few days. These ladies were interesting.

Joan, although from Illinois, is Scottish and at heart she's still a highlander gal, a lass with sass. She's loud and brash, evoking laughter without intending to be funny. She was a stout woman with the figure of a badly beaten barrel, and with Coke-bottle spectacles perched on the bridge of a pointy nose, she could seem pushy, too.

Flo, on the other hand, is quiet and spent most of her time giggling at Joan. She calls herself an artist who does "box" art — creations she makes out of boxes.

The third member of this traveling sisterhood is Shirley, a librarian who appears older than she probably is. Perhaps it was the glasses, or the short, graying hair, or the flowered print dress that seemed somehow dated. Her features were sharp but her manner was pleasant and inviting. Although she's been in Turkey for three years, her Turkish is very limited. This may be because Shirley loses focus occasionally and things get by her.

All of these ladies apologized for invading our space, but we assured them it wasn't our space to invade. So they settled in.

The next day, Sunday, we went to church and didn't see the Sisterhood all day. And therein lies a story.

At 8:30 p.m. Mic stopped up and announced that the ladies were evidently lost. He wondered if I'd be willing to go with him to scout for them. Mic wasn't the sort of fellow who often asked for help for any reason. But driving around at night trying to snare these birds was evidently a task that was daunting, even for him.

So of course I said, "Of course," wondering how one scouted for three old ladies in a city of seven million people, a city located on two continents.

Mic's plan was to go down to the ferry in Üsküdar and see if we could spy them wandering about. He hadn't any other plan.

So we did, to no avail.

Mic's exasperation grew with each passing minute. Mic is above average in height, blondish mop of hair, about 50-something. He's clean-shaven, doesn't wear glasses, skin is fair and his nose bends a bit to the side. He's slender, almost gangly and he affects the air of an intellectual. Not talkative, and when he does talk he can sound dismissive. He's one who — to not coin a phrase — doesn't suffer fools gladly. Chasing three disoriented women around Istanbul at night was definitely not his stein of beer.

We went back to the apartment. There we got news that Sally had called a friend of theirs on the European side. Evidently, the ladies had been there to see her. She said that she'd put them on a ferry at Beşkitaş and that they should have been in Üsküdar some time ago. Hearing this, Mic left to return to the Üsküdar ferry to see if they could be located. This time, I stayed behind.

At about 10 p.m. Mic returned with the Ya-Ya Sisterhood in tow, who trooped in, visibly weary and disgruntled. Mic was silent and remarkably gruntled. The women had been in a taxi for ninety minutes and had been over the Bosphorus Bridge three times!

Sally had given Shirley a card on which was a phone number and an address. Unfortunately, it was the Near East Mission address on the *European* side. So in effect, they took a ferry from Beşkitaş to Üsküdar—from Europe to Asia — then caught a taxi, produced the address on Shirley's card, whereupon the driver promptly took them *back* to the European side over the Bosphorus

Bridge to Europe. You can see the problem.

Of course they had to get back to Asia, but none of them had an address for the "Upper Room." They did not have a phone number (no cell phones, remember), they did not know where we lived in relation to the ferry boat docks, they did not know how to use a dolmus. They couldn't tell a taxi driver how to get them home. In short, they were lucky Mic spotted them.

When they gathered in the kitchen, the story was told and retold with many rhetorical flourishes, and Joan was heard to oft repeat in her high Scottish brogue: "Well, all's well that ends well!"

Later, not finding any brandy in our apartment, she went down to the "Lower Room" and found some with the McCain's—Mic had no doubt already poured himself a snifter—and returned upstairs and prepared a concoction which she called Anglican chicken soup. She raised her glass, and said, "Here, here!" and drained the contents of the chalice in a single gulp.

The reference to chicken soup was appropriate because Shirley had come down with a nasty cold, and Flo seemed to be suffering the same symptoms.

The only one who was well beyond suffering was Joan.

34

We Find a Church

WHILE THE GIRLS WERE OUT AND "ABOOT" THAT DAY, WE went to church, as I said. Church was a very important part of our "routine." We lived now in a country that was thoroughly Islamic. The calls to prayer could be heard five times a day from the minarets. There were minarets everywhere. Going to church was much more than merely going to a place of worship; it was a home for friends with whom we shared a common faith, a common culture, and a common language. We rarely missed church.

We went with the McCains who took us to the 9:30 a.m. service at the Union Protestant Church which convened in the Dutch Chapel at the Dutch Embassy. The church has been a continuous presence in Istanbul for 160 years and worships in this chapel by the permission of Queen Beatrix of the Netherlands with the proviso that the queen be mentioned in prayers every Sunday. The pastor is a Presbyterian from New Zealand, and he did indeed remember the queen in his pastoral prayer along with other weighty matters such as the peace accords, Bosnia, and so on.

We enjoyed the service very much, met other Americans, and English speaking people from other areas of the world. We had been here only a week and our circle of friends was already growing. It's easy to feel "at home" here and I could imagine how someone who has been here for years would find it hard to leave, or at least find American culture a bit alien upon return. We also saw Carol Garn the school teacher whom we had met in Boulder a couple of years ago when she was on furlough and who had later described me as "flamboyant." I didn't bring that up.

Going to church became our custom. It took us about an hour to get to church. After all, we had to travel from Asia to Europe and that involved walking to catch a dolmus, a dolmus to the ferry, a ferry across the Bosphorus to Beşkitaş, another dolmus to the Tunel and more walking.

Often, we got there in time to stop at a pastry shop near the Dutch Embassy where we had a Sunday morning treat. Sometimes we met other church goers there as well. Then it was off to Sunday school at the Union Han, and then Jeanie and I would walk to the chapel itself a couple of blocks away.

The Dutch Chapel was usually full of visitors, some from Wales, or Texas, or immigrants from Ghana. On this occasion, the preacher was holding forth in a series on the book of Exodus. One week the sermon outline had made use of the letter P: The Purpose of, the Power of, the Problem of, and the Promise of. Fill in the blanks. On another occasion the operative letter was I: The Inopportunity of, the Indictment of, and the Importance of. He obviously didn't miss the class on Alliteration when he was taking his seminary class on Homiletics.

The pastor was a Rev. Anderson, a Presbyterian from New Zealand, and a very good-hearted man. His congregation comes and goes so it's no wonder that he had trouble remembering our names. Didn't matter that we'd had a lengthy conversation in his apartment a fortnight ago, or that we'd met once at a reception, or that we shook hands following the service. He would fumble about, and then we'd tell him who we are—because it was obvious we looked vaguely familiar—and then he'd remember, "Oh, yes, yes, quite right, the reception, the pastor from the States, good to see you." Sometimes that ritual would happen as we were entering the sanctuary; no matter, it would be repeated when we left the sanctuary an hour later.

"I think he's cute," Jeanie said once, after we'd just labored through this embarrassment again.

"Cute?" I said, "What do you mean cute? He's quite portly and undistinguished if you ask me."

"I don't mean cute cute," she said laughing. "I mean cute likeable."

He was likeable. Although he could laugh at himself, he also could spot other moments of humor. Once when the liturgist had led us directly from the singing of the hymn to "Words of Assurance" which expressed gratitude for God's forgiveness, overlooking the Prayer of Confession which was a collective prayer asking for that forgiveness, Anderson arose, getting on with the order of worship, after reminding us that God—speaking of errors—forgives even the errors committed by inattentive liturgists who in their enthusiasm for forgiveness forget the solemn duty and necessity of confession.

The congregation tittered with appreciation.

After the service, we would pick up the boys who had a great time in Sunday school with other kids who spoke English. Getting home, we used all the means of transportation (in reverse order) we had used to get to the chapel. At home we would have dinner with baklava and bread pudding for dessert.

The boys had Sunday school classes of their own to attend, so Jeanie and I always went to the adult class. When we got wind of a "choir" that was rehearsing for a Christmas concert, we signed up!

As much as we were committed Christians, we were very interested in and respectful of Islam. When an opportunity arose to observe an Islamic religious rite, we jumped at the chance. The "Sisters," as it happened were in on this one, too.

Jeanie and I were particularly excited about today's scheduled events, especially the evening plan. We were going to visit a *tekke* to see the Mevlevi, or Whirling Dervishes.

But Shirley decided to stay put for the day. She had spent the night coughing and wheezing. In the morning, Taylor and Spenser played games with her. If they had not already been infected with what she had, they almost certainly were now. Joan and Flo agreed to explore the city—in daylight.

At 8:30 a.m. Mic arrived upstairs to take the "deariers" to the Üsküdar ferry, making the pointed observation several times that they "needed to be leaving SOON" if they were to catch the 9 a.m. ferry.

Not to worry. Although the meaning of his words seemed lost on these two birds, they did finally appear. Joan looked like a lollipop in a pink jogging outfit and a white cap; Flo was less conspicuously attired. Joan was in good form, both the brandy and a good night of sleep having the desired effect, and even in their departure, she provoked gales of laughter as they sallied forth. Mic rolled his eyes and left with a pained expression on his face.

In the afternoon, the Merrills stayed at home, too, catching up on school, reading and writing. I was nearly at the end of *The Bostonians*, written shortly after *Portrait of a Lady*, both wonderful. Prior to *Portrait of a Lady*, I'd read Paul Theroux's *My Secret History*, a novel, but highly auto-biographical.

We were to meet Mic and Sally, Flo and Joan at the mission office in Sirkeci at 5 p.m. Since Jeanie wanted to pick up some things at the spice market in Eminönü we set sail at 3:30 p.m., did our shopping and got to the mission office shortly before 5 p.m. Of course, Joan and Flo had not arrived yet but they did show up at 5:20 p.m.

Joan decided that she'd had enough for the day and didn't want to extend it further. Flo, however, wanted to visit the *tekke* with us, so Joan went home with Sally and Mic. I got on the phone with Linda, a friend from the Dutch Chapel who had arranged this for us. She said to meet her in front of the Marmara Hotel in Taksim at 7:45 p.m.

This arranged, I took my little group down the street through some narrow lanes and alleys crowded now with people headed home. We pushed through crowds gathered around small shops, went through the Spice Market, over the Galata Bridge and on to the Tunel and up to the Istiklal Caddessi where we strolled, observed, and then stopped to eat. Later at the Marmara Hotel, we met Linda, caught two taxis and were off to Fatih where the *tekke* was located. We were going to attend the worship service or *sema*.

The Mevlevi or Whirling Dervishes are followers of Medlana Rumi the 13th-century poet, perhaps the greatest of the Islamic philosophers. The *sema* is based on Rumi's occasional habit of whirling in joy in the streets of Konya where he did most of his life's work, although he was born in Afghanistan.

A *tekke* is a center of learning for Muslims. This particular *tekke* describes itself as a cultural center. It's also a place of prayer and worship. This *tekke* is not large and was found on a side street. But when we entered, we found it to be very busy. Jeanie, Flo and Linda had to don scarves. Linda described what was about to happen as a sort of "choir practice," a rehearsal for the worship Thursday evening. In fact, however, you can't practice praying. When one prays, one prays. So we found the experience very moving.

It began with formal prayers. The women couldn't watch, but I was allowed to, so I took the boys and we stood in the doorway while a room the size of a half basketball court was full, really full, of men who fell to their knees and prayed following the lead of the muezzin who stood facing Mecca in the minbar. At a signal in the prayer, their faces all hit the carpet, posteriors rising behind them.

The carpets were then rolled up and the men convened in an adjacent room for singing. I should mention that all the men wore white hats in the shape of a small baker's hat without the puff at the top. Instrumental music, very Middle eastern then began and singing followed for about thirty minutes. Novice dervishes were practicing in another room which we were not allowed to watch. But we did see them standing on boards which had a nail in it. They inserted their foot so that the nail was positioned between the big toe and the fourth toe. Then they whirled.

We were led into a large room where the men had been praying before. Directly across from us, the men were now singing. After thirty minutes, the dervishes, dressed in long black robes filed in and sat down right in front of us. We could've touched them. Beneath their black robes were the white blouses and skirts in which they would whirl, the black and white signifying the death and resurrection theme of their worship.

The dervishes, while perhaps not identifying themselves as Sufi Muslims, certainly fall into this branch of Islam, which is the mystical wing of Islam. The word "dervish" is Arabic and means "threshold," suggesting again that the dervishes regard themselves as "walked upon" or as having lost a sense of self and have offered themselves to God to be "walked upon" or across as necessary.

Their elongated stovepipe hats, narrower at the top than at the bottom, symbolize their tombstone. Dervishes have "died" to themselves, while they are alive to God. As they whirl, one palm is open toward heaven, the other is extended down, showing how in their dance they hope that God's blessing will come down, be received by them, and then extended to others, or "whirled" out to others as they dance.

The dervishes do not whirl particularly fast; the tempo was moderate and it never varied. While the chanting of the men in the prayer room picked up speed, or slowed down, the whirling itself remained constant. What is amazing — and this is no doubt a trite observation—is that they can whirl and not lose their balance. Later, in the apartment, I took three spins and couldn't walk steady when I stopped.

The dervishes also are not in a trance when they dance. They are very much aware of their surroundings, of what they are doing, and at a signal, they all stop whirling at once, take a slow walk around the room, and then, one by one, the whirling begins anew. This happened three times, As they whirl, their leader walks among them, directing traffic so to speak, so that they don't bump into each other (their skirts flare out about three feet).

Several weeks later, we saw another dervish service, but this time it wasn't a practice. Both experiences very much impressed us.

35

The Case of the Mascot Murder

ISTANBUL IS A CITY OF TREASURES. MAGNIFICENT TREASURES. LET ME take time to mention two.

The Blue Mosque, for example. Its real name is SultanAhment Mosque built shortly after the grand Suleymaniye Mosque in the 17th century. It's called the Blue Mosque because of its thousands of blue tiles, mostly from Iznik (former Nicea — the same Nicea as the famed Council of Nicea, 325 A.D.). For architectural achievement, the Suleymaniye Mosque is perhaps the greatest, but for beauty, the Blue Mosque is hard to beat. It's the only mosque here with six minarets. The dome, seventy-seven feet wide and one hundred and forty three feet high, not as large as the Pantheon or the Hagia Sophia, but impressive nonetheless, is supported by four massive columns.

But if that's not ancient enough for you, walk across the street to the Hagia Sofia, or the Ayasofya. St. Sophia, as it's been known in the past, was built 1,500 years ago. It predates just about everything still standing in Istanbul, except perhaps for the aqueduct which dates from the Roman era. The original church was built in the fourth century at the behest of Constantine's mother, Helene, who also ordered the construction of the Church of the Nativity in Bethlehem. But it was destroyed by a fire or earthquake so this present structure dates from Justinian, 532 A.D.

The stunning feature of this Church of the Divine Wisdom is its massive dome which, when it was built, was a wonder of the world, for it appears to rest solely on the forty-some windows at its base. The exquisite effect is that it appears, as some have noted, to be supported on, or hover over, a circle of luminous light. Its cavernous dome is an absolute engineering marvel. It's been a Christian church, then a mosque, and now mostly a museum.

There's so much to do in Istanbul. The mosques. The bazaars. The streets. The museums, including the Archaeological Museum and Topkapi Palace. We visited the church in Chora (frescoes) and underground cisterns, the ancient walls of the city, and more. We weren't sure where to start. But the advantage of an extended stay in Istanbul is that we had plenty of time and we saw much, indeed *all*, of what we wanted to see.

Whatever we did, however, usually involved a ferry ride across the Bosphorus to the European side of the city.

We enjoyed the ferry rides. We took both the large ferry and small ferries. The large ferries were at least three levels high and had ample seating inside and out. Spenser was young enough to get in free because he passed the height test. Anyone able to walk beneath a turnstile got in free.

The small ferries, about the size of a small tug boat, also had seating inside and out but they were crowded, and traveling on these ferries was always an adventure, because they had to flit like water bugs across the Bosphorus dodging the larger ferries as well as huge ocean-bound barges headed to or from the Black Sea to the north. Our little boat looked awfully small against the prow of a flat-deck barge. Sometimes there were collisions. The ferry traffic across the Bosphorus is very heavy.

Quite simply we were in love with this city. We were enthralled by every aspect of our experience, and we still couldn't believe our good fortune in securing a place to live on the banks of the Bosphorus that afforded us such comfort and such beauty.

We talked about it one evening as we sat on a patio table, looking directly west across the shimmering water to Taksim and the Golden Horn, pipe and wine at the ready. The sun hung low in the west like a red Chinese lantern, veiled by a lacy cloud veneer. The sky behind the Blue Mosque and the Ayasofia was a surreal swirl of gold and maroon, as though it had been photo-shopped to achieve a special effect. We came out to the patio almost every evening and were tracking where precisely the sun set over the cityscape of the ancient city known at times as Byzantium, Constantinople and now Istanbul.

"I hope we don't have to leave this," Jeanie said, after we'd been sitting silently for a while.

"If the boys keep running up and down the steps by the McCains, this might not last long," I said.

Jeanie looked at me startled. "What do you mean?"

"They were chasing each other this afternoon on the steps, whooping and hollering. Mic probably wasn't home." I paused. "It's probably okay."

"They're boys."

"I know they're boys. They have a ton of boyness. The question is, 'Is it going to be too much for Mic and Sally to endure for another two months?'"

Jeanie was silent.

I continued. "Frankly, I really don't think there's a problem. It's been great. I haven't noticed any sign of irritation or awkwardness. I just wish we knew what was going to happen."

"Well, you should talk to them."

"It's too early. We've got time. But we need to know by the end of the month. Surely they would give us time to make arrangements." I paused, thinking of something else. My pipe had stopped smoking. I reached for a lighter. "Spenser's birthday is coming, too. We gotta make some plans for that grand occasion."

The sun was now falling between the minarets of the Hagia Sophia. In a few moments it would drop behind the hills. "Maybe they assume that we know that we've got the place for as long as we need it," Jeanie said. "I think if there was a problem, they would say something, wouldn't they? Or at least give us a hint? What are we suppose to think?"

I had the last word: "It'll be okay. It's fine. Not to worry."

Mic and Sally never said anything about it. We were left to wonder. And to think about Spenser's birthday.

❧ ❧ ❧

One chilly Sunday morning in late October, we left for the docks at Üsküdar as per our custom, and got on a large ferry for Eminönü rather than Beşkitaş. We were not going to church; we had some other plans. We sat outside in the prow of the boat on a bench that had been lacquered with white paint many times over. The ferry cut through the water under cloudy skies that looked like rain. The wind swirled and Jeanie tugged on her coat. She'd wrapped her scarf around her neck. Taylor wanted some tea.

"Have you ever had tea, Taylor?" his mom asked.

"No," he said in a defiant and sullen sort of tone that let us know that not ever having tea was no excuse for not having tea now.

Tea was available. It was sold by kids who sallied forth from the kitchen bearing a silver plancher laden with çay glasses. These delicate glasses were about three inches tall, no handles, and usually were ringed with a golden band around the top, and sometimes featured an etched pattern in the glass. Each one sat on its own glass or brass saucer, also no more than three inches in diameter. A small stirring spoon was in each one, and they were all full of hot steaming "çay" or tea. Lumps of sugar were available. In the cooler fall days, and especially in the winter, çay (pronounced "chai") was very popular, and the children and sometimes adults selling the tea had a flourishing business.

"Okay, then," she said. "You have some money? It will cost you about 12,500 Turkish lira."

"I have money, lots of money," he said smiling, and he pulled a fistful of lira out of his pocket. He probably had 150,000 TL in his hands.

"Where'd you get all that money?"

"Timothy."

Jeanie looked at me. "A kid's got to have some ready cash," I said. "You never know when you're going to need tea."

Actually, it wasn't as much as it sounded. When we arrived in Istanbul, the Turkish lira stood at 43,000TL to the dollar. So he had about ten dollars in his hand.

When we left in January, 1996, the Turkish lira was over 100,000 to the dollar. Inflation was a huge problem at that time in Turkey. And it wasn't going to get better anytime soon.

So Taylor got some tea, one lump of sugar. We watched with amusement as he transacted his business.

"Teshike ederim," Taylor said. We were shocked.

It means "thank you," and Göksel had taught this to us, helping us to sound out the syllables and how to say it fast so it appeared that we knew what we were saying.

Nearby, a man and his wife were standing, watching this little drama play out. He was wearing a heavy dark woolen overcoat with the collar turned up and a scarf wrapped around his neck, and she was also wrapped in a coat and wearing a head scarf. His face was dark with what looked to be a three day growth of whiskers, but Turkish men are so dark and their beards grow in so quickly, he might have shaved that very morning.

We appeared to be the only foreigners on the ship. This wasn't always the case, but not too many expats lived on the Asian side, and today we were the only ones traveling across. They attempted a conversation in broken English.

"Amerika?"

"Yes, we're from Colorado."

"Oh, Colorado, we have friend lives in Yuma."

"Arizona?"

"Yes, Arizuma. Yuma."

This conversation continued for a few minutes, and when it broke up, both the husband and wife, in their mid-fifties we thought, extended their hands and gave Spenser's blond little head a good rub.

It was not the first time he'd received such a noggin-nudging and it wouldn't be the last. Blond-haired little boys were very rare in Istanbul and complete strangers had no compunction about running their hands for good luck across his head. After a while, Spenser found it more amusing than abusing, but when it first happened, he looked up at his Mom and wrinkled his nose as though to say, "What was that?"

I loaded my pipe with Turkish tobacco, much finer than the American variety, and enjoyed the trip over, the breeze bracing into my face.

At Eminönü we disembarked and headed for the Spice Market. Here every variety of spice known to humankind could be found, as well as vegetables from stands nearby. Teas and coffee, saffron, curry, paprika, grains and nuts, cinnamon and more. The spices were arranged in large burlap bags or open mouthed jars. Some small shops were devoted to cheese. Others to baklava or candies. People milled about inspecting, sniffing, and sampling and haggling and buying. Always there were rows and rows of young men with their shoeshine boxes waiting for customers to step up, plant a foot on their box to get a shine for a few coins.

A short walk from the Spice Market brought us to the *Kapali Çarsi* or Grand Bazaar or Covered Bazaar, a beehive of commercial activity since the fifteenth century and where today over 4,500 shops await your visit. Here scores of merchants sell everything from souvenirs, to pottery, to carpets, clothes, jewelry, Turkish Nargile (water smoking pipes), Turkish antiquities, clothing, kitchen items. It's sort of a mall in the ancient style and although the bazaar is patronized by the Turks themselves, it was a destination that every tourist had to visit. Outside the bazaar we might encounter dealers selling pencils, tissues, cigarette lighters, pipe tobacco, combs, pigeon seed, and more. Inside, we found silversmiths, tinsmiths, goldsmiths, Meershaum pipe-carvers, basket-weavers, book-sellers, slipper-makers, coffee-grinders, spoon-makers, broom-makers, bakers, potters, flower peddlers and cobblers.

It had begun to rain lightly, so we were glad to get under the cover of the bazaar. As we approached the east entrance a young man greeted us: "Hello? Welcome. Let me help you spend your money."

We smiled and walked on.

"America?"

"Yes, we are from Colorado."

"Oh, I have cousin lives in Boulder. She like very much."

It was a curious fact that every vendor we met had a friend or relative who lived somewhere in the United States. Never failed.

This young man, persisted. "Let me show you my jewelry." The jewelry stores were always brightly lit and gleamed with flashy bracelets arranged in their windows like slices of gold standing on end. We weren't interested.

The chap followed us for a while, so we resorted to a familiar technique. Lifting our head and eyebrows in a quick motion a couple of times, we said something like, "Tsk, tsk" which let him know we wanted him to leave us alone. Usually, it worked.

The bazaar is a fun place to shop if you enjoy the haggle. The price that is offered is never the price you should pay, nor do vendors expect you to pay it. You never show interest in what you're really interested. You low-ball the price, and if you want it, you'll settle on something in between. If you think their offer is still too high, you walk away. If they want to sell you a bracelet, they will shout out their final price which you can accept or reject. If they let you go, then you can be fairly confident that the price they quoted you was their last offer, and you can go back, or move on and hope to get a better deal. "Honey," I said, "They will never sell you something at any price unless they're making some money."

She looked at me. "Seriously," I said.

We bought some tiles using these very techniques. The tiles had a beautiful blue floral pattern, and came from Iznik, the tile capital of Turkey. We bought nine six inch squares and the smaller border and corner tiles as well. Believe it or not, we lugged these tiles all the way back home and I installed them in the wall of our kitchen at Bell Court where they remain, as far as I know, to this day.

"You make very good deal, mister."

Our objective today, however, was really to meet up with some friends, Zacherias and Turkan, and their little girl, Aisha, about three years old. A darling. Zacherias and Turkan wanted to take us to a football game, football as in soccer. We met near the university not far from the Grand Bazaar and piled into their 1974 gold VW Beetle and with their three and our four it felt more crowded than a Japanese camera convention. Zacheria drove, I sat up front with him, Spenser on my lap; the women sat in back with Taylor and Aisha on laps. Off we went.

A major soccer match was scheduled for 7 p.m. that evening and Zacherias felt we needed to be at the stadium by noon to get tickets. We'd then take our seats and wait. I was skeptical but said nothing. Get tickets at noon and wait for seven hours? With three children? In the rain?

As we careened through the streets of Istanbul, not even hitting a single simit vendor, the rain began to fall harder. Undeterred, we drove on. It was a thirty-minute drive.

When we got there it was bedlam. The crowds pressing and pushing toward the ticket offices were impenetrable. Young men were attempting to scale the walls of the stadium in order to see this match which evidently was an important match in the World Cup series. Police were blowing whistles and catching miscreants. Shouting. Lots of shouting. It was a mob scene and our car was engulfed at first, until Zacherias managed to snail through to safety. It seemed clear to me that there was no way we were going to get tickets to this match, and with the rain falling and a seven hour wait ahead of us even if we could get tickets—the whole thing seemed quite impossible.

It took Zacherias longer to reach this conclusion than I, but it's a conclusion he did reach, so we drove off.

He was determined, however, to take his American friends to a soccer match. He knew of another game in a lower division at the Academi Stadi, a much smaller venue, that might be a possibility. Zacherias gunned the engine and we spun out and headed north.

The crowd was much smaller, and we were able to sit in stands with a roof over our heads. The tickets were only 2USD compared to 20USD we'd have paid at the first game and now, at 2:30 p.m., the match was about to begin. We all felt that this was a much better choice, and we were pleased with the outcome. Besides, we'd been inside a VW Beetle for over an hour. It felt good to pile out, stretch our legs and put our face to the rain. We looked forward to being in one spot for a while.

We climbed up into the stands until we were about three-quarters of the way up and found an empty row to occupy. The players had left the field after getting warmed up and we were now awaiting the start of the match. We didn't have to wait long.

The visiting team took the field first to much hooting and hollering. Shortly after they had appeared, two men came out with a sheep. The boys beamed excitedly: they were pleased to see that "our" team had a mascot, a fat, woolly sheep. Back in Colorado, the university football team, the Buffaloes, had a mascot too. Ralphie. A bison. He was at every game. At the beginning of each game, Ralphie, with a team of handlers, charged out on to the field, inciting the crowd of 80,000 into a frenzy.

These "football" fans now stood, too, as the sheep was led out to the side line. We watched with interest. We expected the home team to appear momentarily.

"I hate it when they do this," Turkan whispered. She'd barely uttered the words when we saw the sheep go down. Its legs were pulled from under it, and it was on its side flat on the ground. One of the men pinned it down with his knees, while another took a dagger and slit its throat. Thick blood splurted into a flat pan. Jeanie gasped and turned to the boys who were bug-eyed.

The boys had just been witness to a murder.

A mascot murder.

"Timothy?" Jeanie looked at me saucer-eyed as though to say, "Why don't you do something?" Wishing, for once, I had some control issues and would handle this. Because she certainly didn't know what to do.

"Whaaat?" I mouthed back at her.

We had not yet recovered from this shock when the home team appeared and each player filed by the slain animal, dipped his forefinger in its blood, and applied it to his forehead and then ran out on the field. The forefinger to the forehead. The crowd was going wild.

Zacherias explained that this was a good luck tradition. The Chinese light firecrackers; the Turks slaughter sheep. It also happens occasionally at the dedication of a new building or the purchase of a new piece of machinery or equipment. The meat was donated to the poor.

The match began, and the home team scored twice bearing witness to the efficacy of the superstition. And going in to the last minute of the match the home team preserved its lead on the field, but all was not well in the stands.

Tuesday, October 23, 1995

I saw a sheep sacrificed. I learned they sacrifice animals for good luck. I ate three hamburgers yesterday. I saw a scoccer game and it was raining. I learned the police are at games to stop fights. We squished into a tiny gold bug. I thought the game was neat. —Taylor, 10

A dispute broke out among fans, all men, about eight rows below us. Disputes in a sports arena, whether a ball park in New York City or a soccer stadium in Istanbul are not quiet affairs. This one was no different. It was a loud and boisterous confrontation. Soon it had escalated into a brawl. Punches were thrown, usually missing their targets. Bodies lunged upon bodies. People were shoved out of their seats and into the row above, igniting further loud recriminations. Before long the melee had taken on a life of its own and began to "roll" up toward us, row by row, as other fans became involved along partisan lines.

We watched with amusement, then astonishment, and finally alarm. The fight was now only a couple of rows below us. We were seated in our row Jeanie-Taylor-Timothy-Spenser. At this point I began to think about our options, but just then scuffle was in the row directly in front of us, and I moved to grab Spenser, hoisting him in the air just as one of the brawlers landed in his seat. Jeanie and Taylor had already scootched away from the action and couldn't believe their eyes.

When the fury had played itself out like a typhoon losing steam over land, I looked down the row to Zacherias and Turkan who had been spared the action. He looked at me and shrugged. "We're Turkish," he said, a refrain I'd heard before and would hear again.

We left and returned to Asia via the second, north, Bosphorus bridge and had tea by the Bosphorus at a little outdoor café where the water lapped the walls of our enclave not three yards from our table. It was a calming and delightful respite from the adventures of the day.

Zacherias asked us to call him when we got back from Cappadocia so that we might have dinner at their house. I said that we surely would.

36

The Cappadocian Caper

IT WAS A DARK AND GLOOMY NIGHT WHEN AN ANXIOUS family of a man and a woman and two small children, burdened with heavy backpacks, huddled atop a windswept bluff above the stormy Bosphorus. Beneath them dropped over eighty slippery concrete steps through a deep woods leading to the water and the narrow cement path that meandered beside it.

Gothic description aside, this is pretty much how our Cappadocian adventure began. We had cleaned up the apartment, packing all of our belongings and stowing away as much as possible, shouldered our backpacks and stepped out into a cold and rainy night. For this trip, only Jeanie and I carried packs as we were traveling light. It had been raining for a couple of days and on this day refused to quit, not even for the four of us as we walked about a half mile to the Harem bus station where we were to catch the 9 p.m. bus. We were scheduled to arrive in Göreme in Cappacodia, Central Anatolia at nine the next morning.

We were embarking on an excursion. Until now, we'd been like bear cubs at the mouth of the den: we'd leave our apartment, make a few forays into the city and then scamper back. But now we were leaving our "home away from home" to explore beyond that which had become familiar.

By now it was late October, and we had hoped we would have a word from Mic and Sally about our future. Would we be able to stay in the Upper Room for the months of November and December, or had they decided that it was too much of an inconvenience to have boarders staying for an extended time? We had received no hint that the McCains were unhappy with our presence, or that we had in any way made their work more difficult, or that guests who had stayed with us, like the Sisterhood, or Dr. Barkley Shepherd from Tarsus, had felt uncomfortable bunking with this little family from the United States. In fact, the feedback was positive. The guests that Mic and Sally had to book in the Upper Room with us from time to time had all seemed to enjoy the interaction with us and the children. Still, you never know.

We planned to be gone for about a week from the 23rd to the 30th of October. We wondered if it would be too much to make inquiries before we left as to our status. I sent Jeanie down to do the dirty work.

She came back with a glowing report. They were quite happy to have us and to extend our stay through January 6. The rate would be 500USD per month. Jeanie also had another piece of news: Mic and Sally were leaving. They had a sabbatical coming up and would be leaving as of November 1 and an interim director of the mission would be installed in the Lower Room, the Nielsen's, and it would be the Nielsen's who would have to put up with us for most of our stay in Istanbul, not Mic and Sally after all.

A reception would be held for the Nielson's shortly upon our arrival back in Istanbul. And it would be held in the Upper Room.

This was all good news. Not the part about Mic and Sally leaving of course—they had been wonderful to us. But it was a great relief to know that the question of our lodging had been settled and we could now travel to Cappadoccia without this weighing on our minds.

The bus station was a zoo. I was surprised at all the people traveling to Cappadocia at this time of night. But in fact, they wanted to take the overnight bus as did we, so that they could start their day in Göreme. It was a 12-hour trip. The staging area was full of buses, taxis, people milling about—women in coats and scarves huddled under an eave with their children, and men, each with a cigarette in his mouth or between two fingers, chattering and gesturing about the soccer game, their wives or the government of Tansu Çiller. Vendors were roasting chestnuts over a charcoal fire and simit sellers balanced tall spindles loaded with their pretzel-like treats. The scent of roasted lamb filled the air.

We already had our tickets. Ours was the 9 p.m. bus. We took up a position near the *peron* where our bus was to arrive and then depart with us on it. A few buses at our *peron* came and went. And then, just about 9 p.m. the bus to Göreme drove up.

"Okay, people," I barked joyously, as I picked up my pack, "let's do it."

We walked to the bus; Jeanie had each of the boys by hand. "Go ahead and get on," I suggested. "I'll stow the bags first." Jeanie sent Spenser up the steps and into the cabin of the bus first, Taylor followed, and then she was on.

I found the driver and we threw our red bags into a compartment in the belly of the beast, and then I boarded by a rear door. The bus had come from the Topkapi station on the European side, so passengers for this trip were already on board.

I got inside the bus and noticed that Jeanie and the boys were standing in the aisle. Jeanie seemed confused.

"I think some people are in our seats," she whispered.

"You don't have to whisper," I said. "They aren't going to understand you." I took the tickets from her, checked and double-checked, and even though the tickets were printed in Turkish, numbers are numbers. These people, including an elderly grandmother, were clearly in our seats.

There was a scene.

I began with hand and arm motions, mostly pointing to the numbers on the overhead storage area and pointing to our tickets, pointing to myself and pointing to them, but the grandmother sat in my seat with a totally Stoic expression, clutching a paper sack with provisions for the journey. Her head scarf was still around her head and would stay there, no doubt. And I had a sinking feeling and she would be staying there in my seat, as well.

My pointing seemed not to have the desired effect. I said to Jeanie, "I know they can't understand me, but I'm going to start speaking in English loud and clear and someone who has a smattering of English will hear me and tell these people to get out of our seats." So I turned to the grandmother and her family and said loudly, "I'm sorry, but you are sitting in the wrong seats. There has been a mistake. Let me see your ticket and I can tell you where you should be sitting. Do you understand me? You are sitting in my seat and my family's seats. We have the ticket here, see? It says these are our seats."

This had the desired effect, and soon passengers and drivers—even drivers of other buses—were talking excitedly in Turkish about our situation. From this, I derived a small measure of comfort and satisfaction. This would be worked out. I knew it.

This tactic has worked on other occasions. When I traveled in a dolmus in the city and needed to get off, I simply said in clear, plain English, "I need to get off here," and the driver would whip over to the curb and let me out. It's not that he understood English, it's just that I was saying anything at all. I might have said, "My, what a beautiful day it is today," and the driver would have slammed on his breaks, curbed the dolmus to let me off. So I was quite sure that if I started to speak in clear, forceful English, someone was going to pay attention.

A Turkish gentleman wearing a heavy coat and a Greek fisherman's hat pushed his way to the center of the bus and to the eye of the storm. Behind him came the driver looking very concerned. Suddenly all conversation on the bus stopped.

I explained our situation to this kindly man once again, throwing in a few jabbing gestures toward Grandmother sitting in my seat. "These are our seats," I said, "See here are the numbers—13A and B, C and D." I handed our tickets to him. "See?"

He took our tickets. The dark crust on his old hands was like chicken skin that has baked for too long. He fingered the tickets and examined them closely and then gave them back to me.

"These are our tickets, yes?" I asked.

He made a chomping noise with his teeth before speaking. "Vell, yes und no." He was Turkish, but spoke English with a German accent. Go figure.

"What do you mean yes and no?"

"Yes, yes, yes, dees heer are your teekets and dees heer ees the row, number 13 A, B, C, D for dees 9 o'clock bous to Göreme."

"Yes I know that. So are you going to tell these people to move?"

"Vell, no," he said, making that chomping noise again, "Because you are not on the 9 o'clock bous. You are on the 8 o'clock bous. Ja. Dees bus ees one hour late."

Oh, for Pete's sake!

I made a lot of pointing gestures as I got my family off the bus. "I'm sorry, I'm sorry." We retrieved our bags from the undercarriage compartment and walked beyond the *peron* where we dropped the bags and watched the 8 p.m. bus, leave the station one hour late. At 10 p.m. the 9 p.m. bus arrived, our seats were vacant and we plopped happily in them, although dead tired. A bus assistant came up the aisle squirting a lemon-scented cologne in our hands to both freshen us up or to wake us up. I don't know.

The rain had not subsided. When we pulled out of the station and on to the Trans-European Motorway for Ankara, Jeanie noticed that the windshield wipers were not working. To their credit, the drivers stopped and vainly tried to fix them. But, oh well, they weren't working. We forged ahead anyway. Fortunately the highway was very good: a six lane tollway, to Ankara at least.

The driver pulled off the highway for gas twice and these stops were designated rest times. The twenty minute break gave us a chance to visit the restrooms and stretch. But Spenser had inconveniently decided to sleep through the whole night. The rest of us found sleep difficult because the seats were not comfortable and we found it hard to sleep in a moving coffin of carcinogens—non-smoking buses were unheard of in those days.

On the first of these stops, shortly after midnight, we stepped off the bus, pale and green, thankful to be able to breathe fresh air, but Spenser slept on. As Taylor understood, this presented a problem: one of us needed to stay on the bus with Spenser at all times. The boys could not be left alone. That would leave us vulnerable to an incomprehensible nightmare: What if the bus left before we returned? These were not our thoughts, but Taylor's.

He stood on the gravelly parking area not ten feet from the bus while Jeanie and I got off to discuss logistics. He was wearing shorts with broad green vertical stripes, and a loose, oversized grass-green shirt. He stood knee-locked and flat-footed. His hands hung heavily at his sides pulling his soft, rounded shoulders into an attitude of helplessness. His head was still shaven in the style we'd established in East Shroudsburg, Pennsylvania: He looked like a Buddhist monk in training without the saffron robe. "Who's going to stay?" he asked.

He was very concerned that the bus was going to depart with Spenser but without us. Where does he get these ideas? So if his mother was on the bus with Spenser, it was hard for Taylor to not be on the bus too. And if he was off the bus with his mother, it still was hard, knowing that Spenser and Timothy were on the bus and that if the bus left, he was stranded with his mother—for whom he would then be responsible—in the middle of Anatolia. Stranded with his mother; saddled with responsibility: it was too much for this gentle child to contemplate. He didn't really want to get off the bus, but we made him.

By 6:30 a.m. the eastern sky had turned salmon pink. Sun would be up soon. I peered out the dusty window. We were traveling through country that reminded me a lot of northern Utah, or southern Wyoming. We traveled past Tuz Guloz which looks much like the Great Salt Lake. It had been a long time since we were on a six lane toll way; the road here was a narrow asphalt lane that stretched for countless miles across the Anatolian plain. Not even a white center strip. We had the road pretty much to ourselves. By now Spenser was rousing. Jeanie motioned at me.

"Spenser's not feeling well," she mouthed at me. Passengers were asleep. I looked at him. His eyes were half open. He looked pale and pukish. He needed to go to the bathroom.

"He needs to go to the bathroom?" I whispered. "We aren't going to have another stop for an hour until we get to Neveshir."

Jeanie turned to Spenser who was now nestled on his mother's lap: "Can you hold it for a while, sweetie?" she asked. Spenser nodded. His hand was in his lap; he was already quite literally "holding it."

We drove on. But before fifteen minutes had passed, Spenser was showing signs of nausea and the fidgeting that affects someone with a full bladder. Jeanie looked at me. So I got up and stumbled down the aisle of the Mercedes bus and spoke to the driver, in English, of course.

He was clearly puzzled as to my meaning. I made a gagging noise and put my hand to my throat. The meaning was clear. "Immediately?" he asked. He knew some English.

"Evit," I said. I knew some Turkish.

He muttered something and downshifted the bus and slowly brought it to a stop in the road. He didn't attempt to pull over to the side. No shoulders on this road. He simply stopped. If another vehicle approached it would have to pass us and go by. There we were. We had brought the bus to a halt.

The bus idled, the only noise in a quiet dawn. I motioned for Jeanie to send the ailing lad up the aisle to me. He arrived and I grabbed his hand and helped him off. We took a couple of steps on to the pale Cappadocian soil and walked back beside the bus, turned our backs to the bus and waited. Spense knew the drill. I stood there and looked across the Anatolian landscape to the distant low hills that even now were coming into view like an image in a darkroom developing tray. The apostle Paul and his pals had wandered through here, pushing Christianity to the west for the first time. I thought about the armies of Crusaders and the support staff, including people in all the trades and professions needed to keep an army in business, that had tramped through here in 1096 and 1097 A.D. almost a thousand years ago. This area had echoed with the sounds of war, the cry of death, and it was all silent now. History had folded on itself; buried beneath this dirt were lessons to be learned.

I scraped the earth with my foot and then realized that I had not heard or seen any action from Spense. He was standing beside me, feet spread, head bowed, shoulders stooped, hands in front of him, but nothing was happening.

"Spense."

"Yeah?"

"What's happening?"

"I can't go," he said.

"Sure you can," I said brightly, wanting to encourage the lad. "Keep trying." I glanced backward at the bus. Faces were at every window. The stop had awakened everyone. They no doubt thought we'd arrived at Neveshir. But we hadn't. The little blond-haired American kid had to pee.

"Try again," I said.

We stood again in silence. But nothing.

"Come on, Spense."

"I'm trying."

I waited. Jeanie waited, watching anxiously from the first step of the bus door. Nothing.

"I think I can wait," Spense said.

I was afraid this would happen. I'd go to the front of the bus, I would get the bus driver to stop the bus. Spense would get out to pee, and then he wouldn't pee. It's not an uncommon phenomenon. You're in the doctor's office and you're told to provide a sample. But you cannot provide a sample. Can't do it.

Perhaps Spenser could not provide a sample, but we were not going to get on that bus without trying one more time. I addressed the seven-year old one more time in a voice as authoritative as I could possibly make. Being nice had not worked.

"Spenser!"

"What?"

"We have stopped this bus in the middle of Cappadocia for no reason in the world except you said you had to pee. There are forty-five Turkish people staring out the window right now and every last one of them is waiting for you to pee. You. Will. PEE!"

He said nothing but stared at the ground. A few seconds later he started to pee.

I fully expected the bus to erupt in cheers when we boarded a few moments later. The driver didn't wait for us to get to our seats. He closed the door and geared up and sent us flying down the road—not to speak of the aisle—again. He had time to make up. We had already started an hour late.

Americans!

37

Fairy Chimneys and an Underground Hittite City

WE ARRIVED IN GÖREME, OUR DESTINATION, WITHOUT FURTHER ADO. It's a destination of desolation.

The landscape is pocked with needle-like rock formations, as though the earth was a pin cushion and these were the needles pushed through the fabric of the landscape. Domes, pillars, and stalagtite columns with granite caps on top, like an Oxford don in academic regalia. In many of the cliffs, ancient dwellers had carved out homes in the limestone, complete with dining rooms, common areas and bedrooms. Nearby might be a monastery, or a chapel. Although rich in history, many of these dwellings had been occupied as late as seventy-five years ago.

It was a strange moonscape of a scene; we expected Kirk and Spock, or the Starship Enterprise, to materialize before our eyes to greet us before returning to the Enterprise. The area seemed at once futuristic and a glimpse into an intriguing past.

We stood gawking in the small gravel lot of the bus station for a while until a slight man, in stained trousers and a torn white shirt, and cap atilt on his head, offered to take us ten kilometers into Avanos for 200,000TL. We agreed, and off we went.

Our reservations were at the Sofa Hotel. Our driver took us directly there. We paid him with a handsome tip and walked through an arch into the courtyard. Immediately a young man greeted us in Turkish and motioned for us to follow him. We wondered how he could possibly know who we were. The place had a pronounced Mediterranean air to it: the red tiles, the whitewash on the adobe or stucco walls, pottery everywhere. He led us up some stone stairs, beneath more arches, more stairs. We are still outdoors. Then around a corner, through another arch and then a descent of ten steps into a cave and more arches, and then up, up, up through the cave to a landing until we reached our room, the "Zurich" room which overlooks Avanos and the Red River and, we could say, the "Red River Valley."

It was entrancing and exciting for us, a welcome change for now, at least, from the busy city of Istanbul. Welcome, I say, for all of us except for Taylor, because Taylor, nursing all the fears of the unknown, braving the trauma of the rest stops on the trip from Istanbul and the uncertainty of whether someone would get left behind, all of this had turned his stomach into a nervous tizzy and what with the lack of sleep, the *sturm und drang* of the unfamiliar, he would not be 100 percent for another twenty-four hours.

We left the hotel and rented two scooters so that we could quickly tour the area or parts of it, and get a "lay of the land." With Taylor sitting behind me and Jeanie on a bike with Spenser, we sputtered off from Avanos in search of an adventure in Cappadocia.

The roads are not smooth. Even the paved ones have terrible ruts in them. Buses and vans could be seen motoring down the wash board roads often on the wrong side in the belief that that the road is always smoother on the other side. We puttered around some slow-moving vehicles and came to the small village of Uchisar which is dominated by a large "castle" rock which was inhabited by Anatolians of centuries past and by Byzantine monks. Over three thousand cave churches exist in this Göreme Valley area, many of them decorated with frescoes. In fact, the next day we visited the cave church of St. Barbara of which we took several pictures so that the boys could show their Grandma Barbara. The Barbara after whom this church was named achieved sainthood, but only after she'd also achieved martyrdom.

We returned our scooters at the appointed hour and straggled back to the hotel. By now a severe case of bus lag had caught up with us and we all laid down for an afternoon nap which lasted about three hours. You do what your body is telling you to do. It's not worth it to ignore what your body is saying. So we slept—right there in the middle of the afternoon. Taylor was now entrenched in the melodrama of his illness, and we hoped that a good sleep might help him, which it did.

We departed late afternoon with about an hour of sunlight left to the town square of Avanos. This region has had a strong French presence in the past and many stores and restaurants posted signs in French. Like their Hittite ancestors, the people here make and sell mugs, jugs and rugs.

We walked up a side street and saw in the distance a small light burning. We approached and I peered inside finding there a potter working alone in a cave at a wheel. I motioned to Jeanie and the boys to come over and we went inside and watched him throw a couple pots. He was incredibly fast and was throwing the same type of pot, over and over. Each pot came out the same size and height as the one before it. No measurements, no trimming. He took us further back into the cave showing us three rooms with pots arranged on shelves, thousands of them. Incredible. We bought a pot, expressed our admiration and left. Two days later, we returned to film him at work, but the shop was closed and we never saw him again.

We visited a commercial operation the day before we left, the type of place where tour operators send their large tour buses. Indeed this is exactly what happened as we were there. Three buses drove in and unloaded their occupants. They were in a buying mood. A staff person took us below to where the potters were at work throwing pots, bowls, plates, etc. It was fascinating to go into the room where they make the clay, dug out, he said, from the Red River.

The next building over was an onyx factory and one of the workers there showed us around his workshop and explained the difference between marble and onyx and alabaster. Onyx is harder than marble and older. It takes 20,000 years for marble to develop into onyx and the stage in between, he said, is alabaster. He showed us how they cut it with diamond saws, put it on a lathe to create the desired shaped and polish it.

Even the boys found this demonstration interesting.

Finally, while there, we visited a meerschaum carver's shop. Meerschaum is actually mined in another part of Turkey but this shop gets it meerschaum from Elkeshir and then produces pipes and other articles. I was tempted to buy a meerschaum pipe, but as I hadn't priced them yet, I was reluctant to buy.

At dinner that night, we agreed to hire a guide and spent the next day exploring the region. Therefore, at 8 a.m. we met our guide, Ali, and the driver, Yasha. Ali has several enterprises going in the Göreme area: a Turkish travel agency, carpet shop, tour business and other odds and ends. Educated in Ankara, he speaks good English without a heavy, distracting accent. He was a good guide for us.

He had arranged for a van, so we piled in and took off for Derinkuyu about fifty kilometers away. There we would visit one of Cappadocia's underground "cities." Only two such cities are now open to the public and this one has eight levels underground to visit. It was by far the deepest of the cities.

The topography is flat in and around Derinkuyu. One would never suspect that beneath the surface of much of this area are deep labyrinthine networks of tunnels leading to kitchens, bedrooms, churches, schools, wine cellars and more. Anatolians discovered that the tuff, volcanic rock that fell from Mount Argaeus eons ago, was soft enough to excavate but hard enough, when exposed to air, to provide safe and relatively comfortable living quarters. It was fascinating to see the ventilation shafts and the cisterns which appear bottomless as we peered down, and other accommodations these trogdolytes had made in order to survive underground.

Of course, they did not and could not live underground permanently. Some think that three months was the outside limit. One has to have sunlight, and supplies were limited. It was more likely that most lived in houses above, used some of the underground space regularly, but when the enemy swooped through the valley, the village disappeared into their "city" beneath the ground, stopping up the entrance behind them. Or, if attacked, the men stayed above and fought the battle and the underground city was a place of refuge for women, children and animals.

Ali said that the cities were constructed about the 7-6th century A.D. but I believe he's wrong, that they are in fact older.

The boys enjoyed the underground cities immensely as they provided fodder for the imagination. For example, Ali explained that some of the tunnels were long, narrow and short for strategic reasons: if their enemy should chase them into the underground caverns, they could be led through these tunnels and then as each invader emerged single file, stooped and defenseless, the defenders could lop off their heads one by one, or in some other gruesome fashion dispatch their foes handily. For Spenser, particularly, these are powerful and fertile ideas for his action heroes with which he plays for hours on end.

The rest of the day was spent touring the Göreme Open Air Museum and Zelve Open Air Museum, both studies in the trogdolytic existence of the Anatolians and Greek monks who lived here in the Middle Ages. We explored caves and monastries, paused in churches and refectories, walked narrow gorges, climbed up steep trails and of course took millions of photos.

One morning, we spent 300,000TL returning by taxi to Uçhisar, a cave village near Göreme. When we arrived it wasn't a cave that snapped us to attention; it was a camel.

"A camel," Taylor shouted.

"A camel," Spenser shouted.

"A camel," I shouted.

Jeanie said nothing. She knew what was going to happen next.

"Let's ride the camel," Spenser suggested. You could hear the whine in his voice. But, since we were tourists, we thought we should behave like tourists, so we paid the man 100,000TL for a ride.

It was Spenser's idea, so he was the first to accept the challenge. The beast sank to the earth, its legs tucked beneath it. The owner presented a ladder and leaned it against the camel's enormous hump on which an ornate saddle had been strapped. Spenser grabbed the ladder and climbed up until he was perched, if not precariously, atop this camel having the time of his life. Spenser, not the camel.

I snapped pictures, Jeanie filmed. The kindly Turkish man led the camel up and down the road a few meters, Spenser a top, lurching with each step, smiling broadly and yelling loudly.

Then Jeanie went. The camel went down, Jeanie went up. This time the owner let go of the reins. She was on her own. Great fun.

By now Taylor had decided that it wouldn't do for his younger brother and his mother to have the courage to confront the beast, so bless him, he clambered aboard the camel and it was the highlight of his day.

Finally the family prevailed upon me to make us fools four, so our album will testify that I, too, steered a ship of the desert in my best sultanly manner for at least a little while!

We did some souvenir shopping but tired of this quickly and wondered what to do next.

"Let's just hike back down to the road," I said. Göreme wasn't too far. This proposal wasn't met with much enthusiasm, but as there were no taxis in sight in this little village, it was our only option. When we arrived in Göreme, we had some lunch and walked around the town, by now completely tired. I once again suggested a hike back to Avanos about 10 kilometers down the road.

"Why don't we get a taxi?" Taylor asked.

"I would gladly get a taxi if I could find a taxi," I replied, stating what I thought was obvious.

"Why don't we get a camel?" Spenser asked. We were in one of those traveling situations where the edge of experience wasn't aligned with the frame of expectations. We'd love to have a personal driver to take us hither and yon, but with our budget travel plan, we had to do hither and yon by ourselves sometimes.

"Let's get started, and perhaps we can flag down an ox-cart or something." That piqued some interest, but not much.

So we started.

"They have a good marriage," I noted. We had come upon a Turkish man astride a small donkey, his feet nearly scrapping the hard-scrabble earth. A woman—we assumed it was his wife—followed behind. We had noticed on other occasions that Turkish men in this area at least seemed somewhat indolent. They sat in smoky pubs playing blackjack, dragging on hand-rolled cigarettes and drinking coffee while the women-folk were in the fields hoeing crops. We asked the hotel manager about it.

"It's their job," he said.

"Whose job?" I asked.

"The men," he replied with a shrug. "They have to make plans, take care of business. They do this in the coffee shops. The women work in the fields."

Jeanie said nothing.

Two kilometers down the road, a local bus came into view. I flagged it down and the four of us piled in the back. I paid the driver 40,000TL and soon we were back at the Sofa Hotel in Avanos for much needed rest.

Our last day we prepared to leave, packing our bags and storing them in a room at the hotel. But we were not finished with Cappadocia. We had reservations for the 6 p.m. bus out of Avanos for Istanbul. But the day was ours until then. We hired the same taxi as the day before to take us down the road between Avanos and Urgup to the Valley of the Fairy Chimneys. The driver dropped us off in the middle of Nowhere, Cappadocia and promised to return in two hours. This arrangement was secured through a variety of comical and intensive communication tricks, but it succeeded, we hoped, nonetheless.

> **October 26, 1995**
> *"I saw the Turkish post ofise. I got a bledy nose! I got to ride on a camel!!! I went in a rock. I went walking with my family."* —Spenser, 7

The taxi gone, we looked about us and this moonscape of pillars and chimneys with small stones or rocks sitting atop them, rocks of granite or some other igneous substance which protected the softer tuff below from the elements of nature over the centuries and millennia. We started to climb up and away from the road, the boys jumping and leaping, bobbing and weaving up ahead of us, shouting and throwing their voices into the canyons and gullies.

After photographing and hiking for about an hour, we found a spot deep in the chimneys where it occurred to me that we could have a good game of Hide 'N Go Seek. So we did and had great fun. This activity became an entry in the boys' journal.

When the two hours elapsed, our driver showed up two minutes early, quite proud of himself and delivered us back to the Sofa Hotel, and our time in Avanos and Cappadocia came to an end.

There is much more to explore in Cappadocia than we did. The Ilhara Valley and the Soganli Valley, for example. But we saw as much as we could comprehend for now. We found it amusing to be looking forward to our return "home" which for us, now, is Istanbul. We were going back to Istanbul, to the apartment, our beds, a kitchen.

Our home.

38

Wherein Someone Gets Groped

T HE "DARK AND STORMY NIGHT" THAT HAD VISITED US WHEN we left Istanbul was nothing compared to the storm that washed over Istanbul the night we arrived home.

The winds flew in bringing furious rain, lightning and thunder. Unable to sleep, I peered out across the Bosphorus about 5 a.m. The lights of the European city were laid out, as F. Scott Fitzgerald would write, like a bracelet along the water. The spires of the mosques hung like pendants in a dark sky. When dawn broke, branches and trees lay awash on the patio and when the boys went down the bluff through the woods to the water's edge below, they discovered to their utter amazement that a ferry boat had been tossed by the wind against the abutment rocks like Noah's Ark on Ararat. Of course, when Jeanie and I heard the news, we, too, rushed down the steps to survey the damage and take pictures. We were saddened to hear that this same storm had taken fifty-five lives in Izmir, Turkey's second largest city.

It wasn't the only news we would hear within the first week home. On November 4, Yitzhak Rabin, a winner of the Nobel Peace Prize, was assassinated by a right-wing Jewish student who pumped three bullets into the Israeli Prime Minister. Rabin was in Tel Aviv where he had been speaking to a crowd of 10,000. Tensions had been running high in Israel in the wake of the government's negotiations with Arafat and the Palestinian National Authority. The "Declaration of Principles" Rabin and Arafat had signed in the Rose Garden in September of 1993 now seemed like feeble murmurs.

The world, with the exception of Iran who said Rabin had been "paid in his own coin," generally mourned his death as they had the death of Sadat some years earlier. I was shocked. The prophet without honor in his own country. The dove slaughtered and the olive leaves scattered to the winds. A martyr for peace.

Our plans for the Israel trip were now threatened. We didn't know whether the new government of Shimon Peres would continue with plans to withdraw troops from the West Bank, continue the construction and paving of the bypass around Bethlehem, and stay the course with the PNA. We determined to move forward, financies permitting, to travel to Israel over Christmas, and if that was possible, we would most certainly visit the freshly dug grave of this "warrior for freedom."

It was still storming on our first Sunday back, October 29, and we were inclined not to hop over to another continent to go to church as was our custom. But the choir was depending on us so we trooped off in the rain, got a dolmus, and a ferry and a dolmus and went to church and choir practice. Barbara Noscroft, the director, had assigned a solo to me for *O Holy Night,* and Jeanie had a solo as well. The choir was working hard to be ready for our grand concert and performance at the Swiss Hotel come Christmas.

Prior to these events, we had important matters to attend to, including our preparations for Halloween. We were determined that the boys should have a proper Halloween — don't ask me why — just as they might back home. Halloween is not observed in Turkey, and therefore going from apartment to apartment dressed as Ninja Turtles or Power Rangers asking for treats was not an option.

"So what are we going to do?" Jeanie asked, after the boys were in bed. She was sitting in the armchair with her embroidery over her lap. I had the *Turkish Daily News* in my hands and I'm generally not a good conversationalist when I'm reading the paper.

"Why can't we just cancel Halloween?" I said. The Colorado Avalanche had beaten the St. Louis Blues 3-1.

"We can't cancel Halloween."

I didn't think so. "Okay, I have a plan," I said. I love having plans. I waited for her to ask me what the plan was.

"So what's the plan?" she asked.

"Okay, there are three external entrances to this apartment, one there, there and there." I pointed to the main entry, a west patio entrance and a south patio entrance. "And there's Mic and Sally downstairs, so we have four doors they can knock on to go trick or treating. I'm sure Mic and Sally will play along. We'll give them some candy so they don't have to spend any of their own money—not that they wouldn't be happy to."

"So the boys will go out and knock on our doors, and we give them candy?" she asked.

"Exactly. It will be part pretend, part real, and since the end result is candy in their sacks I don't think they'll much care as to how it gets there."

"But they want to show off their outfits," said the mother.

"Well, they can impress Mic and Sally and maybe the Merhaba man. And we can pretend to be surprised and impressed, too, and pretend we don't know who they are. It'll be fine."

"But we don't have a pumpkin," she said, looking up from her embroidery.

"First, the plan; then the pumpkin," I said, removing the objection.

This, then, was our plan. We now needed a pumpkin. Turkey doesn't have orange pumpkins. Their pumpkins are green. Nevertheless, on Saturday, October 28, we set out in search of pumpkins. We didn't have far to walk to find the crowded Saturday street markets. I left the group momentarily in search of baklava, and promised to rejoin them at the pumpkin stall up the street.

After I left, Jeanie and the boys moved through the crowd. Actually, they moved *with* the crowd. If the crowd didn't move, they didn't move. Markets and stalls lined both sides of the streets, some with awnings from which hung blouses, purses, jackets and caps. Some vendors sold vegetables, other plastic kitchenware, meat, kebabs, spices or shoes. The street was thick with people— women in headscarves or the chador, babies in arms, men in heavy coats, children running on the edges. It wasn't a moving crowd; it was a *milling* crowd. And it was in this crunch of humanity that Jeanie got groped as she shuffled baby-step by baby-step toward the pumpkin stand.

At first Jeanie thought the grope was merely accidental and incidental contact. Then it unmistakably happened again. The man was pressing close to her, hanging on her like a cheap suit. She was using both hands to grasp the hands of each of the boys. She forged ahead.

Then the rascal grabbed her butt again. "Stay close, boys," she said, quietly, and she released her grip on their hands. Cocking her arm so that her elbow became a weapon, she moved it forward slightly, and then slammed it backward into the chest of the man behind her. The impact was like that of a SWAT battering ram forced-entry tool on a three-quarter inch plywood door. Her elbow hit him with such force that the pervert stumbled backward and lost his footing. He didn't fall to the ground, as the crowd was too thick. But he didn't harass her again. What's more, two men who had witnessed the incident grabbed the knave and gave him a very vocal and public scolding and sent him packing down the street.

They then shouldered their way to Jeanie, caps in hand to apologize. They were older men, in their fifties, both wearing old suits, the kind that you might find at Goodwill.

"We are sorry for what happened," said the taller one. "We hope you do not think this is the way Turkish people are. Turkish people are generally not so rude to their guests." He paused and looked at his friend. "Rude to each other, perhaps. But not rude to our guests."

Jeanie was surprised that anyone had noticed her ordeal. "Oh, no. We love our Turkish friends. But he was not a nice man."

"No, he was not. He's Kurdish." They nodded to her and disappeared into the crowd.

I showed up soon after and got the story. It's what might happen when a woman goes out in public without her husband. Jeanie has had similar experiences at the post office. She's in line at the window, and finally gets up to the window, and men will come out of nowhere, shove their mail under the window to the clerk, complete their transaction as though Jeanie were completely invisible. It's a cultural issue, not a personal one. Years later, we would find that the same sort of thing happens in China.

We found the pumpkins. They were being sold by a jolly man who was standing on a platform of melons clad in a woman's pink nightgown. He was dressed as a typical Turkish man, but he was also selling sleepwear. He decided that his sales might increase if he modeled the product.

He was talking loudly and enthusiastically about something. But he was doing a brisk business selling pumpkins. When a person bought a pumpkin, he'd take it, slice off the stem with one stroke of a machete, and the transaction would be complete. We didn't want him to slice off the stem. So we found a pumpkin we liked and handed it to the man in pink.

"Don't cut the stem," I said. I didn't' know Turkish for this. But I covered the stem with my hand, made waving signs with my hand, shook my head and scowled. Everything possible to express negativity.

The man in pink smiled and said, "Evit, evit." Took the pumpkin and sliced off the stem.

We bought three stem-less, green pumpkins and lugged them back to the Upper Room. They were carved, candles were inserted in the interior and at night they gave off a friendly, if not toothy, Halloween grin.

The strategy for Halloween was simple. We send the Ninja Turtle and Power Ranger out into the night and they would appear at one of the doors and ring the bell. We'd answer it, be all scared and amazed, give them candy, and wait for them to appear at another door. Then they'd go down to Mic and Sally's who would react similarly.

The boys went to all of our doors at least twice and we all had great fun.

They got a ton of candy, too.

CROSCROS

Then Mic and Sally were gone. We were sorry to see them go. Jeanie and Sally embraced. Sally and I embraced. Mic and I shook hands. This was well before hugging became an acceptable way for men to greet each other or say farewell. I am not sure that Mic ever became a hugger. They would return, of course, but long after our own departure for the States.

We later welcomed Paul and Jean Nilson who were past directors of the Near East Mission. They were now retired back in the States but welcomed the opportunity to fill in as Directors *pro tem* and spend some time in Istanbul. Jean was tall and thin, the model of efficiency. Details did not escape her attention. Paul was as laid back as his wife was energetic. In this respect, they were much like Mic and Sally. Paul, however, was more affable than Mic. Not that Mic wasn't likeable. He was. Mic had the reserve of an upper crust Englishman; Paul was a thorough-going American—welcoming, friendly and open. We enjoyed Paul and Jean very much, as indeed we had loved Mic and Sally. Without the cooperation of the McCain's our Turkish adventure could not have happened.

It's been well over two months, almost three, since we left Colorado, and with the departure of the McCain's, our final plans began to crystallize. We had been saving carefully so that we could experience the one trip we did not want to abandon: a week or so in Jerusalem. We had already given up on plans for a side trip to Athens, and I relinquished a dream to spend a week in the Mt. Athos Monastery in Greece. It would have been wonderful. In order to spend time with the monks there, one has to have some kind of ecclesiastical preferment, letters of reference and recommendations. I had prepared all of these in advance and had made the arrangements. But it just wasn't convenient; there was no way, really, that I could leave the family. So those two trips were out.

We could see, however, that financially we could afford one more excursion in addition to the Jerusalem foray, and that was a trip southward to Parmukule, Ephesus, and Izmir. And we also hoped to go south from Izmir, take a ferry and get over to the Isle of Patmos, the site of St. John's revelation and where he wrote the New Testament book of the same name. Following that visit, we'd then return to Istanbul and stay through the 18th of December, culminating in our choir concert at the Swiss Hotel, and then we would leave for Jerusalem. We'd be there ten days, return to Istanbul for six days and then head back for the States.

So with the departure of the McCains, we began to see the *terminus ad quo* of our own trip, and our Great Adventure was suddenly shrinking. We were now conscious that these wonderful days were, in some sense, more precious, that while all of them had been rare, only now were we beginning to realize how rare and blessed they were.

C3C3C3

We also had just received some more news: *Grandmother was coming for a visit and she'd be arriving November 20.*

This news was greeted with general joy, but not without some misgivings— mostly on my part. Barbara is grandmother to the boys. No problem there. But she's Jeanie's mother, and mothers and daughters always have issues. They have more issues than politicians in Congress. And Barbara is my mother-in-law, and we all know about mothers-in-law.

My relationship with Barbara had always been warm. I knew her before Jeanie and I were married. No problems. But Jeanie's divorce had been a shock to the entire clan. She'd been married for fourteen years, had two small boys and a comfortable life with all the appearances of the "perfect" marriage. Moreover, of the three children, she, the middle child and only daughter, was the one blessed with common sense, although she'd had her own period of rebellion as an older teenager. Still, through fourteen years of marriage, her life had seemed somewhat more stable than that of both of her brothers.

Her divorce was utterly incomprehensible.

Then, she married a man much older than herself. This was equally, if not more, incomprehensible, as likeable as I may have been. Truth is, both of our families thought we were nuts.

At first, Barbara, a psychologist, had tried to fix it. She'd tried to help Jeanie see where she wasn't thinking straight. Barbara, herself divorced for many years, thought that whatever it was Jeanie was going through, divorce was not the answer. Jeanie found these ministrations on the part of her family irritating. She felt then, as she had for most of her adult life, that her ex-husband and her extended family, still considered her to be a child, with no intellectual resources of her own, as someone who still needed their help, and as someone who would profit from their advice, however unwanted and unnecessary.

Jeanie was implacable.

It was difficult for her to see that her mother's reaction was probably not much different from any mother who thought her daughter was making a mistake. Barbara's problem was that she could state her case so articulately; she was a meddler. Articulate, good-natured and well-meaning, but a meddler.

But when the marriage took place, Barbara stepped up, generous to a fault. She paid for our stay at the Hyatt hotel in Denver where Jeanie and I hosted a wedding reception. She offered abundant verbal support and encouragement, and she was enthusiastic about the marriage now, seeing opportunities for Jeanie to experience a greater degree of self-actualization than had hitherto been possible.

Jeanie even found these kinds of expressions irritating and patronizing. So it's been dicey.

I was on the frontier of all this wrangling. And now, years later, I've still been able to stay above the fray. When I heard that she was headed for Istanbul, it gave me pause. I had no fear that she and I wouldn't get along; we would. We always had. There'd be no problem. But I wondered what Jeanie's reaction would be, and how it would play out.

The news, however, was greeted with genuine excitement. I was relieved. Jeanie was genuinely pleased. I thought this trip might be the perfect opportunity permanently to file any issues still on the table.

We'd see.

39

Spenser Has a Birthday

BEFORE SPENSER'S BIRTHDAY, WE WANTED TO DO SOME PRELIMINARY SHOPPING. So one day, we set out for the Üsküdar docks when suddenly we heard sirens. Immediately all traffic ceased. People began laying on their horns, or they got out of their cars and stood beside them. Taxis, trucks, buses. Everything stopped. Pedestrians stopped dead in their tracks and stood at attention.

We learned later that this is an annual ritual that occurs at 9:05 a.m. on November 10 which is the anniversary of the death of the great Ataturk, the founder of the modern nation of Turkey. His picture's everywhere in Turkey. He's greatly revered. It is he who secularized the country, he who changed the basic language structure of Turkish from a language written in Arabic script to the Latin letters it uses today. And while the country is thoroughly Islamic, it's a secular state and the wisdom of this policy has been seen time and again.

After one minute, it was all over and life resumed. Traffic lurched forward, pedestrians continued on their errands and we continued toward the Üsküdar docks.

Spenser's 8th birthday was celebrated in grand style. We purchased the birthday necessaries for a good birthday dinner, but in addition decided to stretch out the celebration over a two day period.

Quite honestly, parental guilt was involved. You don't want to have this great adventure and feel that your kids are going to suffer for the choices you've made. Back home, Spenser would've had all his friends over, and there'd be this huge cake that said, "Happy 8th Birthday, Spenser!" And there'd be yellow, red, orange and blue balloons festooned all over the kitchen, and Grandmas would be over and aunts and uncles and neighbors, and the parents of all the children coming to the party would make sure their child brought over an age-appropriate gift, and Spense would be reveling in all the wrapping, and bows, cards and gifts. In short, in the U.S. Spenser would be King for a day, or at least the Little Prince.

Here, it was just us, and even Mic and Sally were gone.

So, guilt kicks in and we were darn certain that we'd do everything we could to make Spenser feel like he was a Prince for a day. We would serve him, cater to his every desire, respond to his every request.

His first request was for a trip to the Capitol Mall. Okay, then. Off we went. First, we stopped at McDonald's for a Happy Meal. The toy in the box is always exciting. *Forrest Gump* had yet to be filmed, but in a Happy Meal, you're never sure what you're going to get. Spenser was always delighted with what he got. Jeanie's getting all of this on video, of course, just as she would've had we been in the States.

The next stop was the bowling alley. Bowl-lingo it was called. The balls are half the size of U.S. balls, perhaps a little bigger than a shot put, but not weighing as much. No holes in the ball; one simply grasps the ball and tosses it down the alley. So there's no messing and mucking about trying to find a light ball a kid can throw. A 90-year grandma can toss this bowl-lingo ball.

Another difference is that there's no special requirement for shoes. On this particular synthetic surface, any type of sole was permissible, so that all souls could wear whatever soles they wanted. Other than those differences, the game was played just as in the States, and an automatic scoreboard kept track of the score for us. We had great fun with this, and Taylor beat us all.

Our next stop with the Little Prince was a visit to the arcade where both boys played Mortal Combat and other such games.

Of course, there were also presents. Spenser was expecting a box from his dad, but it had not yet arrived. So the next day, before leaving for church, Spense began to open presents.

"A jump rope!" he exclaimed. He was happy with anything. He unwrapped a coloring book, an action figure, a Turkish army knife, and money from various sources.

We finished up with the gift opening, and left for church. But the celebration wasn't over. Jeanie made a cake and pizza was ordered, and guests arrived that evening. Neredin and Göksel showed up about 7:30 p.m. Göksel brought a present from UNICEF, a neat little magnetic board with pieces to move around to create different designs.

I was in some difficulty. After church, we had gone to Burger King, and I'd ordered a triple-decker cheeseburger. I was now paying for it with some serious indigestion.

"You need to go to bed, Timothy," Jeanie said, alarmed, after I had retreated to the kitchen.

"I want to stay," I moaned, grimacing and clutching my abdomen. "Goksel is here, I don't want to just disappear."

"He'll understand," she said, shoving me toward the bedroom.

I went to bed, doubled over, cursing my immoderation. Beyond the bedroom door I could hear the gaiety continuing without me. Jeanie brought out the cake. We couldn't find birthday candles anywhere, so we'd gathered standard-sized candles from various cupboards throughout the apartment and stuck them on the cake. To make this work, the space between the candles had to be much farther than normal. So when Spense attempted to blow them out, even he, with his universally-acclaimed boisterous and prodigious lungs, failed to do so. Three of the eight candles remained aflame, and Taylor announced that, according to folklore, this meant that Spenser had three girlfriends, an assertion that Spenser stoutly denied.

The guests left, but the celebration was still not yet over. The next day, we learned that the package from his dad had arrived, but it was being held in customs at Topkapi at the postal office there and we would need to retrieve it. Paul Nilson said that it would probably be best if a man from the mission accompanied us. Sometimes, what we'd expect to be a simple transaction, is quite difficult if you're traveling and overseas.

Jeanie and the boys went without me. I repaired to the patio to read and write. While there, Jean Nilson happened to troop up the stairs from the Lower Room on her way to the street and the market. She saw me on the patio, smoking my pipe.

"Hey, there!" she called out.

"Hi, Jean," I said.

"I thought you'd gone to get your package." She had stopped and I could see that there was going to be a brief conversation. I laid down my book.

"No, Jeanie and the boys went," I said, knowing this was an insufficient explanation.

"You didn't want to go?" she asked. I don't know why she was prying.

"Let me put it to you this way, Jean." I paused, and then launched: "If you had two of the following choices, which would you make, or which do you think I would make: First, I accompany my wife and two children across the Bosphorus, walk to the mission, take a taxi to Topkapi, wait in line at the post office, fill out innumerable forms, and probably consume a good four hours of the day, or, second, I stay at home, which is now quieted by the absence—almost—of human society and sit on the patio and read a novel by Henry James. So, I say, what would you do?"

Left: Car trouble 45 minutes into our trip;

Below: The home of Harvey and Peggy Knott in Beaver City, Nebraska;

Bottom: Beach at St. Malo, Brittany, France and two writers at work.

Clockwise from top left: We prepare to board a plane at Thessalonika for Istanbul; Timothy in the "Fairy Chimneys" of the Goreme Valley; the Ayasofia in Istanbul; boarding the Pammukele Express in Denizli; the entrance to the Sofa Hotel in Avanos.

Top: More of the Fairy Chimneys in the Goreme valley of Cappadocia;

Middle: The Library of Celsus at Ephesus.

Bottom: We pose with our new headgear which we would actually wear when the weather got colder in Istanbul.

Top: On top of Masada, with the Dead Sea in the background;

Middle: View of the Hotel Esmeralda and the Place Rene Viviani from the north tower of Notre Dame;

Bottom: The Dome of the Rock.

She was quiet for just a moment, and then said, "Well, I see your point." She turned away. "I'll be going then."

"Bye, Jean."

She left, but then yelled over her shoulder, "You've been reading too much of Henry James, I'd say."

I really think she understood. Truth is, Jeanie doesn't need as much personal space and time as I do. Sometimes I think she feeds on the energy of other people. It makes her stronger. She's like the robots of the old science fiction movies of the 40s and 50s: when they went beserk the good guys would zap them with electrical charges, but rather than immobilizing them, the zapping only gave them more energy and power. She's like that. I'm the opposite. People drain my energy fields. I need to get apart from everything and everyone once-in-a-while. I knew that these four hours would be a perfect time to breathe deeply and quietly and get recharged. The three-day birthday bacchanalia had pretty much depleted my reserves.

Fortunately, Jeanie understands this about me, and I understand this about her. And if spouses don't understand each other, it can be hell to travel together, that's for sure.

I once had a couple of parishioners who were a case in point: Harry and Martha. Both were retired, and both had their own special interests. She was a political activist, and particularly active in the local United Nations chapter. Harry was a farmer who had a rock collection. He love to polish rocks and was an avid fisherman. While he was supportive of his wife's interests, he didn't often participate with her in them.

One summer, I learned that they were going on an extended road trip, vacationing in the west, traveling up into British Columbia and going as far as the Yukon. It sounded like an enormous undertaking. They were going to haul a little trailer behind their pickup truck. I asked Martha about it.

"How are you going to do, Martha?"

She laughed and waved her arm at me dismissively. "Oh, I'll be fine. We'll stop by a river, and Harry will go down and fish, and I'll stay up by the camp and read my books."

They were fine. They had a good and long marriage. They knew each other. They embraced their differences. It made them whole.

So Jeanie and the boys went to the post office. I read Henry James and smoked my pipe and regained my sanity.

At the post office, Jeanie was losing hers.

They left the Upper Room at 9 a.m. and stuffed themselves on to a crowded ferry—particularly crowded because early morning fog had shut

215

the ferry system down. They arrived at the mission office about 10 a.m. The gentleman from the mission office who was to accompany them was delayed likewise by the fog. By 11 a.m. they were on their way to Topkapi.

Once inside the main postal terminal they approached the first window and gave a "notice slip" to the clerk who pawed through a box looking for paperwork that corresponded with the notice. She then filled out a form in duplicate, stamped it, and Jeanie signed it and then they left, clutching a copy of the signed form and walked down a hall to a room with four service windows. Only the fourth window was open, however. Jeanie learned that it was the only window that was ever open. They waited in a line to give the paperwork secured at the earlier station to a woman who passed it back to someone who wasn't there. Then the mission man motioned to Jeanie that she should sit on some chairs arranged along the far wall. She realized then that they'd be waiting for a while.

While they were waiting, the post office had sent a messenger to retrieve a batch of parcels from wherever they were stored. Spenser's package was among them. After an interminable delay, the large bay doors opened and everyone in the waiting area got up expectantly and crowded around Window #4.

As the mission man and Jeanie approached the window, he looked at her and said, "Passport."

Jeanie stared at him blankly. No one had suggested that she'd need her passport to pick up a package. She didn't have it.

"I don't have it," she said lamely. "I didn't know I needed to bring it with me."

"You must have your passport to get package." The mission man, a Turk, said it kindly—even though he must have been amazed, if not chagrined that four hours of his own day had been involved in a lost cause.

Jeanie fumbled about in her bag and produced another document. "Will they accept my driver's license?" she asked.

They huddled around the window with about ten others and watched as a postal official opened each parcel and pulled out the contents. When he opened a box and removed some gifts with Batman wrapping paper, they were quite sure that Spenser's package had been found. The inspector only opened one of the presents, and since the boys were so small, they couldn't see what it was because of the crowd.

"I'm glad I couldn't see," Spenser said, "because then it wouldn't be a surprise."

Spenser's name was called, so they pushed to the front. The mission man spoke with the postal authorities in an animated fashion, convincing them to accept Jeanie's driver's license as sufficient documentation. A woman now appeared and prepared another form in duplicate which Jeanie signed. The mission man then showed Jeanie a calculator which read 370,000TL. Jeanie gave him a 1,000,000TL bill. The mission man took it and the paperwork back to the first window. He had to go there to get change. Then he ran to another window to purchase stamps. Then he came back to Window #4 and gave the stamps to the woman who put them on yet another form, stamped it, and asked for Jeanie's signature.

"When do we get the box, Mom?" Spenser asked, tugging on her arm.

"Not yet," she said. "Patience."

The mission man returned now to the first window, paperwork in hand as well as Jeanie's license, and then scurried to another window across the hall.

"Shouldn't we go with him?" Taylor asked.

"No, we'll stay put," Jeanie said. "If he needs us, he will come get us."

She had no sooner uttered these words than she saw the mission man waving from down the hall, so the three of them ran to yet another window and paid the clerk there 60,000TL. Another form was attached to the previous paperwork. It was also stamped and authenticated with Jeanie's signature.

The group shuffled to another window where the box appeared. Jeanie presented the paperwork to the clerk who okayed it, stamping it a final time. He then gave Jeanie—the box.

But the ordeal was not over. Just as they were about to leave, a security officer met them at the doors demanding to see a receipt. He checked the receipt as well as Jeanie's driver's license. Another guard from inside a nearby cubicle had to give his permission before Jeanie and the boys and the mission man could proceed.

Total monetary damages were about $16USD in fees plus taxi fare. The fees, we learned later, were for customs and storage.

They were gone about six hours, getting home at 4 p.m. Although I did not spend all of that time on the patio, reading and smoking my pipe, by 4 o'clock in the afternoon I was back on the patio, feet kicked back in company with Henry James, a delightful Mr. Maduro—a Dominican, and a very smooth Mr. Courvoisier. I heard them arrive, and looked up as they trooped by.

"So how was your trip?" I inquired brightly, feeling rested and renewed.

"Don't ask," Jeanie said. Then she blew the hair out of her eyes.

40

Grandmother Comes to the Bosphorus

THE BOX CAUSED A SENSATION AT HOME. SPENSER'S DAD DID a great job in packing some gifts that helped both Spenser and Taylor spend many hours playing.

The biggest hit was a box of magic tricks. And what are magic tricks if you cannot demonstrate your magic to an interested audience? So during the month of November, several magic shows occurred in the Upper Room. The dining table was cleared and the stuff of magic was laid out before the magician including brightly-colored cloths, rings, boxes, books, wands, rope and string, playing cards and much more. Taylor was the assistant—a suitable young lady in black tights was not available. Jeanie and I sat on two chairs facing the table. Spense and Taylor stood behind the table and performed the magic.

It was very much a scene we might have had in Colorado. Jeanie and I were always quite aware that we were living in a pair of parentheses: this adventure from August, 1995, to January, 1996, was essentially parenthetical. Our lives—work, shelter and friends—were in Colorado, and it was a world to which we would soon return.

For the boys, however, no such concept of a bracketed life existed. Their world was very much in the present, and didn't have much of a past, and nothing of a future. This was more true for Spenser than Taylor, but essentially true for both of them. Children don't understand history. When you are at the center of the universe, there is no history because everything is happening right now. As they did their magic tricks, I understood again that our job as parents traveling with children was to help them to feel as though they were not traveling at all, but to keep the universe properly focused on them in the same way we might have if we were in Colorado.

This didn't mean that in Colorado we let them run the world; it meant that, as in Colorado, everything that happened had some kind of relevance

218

for them. So in Istanbul, we understood that they continued to interpret life by means of an existential hermeneutic that was ego-centric. Our job was and is to manage that and—over their childhood years—gradually move other people, things and ideas on to center stage.

But right now, they were center stage and all was well in their world—as it should be.

We had just retrieved a box from the post office; soon we would be retrieving a grandma from the airport. This event, likewise, fit in with their worldview perfectly: Grandma was coming to visit *them*! Wonderful!

The excitement had been building. Barbara is a very interesting person. I suppose most husbands say that about their mothers-in-law. Highly educated, she was at the time, finishing up on a Ph.D. in Psychology. She was a professor, seminar speaker and leader, and active in a number of organizations. Always curious about the world around her, she was a voracious reader, and traveled as much as she could, including a trip to China. She had been thrilled when we first talked about this trip, and thought it would be wonderful for all of us. She was very pleased that Jeanie had the opportunity to experience travel and foreign cultures; Jeanie had not spent too much time out of Colorado, and none outside of the U.S. except for an occasional visit to the Caribbean.

I was nervous. I had my hands full with my stepsons. My young wife. The Martin family and the Dalberg family were still suspicious, I thought, of this interloper who has taken their Jeanie and two little boys halfway around the world to an Islamic country. Jeanie, of course, saw it completely different: I hadn't "taken" her anywhere. She had a mind; she'd made these decisions on her own. No one made them for her. She could think for herself. She wasn't a child. I thought back to our argument at the Rodin museum in Paris: "I'm not a child," she said, angrily.

The son-in-law. The mother-in-law. The mother. The grandmother. A ton of stuff floating like flotsam on this relational ocean, and who knew what lay beneath?

On November 20, we caught a taxi and headed for Ataturk International Airport. Her plane was due in at 4:10 p.m.

"What time is it, Timothy?" The question was posed by Taylor. He needed the time because he and Spenser had prepared a sign for grandmother's arrival. The sign read, simply, "Grandma Barbara." They thought their hand-lettered sign, wrought with a rainbow of crayon colors would help their grandmother spot them more quickly. We were separated from the baggage claim by a plexi-glass partition; while we would not be able to greet her in the baggage-claim area, she should be able to see us after she retrieved her luggage.

"It's about 4:20, Taylor," I said. "About five minutes later than the last time you asked me."

"Shouldn't she be here by now?" he asked.

"No, because it takes some time for the plane to taxi to the gate, and then she has to clear customs, and go through passport check, and then get her luggage. It'll probably be another 10 minutes."

A day is as a thousand years and a thousand years as a day, saith the Lord. To a 10-year-old, 10 minutes can be as 10 years.

Lord, I hoped this visit would go well.

৵৵৵

The moment Barbara arrived, the sun disappeared. I don't think the sun shone for the entire length of her visit. I mean this quite literally, not metaphorically. The weather turned cold and rainy. So when we gathered Barbara and her luggage and stepped outside, the air was misty and cold, and a breeze was sweeping in from the Marmara Sea to the south. We snapped open our umbrellas and they stayed open for the next seven days. It rained continuously. Even the locals could not remember a time when the rain had been so relentless. Certainly, there'd had been nothing like it since our arrival almost two months prior.

The boys bounded to their grandmother with arms outstretched and tugged at her overcoat and clamored for her attention like hungry bear cubs, both of them speaking at once, their words tumbling all over each other. Jeanie and I held back while she set her bags down, laughed, told them how big they'd grown and gave them affectionate hugs and kisses. Then we all had a group hug; the inevitable questions about the flight and the trip poured forth and continued in the taxi as we journeyed home. We took the taxi to Eminönü and the ferry across the Bosphorus to Üsküdar. Barbara loved it. She was not going to have a problem in Istanbul.

41

Taxi Terror

I HAVE RULES ABOUT TAXIS.

THIS COMES FROM MANY YEARS of experience traveling in public transportation in the third world. Not that I'm a great world-traveler, but I've done my share. Call me stupid, but I will try a mode of conveyance simply to see where it takes me and how it works.

Once in Venice, I thought it would be fun to hop in a *vaporetto* and see where it goes. So I did. It took off for the open sea and after about thirty minutes, we docked on an island. I hopped out, and hopped right back on, hoping the *vaporetto* was returning whence it came and not on the way to another stop of a multi-stop trip.

Another time, I was in Beskitas, Istanbul, near the ferry dock. It was also where a number of different buses took off. I had been given some instructions about the buses, but I could not read Turkish. Could not speak Turkish. And I couldn't remember what I'd been told. I wanted to get to Taksim. Couldn't find a dolmus, and at 5 p.m. everyone wanted a taxi, so I decided to take a bus. Where could it possibly go? Couldn't take me too far away from Taksim, a business district on the European side, could it?

The bus was full. I stood near the driver after stuffing a couple of Turkish lira into the fare box. We lurched out on to the main road. So far so good. It was midnight black outside, even at 5 p.m. Yet, it wasn't long until I had a feeling I wasn't going to be happy with this bus. After that feeling had passed, it was replaced with another one: regret. Why did I take *this* bus? This bus, I knew now, was headed for the Bosphorus Bridge, and would take me to Üsküdar, but miles from our villa on the Bosphorus. And besides I needed to get to Taksim.

The bus didn't stop until after we'd crossed the bridge in Asia. I got off and, mindful that it was dark and freeway drivers likely would not be able to see me, scurried across the freeway without mishap and took a bus back.

In Sofia, Bulgaria, at midnight New Year's Eve, in 1989, I caught probably the last cab from Alexander Nevski Cathedral Square. Snowpack on the ground. Dead cold out. I was freezing. This cab stops. A white Fiat, with wheels so small, they looked like they belonged on a baby buggy. Unshaven driver with a knit cap pulled over his head to just above his black bushy eyebrows. He had on a heavy navy jacket. Back seat, a blonde women taking a drag on a Marlboro. I thought I was in a *film noir* movie. I got in back with the blonde. I'm Humphrey Bogart. She's Lauren Bacall. Turned out her name was Bennislava. She and the driver were lovers. They were headed back to her parent's apartment to celebrate the New Year. Moments later I was there with them, drinking plum wine, and eating Bulgarian baklava.

Incidents such as these, although not all involving taxis, have led me to adopt the following taxi rules:

Rule No. 1: *Don't take a taxi if your last blood pressure reading was 160/100 or higher.*

Rule No. 2: *Have someone write your destination in the local language on a card which you can give the driver.* Have a phone number for your destination so that, if necessary, the driver can call it. Remember, while people on the street may know a little English, this is less likely for taxi drivers in the third world. Heck, you're lucky to get a driver in New York City who can speak English.

Rule No. 3: *Knowledge of useful phrases is helpful but not necessary.* Try to memorize phrases like, Left, Right, Straight Ahead, Turn Around, Slow Down You Bloody Fool.

Rule No. 4: *Always know from whence you came.* Do you have a card with your hotel printed on it? Do you have a phone number for the hotel or a phone number of friends who can render assistance?

Rule No 5: *Always carry a map.*

Rule No. 6: *If, when you get in, you notice that there are no door handles, get out.*

We got grandmother home that wet Monday evening and put grandmother to bed.

The next day, the rains came down and the floods came up. Although Barbara's time was limited, we nonetheless felt that it would be a good day for her to catch up on some rest, to stay indoors, get reacquainted, tell stories, catch up on what had been happening back in Colorado. So we did. No need to push it.

On Wednesday, however, the rain was still coming down, and we decided that when life gives you rain, you find a good umbrella. Rain or no rain, we needed to get out into the city. There was too much to do and see, and Barbara was eager to explore.

So we set out.

Usually, I was out front and ahead as the family brood—grandmother, daughter, grandchildren—waddled, or waded—behind. We got on a car ferry to Eminönü and from there a taxi to the Grand Bazaar, sometimes known as the Covered Bazaar, or, in Turkish, the *Kapalı çarşı*. Barbara was particularly interested in the booksellers, and found a copy of the Qu'ran which she loved. Jeanie and I bought it for her as a small way of thanking her for all the assistance she'd given us on this trip—mailing journal pages to relatives, for example. Jeanie didn't leave the bazaar empty-handed either: she found a denim dress she couldn't live without.

From the bazaar we trooped, umbrellas sprung, to Sultanahmet to visit the Blue Mosque. Following this sojourn it was about time to head back to Üsküdar. I thought I would look for a FedEx office near the Piyale cami or mosque, since I had some materials that needed to get back to the home office of Communication Resources, Inc., in Canton, Ohio, the publishers of *Homiletics*. As an assistant editor at the time, I had some materials I needed to get back to them, and sending PDFs as I might do now, was not then an option.

The group, however, wanted to tag along. So we found a taxi, but then discovered it was a taxi without a meter. The driver said he'd take us for 250,000TL. Too much, but we said, "Tamen." Okay.

He took us alright.

Taxi rule No. 7: *Don't take an unlicensed taxi.* There are good reasons why municipalities require their taxis and taxi drivers to be licensed.

We broke Rule No. 7.

Then we promptly broke Rule No. 8: *Don't get out of the taxi unless you're positive that the driver has delivered you to the desired destination.*

I had a map. I was not map-less. I'd become suspicious because the driver seemed to be making a lot of turns and what appeared to me as "back-tracking." But I am not a native. And I have another problem: I am too trusting of people—especially if they're locals in our host country.

We've noticed this before. We assume that locals are eager to befriend and help the foreigner, and in 99% of cases, this is correct. Someone speaks to us in broken English or even in incomprehensible Turkish, we're going to believe that person because we're convinced that they'd not cheat or deceive us or knowingly lead us astray.

I'm not sure where this optimism comes from. Well, perhaps I am. The

Golden Rule applies here. As I would do for others, I assume others will do for me. Especially if they speak in a foreign accent.

We'd run into this problem in Bari. We talked to a policeman, no less, who had no idea how to direct us to the waterfront—or, to give him the benefit of the doubt—didn't understand what we were asking. Of course, it's quite possible we didn't understand what he said.

Now, we're all in this taxi with Mahmoud. He pulls to the curb, points to a mosque and says, "Piyale." As I said, I had a map, and this didn't look like Piyale to me. But why would he tell us this was Piyale cami unless it was Piyale cami?

We got out. We should have stayed in. I should have told the driver to wait, asked the family to stay in the taxi, until I had determined whether this mosque was indeed the Piyale cami.

It wasn't.

The driver was a scoundrel. We'd been in heavy traffic. We were paying a flat fee. He was losing money. He dumped us.

"Are we lost, Timothy?" Taylor asked, as he always does.

"Yes," I said, as I looked about to see if I could get any bearings at all.

Taylor was surprised at this frank admission, because I had hitherto always denied being lost, even if we were lost. This was unsettling. He grabbed grandmother's coat and waited.

"So, what are we going to do?" he asked.

"I don't know," I snapped. Taylor stepped back. I looked at him, and softened, and said, "Ferme le bouche!" smiling. He smiled back.

I had a suggestion: "Why don't you all duck into this pastry shop and get some coffee and pastries, while I take a look around to see where we are and what's going on?"

I walked hard for thirty minutes scouting every building, eying every street sign, looking for any clue that would get me to the Piyale mosque. I stopped on three occasions and asked directions, and finally found the mosque and the FedEx office nearby. I decided, however, not to keep the family waiting longer—it would be an hour of waiting in that pastry shop—so rather than getting my business done, I returned to the shop, thinking I could return on the next day alone.

The next day it was no longer raining; it was snowing! But we all set out for the city again nonetheless. This time the family did some exploring on their own. Jeanie was quite familiar with the haunts in Eminönü by now, and I had no fear that she couldn't get everyone around just fine without me. So while they went to the Hagia Sophia and the Spice Market and the underground cistern, I grabbed a taxi at Beşkitaş, quite clear as to where I needed to go.

Unfortunately, for the second day in a row, I'd found a rotten apple in the taxi queue. This driver didn't know where he was going, but agreed to take me anyway and we set out, like Abraham from Haran to a "land that he knew not of." I assumed taxi drivers knew their land. But this one didn't. When he didn't make the turn at Inonu stadium, I made a mental note of it, but gave him the benefit of the doubt. He could have thought that going around to Karakoy, then Galatasaray would be quicker, if a bit longer. But when he turned and drove over the Galata Bridge, I had had enough. I knew he would either need to turn around and come back over the bridge, or return via a bridge further up the Golden Horn, which he did. He then pulled over and looked at the map. I had circled Piyale cami. The poor soul looked confused. I paid my fare and got out, flagged another taxi who delivered me to the mosque within minutes.

I was disgruntled. I delivered my package to the FedEx office and then, pipe in hand, strolled over to the Istiklahl Caddesi and from there to the Spice Market, no small journey, picked up a *USA Yesterday*, got some coffee and read the paper.

Soon I was gruntled again.

And why not? It was Thanksgiving Day in the States, and back in Üsküdar, preparations were underway for a Thanksgiving feast in the Upper Room.

I had many reasons to be thankful.

42

Goodbye to Grandmother

AMONG THE MANY REASONS TO BE THANKFUL WAS THAT MY mother-in-law was leaving in four days.

Kidding.

Jean Nilson had everything ready for Thanksgiving Dinner when we discovered that the plumbing was on the fritz. Without being indelicate, I can say that the plumbing worked if you had a bucket of water to throw in the bowl every time there was an emergency.

Plans went ahead for the dinner in spite of the toilet issues. Jean had procured a white linen tablecloth, flower centerpiece, and place settings cobbled together from the Upper and Lower Rooms. The aroma of allspice, nutmeg, pumpkin, and turkey warmly permeated every atom of air in the apartment like bread baking at 6 o'clock in the morning. The smells and scents were nostalgic, like Thanksgiving aromatherapy, with the turkey and stuffing baking in the oven, with the potatoes and yams cooking, and the brown sugar burning slightly.

Hans and Sylvia Meyers arrived from Tarsus, Sylvia being Paul Nilson's sister. They're retired teachers and the parents of Helene who was one of the students we met at Mic and Sally's our first night in Istanbul. Hans is a sharp-nosed, middle-aged man of thinning hair and speaks English very well but with a heavy accent. The two of them are quite cute together, but walk and talk quite heavily as Germans often seem to do, banging doors and cupboards and speaking loudly as though others share the same hearing loss as they do. "Die Toiletten arbeiten nicht, Hans, so verwenden Sie nicht, wenn Sie dazu haben."

"Ja, Ja, I know."

Two other couples were there as well, one with a six year-old boy with whom Spenser played called, curiously, Merrill. Colin Edmonds and his Turkish wife were also at the table, Colin the son of Bill and Ann Edmonds, missionaries now retired at Bainbridge Island, Washington; and Whyte Shepherd, also with his Turkish wife, nephew of Dr. Barkley Shepherd who had stayed at the Upper Room for a few weeks. Both the Edmonds and Whytes were on the faculty of Roberts College in Istanbul. It was a fabulous dinner and when it was done, the sixteen-pound turkey, scrawny by U.S. standards, what with the breast injections turkeys get, was nothing but a dry carcass on a greasy platter surrounded with stuffing crumbs.

We had had a wonderful time with Grandmother Barbara. She was enjoying herself immensely, the boys were happy, and Jeanie was pleased to have her in our little "home" on the Bosphorus. All good.

One of the benefits of hosting guests is that you're compelled to compress the huge number of events and outings into the calendar space available.

This is both a good thing and a bad thing. You can only remember so much from museums. You should focus on one or two things and learn the story, and then just appreciate the rest. For example, I've been to the Louvre several times. What can I tell you? I saw the *Mona Lisa* and *Winged Victory*. The Uffizzi in Florence: I remember Botticelli's *The Birth of Venus*, and Albrecht Durer's *Martin Luther*, and a ton of "annunciation" paintings. In the Musee D'Orsay in Paris, I remember that *Whistler's Mother* was visiting.

Topkapi Palace, Istanbul?

The Harem.

I have a very low MSQ. My "Museum Staying Quotient." To arrive at your MSQ, you take the number of art history classes you've taken times the number of history books you've read, times the number of Rick Steves' shows you've seen, divided by the hours of TV you watched yesterday plus the number of other things you'd rather be doing divided by the hours since you last had a bite to eat.

My MSQ, quite frankly is about forty-three minutes. Then I am bored to tears. What can I actually remember? Not much as you now know. It's kind of pathetic, especially since I'm only one nervous breakdown and a psychotic episode away from a Ph.D. in Medieval History, but I can't tell you much. I do know that Rodin's *The Thinker* is in Rodin Hall at the Metropolitan Museum of Art in New York City, and that there's a copy at the Rodin Museum in Paris. *That much I know.*

I actually prefer the world … as a living museum. Never, ever get bored seeing the world, outside the walls. But inside it can get tedious—even though I completely support the idea of museums, and I am glad we have them.

Still, I can only really enjoy the experience for forty-three minutes at a time.

తతత

We had taken a leisurely approach to seeing what there was to see in Istanbul, but now, with Grandmother Barbara in town, we needed to see these things now—rain or shine.

It was still raining, but we nonetheless persevered. Some excursions were repeat visits, like to the Kariye mosque where one can find the greatest mosaics in the world. Barbara bought prints and books. We went to the huge Suliemaniye mosque with its oil lamps and the ostrich eggs suspended above each lamp to catch the carbon in the smoke (for use in making calligrapher's ink), and then on to the booksellers where Barbara bought a Qur'an and then to the Covered Bazaar. We ate at a traditional Turkish restaurant where tourists wore the fez. Then onward to the Hagia Sophia, through the walls behind it, past Hagia Irene to Topkapi Palace.

The palace is an ornamental history of the Ottoman Empire, especially in its early years. It was built by the sultans after Mehmet the Conqueror rode his steed into St. Sophia in 1453. It served as the center for the extended family of the sultan, quarters for slaves and eunuchs of the Harem, and a palace for the receiving of foreign dignitaries. It now functions as not only a visible reminder of the opulence of the sultan's lifestyle, but as a museum for some of the best examples of Ottoman treasures in the world, including fabulous collections of jewels, daggers, swords inlaid with mother-of-pearl and other gemstones, various thrones adorned with ivory and gold. We saw the Spoon-maker's Diamond, a colossal rock of umpteen carats, and interesting pen-and-quill writing sets, and Islamic manuscripts and copies of the Qur'an. In one chamber devoted to the sacred relics of Islam, we saw a reliquary (they prefer the word "casket") for a tooth of the Prophet himself, and saw swatches of beard and a cast of his footprint, some soil from his grave, his sword, his bow. Also saw an ancient door from the Kaaba in Mecca, this one the "door of repentance" and in a glass case nearby was a rusty key identified as the key to the door of repentance.

We paid extra to go through the Harem, but I wasn't about to leave the palace without a tour. It was dark and cold, and one has to remember that the stone floors in the castles and palaces were covered with carpets back in the day, and in some cases, carpets and tapestries hung on the walls, and fires were lit in the fireplaces. It was not as dark and dank then, when occupied, as it was on this cold and gloomy day when we visited.

The Harem was really the center of the family life of the Sultan. The men lived in the palace at large, but the women for the most part lived in the Harem, guarded by white eunuchs outside and black eunuchs inside. The Harem was administered by the Sultan's mother, and slave girls were brought from all parts of the empire to the Harem to enter its discipline and to be groomed as possible wives for the crown princes, or to someday share the bed of the Sultan himself.

If this happened, the concubine in question was rewarded with some sort of "promotion." I'm not quite sure what that "promotion" involved.

The Harem was our last stop, so we left, the day darkening, clouds of snow seemed lower than ever, and we all despaired of ever seeing the sun again.

We were sorry to see Grandmother go. She was a trooper, walking through rain and sleet, visiting museums and mosques, shopping and sightseeing, reading with the grandchildren—she did it all. It was a special visit.

Two days before she left, we awoke to glorious sunlight. The fog had rolled back and the morning opened before us, as hopeful and promising as a newborn baby. Barbara had expressed interest in the Peras Palas, or Pera Hotel.[1] So at 10 a.m. we set out for the European side, but not before Paul Nilson stopped by to say the plumbers today were fixing the toilets.

I shrugged. I've heard this before. The proof will be in the flushing.

With Grandmother in tow, we walked out to the main street, found an empty dolmus, got down to the ferry dock, took a small ferry over to Eminönü, sitting on the roof of the boat which afforded great views for Grandmother on the way across the Bosphorus, dodging two big tankers en route. At Eminönü, we walked across the Galata Bridge as we've done so many time before, went up the Tünel subway and from thence it was but a short walk to the hotel made famous by Agatha Christie. It was here in Room 411, the most sought-after room in the hotel, that the creator of Miss Marple and Hercule Poirot wrote *Murder on the Orient Express*. The hotel, however, was patronized by many notable figures in the twentieth century, among them Greta Garbo (Room 103), Mata Hari (Room 104), Sarah Bernhardt (Room 304), Trotsky (Room 204), the Shah of Iran (Room 202), Ernest Hemingway, (Room 218), Jacqueline Kennedy Onassis (Room 308), and others.

Although once a luxury hotel, it has clearly seen better days. Once frequented by writers, kings, courtesans, aristocrats and spies, today it's merely an icon testifying to its fabled past, a pale green ghost looking like it's ten years overdue for a paint job. Yet, inside, despite the tiled walls and marble columns, its luxurious appearance had faded, its vaguely dilapidated appearance only served to raise visions of what this place must have been like back in the day. One feature we enjoyed inspecting was a beautiful elevator cage with its rich walnut wood finish.

We settled in around a table for six for high tea and scones—pinky fingers pointing ("When in doubt, stick it out," Spense would say)—and a fabulous chocolate cake, all of which was on Grandmother Barbara, generous and gracious, who insisted on paying the bill.

We left the hotel and walked quickly to the Union Hall where the Union Church which worships on Sundays in the Dutch Chapel, has offices. It was here that a carpet sale was in progress, and Jeanie and I, having done some carpet shopping already, thought we might be able to strike a deal. The sale was sponsored by the church itself, so we felt this was some protection against being duped by an unscrupulous dealer elsewhere.

The room was small and crowded with church people, all prospective buyers. The dealers threw carpet after carpet on the floor, some beautiful, others breathtaking. The dealer's helper would unfurl a carpet, and after we'd looked at it, he'd furl or fold it up again, asking if anyone wanted it held out for future consideration.

Jeanie and I accrued a pile of six or seven pieces. During a break in the action we hauled them into another room and consulted with each other about the merits of each, and just where, exactly, the carpets would go once we got them home. Finally we agree on three kilims and one carpet. The carpet piece is a beautiful runner of reds and blues which we knew would fit perfectly in a hallway at Bell Court. One large kilim, over 50 years old, would go on the hardwood floor in our music room.

The helper folded these up and tried to wrap them in strong, brown wrapping paper. We asked him if it would stand up to airport transport. He said, "Evit," but later produced a large sports bag and put them in there, and gave us the bag for nothing.

Grandmother even bought a kilim.

They were flying carpets. The next morning we were up early to get Grandmother on a 7:50 a.m. plane for Frankfurt. There she'd connect with a flight to New York and from there to Denver.

She took her carpet, and ours, with her.

---

[1] The Pera Hotel is now known as the 4-star Marmara Pera Hotel and has evidently gone through a major renovation since we were there. http://www.themarmarahotels.com/The-Marmara-Pera/index.asp.

43

Midnight on the Pammukele Express

THE SUN HAD JUST SET ON A GOLDEN DAY, WHEN we hit the streets with our packs to catch a taxi to the Haydarpaşa gar. Just a ten minute ride to Kadacoy. We were there in no time, certainly adequate to catch the 5:30 p.m. train to Denizli.

The Haydarpaşa station is a huge stately building circa 1920 from which all trains heading eastbound into Asia begin their journey. Westbound trains depart from a station on the European side. The rustic trains here appear to be of a World War II vintage or even pre-WWII models. One can easily imagine, as I did, the scene during the war years as young men yanked from schools or occupations, fields and farm, boarded flatcars and cargo-trailers bound for the front and these were the trains they boarded. Turkey was neutral during WWII (unlike WWI when the Ottoman Empire breathed its last). Nevertheless, we're talking old Pullman cars here and with the antiquity, a certain aura of romance and adventure.

The entire trip for the four of us on the overnight Pamukkale Express with the sleeping couchette was $31—for all of us! We found our car and settled in kusetli 13-16.

We had planned to grab some snacks from a stand before boarding, but in our excitement about getting on, exploring the train and so on, neglected to do so. At 5:30 p.m. the train pulled out of the station with uncharacteristic punctuality and we faced a long trip without food, although we knew there might be a diner somewhere.

In search, therefore, of victuals, Taylor and I set forth to determine what might be available. I had for some time relied on Taylor when I needed help with a task, and his willing and eager spirit made it easy to call for his help, even if sometimes he shrank from the novel and intrepid enterprises to which I summoned him.

231

It was now completely dark outside, the sun well on its way to lighting up the western seaboard of the United States—it was midday in Denver. The cabin lights were on, dimly enough to be sure, and after lurching through two cars, we came upon the diner.

The car was a Dantesque inferno of curling smoke vented from the hairy nostrils of unshaven Turks who crowded every available table or from the cigarettes smoldering like cinders between their fingers. They sat at their tables each with a plate of borek and a tall glass of raki and when we entered, a car which had hummed with conversation suddenly went quiet and every face turned toward us, somehow instinctively sensing our presence, and in this brief moment of time and space immobilized by surprise, Taylor and I stood there taking it all in, amused and still quite mindful of the mission that had brought us: Where is the food?

The conversation quickly resumed. We ordered some snacks and chicken plates and a white villa duoca wine. Later, a waiter brought it to our *kusetli* where we had our fill and Jeanie and I had another memorable toast.

"Here's to you, baby!" I said.

"And to you, my love," she said.

Soon the conductor came by with some sheets and pillows; Jeanie and I took low bunks and the boys the high ones. The middle bunks went unused because we had the compartment to ourselves.

When we awoke, the train was chugging through a valley flanked by snowcapped mountains. And by 8 a.m. we were in Denzili, a city of 200,000. The boys had slept, but Jeanie and I caught only fitful sleep, the train clackety-clack and the Pullman car swaying drunkenly on uneven tracks made for an evening of raucous rest and untidy slumber. Still, it had been much better than an overnight trip by bus and travel by boat, of course, to Denizli was not an option.

We were accosted outside the station by a lad who said he was "Michael." Had we been German, I'm sure his name would've been Hans. Had we been French, it would have been Jean or Pierre. Michael led us across the street to the bus station for our transfer to Pammukele, about 10 miles out of town. We knew Michael had a scam of some kind but he was helpful, got us right on a minibus and we were off. Michael traveled with us, and we discovered that among the "businesses" he had going was a travel agency of sorts with an office that tries to get tourists to the places they want to go in and around Pammukele. When we were dropped off, Michael took us to his office and there we decided at his suggestion to purchase our bus fare to Izmir for 1 million TL and then he got his car, in not so bad shape and drove us up to the ridge above the "cotton castle" of calcium cliffs to our motel, the Pammukele Motel. We paid him 300,000TL to take us up the back way, thus avoiding the entrance to the national park and its fees which would have amounted to 700,000TL. At least that's what we were told.

So off we went. Soon we were on the "back way," bouncing over roads with sharp rocks jutting through the packed surface and deep ruts and rain-washed gullies. As we twisted around hill and dale, we came across a crowd gathered at the edge of a cliff and a *polis* car with its blue light flashing was there as well. At the bottom of the gully, a considerable distance, lay a bus which had plunged off the road and to the bottom. Of course it was probably packed with people and surely there must have been some loss of life.

We continued to drive, and the villagers continued to walk, ride bicycles, or motorcycles with a side car full of people. We saw one such contraption which must have had eight people including some children piled in to it, sputtering down the mountain to visit the crash site, worried no doubt about possible family and friends who may have been on the bus. Later, we learned from Michael that the bus was loaded with eighteen workers, crazy and inexperienced, and that eight people had been killed. It was sobering. I remembered the crash in Ecuador, South America, while traveling in a van in the Andes above Quito and a car hit us on a blind curve in our lane. I had escaped without physical injury but the psychological damage was lasting. I am still uneasy about riding with other drivers, and even more leery of riding with a driver whose immediate previous driving experience was on the back of a donkey. I breathed another prayer of thanksgiving for having survived Mad Max, Crazy Cyril and Blind Basil in northern Greece.

We inquired at the motel about how to get to the ruins at Aphrodesias some sixty miles away. We were told that we would need to go back to Denzili and get transportation there. So we arranged with Michael to pick us up at 9 a.m. the next day and he would, for $40, take us all both to Laodecia and to Aphrodesias, a full day's outing. Having settled this matter, we got our room, extremely overpriced, $100, for the off season and given the shabbiness of parts of the motel. Still, we were all in one room with toilet and shower.

The attraction of the Pammukele Motel was its minieral water pool which dates from Roman times; a ceremonial pool where people came for healing and rest. The area had a number of hot springs, and as these waters flowed out and over the nearby cliffs, the calcium content of the water remained as the water itself evaporated leaving the calcium residue which, over the centuries has built up into cliffs of what appear to be "cotton" perhaps even snow. It's a fascinating geothermal site and a new experience for the boys who've not yet been to Yellowstone. Anyway, we knew the motel had this great pool that had formed around ruins from the Roman period, mossy Corinthian capitals, fluted columns of marble, abandoned bases of pillars, blocks of marble, under water that was so clear that it looked ice cold, except for the steam that fuzzied its surface, especially in the cool morning or evening hours. The pool was deep in some areas, ten to twelve feet. Most areas, the depth was three to five feet. And oh! How good it felt to slip into this very warm water and soak tired muscles and a weary body!

Of course, the boys never interpreted the experience in such terms; for them it was just "neat" because the pool was large, had underwater things to see and sit upon, bridges to paddle beneath and so forth. But for me, the water was wonderfully curative and I wondered at how many thousands of people of different nationalities and kingdoms had passed through these waters in its existence through Hittite, Persian, Greek, Roman, Byzantine, Ottoman, Turkish history. I could see the Roman soldiers, stopping off for a bath, arriving at Hieropolis (mentioned in Colossians 4:13 as the site of the labors of Epaphrus) a city of considerable size and influence in the ancient Roman world.

Indeed, in the afternoon we walked out of the motel a short distance to these very ruins which are spread out for a couple of miles on the brown, dry hills overlooking the Lycus river valley. We visited the theatre, still in rather good condition, and walked some distance to the chalky ruins of the church associated with apostle Philip who, according to strong church tradition came here and died here. The church was impressive; one could visualize the basilica itself and see where the fluted columns had reached to the dome. Spenser videoed some donkeys. Taylor shot this and that and we ambled over pillars and posts in a leisurely fashion until the sun set across the valley and the distant mountains.

❧ ❧ ❧

That night we had dinner in the dining room and we ordered a red wine which cost us $14. The wine was good, but not that good. The boys watched a bit of TV in the room, something they'd not had a chance to do for a long time. We noticed that the tireless Spenser was beginning to cough, but nothing outrageous.

Michael met us at 9 a.m. and we set out for Laodecia and Aphrodesias. Within ten minutes we were at Laodecia, accessible only by four-wheel drive dirt road leading through some hilly farm land. Michael of course did not have a four-wheel drive vehicle, but the car he had did admirably anyway. There's little left of this ancient city which is mentioned at length in Revelation 2-3. The words of Christ to the church of Laodecia in Revelation 3 are better understood in the historical and geothermal realities of this area. Part of the Revelations text reads: "I know that you are neither hot nor cold. How I wish you were one or the other. But because you are lukewarm, neither hot nor cold, I am going to spit you out of my mouth." The water from the hot springs in the hills above Laodecia at Hierapolis, stream downhill to Laodecia but having left Heirapolis hot, ten miles downstream the water is merely tepid. Thus the reference which the contemporary Laodecians must have clearly understood. All that is left are ruins of a church, the city gates, a theatre and a few pillars scattered about, but it is cast over a number of acres, and no work is being done at all and the land is obviously being farmed by someone.

On to Aphrodesias, an hour away. We enjoyed Aphrodisias, the most well-preserved site we have visited so far. The excavations have only been done in earnest in the past thirty years. A village existed on the site until the Turkish government relocated it. The theatre was literally uncovered and the marble, protected from the elements over the centuries is almost as white as the day it was laid in place. This city is not mentioned in the Bible as far as I know, but it was interesting nonetheless.

We spent about three hours there, including the museum. Michael took us to a café nearby for lunch and then we had another ninety minutes and went back to Pamukkale. I shouldn't forget to mention the Hippodrome or stadium. It is perhaps the best preserved of any of the ancient world, certainly better than Rome or Istanbul. You could hold chariot races there today. The boys took a lap around the stadium to the cheers of thousands of imaginary spectators, and Jeanie and I who were filming the event.

At 4 a.m. the next morning, Taylor got up to go to the bathroom, and at 4:10 a.m. he did it again, repeating this pattern every ten minutes for the next two hours. Jeanie started pumping medicine into him at 4:30 a.m. because we knew we had to be on a bus for four hours beginning at 8 a.m. By 7 a.m. Taylor was not feeling any better but at least the bathroom intervals were now 30 minutes apart. Jeanie, after all, had given him enough medicine to dry up the Hoover dam.

We caught the bus to Denizli and Taylor managed to survive. The transfer in Denizli was quick; we had no more than five minutes. The engine had been started, the driver was in his air-cushioned seat, and four Americans were scrambling to get in a potty stop and their luggage stowed. We boarded and ere we had taken our seats, the bus was backing out and lurching on to the highway.

Jeanie and I both had received some indication that the discomfort now afflicting Taylor might also be visiting us. Nevertheless, the trip passed uneventfully, although Spenser seemed to be coughing more now.

We arrived at the Otogar in Izmir (ancient Symrna) about 12:30 p.m. and had a bite to eat. Taylor was now evidently plugged up, still not feeling 100% but glad we were at a stopping-off-point. We caught a taxi to the Ozel Amerikan Lisesi (American Collegiate Institute) where Shirley and Douglas Stenberg had offered to put us up. I think it was my Diet Coke addiction that created the bond: Shirley is a fellow fiend and while in Üsküdar she drained a number of Cokes from my own stash. She invited us to stay with them when we traveled south to give me a chance to raid her refrigerator in a similarly ruthless fashion. So we arrived at the school, explained to the security office who we were and were directed to the new library where Shirley was directing the process of getting everything on computers, brand new computers made available through some grant. We stayed in the library for about an hour, I catching up on reading material and Jeanie immediately offering to help in the conversion process.

At 3:15 p.m. we left and Shirley took us on a short walk through their beautiful campus to their home. Douglas is the director of the school, so they live in this beautiful old house, just three blocks from the bay: high ceiling, hardwood floors, large rooms. It was very comfortably furnished and Douglas, knowing I would surely enjoy reading the *Sunday New York Times,* had a copy sitting on the coffee table. It was a good excuse for him to buy one, because they cost 700,000 TL, about $14! I told him that I subscribe at home in the states. We later had a very enjoyable chat, he and Ken Franks, a United Church of Christ board appointee teaching at the school.

Indeed, Shirley had invited Ken and Betty Franks and their two children, and Fernie Scovil for dinner to help receive us to Izmir. Fernie is a widow, retired, came to Turkey in 1945. Taught math. Now she is back just for four months to help as a volunteer on this conversion project. She had wonderful stories and adventures to share. Her home is now in South Dakota, Hill City, actually in the Black Hills. I told her that we had been through there.

The next morning, after an interminable dalliance around the breakfast table, what with Shirley and Jeanie chatting about innumerable topics in a leisurely fashion when the ruins of Ephesus beckoned, we were not out the door until 11 a.m.! I felt I muffled my impatience rather well. We caught a cab to the Otogar and from there a bus to Selcuk. We had decided because of Spenser's incessant, allergic cough to return at the invitation of Douglas to

Izmir in the evening, rather than proceeding to Kudasasi to scrounge around for a ferry to Patmos. It looked a little dicey in terms of getting to Patmos and trying to do it might prove exhausting, especially when Spenser was not feeling his best. So, we got to Ephesus about 1 p.m. with plenty of time to have a good look at everything: the magnificient theatre, the best preserved city streets in the ancient world, the beautiful library of Celsus, the Odeon, and many fountains, and other buildings, including a restored bath house and latrine, with the sewer system exposed—something the boys found fascinating. Spenser was very tired because coughing during the night had robbed him of sleep and it had started to wear him down. His weariness might have saved his life because at Ephesus instead of running around leaping and jumping from pillar to post, and springing from capitals to blocks as gaily as a spring fawn, he moped and mostly sat here and there and was thereby saved from injuring himself.

It was fun to step on the stage of the theatre and to recall the tremendous riot described in Acts 19 when friends of the apostle Paul were hauled to the theatre and the town met in an uproar to debate the decline in silver sales. Paul himself tried to get to the theatre but was dissuaded by friends because they thought he would be killed. Not long after that, he slipped out of town and headed north. He had been in Ephesus for over two years.

After grabbing some Turkish pizza in Selçuk, we boarded a mini bus for Izmir about 5 p.m. This mini-bus, essentially a larger dolmus, was a dilapidated affair and when we were about forty-five minutes out of Selçuk, perhaps thirty minutes from Izmir, the radiator overheated and we stopped for water. The driver removed the engine cover inside the mini-bus and a number of "technicians" began to work, spilling water into the radiator and trying to reconnect a blown hose. This was a humorous scene which lasted about half an hour and then we proceeded to Izmir without further incident.

The next morning, we returned to the otogar and caught a bus for Denizli where we would then catch the 6 p.m. Pammukele Express for Istanbul. The trip to Denizli was fast: no potty stops. Got there in about three hours. We had a three hour wait in Denizli where we ate, walked around, watched Turkish TV, drank cay and NesCafe.

When we bought the ticket for Istanbul, the couchettes were full, but they found something else for us. When we boarded, we discovered that our compartments were first class. We didn't realize the Pammukele Express had first class! It was a nice upgrade from the cabin we'd had before. Instead of six beds in the cabin, there were only three, and they all had mattresses with sheets and blankets, not just a seat pulled down, and a sheet to cover yourself.

Each cabin had a nifty little fold down sink the boys found fascinating, and in the compartment behind the mirror was a fresh-sealed bottle of water. The steward came around and brought clean towels. The boys had their own cabin since we couldn't all sleep together. So Jeanie and I had a berth to ourselves as well, and although the beds where single beds, we were able to share a bed, at least for a while on the trip home.

The car we traveled in was dark, and the narrow aisle outside the cabins carpeted with curtains over the windows, and even in the cabins themselves, the motif was mahogany and all in all a romantic conclusion to another adventure, an adventure we will always remember as having begun and concluded on the Pammukele Express.

44

Belly-dancing on the Bosphorus

W<small>E TRIED TO DO SOME CULTURALLY-UPLIFTING THINGS ON THIS</small> trip. By the time we got back to Istanbul, it was Advent.

Not that Istanbul really noticed, but as Christians, we knew we were in the season of Advent. And the business community in town knew it too. We saw signs that Christmas was coming, especially on the European side of the city. Santa Claus was showing up everywhere, Taksim especially, in the fancy boutiques and shops. Reindeer, snowmen, a few angels, brightly decorated gift boxes.

No nativity scenes, however.

So we had little time left in Istanbul. Now we knew it. We'd be bugging to Bethlehem soon, and after that, we'd come back to Istanbul for little other reason than to get our bags and head for the U.S. We were running out of time.

We took a look at some of the things we wanted to do, made a list, and then tried to cram it all in our calendar like compressing files on a zip drive. Two things stood out: The choir concert at the Swiss hotel, and belly-dancers. By gawd, we were not going to live in Istanbul for four months and not see some belly dancers.

Not long after returning from the south, we set out on a Saturday morning via dolmus-ferry-dolmus to Taksim and found ourselves in the Ataturk Concert Hall for an 11 a.m. concert. This concert featured a pianist playing a Rachmanioff concerto and it was very well done. The concert concluded with a contemporary piece composed by a Turkish musician and it was a pleasant surprise. The concert had opened with a Mozart number that was the overture of an opera but for me sounded very un-Mozart—lots of percussion and brass, weird stuff for Wolfgang.

After the musical experience, we tried an educational one. Göksel had invited us to the Istanbul Technical Institute where he teaches. He invited us to speak to his class of English students. We had some trouble finding the place, i.e. the specific building where his classroom was located, but as we passed by, headed in the wrong direction, he spotted us and called out. He has about thirty students in his class; they meet all day (seven hours) on Saturday and Sunday from October to May to study English. We came in at the end of their day. I introduced the family, saying a bit about where we lived and why we were in Istanbul, and then opened it up for some Q & A. In the course of answering questions, Jeanie spoke and I had Taylor stand in front of the class, introduce himself, tell his grade in school, and what he liked to do. Later, Taylor counted to ten in French and then in Turkish. Spenser also introduced himself, and went through the same routine, both lads doing very well.

But the day was not done. After class we walked in the rain to Göksel's apartment not far away and we met his roommate Ahmed, a very pleasant fellow who teaches English in a private school and who had taught for a year in Anacortes, Washington. We had tea, and then ventured out into the rain. We had a terrible time getting a taxi and finally caught a dolmus to Taksim instead and from there a taxi to Sultanahmet where we were to have our evenings' entertainment.

We found the Orient House, walking by a tea garden and smoking den where Turkish men were sitting in a smoked-filled room sucking on water pipes, or the hookah. I resolved that before we left Istanbul, I, too, would smoke the hookah. We met up with Zecharia and Turkan who had already arrived. The Orient House is a large dinner house which has a nightly floor show with belly-dancing. We heard it had great food, but Göksel assured me the belly-dancers were phenomenal. I tried to act indifferent around Jeanie.

Dinner was served and the show began. The place was packed with people from many countries: France, Germany, Israel, Morocco and more. It clearly catered to the tourists. But that was fine. Tourists serve an important function in any country: they help to keep native and traditional customs alive. Folk dancers from different regions of Turkey appeared on the stage and danced and sang and a small cadre of musicians provided live instrumental accompaniment. The belly dancers themselves were very good actually. They could really shake their castenents.

Later, the first belly dancers came around to the tables and posed with patrons and a professional photographer was with her taking pictures which would be printed on the premises. This is how we came to have a photo of Taylor and Spenser with this gorgeous belly dancer and how we also have one of her standing over Jeanie, Taylor and myself at our table.

It was a fun evening with these friends: Zecharia, Turkan, Göksel, Ahmet and his girlfriend, and Neretin and his girlfriend. We drank wine, and indeed Jeanie drank an entire half-bottle herself. I had two glasses of raki.

At one point, the floor was cleared for people to get up from their tables and to dance. Göksel who loves to dance, was out there first, and then he and I and Zecharia. Jeanie tried to get a picture. It wasn't long before she was on the dance floor with the rest.

45

We Sing for Our Supper

THE NEXT DAY, SUNDAY, WE PAID OUR RESPECTS TO GOD in the Dutch Chapel, pastor Doug preaching as usual. This was preceded by a dismal choir practice and with a week to go before the concert, I could not fathom how this was all going to come together. The director does not know how to direct, by her own admission, and often is lost trying to ascertain the count while the choir itself is charging bravely ahead fortissimo and when perchance she lights upon the count and wishes us to break, she jabs the air with an uncertain finger and we halt by sections whensoever it seems right. I don't mean to belittle her talents; indeed, it is quite impossible to belittle what there is lacking either to praise or disparage.

We trooped into the service following the rehearsal, for we were to bless the congregation with a few selections, a tune-up before the grand appearance at the Swiss Hotel later. The children presented a small Christmas program of song in which Spenser and Taylor participated. When their little performance was over, the congregation sang a rousing rendition of "Hark, the Herald Angels Sing"—all three verses. Pastor Doug, then announced that the children should leave the platform during the singing of the last verse and rejoin their parents. Then in confusion, it was brought to his attention that we'd already sung the last verse. The kiwi pastor stammered about, "What, eh, mate? We've already sung the last verse? Right, then! Well, then, we'll sing it again. Come along, children." And we sang the bloody verse again while the children traipsed down from the platform to sit by their parents.

Then it was time for our own concert. We were introduced to a full house, processing from the rear, and the programme began. My solo came early and I hit every note, but being a tenor singing a low baritone part, I was unable to hit the low A with the resonance and volume, or "majesty" (as Barbel, the director, called it,) that I had hoped. Nevertheless, I did not embarrass myself or others. Jeanie's solo was superb. Perhaps the concert at the Swiss hotel would be okay.

At 4 p.m. we left for the hotel on the European side, getting there at 4:30 p.m. We spiffed up the boys, dressing them in white shirts and little red ties. This was no easy task. It recalled the trial we'd endured, especially with Taylor, when we attended the wedding of Jeanie's cousin in San Diego. The boys were in the wedding party and thus had to be fitted for tuxedos. Taylor had a fit. Did not want to wear that monkey suit. But it wasn't up to him. His chubby face got red, tears flowed, but he wore the suit, stood stiffly at attention as he was required to do, posed for all the pictures, but no sooner had the groom kissed the bride, most of it came off, and we let it be. Now, he had to be dressed up again, like it or not.

Taylor's dislike for formal attire continues to this day. He might be persuaded to dress up for his wedding, but even that's doubtful.

The boys were to sing and did sing in the Children's Choir. The hotel had a huge buffet going in a large central banquet hall, featuring several stories of glass that looked out upon the Bosphorus. A grand piano sat on a marble platform surrounded by water and fountains in the center of all of this, guests seated elegantly at tables all around, the entire area decorated with poinsettias, Santa Clauses, and snowmen with Turkish fezs, candy canes and the like. The children sounded wonderful.

The adult choir then sang, gathered around the grand piano. The hotel had set up microphones, but when I went to the microphone the night didn't get close to being holy until about the second verse when the mike suddenly went on just about when I was singing, "Fall on your knees, O hear the angel voices …" Jeanie's solo was exceptional and the microphone gave her added power that singing in such a large open room required.

Following the performance we were shown to the Geneva Room on the lower level where the hotel had prepared beautifully appointed circular tables for our dining pleasure, and a table, 40-feet long decked with all manner of delicacies. We were provided with a plate for salad, main entrees and desserts and we availed ourselves richly of the opportunity. We had never stayed or even visited a hotel of this caliber on our voyage and I reminded the family that the only way we could enjoy such opulence was to sing for our food. Jean and Paul Nilson sat at our table, as well as the piano player and her husband, and a young man from Nigeria and a Turk from Redhouse Press.

Singing the Christmas carols and visiting this hotel where everything was so festively decorated for the Christmas holiday was indeed a touching experience, and we felt buoyed by the spirit in the air. There were only eight days until Christmas. It seemed unreal since we'd seen so little of Christmas.

But the calendar said so, and we also knew that with this concert, these songs, the gaiety and laughter, we had brought our time in Istanbul to a grand conclusion. We'd spent our time in Turkey. It was over. The "turkey" was basted, cooked and eaten.

Now we would be taking Christmas to Bethlehem, because tomorrow, we were scheduled to fly out and head to the land of Christ's birth.

Part Six
O Little Town of Bethlehem

O holy Child of Bethlehem, descend to us, we pray;
Cast out our sin, and enter in, be born in us today.
We hear the Christmas angels the great glad tidings tell;
O come to us, abide with us, our Lord Emmanuel!
                                    —Phillips Brooks

"We ... grabbed a *yarmulke* and put it on our heads. Respectfully, we approached the walls where Orthodox and ultra-Orthodox were praying with the *tallit*, or prayer shawls draped over their shoulders, the *tefillin*, or phylacteries, wrapped about their foreheads and forearms." —p. 255.

46

Tantur Ecumenical Institute

W<small>E ARRIVED AT THE</small> A<small>TATURK</small> I<small>NTERNATIONAL</small> A<small>IRPORT ON</small> M<small>ONDAY,</small> D<small>ECEMBER</small> 18, 2005, at 8:15 a.m. precisely two hours in advance of our scheduled departure for Tel Aviv on Turkish Airlines. After going through the usual checks and cross-checks, passport control, we found our gate and sat ourselves down to wait. The boys were quiet with their Game Boys, not paying attention to us or what was going on around them. Fine.

We waited. When an Iranian Airlines 747 pulled into our gate, we began to suspect that our departure would be delayed. I checked with a monitor and discovered that our flight had been moved from gate 106 to 103!

"Boys! We got to go," I barked. "Our gate's been changed," I explained to Jeanie. The wife sighed. There's always something. It can't just go the way it's supposed to go. You'd think that after this much traveling we would've learned that there is no "way-it's-supposed-to-go." But, no. We got to the airport and expected the next couple of hours to unfold precisely as we had planned that they should.

Gathering our possessions quickly we migrated down the terminal corridor to gate 103 where flights were departing to Rome and Amsterdam, but not to Tel Aviv. Further, the staff there had no clue about our particular flight. The word we received was that the monitor was in error and that the correct gate was, after all, gate 106. Perhaps it *was* going the way things were supposed to go.

We trudged back to Gate 106 muttering nasty things about Turkish inefficiency, when we noticed gate attendants gesticulating at us. We picked up the pace when we realized that our flight was leaving, not from Gate 106, nor 103, but 105! Indeed the waiting area had emptied and the doors were literally closed behind us as we dashed down the stairs to a bus that was waiting to take us to our plane. Thus, with a lemony taste of excitement rolling about in our mouths like tart candy, we settled into our seats, and were soon in the air, but an hour late.

The flight itself was uneventful, although we were surprised by the number of snow-capped mountains we saw below us. We also spotted the highway we had taken into Capadoccia passing the Tuz Golu, near where Spenser had stopped the bus to pee.

It was a two hour trip with lunch. At 1 p.m. we were in Israel at Ben Gurion International Airport, Tel Aviv. We filled out some entry forms, and then went through passport control.

"Boys, stand here," I said. Seems like I was always telling the boys what to do, how to do it, where and when to go. They used to call me Mr. Bossy. Maybe they were right. With the wife a few Hindu feet away and behind me and the boys beside me, I surrendered our passports and watched the agent rifle through their pages, pausing to inspect the Turkish visas. Finally he returned our documents to us, and as he did so, I gratefully and absent-mindedly said, "Teseker ederim."

Taylor laughed out loud. "You said 'tesekerim ederim,' Timothy!"

I looked at him puzzled, and then laughed with everyone else. "Well, I guess I did, didn't I!" Later, we learned to say "Thank you" in Hebrew ("todah") and now can say "thank you" in seven languages.

Our luggage came immediately. We spotted an ATM and withdrew 600 NS (new shekels) — about $200 USD — and then walked into the sunshine outside. We looked for a *sheroot,* similar to a Turkish *dolmus*, but with four of us, the cost was higher than hiring a taxi. We approached the taxi stand and came to an agreement for 125 NS with a driver to take us to Jerusalem and from there to Bethlehem and the Tantur Ecumenical Institute. The haggling took about ten minutes, due in part to the *sheroot* driver who still wanted us to travel in his vehicle — which we stoutly refused to do. We crawled into the new Mercedes taxi, and after we were on the road, I gave the driver a phone number for Tantur, and he reached for the cellular phone—very uptown for 1995—and called them to get specific directions. In forty-five minutes we were at our destination.

After Vatican II, Protestant and Catholic observers to the council thought that there should be some place where they could study together and what better place than Jerusalem? So Pope Paul VI bought some land outside of Jerusalem, situated on a hill overlooking Bethlehem, actually, and to the east one can see the golden hills of Jordon (ancient Moab) beyond the river, and a small section of the Dead Sea. Tantur itself is a beautiful oasis of olive and pine trees, beautiful gardens of roses, geraniums, rosemary, long promenades lined with cypress trees and much more. The buildings are of Jerusalem stone.

At the reception desk we ran into Martin Bailey, a United Church of Christ board appointee as the Jerusalem representative to the Middle East Council of Churches. He facilitated procedures and soon we were in our two bedroom apartment, complete with bath and kitchen. Wonderful! Tantur operates on a semester basis and holds seminars and classes for visiting scholars, clergy who visit on study leave, or as a part of their coursework in pursuing a degree. The policy of Tantur is not to accommodate tourists, but inasmuch as we were visiting during the semester break, and my leave was a sabbatical, and I was clergy, prior to our departure from the States they'd readily agreed to accommodate us.

So we moved into Apartment #8 and shortly thereafter made a quick trip to the market for foodstuffs. We were then invited to the dinner that Tantur was preparing for a conference just coming in. No charge! So we accepted! We ate with the Baileys and met their daughter, her husband and their two boys ages 8 and 5. Once again, we were meeting good people, as we had throughout our journey.

"I was thinking about her, not about the birth of the baby Jesus. ... [W]hat a gift to me she was as a wife and friend. Her patience and steadiness was such a valuable contrast to my flammable nature. She was the oil of gladness, a balm for our tired spirits; ... She'd endured much, loved me resolutely and with passion. ... She was remarkable! I was not worthy of such love and loyalty." —p. 285.

47

Is the Holy Land Holy?

I HAVE ON MY BOOKSHELF A LITTLE CLAY PINCH POT that Jeanie glazed and fired in her kiln. I've had this little knick-knack for about ten years now, and at any given time it might hold some paper clips, a push pin, small change, and a rubber band or two.

It doesn't have any monetary value whatsoever, and no one else would ever want to have it. But it has value to me. Spenser made it with his own little clumsy hands when he was in pre-kindergarten.

I also have a wooden box in which I keep shoe-shining items, like black polish, cordovan polish, some rags to apply the shoe ointments, and a couple of brushes. My son, Jon, made the box when he was 11 years old. I'm still hanging on to drawings the girls made for me.

Because they're holy.

Why are some things holy and others aren't? Because only I can decide what is holy to me.

That said, I can recognize and respect that things which might not be holy to me, are holy to someone else. My friends have children, too. Their children have drawn pictures, made pinch pots, written stories, and these things are holy to my friends. But not to me. I understand, however, their value.

The Holy Land is holy if you say it is. Of course, you might be asked why you say it is holy. Even if the geographical area we call Israel and the West Bank today is not holy to you, you must acknowledge, if you're a reasonable person, that—for better or worse—it is holy to the devoted adherents of the three major religions of the world: Judaism, Christianity and Islam.

We might wish it weren't. We might feel that the passions that run so high with respect to this piece of land have resulted in horrible consequences and loss of life for so many thousands, it might be best to de-sanctify the whole area and be done with it.

It doesn't work that way. This land and many locations within it have been assigned such importance and significance that it is indeed considered holy.

The land for all three religions is linked to sacred texts. For the Jews, the land is linked to the Torah and what some call the Hebrew Bible. For Christians, the land is linked to the New Testament and particularly the gospels that tell the story of Jesus. Christians also believe the Hebrew Bible which they call the Old Testament, to be the sacred divine word of God as well. For Muslims, the land is linked to the Qur'an which tells the story of Abraham and Ishmael as well as some stories about Jesus.

As early as the Genesis account, people were erecting monuments and stones to memorialize an event in their national history. Stones were piled high as a monument when the Israelites crossed the Jordan River into the "Promised Land." "Joshua said to them, 'Pass on before the ark of the Lord your God into the middle of the Jordan, and each of you take up a stone on his shoulder, one for each of the tribes of the Israelites, so that this may be a sign among you. When your children ask in time to come, "What do those stones mean to you?" then you shall tell them that the waters of the Jordan were cut off in front of the ark of the covenant of the Lord. When it crossed over the Jordan, the waters of the Jordan were cut off. So these stones shall be to the Israelites a memorial for ever'" (Joshua 4:5-7). Laban and Jacob erected a monument to signify the covenant made between them: "'Come now, let us make a covenant, you and I; and let it be a witness between you and me.' So Jacob took a stone, and set it up as a pillar. And Jacob said to his kinsfolk, 'Gather stones,' and they took stones, and made a heap … Laban said, 'This heap is a witness between you and me today.' Therefore he called it Galeed, and the pillar Mizpah, for he said, 'The Lord watch between you and me, when we are absent one from the other'" (Genesis 31: 44-49). Hundreds of years later, Israel battled the Philistines at this same place, Mizpah, and after a victory, the last Judge of Israel, Samuel, erected another memorial and called it Ebenezer, meaning "stone of help," as a reminder of how God had saved them on this day: "Then Samuel took a stone and set it up between Mizpah and Jeshanah, and named it Ebenezer; for he said, 'Thus far the Lord has helped us'" (1 Samuel 7:12).

These were holy events and were designated as such by the stones and pillars erected to memorialize them.

Even today, we take similar action when something extraordinary happens in our communities. In Littleton, Colorado, the events of April 20, 1998, have been memorialized near Columbine High School with a park and thirteen crosses. Washington, D.C. is home to many monuments which we wouldn't say are "holy," because in the secular and political world we don't use words like this, but at the very least they're "places of respect," like the Vietnam War Memorial, for example.

Most churches refer to their worship area as "the sanctuary," that is, a holy place. It is holy because we say it is holy. It is a place designated for a special, revered purpose: to worship God.

The word "holy," in fact, comes from a Hebrew word meaning to "set apart." In Exodus, the tabernacle and the instruments and utensils of worship were "sanctified" or "made holy." That is, a wash basin, or laver, was declared not to be just a wash basin, but a holy object to be used only in the worship rituals of the Israelites. It was a holy object because it was set apart for particular service that was a part of the people's relationship with God.

The Bible even says that we ourselves, as living vessels, or temples, are to be "holy," that is, we, too, have been "set apart" for special divine purposes. We are holy to the extent that we observe and recognize the divine purpose that is embodied in God's intention for us as a person.

The phrase "holy land" may have been used in the first millennium but we know for certain that by the end of the 11th century, chroniclers and theologians were referring to Palestine as "the Holy Land." The First Crusade, begun in 1096 A.D. was an attempt, in part, to recapture Jerusalem which had fallen into the hands of those who likewise considered Jerusalem a holy city, the Muslims. And therein lay a problem that has beset the world: an unwillingness to share holy sites. Fanatical adherents to the faith have wanted to be the sole possessors of holy places and to secure possession, "holy wars,"—an oxymoron if there ever was one, have been launched at enormous cost to life, liberty and limbs.

No wonder, then, that in the western world in the past thirty years, there's been a tendency to stop calling Israel "the Holy Land," as though if we just whisper it, or don't talk about it, we'll at least not exacerbate the problem. Secularists aren't comfortable with language of the holy, and they simplistically assign the blame for the conflict in the Middle East to religious causes.

It would be better for all parties concerned to state the obvious up front: This land is holy land, and like Moses of old, we should remove our shoes, and tread softly and with respect. We should acknowledge that what is a pinch pot to one, is a relic to someone else.

As we traveled throughout Israel, Jeanie and I were aware that this land, as well as many of its particular sites, tombs, wells, churches, synagogues and mosques, were holy places. We were always respectful of that which others called holy.

Is the Holy Land holy? Yes, it is holy to millions of people around the world. And as we walked the land where Jesus walked, we knew that it was also holy for us.

48
Via Dolorossa

A FTER A BREAKFAST OF YOGURT AND TOAST, WE WALKED OUT to Hebron Road, so-called because it's the major highway between Jerusalem and Beersheba running through Hebron and Bethlehem. We caught an Arab bus and took it all the way to Damascus Gate of the Old City. There'd been plenty of bus bombings in the news, but they're never the blue Arab buses; they were always the red Jewish buses. Sounds awfully racist, but it's essentially true. We felt safe on a blue Arab bus.

The walls of Jerusalem including the Damascus Gate were built or repaired by Sulieman the Magnificent in the 16th century. So the Ottoman-Jerusalem connection is still quite visible when visiting the holy city. Because he did so, twentieth-century visitors, as we were then, are able to envision the Jerusalem of Jesus' day much better than were the walls either in shambles or gone altogether. The Old City is a fascinating "city" of several ethnic neighborhoods, including Muslim, Armenian, Jewish and Christian quarters. On this day, we headed through the Muslim quarter on the way to the Wailing Wall, the holiest of Jewish shrines. We weren't inside the gate two minutes, and Spenser had to spend some money. The transaction completed, we were soon at the Wall.

Not much had changed in the twenty years since I had been to the Wall. After the Israelis took the Old City in the Six-Day War of 1967, wresting it from Jordanian control, they cleared a couple of blocks of Arab housing to create the plaza that one now walks about. I was there in 1973 and 1975. The Wall had formerly been accessible only through an alley, and was visited by Jews as often as Jordanian authorities would permit them.

Now it's a large plaza and is often the site of *bar mitzpahs* and I suppose that Jewish parents would want their sons to be bar mitzvahed at the Wailing Wall just as devout Catholics would want their children to be baptized at the Vatican. It appeared that tourists were not allowed to go to the Wall, at least we didn't see any. But I threw off my pack and gave it to Jeanie, and Taylor and I went in anyway (women were not allowed), casually shuffling past two Israeli soldiers, Uzi's at the ready. Assiduously avoiding eye contact, we moved forward to a gated entrance, grabbed a *yarmulke* and put it on our heads. Respectfully, we approached the walls where Orthodox and ultra-Orthodox were praying with the *tallit*, or prayer shawls draped over their shoulders, the *tefillin*, or phylacteries, wrapped about their foreheads and forearms. In the boxes are parchment scraps of the Torah describing duties and religious obligations. We noticed all the prayers that had been written on bits of paper and inserted into cracks. We saw a 13-year old boy being bar mitzpahed and saw him carrying the Torah, and we listened to the rabbis reading the Torah while Israeli soldiers patrolled the rooftops nearby, Uzi's at the ready. It was an odd mix—the Jewish star and Israeli snipers, walls and barricades around a "wailing wall." One tried to at least imagine a sense of the Holy, but it was rather difficult.

After discreetly taking some pictures, we left the area.

The Dome of the Rock was closed to all except Muslims until the next day. We subsequently discovered that the Dome of the Rock area is closed to tourists more often than not, reserved for Muslims for prayer at the Al Asqa mosque. There continue to be concerns about Jewish disturbances. We decided to see the Dome of the Rock on another day, so we departed the temple mount area through the Dung Gate, so-called because city's garbage was carried through this gate and dumped in the valley of Hinnom where it was burned. There was a time when *gehinnom*, or *gehenna*, was always burning. Thus the biblical reference to *gehenna* as hell, a burning garbage pit of torment.

We walked *outside* of the walls around the SE corner and through a Muslim cemetery, placed there in the belief that invading armies would not desecrate a cemetery. Still walking, we reached the Lion's Gate, or St. Stephen's Gate, so called because of a tradition that Stephen was stoned near this gate. Here we re-entered the Old City and soon we were on the Via Dolorosa or "Way of Sorrows," the approximate path that Jesus would have taken on his journey from the hall of judgment to Golgotha, in this case, across town to the Church of the Holy Sepulcher.

This church, commissioned by Constantine in 326 A.D. was built on the site of a Roman temple to Venus, long considered the location of both the hill where Jesus was crucified and the place where he was buried in a nearby tomb. Indeed, inside the church one can see both caves and the granite protrusions of rock, indicating the manner in which this church was built into the side of the hill.

The archaeological evidence also shows that this church was outside the original, or Roman walls of the city as the biblical account indicate. And it's probable that the Romans built the temple to Venus with its concomitant sordid and licentious practices over a spot that had been revered by early Christians in an attempt to both discredit their faith and discourage its practice. So there is much to commend the Church of the Holy Sepulcher as marking the area where the crucifixion of Jesus took place as well as his burial.

The church has been built, rebuilt and remodeled over the centuries by a coalition of denominational entities, and is jointly "operated" by both the Catholic, and the Orthodox (Syrian, Armenian and Greek) churches. The Ethiopian Coptic church has a claim in as well. Nothing gets done to the church itself with the approval of these ecclesiastical bodies. Even the most holy church in all of Christendom, like most other churches, is operated by committee.[1]

For a church of this size and importance, the entrance is small. As soon as we were inside, I had something I wanted to show Spenser: "Come over here, Spense."

I squatted down to one knee and ran my finger over the stone flooring. "Do you see this?" I asked.

"It looks like a cross," Spense said. He got down on his knees beside me.

"That's right. You can see these crosses etched in the stone all over. This is where Stephen of Blois and Raymond of Toulouse and many other knights in the First Crusade left their mark. One of the things they wanted to do the most when they got to the Holy Land, was to worship in this very church. And when they did, many of them made the sign of the cross in the stone."

Spenser ran his finger over a stone-etched cross. "Know how old that mark is?" I asked. "It's about 900 years old. And what does the shape of this cross remind you of?"

"A sword?"

"That's right! Sometimes, when a knight couldn't get to a church, or while he was out on the battlefield, he would thrust his sword in the soft ground, and then kneel before it and pray."

We got up and walked over to a nearby slab of marble where tradition says the body of Jesus was laid out and anointed when taken off the cross. We went into the tomb area as well, accessible through a low, narrow opening, reeking of incense and lit by candlelight. Nothing really to see, except the shrine itself. Yet we saw many devout Orthodox enter, and kiss that stone or this relic, as obvious acts of piety and devotion.

For us Protestants, though, while we could appreciate the piety associated with this church and the centuries of tradition, it was harder to appreciate with the eyes of imagination than our Catholic and Orthodox friends for whom the drama of the mass and symbols and imagery has always been more significant. When we later went to the Garden tomb, we found ourselves able to appreciate it much more because the Garden Tomb requires less imagination, even though in terms of archaeology and history, the Church of the Holy Sepulcher, has more of a claim to being the actual site of the passion of the Christ.

When we left the church, the wind, which had been chilly before, had really picked up. We ate lunch nearby and then walked out Jaffa Gate and caught a bus for the military cemetery and paid our respects to Yitzak Rabin who was recently buried there. We didn't fail to notice the symmetry: We'd just left the site commemorating the death of one Jew who died reconciling humanity to God; now we were at the grave of another Jew who had died attempting to reconcile humans to each other. Flowers were heaped over his grave and scores of mourners were there. He lies in a grave with pine trees all about, on a hill, with the father of Zionism, Theodore Herzl, lying nearby.

Fifteen minutes later we were at Yad Vashem, the Holocaust museum, going from a church built to memorialize the death of one Jew, to a museum memorializing the death of millions of Jews. The name comes from Isaiah 56:5, *"And to them will I give in my house and within my walls a memorial and a name [a 'yad vashem'] ... that shall not be cut off."* It's full name is *Yad Vashem, the Holocaust Martyrs' and Heroes' Remembrance Authority*, and it was established in 1953, only five years after Israel was reconstituted a state, by an act of the Israeli Knesset. It's stated purpose is to document the "history of the Jewish people during the Holocaust period, preserving the memory and story of each of the six million victims, and imparting the legacy of the Holocaust for generations to come through its archives, library, school, museums and recognition of the Righteous Among the Nations." It's a very impressive site, and we could have stayed much longer than we did. We weren't sure the boys were quite ready to see or understand everything in the museum. It was gory enough that we wanted to shield the children from some of it. Still, they were impressed by much of what we were able to explain to them.[2]

At home that night we talked about Yad Vasheem, and we told the boys that the next day we were going to the Mount of Olives.

"I don't like olives," Spenser said.

---

[1]For more on the Church of the Holy Sepulchre, see Appendix II.
[2]For more on Yad Vashem, see Appendix III.

49

The Mount of Olives

T HE PEOPLE AT TANTUR, MARTIN AND BETTY BAILEY, for example, were still unsure of when exactly Bethlehem was going to be turned over to the Palestinians. The best money was on Thursday, December 21, as the town would be sealed off for two days and "they certainly wouldn't attempt a transfer on Christmas Eve or Christmas Day when the eyes of the world will be upon them." So our plans began to take shape. We'd probably rent a car for three days and go to Galilee for two days, and then the Dead Sea and Masada for another day. By then, Bethlehem would no doubt be in Palestinian hands and have self-rule for the first time in well over 2,000 years. It was going to be crazy.

Bethlehem, inhabited overwhelmingly by Arabs, but religiously consisting of 60% Muslims, 40% Christians, has been occupied for twenty-eight years by the Israelis. Before them the occupiers were the Jordanians, before them the British, before them the Turks, before them a patchwork of Crusader and Muslim entities, before them the Byzantines, before them the Romans, as was the case in the days of Jesus. So self-rule is a big deal here: the town's been occupied by a foreign power for over 2,000 years. Now, things are really happening. Below Tantur is the Israeli checkpoint for Bethlehem, for no Jews are allowed in Bethlehem for the indefinite future, and security is very tight.

This morning we're up at 7 a.m. and off on an Arab bus by 8 a.m. for Jerusalem. The people of Jerusalem are interesting to say the least: Arabs who (the males) frequently wear the *keffiyeh* held in place by an *ogal*, a black cord wrapped twice about the head (they were usually attired in long robes, and the women just as frequently scarved or wearing *burkas*); Jews appearing in a variety of dress but overwhelmingly "western" in their attire; and the ultra-orthodox especially interesting with their leggings, long black coats to below the knee, stockings, side curls, shaved heads and black fedoras.

We took the bus to the Damascus Gate again and walked to Lion's Gate looking for an ATM and film since we were out of both money and film. We bought some Agfa for 20 NS, still too much but better than 25NS demanded for a roll of Kodak film. We were headed for the Mount of Olives proceeding on the Via Dolorosa toward Lion's Gate. Cars sped by on this one lane alley forward and backward, a major entrance to the Arab section of Old Jerusalem and the Via Dolorosa. It's called the "way of sorrows," we decided, because of the motorists who terrorize pedestrians as they do. Out Lion's Gate, down the hill, and then failing to look to the right, I instructed the party to proceed to the left in order to hook up in vain to the road up the Mount of Olives. It soon became apparent that we had walked the WRONG direction. I quickly admitted the error, but was reminded of it frequently in the days ahead. We soon were at the foot of the Mount of Olives and chanced upon the underground church of the tomb of Mary for no other reason than that we were looking for a bathroom.

We walked into the dimly lit, incense-filled church where a service of some kind was going on: priests were chanting and singing from several different points in the altar area. The tomb itself is behind the altar and in itself not very impressive except to those for whom the tradition itself is impressive. Not finding a bathroom and not in possession of excessive devotion to Mary herself, we departed and found what we required a short distance away, near the Church of All Nations, build on the site of an ancient Romanesque chapel honoring Gethsemane and the agony of Jesus the night before he was killed. Indeed, in this garden area are many olive trees of such massive size that there's little doubt of their being 2,000 years old as the naturalists claim.

We left these precincts and trudged up the busy Mount of Olives road (situated now in East Jerusalem). I recant my earlier testimony about the Mount of Olives not being a "mountain." It's probably not a mountain, but this walk was definitely uphill. So *Mount* of Olives is fine with me. *Hill of Olives* doesn't have the same ring to it. After a while, we thought we might cut through the Mount of Olives cemetery. While on this detour, we were accosted by a care-taker who answered our questions and then took us to the tomb of Menachem Begin, a terrorist during the 1948 War of Independence and later Prime Minister, signing the Camp David peace accords with Anwar Sadat at the behest of then President Jimmy Carter.

We also saw the grave of Oscar Schindler, of *Schindler's List* fame, and also the final resting place of Robert Maxwell, the publishing tycoon who had the misfortune to slip off the deck of his yacht into the ocean a few years ago and was, in his obese state, unable to take advantage of the ballast, and sank. A plot in the Mount of Olives cemetery costs about $10,000 we were told, and it's of course a desirable spot to be buried facing as it does the Golden Gate through which the Messiah is to march some day and where the Resurrection of the Dead will occur. When this latter event takes place, the dead on the Mount of Olives will therefore be first in line to accompany the Messiah through the gates of Jerusalem.

This little tour cost us about 20 NS and soon we were atop the Mount of Olives which today doesn't look like a "mountain" at all, as I said, and there are very few olives around. But it's higher than the Temple Mount area and affords an excellent view of the old city, and millions of photos have been taken from this spot of the Dome on the Rock and the Old City and we took a number ourselves, although we were there at a poor time of day for good pictures: mid-day, lots of sun, washed out sky.

December 20, 1995

I saw the Lion's Gate. I went to the top of the Mount of Olives. I saw the Gethsemane. I saw the Dome-of-the-Rock. I walked on the walls of the old city. I learned that New York has more Jews then Jerusalem. I thought walking on the walls was fun. —*Spenser, 8*

We flew from Istanbul to Israel. I touched the wailing wall. We went to the church of the Holy Sepulcher and saw Jesus' tomb. I learned the jews put there prayers in the wailing walls' cracks. —*Taylor, 10*

We were told the Dome would not be open until 12:30 p.m. and then, for only an hour. So we got something to eat in the old city and then went to the Wailing Wall to sit and chat until we were able to go in. At the appointed hour, we queued up like everyone else and marched through the Morocco Gate near the remains of Robinson's Arch and were on the Temple Mount, an area of Mediterranean cypress, pine gardens and flower and Roman-style porticos. We took innumerable photos of the Dome before Jeanie went inside to see the rock upon which Abraham had nearly sacrificed Isaac, which had then become a threshing floor purchased by David, the rock from whence Mohammad had made a night journey to heaven. I told Jeanie to look for the fingerprints of Gabriel when he restrained Abraham and the heels prints of Mohammad when he pushed off on his night journey. She said later she couldn't be sure if she saw them or not.

After some discussion with the locals as to where we could find an ATM machine, we walked out of the old city up Jaffa Road a ways and found one and extracted some money. We then walked back to the Damascus Gate and climbed the ramparts and walked the walls to the east, past Herod's Gate, to Lion's gate. Then we walked back up the Mount of Olives. I wanted to get a picture of the Old City at dusk. I don't know why I dragged the family back up there with me. Probably because I wanted them to see the beauty of it. We stayed on the Mt. of Olives about 30 minutes. The sunset was beautiful and the city seemed peaceful, yet as we knew, a city that above all cities in the world, evokes controversy and war. "O Jerusalem, Jerusalem."

We were reminded to "pray for the peace of Jerusalem."

Dec. 22, 1995.

I saw the Sea of Galilee. I got to swim in it, I stai-
d in Tiberias, I went to Mount of Beatit-
udes, I went to Caper-naum, I ate at a restaurant with a playground, I saw the Chu___ the Annuu___ thoug___ fun.

T___
wo___

December 19 and 18, 1995

We flew from Istanbul to Israel. I touched the wailing wall. We went to the church of the Holy Sepulcher and saw Jesus' tomb. I learned the Jews put there prayers in the wailing wall's cracks.

50

Into the West Bank

W E AWOKE TO THE SOUND OF HELICOPTERS FLYING OVERHEAD, buzzing over Bethlehem, and we knew that the City of David would be transferred to the Palestinian National Authority today and tomorrow. Therefore, the next two days would be ideal for traveling north through the West Bank to Galilee where we could visit Nazareth, Tiberius and other areas around the Sea of Galilee.

After some negotiating with the car rental agency (they didn't want to rent us a car because we had a Bethlehem address) we secured a little green Fiat and prepared to leave.

Our route would not actually take us "into" the West Bank because as temporary residents of Bethlehem we were already *in* the West Bank.

What, you ask, is the "West Bank"? Is there an East Bank?

Of course, there's an east bank, and it's called the country of Jordan which lies east of the Jordan River.

We drove north in Jerusalem and out of Jerusalem through Ramallah (which was due for transfer soon) and there had our first moment of directional uncertainty. I recalled that we were taking pretty much the same route as Mary and Joseph took when they'd been down to Jerusalem for the Passover, and at the conclusion of the observance, had left in a huge caravan of people thinking that their 12-year old was with relatives. He wasn't, and when his mother found him in the temple talking theology with the elders she was peeved. No matter she had a gifted-and-talented child. This was too much. Jesus, for his part, had a quick answer, and it wouldn't be the first time he had a confrontation with his mother. Check out the story of the wedding at Cana. One can only imagine the contretemps those two had during those biblically silent years of Jesus' life: age 12-30. In fact, I believe the only time Scripture shows him having compassion for his mother was when he was dying on a Roman cross.

Anyway, I stopped at a grocery market, and with map in hand, inquired of the Palestinian proprietor about directions to Nazareth. He happily provided it, especially after we purchased some fruit for the trip.

Our route took us north toward the ancient city of Shechem (now Nablus). Here we missed a turn, however, following a road which seemed to be more easterly than northward and as the road narrowed and became more bumpy and more winding, my co-pilot likewise became more bumpy and whining.

"Honey, are you sure we're on the right road?" she asked sweetly.

"No, my pet, I am not sure."

"Because this sure doesn't look like a main road to me," she said less sweetly.

I was silent for a minute or two, as we drove around another bend in the road where I hoped there'd be some signage that indicated that we were indeed on the right road. But there wasn't. "Well, I'm not sure that in this neck of the woods there *are* 'main roads' you know," I said, quite certain now that we were not on a main road, and not on the right road either.

We drove on unwilling to turn around and go back to Nablus and lose so much time. But when we came to a small nameless village, we pulled over to the side of the road near some people who were resting under a shade tree. One young man was sitting idly on the bars of his bicycle watching us with what seemed to me as dark interest. These people didn't seem particularly friendly, but I decided it was probably because no white fools like us pass through these parts very often.

"We're lost, huh?" Taylor said nervously, stating the obvious.

"Yup."

Their knowledge of English was limited and my Arabic was non-existent. But one thing was clear: we were lost. We jabbered incomprehensively to each other in our respective languages, but with the map, they were able to point out where we needed to go, and in fact, suggested we turn off on a road that was just a few meters away.

So we did. We were now driving north on some side roads, not main roads, toward the city of Jenin, the first Palestinian town (except for Jericho) to be given self-rule, the first of a scheduled six or eight. Soon we could see Jenin in the far distance, and we could also see up the road a couple of Israeli soldiers. At least we thought they were Israelis.

They were hitch-hiking. I slowed down and saw that they were indeed Israelis, each with a small backpack, and each with an Uzi slung over their shoulders. Taylor and Spenser pressed their noses to the glass in the back seat.

"Honey, what are you doing?"

"I'm stopping to give these boys a lift."

"Honey—"

We were alongside the soldiers now. "Hi, boys!" I said brightly. This was *so* cool. They were young, good-looking lads, obviously tired. "We're on holiday," said one, leaning over and peering into the car on Jeanie's side. "Just need a lift to Nazareth," he said, smiling.

"And that's just where we're headed," I said, smiling.

"But, as you can see," the mother of two pre-teen children interjected, "we don't have any room."

"Yeah, yeah, yeah, but we could squeeze in with the lads, couldn't we boys?" The boys were bug-eyed.

Jeanie's voice turned hard as quik-cement in Phoenix in July. "I'm sorry, but we have luggage, and you have packs, and it's still some distance to Nazareth. It's not going to work."

The young man pulled away from the car, straightened up, adjusted his automatic weapon, and said, "Okay, thanks. Have a good trip," and I applied the gas and we sped off. They recognized a Jewish mother when they saw one.

I could feel Jeanie looking at me. The boys were quiet in the back seat. "What were you thinking?" she asked.

"I was thinking we could give them a lift," I said. "They're not going to get a Palestinian to stop for them, and there's not a whole lot of traffic on this road."

"They're SOLDIERS, Timothy, Holy Jesus, Mary-Mother-of-God, with *live* ammo, and we're going to put them into our car with children? We might as well put a bulls-eye on the car for some Palestinian whack job to lob a grenade and get two soldiers and four Americans at the same time."

Sometimes I don't think things through.

From Jenin we motored steadily—in silence—to Afula, now out of the West Bank, and drove up to Nazareth situated on a high bluff overlooking the Plains of Jezreel. Looking up at Nazareth perched on this aerie atop the Galilean hills, the story of Jesus reading the Scriptures in the synagogue made perfect sense. He'd read from Isaiah in his hometown, said something about "Today this scripture has been fulfilled in your hearing." The audience then questioned his claim, and Jesus retorted by saying that Elijah was a great prophet, and there were many widows in Israel, but he was sent to only one, a foreigner. And Elisha was a great prophet in Israel, but although there were many lepers in Israel, he was sent to only one man and he was the gentile,

Namaan the Syrian. He threw in that "a prophet is accepted save in his own country." By then, the crowd, thinking they'd just been insulted by a lunatic, was determined to throw the irreligious fellow over a cliff. They "drove him out of the town, and led him to the brow of the hill on which their town was built, so that they might hurl him off the cliff." Jesus managed to escape (see Luke 4:16-30). The "brow" is easily visible when approaching Nazareth from the south.

While there were times when we were again unsure of the route, I stopped and consulted the map or asked for directions and Jeanie applauded my willingness to listen to the feminine side of my nature. We arrived in Nazareth and the day was sunny and clear. We first ate lunch leisurely at a place that commended itself for no other reason than that it was the first bathroom Jeanie could find. Sometimes I thought that our trip was not much more than a journey from one bathroom to the next and we tried to work in what sights we could see en route.

The major point of interest for Christians is the Basilica of the Annunciation, the parish church for about 7,000 Catholic Christians who live in Nazareth. It's a beautiful structure of white stone, with a dome that rises over 150 feet built in the shape of the so-called Madonna lily, a symbol for the Virgin Mary. The church was consecrated in 1969, built over an earlier Franciscan church. A church of some kind has occupied the spot for well over a millennium. It consists of an upper and a lower church. In the upper church one can find mosaics of the Virgin contributed by artists from around the world. The lower church consists of the Grotto or Cave of Annunciation where Mary is said to have been visited by the angel Gabriel. You can also see the remains of Byzantine and Crusader churches which once occupied the site. The interior is designed so that one can peer from the upper church into the Grotto below.

Outside on the walls of the church are several verses of Scripture in Latin: *Verbum caro factum est et habitavit in nobis.* (The Word was made flesh and dwelt among us.) And: *Angelus domini annuniviat Mariae"* (The angel of the Lord said unto Mary).

Today Nazareth is a large city of tens of thousands of Israeli Arabs and Jews. Back in the day, it was just a small village, so obscure that some Galileans who grew up in the region didn't know where it was (see John 1:46). We left Nazareth about 3 p.m. and drove through Cana where Jesus performed his first miracle and had a few words with his mother. We had tarried too long in Nazareth so I felt some pressure to move forward expeditiously. While the route to Tiberias was somewhat vague to me, I had a sense of the way to go, and didn't want to spend time second-guessing myself or stopping to consult with locals. So I said to Jeanie, "Would it be okay, my petunia, my feminine side notwithstanding, if I listened to my testosterone, and just floored it, and head down the road?"

She laughed. "Go for it, Timothy."

So we did, driving fast and furious, most of it down, down, down from high in the hills above the sea of Galilee to the lakeshore itself and then on to Tiberias on the western shore, a town that was built during Jesus' lifetime by Herod Antipas in honor of the then current emperor in Rome. It's the only town of those that ringed the lake in Jesus' day to have survived up to the present, now as a primarily resort area.

We decided, since there was only about an hour of daylight left that we should head directly for the waterfront to enjoy the lake as the sun set behind the hills to the west of Tiberias. So this we did. We would then attempt to discover the location of our lodging at the Church of Scotland hostel where we had a reservation. But it was best that we get to the lake now.

We found a table on the shore and had tea and cokes and relaxed for a while as the late afternoon dissolved into dusk. Before night fell, I pulled a New Testament out of my pack.

"Taylor, here," I said, handing him the Bible. "Read this for us." The little fourth-grader began to read from John gospel, chapter 21:

> *After these things Jesus showed himself again to the disciples by the Sea of Tiberias; … Just after daybreak, Jesus stood on the beach; but the disciples did not know that it was Jesus. … When they had gone ashore, they saw a charcoal fire there, with fish on it, and bread. Jesus said to them, "Bring some of the fish that you have just caught. So Simon Peter went aboard and hauled the net ashore, full of large fish, a hundred and fifty-three of them; and though there were so many, the net was not torn. Jesus said to them, 'Come and have breakfast.' Now none of the disciples dared to ask him, 'Who are you?' because they knew it was the Lord. Jesus came and took the bread and gave it to them, and did the same with the fish. This was now the third time that Jesus appeared to the disciples after he was raised from the dead.*

"The 'sea of Tiberias' that Taylor read about was this very lake by which we were sitting, also called the 'sea of Galilee,' and the fish that the disciples caught," I said, "they caught right here in this lake, and today they call the small little fish that's common here, 'Saint Peter's Fish'."

"Saint Peter's fish," Spense echoed, wrinkling his nose and jabbing inexplicably at his eye.

"That's right, and I think we need to find where we're staying for the night, and then we'll go to a restaurant and we'll eat some of St. Peter's fish."

"You'll eat St. Peter's fish," Taylor said, sticking his tongue out in disgust. "Yuk."

It was now dark and the task fell upon us of finding our lodging for the night. We walked back to the car and noticed St. Andrew's Church and a "Galilee Center"—words which rang a bell because the lady on the phone had used them. But we saw nothing else. Not far off, however, Taylor saw a sign that said, "GUEST HOUSE," something about the Church of Scotland. It was too far away for me to read the phone number listed, but Taylor could. I compared it to the one I had scribbled on my paper, and they were the same! We walked over to the establishment and asked them if they had a reservation for the Merrill's and they did! So here we were. By incredible good fortune, we had careened down the hill as fast as possible to the lake and had at the same time found our lodgings for the night.

The hostel was a beautiful place, situated a block off the shore, although they have a private beach which was used the next morning. It used to be a hospital, but it closed about thirty years ago and has since been used as a hostel and as a retreat for small conferences. The stone is old as the Church of Scotland itself, which has had a presence here for over 100 years. We were quartered all together in a room with a vaulted, arched ceiling and private bath. We were very pleased and excited. Breakfast the next morning would be included.

After bringing our packs inside, we went back out for dinner. Jeanie and I had St. Peter's fish which was served head, eyeballs and tail *en toto*. The boys declined and instead had the usual, something greasy. Back at the hostel, we tucked the boys into bed, and then walked out, leaving them! We told them both, of course, exactly what we were doing, where we were going and how long we'd be gone.

Truth is, we were looking for Margarita-ville where we could relax just the two of us. So we migrated down to the waterfront and finding a bar, ordered a couple of margaritas. They had to be the worst, worst margaritas of our lives. To this day, we talk about the "Margaritas of Tiberias." But being together without background chatter was fabulous and it was a very special moment, a fountain from which we drank, deep and rich.

51

The Twos Seas

I AROSE WELL BEFORE DAWN TO GO OUT TO THE LAKESHORE and watch the sun rise over the Golan Heights. I encamped myself on a rocky shelf not far away to watch as fisherman who had let down their nets the night before, draw them in, with little success, I noted. I resisted the temptation to shout: "Let down your nets on the other side!" The air was quiet and the lake surface still. Sea gulls shrieked and flew nearby, following a boat here or there, diving for a minnow. I lit my pipe and enjoyed about forty-five minutes of undisturbed, quiet reflection. The sun emerged for another day's work at 6:50 a.m. and shortly thereafter I returned to the hostel. The family was up and about to go out, so I joined them and we went to the private beach for another forty-five minutes. Then on to a delicious breakfast of granola, eggs, bread, juice, cheese, coffee and yogurt.

After this breakfast, we took another hour for the boys to swim in the Sea of Galilee or to play in the sand.

> **December 22, 1995**
> I saw the Sea of Galilee. I got to swim in it. I stayed in Tiberias. I went to Mount of Beatitudes. I went to Caper-naum. I ate at a restaurant with a playground. I saw the Church of the Annunciation. I thought the day was fun.
> .—*Spenser, 8*

On our way back through the garden we saw the graves of those who gave their lives to get this work of the Church of Scotland going 100 years ago. The founder of the hospital was David Watt Torrance who came to Tiberius in 1880s and died there in 1923. His wife, Lydia, born the same year as he, 1862, died in 1892, and was preceded in death by their twin sons, in 1890. David remarried Eleanor, but their son died too, and she herself died in 1909. So life was hard and the price was high in those days. It was moving for us to piece

269

together a bit of their life by reading the information on their tombstones.[1]

We left the hostel and headed along the north shore by car. Our original plan had been to take a boat from Tiberias to Capernaum, but in the off season they don't run. So we drove and stopped first at the Mount of the Beatitudes chapel, visited by Pope Paul VI in 1965. It was built to immortalize Jesus' Sermon on the Mount, not that the "Sermon" wasn't sufficiently immortal in its own right, surviving as it has for 2,000 years. The spot is situated above the Sea of Galilee on green, gently sloping hills, and, with the implements of farming lying about and workers toiling in the fields, it's quite easy to envision Jesus sitting under a shade tree with a curious crowd gathered about him, and saying something like, "A sower went forth to sow and some seed fell on stony ground…" We found a quiet nook and when Jeanie and the boys found some quiet personal space to sit and look out over the hills and the lake, I read the Beatitudes from St. Matthew's gospel, chapter 5.

> *Blessed are the poor in spirit: for theirs is the kingdom of heaven.*
> *Blessed are they that mourn: for they shall be comforted.*
> *Blessed are the meek: for they shall inherit the earth.*
> *Blessed are they which do hunger and thirst after righteousness: for they shall be filled.*
> *Blessed are the merciful: for they shall obtain mercy.*
> *Blessed are the pure in heart: for they shall see God.*
> *Blessed are the peacemakers: for they shall be called the children of God.*
> *Blessed are they which are persecuted for righteousness' sake: for theirs is the kingdom of heaven.*
> *Blessed are ye, when men shall revile you, and persecute you, and shall say all manner of evil against you falsely, for my sake.*

On to Kaper Naum, or Capernaum, nothing but ruins now, but the city to which Jesus went after wearing out his welcome in Nazareth. Located on the north shore, it was his base of operations while he was in Galilee traveling north to Bethsaida, or Chorizim and other villages. When I was here twenty years earlier, one could see the house of St. Peter quite clearly, but "they" have now built a shrine directly above it, supported by pillars, a structure so monstrous in appearance, it looks like a flying saucer. Absolutely terrible. We saw the synagogue, built on the site of the synagogue where Jesus read the Scriptures.

Back in the car, we crossed the Jordan River and drove down the east side of the river and then connected with the main road going down the Jordan River Valley through the West Bank. This is a heavily agricultural area: dates, bananas, oranges, grapefruit, lemon, egg plant, etc. There were numerous checkpoints along the way, barriers set up through which one had to weave, soldiers to smile at, or some soldiers hitching a ride back to their base—who didn't get a ride from us.

We had lunch in Jericho. We didn't bother to stop and peer into the archaeological ruins of Jericho. The tel is quite boring actually. A big hole in the ground, bricks etc., protruding at different intervals showing that this city, perhaps the oldest active city in the world, has been built, destroyed and rebuilt numerous times, destroyed by earthquakes as often as by invaders.

After lunch we drove up through the Judean wilderness to Jerusalem, spun around the Mount of Olives arriving home by 4 p.m.

By 8:30 a.m. the next day, we were off again, this time to the Dead Sea. We took the main road behind the Mount of Olives, down through the Judean Wilderness, but rather than going into Jericho, we angled off to the Dead Sea. We were there by 9:15 a.m. but there were few signs of life that early.

The beach seemed closed. We asked someone if things were open and he replied, "Be an Israeli. If it's open, go through and see what happens." The gate was open, so we drove through it down to a section of "beach" on the Dead Sea. The boys got into the water, Taylor even slipped in the black mud and was a mess, but about that time we heard a holler. A security fellow told us we couldn't swim there. He was quite incensed.

"Do you see any other cars here?" he asked.

Well, no we didn't. But we also didn't see a sign saying the beach was closed and the ticket windows were closed. So where did he want us to go? We gave him a lift back to the *proper* area. I had to roust someone to whom I could pay a fee of 60 NS, rather steep I thought. I bought some Cokes and a Sprite for us all while the rest went on in.

This fellow had now softened, seeing the boys and our excitement, and also seeing perhaps some tourists he could fleece for a few bucks. After the boys had been swimming and floating for a while, he motioned for the boys to get out of the water, which they did, and then he smeared some of this black Dead Sea mineral mud, supposed to have wonderful medicinal, healing properties, all over their bodies. They looked like little black children. After allowing it to dry for about ten minutes, they washed it off in the Dead Sea. They really enjoyed swimming. The sense of weightlessness was a novel feeling for them. They were in water well over their heads, but they didn't need to tread water;

they just floated.

The lifeguard *cum* security fellow hosed them down with fresh water and with his hand held out, I pressed a NS 20 bill into his hand for the little bag of mineral mud he had given Jeanie and so his day didn't turn out so bad after all.

From this particular beach on the northwest corner of the Dead Sea, which incidentally is the lowest, deepest spot on the face of the earth at 1200 feet below Sea level, and where there is 15% more oxygen than might be found elsewhere, we motored to Qumran, where the Dead Sea scrolls were found by a goat herder in 1947 and where they continue to find evidence of an ancient monastic community, the Essenes, who lived there in the biblical world of Jesus. They have now found another cave which they're excavating. Anyway, we looked around, read up a bit on the history of the area, and took some pictures of the hills and caves of the area.

From Qumran we drove south thirty minutes to Masada, the site of the last Jewish resistance of A.D. 70. Masada was also a fortress for Herod. Rather than hike up the trail with its numerous switchbacks, we took the tram and that's always fun. I'll not go into the detail of Masada's history, for it's well-told in other places. From the top, you can see the outline of the camps where Roman legions lived during the three year siege. From certain viewpoints, one can also see the ramp they built during those three years on which they were able to breach the fortress. Once they had, they found over 900 dead—a mass suicide. It's a dramatic story and has been retold in literature and depicted in film. Since my last visit, spectacular work has been done on the northern palace and it's now possible to walk down to the middle and lower terraces, which we did, although the wind was fierce. We also went down in a large underground cistern, stairs cut out from the wall. Herod had build storehouses for grain, tools, and equipment and the rebels had filled them so that, with a system to catch rainfall and store the water, they were able to survive for three years, trapped by the Romans, and could have lived longer but for the breach. It was a good experience for all of us.

Back down off the tram we had ice cream and relaxed for a while. Then we took off, and going further south, we motored through Ein Bokek, a resort community where the Hyatt Regency was building a posh, 600-room hotel—out in the middle of nowhere. It was later bought by the Hiltons but today is the Le Meridien Dead Sea Hotel. At Ein Bokek, we turned left, heading for Arad and in the general direction of Beersheba where we stopped briefly to visit the "camel market" where one can buy camels and sheep, although most visitors prefer the copperware, or spices, cloth, embroidered cushions, and more.

Being in Beersheba just seemed so weird to me. It's a biblical place name with which I've been familiar since a kid. Like Bethlehem. To be in Beersheba and Bethlehem and Jerusalem was like being inside the covers of a 4,000 year old history book. A sense of the unreal. Can one's mind telescope back that far in time to imagine Abraham and his company migrated this far south making Beersheba home for a while? It was here Sarah booted Hagar and the son she'd had with Abraham out into the "wilderness of Beersheba." Abraham's well is still visible in the area, although we didn't see it ourselves. The city today is the capital of the Negev Desert region.

North of Beersheba we connected with the Hebron highway. We were stopped by Israeli soldiers at a checkpoint. They advised us to turn back. "It's a bit dangerous," they said. Turning back would've meant a lengthy detour up to Tel Aviv and back. Since the soldiers did not order us to turn around, we drove on.

Shortly thereafter we wondered if we'd made the right decision.

"I wonder if we've made the right decision," I mumbled as we drove into a little village south of Hebron.

"Actually, *we* didn't make this decision," Jeanie correctly pointed out.

Evidently the markets had just closed because there was a great deal of activity and driving became difficult—not because there were so many cars but because there were so many people. As we peered ahead, the street was filled with people making the road completely invisible. People walking, riding bicycles, pulling carts, tapping sheep or leading goats, women with lambs slung over their shoulders, vendors carrying produce. We needed a "Red Sea" miracle here as I dipped the car into a sea of Palestinians as light began to fade from day, as sand seeps through an hourglass.

Soon we were surrounded by people. I checked the rear view mirror: Saw nothing but people. To the left, right, and ahead: People. Then they noticed us.

"Boys, roll up your windows!" I said. Jeanie was already getting hers up. Not a moment too soon. Beggars and trinket-sellers now began tapping on our windows wanting us to buy something.

"We're never going to get out of here," Jeanie said, amazed, staring firmly straight ahead. She couldn't look at the faces inches away from her pressed against her window, their noses like pig snouts against the glass. The boys cowered in the back seats.

"The secret is to keep moving, keep honking, and keep hoping," I said, as though I'd done this many times. Moving, honking and hoping: the strategy got us through this village although it took us twenty minutes to do it. As we came out of this sea of people and applied some speed we realized how tense our bodies were. We had to consciously relax our muscles, take some deep breaths before we felt okay again.

"Crack your windows, boys," I suggested. "Let's get some fresh air in here."

❧❧❧

We got lost in Hebron. This city is a flashpoint for Israelis and Palestinians because of its historic importance. It is mentioned frequently in the Old Testament, especially Genesis, and is the site of the Tomb of Abraham, a holy place for both Muslims and Jews.

We asked some soldiers for directions and soon found the highway and it wasn't long before we were nearing Bethlehem. Rather than take the new bypass road which was built so that Israelis could bypass Bethlehem and go directly to Jerusalem (and indeed, Israelis are barred from entering Bethlehem for the indefinite future fearing possible protests or violence) we decided to go into Bethlehem since this was the first day after the city was reopened.

December 23, 1995

I swam in the Dead Sea which is 1,200 feet below sealevel. In the Dead Sea I can float without treading water in water that's ten feet deep. We went to Masada in a cable car. We got pulled over by a soldier that had a machine gun and asked for our passports. I thought it was neat when the soldier came up. I got covered in mud by the lifeguard. I thought the mud felt good.   —*Taylor, 10*

It was an unbelievable scene. The checkpoint was a mass of cars, beeping horns, and soldiers dressed in black boots, green dungarees, and beret, and armed to the teeth were everywhere, with tanks nearby on standby.

It was crazy. We were flagged on, stopped, flagged on and stopped again. A soldier approached us and asked for our passports.

"Who are you?" he asked, as I handed him my documents. This soldier had some rank. He was older, in his forties I think, and had some girth to him. I suspected he was in charge of some aspect of the operations going on right now. I also knew that Yasser Arafat was in town, so I wasn't surprised to see the strong military presence, and I also knew that the Israelis wanted nothing to happen to the Palestinian leader.

"He motioned for the boys to get out of the water ... and then he smeared some of this black Dead Sea mineral mud, supposed to have wonderful medicinal, healing qualities, all over their bodies."—p. 271

"We're from the U.S. on sabbatical," I said.

"You're staying in Bethlehem?" he said.

"At Tantur."

He didn't really look at my passport. He leaned forward peering into the car to give my passengers the once-over, first Jeanie and then the boys in the backseat.

"It's a good picture, don't you think?" I asked.

"What?"

"My passport picture."

"Honey—" Jeanie interjecting. Seemed to me like she'd done a lot of "honey-ing" on this trip.

"Wait," he said. He looked at my passport again, and laughed. "Good picture."

He returned my passport. "Have a good time. Be careful."

So we went on into town.

But the traffic was impossible. We had thought we might have supper in Bethlehem, but abandoned that idea fast. Parking was not an option. Palestinians were in the streets whooping and hollering and waving the new flag of the Palestinian National Authority.

"This is no time for estrogen or for 'listening to the feminine side of my nature'," I said. "There's nothing but testosterone on these streets right now, and it's going to take some testosterone to get us out of here."

"So a woman couldn't drive through this?" Jeanie asked pointedly.

"Hey, I'll pull over, and you drive," I offered.

"No thanks," she said.

To drive in Bethlehem at the height of this Palestinian exuberance required massive doses of testosterone, as I was saying. Cars were darting in and out of traffic and we saw Arab drivers sunk low in their Mercedes with the red *keffiyeh* wrapped around their faces, two hands gripping the wheel and with Allah as their co-pilot. We either got out of the way, or honked our horn and drove straight at them, swerving at the last minute. No hesitation here, no consideration of options, no polite deference to the other guy, no time for driving manners. We had one objective and one objective alone: to get our vehicle through the bedlam quicker, sooner, faster than anyone else. No being nice and allowing the other guy to cut in front of us. It was a cut-in or be cut-out world right now. This was not an occasion to be nice: we'd not be thanked by the person who cuts in, and we'd be cursed by the irate driver behind us whom we'd cut off. In Bethlehem, right now on these streets, there was no "peace on earth, good will toward all."

When we went through the Israeli checkpoint on the other side, we weren't clear just how far we would need to travel to get to Tantur. But when we looked around, we recognized the intersection. The checkpoint was right below Tantur. We were home!

We had hamburgers and corn for supper!

---

[1]For more on the life of David Watt Torrance, see Appendix IV.

52

Hezekiah's Tunnel

O NE DAY, WE WENT OUT TO THE BUS STOP BELOW TANTUR and rode an Arab bus into Jerusalem. We got off at Jaffa Gate and then walked through the Armenian quarter to Zion Gate where one can still see the results of the Six-Day War in 1967 in the rocket-shelled walls. This is also the location where Count Raymond of Toulouse breached the walls during the First Crusade in 1099. Anyway, from there we walked along the walls and then down a hill toward the Kidron Valley to the pool of Siloam.

Here we were to begin our hike through Hezekiah's Tunnel.

The bore is not more than 30 inches wide and the height varies from 10 feet to five feet in some places. When we walked through it, the water depth came only to our knees. At different points during the day, the water level rose considerably, depending upon what was happening in the spring. That concerned us somewhat.

"This is safe?" Jeanie asked the Arab man sitting at a little wood table. The green paint was peeling off revealing bare wood beneath. From the table hung a sign with black letters on a white background. The words were written in Hebrew and I had managed to get through seminary and through a doctoral program without learning Hebrew. The sign probably said, "This is safe."

"Yes, yes, safe," he said, passing his hand over his unshaved chin. The whiskers on his three day growth were white like the bristles on a tile brush, and contrasted sharply with the deep leather hue of his skin. "Very safe. No problem."

"How long—to walk—to the other side?" I asked. I was fumbling around for some shekels. I needed to pay the man.

"You walk twenty minutes. No problem," he said. I gave him some money and he gave me four candles not more than a third inch thick and about five inches long. These candles were to provide light for the twenty minutes it would take to slosh through Hezekiah's tunnel.

"Boys, why don't you just take off your pants and I'll carry them in my pack to keep them dry?" Spenser immediately began to de-pants himself, but Taylor stood there.

"Okay," I said to him, "roll up your pant-legs."

I had shorts on, Taylor and Jeanie rolled up their pant legs, and Spenser stood there in his Ninja Turtle skivvies. The little man smiled at us. We walked down a flight of stone steps to a small dark opening, and stepped into the water and then set out into the darkness, candles flickering. This was not an experience for those who get claustrophobic. We felt like explorers in an Indiana Jones movie. I warned the boys not to spring a secret door in the rock or else we'd slide into a pit of vipers.

"No we won't," said Taylor, ever the skeptic. But there was a quaver in his voice.

Our candles illuminated only the tunnel a few feet at a time. Most of the time we were slightly bent over and the shaft was not high enough to accommodate our height. After ten minutes of wading through the water, I began to think this trip might take longer than twenty minutes. I decided to blow out my candle. Since I was the last one—Spenser went first, then his mother, followed by Taylor and me—I had no trouble following Jeanie and the boys. Besides, I thought we might need my candle if the others' went out. After fifteen minutes of sloshing through the tunnel, following its curves and bouncing against its cold sides, ducking to avoid bumping our heads, I noticed that Jeanie was getting a little edgy.

"Would you like to hear some of the history of the tunnel?" I asked, hoping to distract them from any feelings of panic and claustrophobia they might be experiencing.

"No," said Taylor.

"Sure," said Jeanie.

"Well," I began, clearing my throat importantly, "almost 3,000 years ago there was this kingdom called the Assyrian empire. It's located sort of where Syria and Iraq is today. They marched west and destroyed the northern kingdom of Israel in 723 BC. After they did this, they had the bright idea that they could also conquer the little kingdom of Judea to the south as well. But the Jewish king—his name was Hezekiah—had been afraid something like this would happen. He knew that if an enemy attacked them, the first thing the enemy would do would be to cut off the water supply to the city. Back in those days the water supply for Jerusalem came from the spring of Siloam where we got into this tunnel. So King Hezekiah also had a bright idea, a brilliant idea.

Since the Gihon spring that fed the pool of Siloam was outside the walls at the time, making the city vulnerable during a siege, he had his engineers carve a 2,000 foot tunnel from the pool to within the walls. They then sunk a shaft to the end of the tunnel so that they could access the water after which they also plugged the exterior access to the spring. They now had water inside the city, although the source was outside the city. Pretty cool, huh?"

Nobody said anything. So I continued. "The engineers began at opposite ends, and met in the middle, 2,700 years ago. When they met, they wrote an inscription celebrating the event, and the inscription is in the Archeological Museum in Istanbul today because when the Ottoman Turks were still occupying Palestine they took it."

"Like they stole it?" Spenser asked.

"Sorta, kind of," I said. "It was an amazing feat of engineering for those days."

Twenty minutes elapsed and we were still in the tunnel and no there was no indication that we were close to the end. Twenty-five minutes passed, thirty minutes and now the candles were just about out. Spenser's did burn out and we had only Jeanie's and Taylor's. Thirty-five minutes.

"We just about out of candles," Taylor said nervously.

"I think you should blow yours out," I said. So he did.

"Are we ever going to get out of here?" Jeanie muttered?

"Are we lost?" Taylor asked.

"We're going to get out of here," I said brightly. "The end is near! And no we're not lost. How can we get lost? There's only one way, to go. Right, buddy?"

"Straight ahead," said Taylor.

"Straight ahead," I said.

Jeanie's candle was just about gone, and I was about to produce my candle when, at forty minutes, we felt a rush of cool air and heard the sound of water flowing. This development energized our flagging spirits and we pressed on with fresh zeal. Soon we were at the other end of Hezekiah's tunnel!

"Let's do that again!" Spenser said.

53

Bedlam in Bethlehem

ON CHRISTMAS EVE, WE MET MARTIN AND BETTY BAILEY after lunch in their apartment, together with their daughter and her husband (Chris and Bob) and their boys Jimmy, 8, and Jason, 5. I should say something here about the Bailey's. They are both both Ph.D.s, both retired, and both volunteers in Israel, board-appointed by the UCC, not wanting to sit on the front porch of their home in New Jersey, out to pasture, as it were. Martin, is of medium height, balding and what hair he has is gray, but the goatee is very white. His sharp features give him a piercing countenance at times, yet he was quite affable and open, and very cordial to us during our entire visit. Formerly the editor of A.D. magazine and also *UCC News*, Martin worked as a communications coordinator of the National Council of Church. I'm not sure what Betty's field or discipline was at the time, but she as well is very capable and was extremely helpful to us. An anorexic-thin, odd-looking woman, she gave the appearance of being tall, but is not much taller than Martin, if at all. She is one of those persons who's born with a smile creased into the face. Her hair is short and easily kept as she wears it in bangs that are cut evenly much like Moe appeared years ago in the *Three Stooges*. She is no stooge however, and very much knows her way around. We found their friendship delightful and at the conclusion of our visit exchanged addresses, e-mail boxes, etc.

We met them in the airy reception area of the institute, and shortly were off, out the back gate of Tantur, thus avoiding the IDF checkpoint down below. We thought we could walk along the road and catch a ride on an Arab bus which is exactly what we did. The bus, in fact, was empty, and the driver took us all the way to Manger Square.

Our thought was simply to see what was going on and then to walk to the Lutheran church for the service at 5 p.m. Of course, there was a continual commotion and the closer we got to Manger Square the more crowded the conditions. Admittance to the square proper was possible only with a ticket

281

which we did not have. The square is not large—thus the ticket requirement—so we were able to peer over some heads and see much of the action. The Latin patriarch had made a pilgrimage to Bethlehem and was received at Manger Square, and there were all sorts of bands, and school groups marching through the streets and the square itself. An Arab band was playing bagpipes! We moved about, and got caught in an incredible rush of people. This, after all, was their Independence Day! One could easily imagine the Biblical accounts which told of the multitudes pressing upon Jesus as he went from city to city. We were "carried" downstream as it were, toward the square but were able to get off to the side, and the street being elevated somewhat we were able from our viewpoint on the perimeter of the square to witness history unfold.

Palestinian flags were everywhere, giving the appearance of a Fourth of July celebration. A two-story banner of Arafat was draped over one building in the square opposite the police station.

"Do you have a piece of paper?" Betty asked us.

I looked at Jeanie. "You got something, honey?" She reached into her bag and produced a small yellow sheet of lined paper. We gave it to Betty.

"I'm going over to the post office to see if I can get some Palestinian statehood stamps and ask them to cancel them with today's date." It was a great idea!

We waited about forty-five minutes until she'd returned with two yellow sheets, PNA stamps canceled on each of them with the date: December 24, 1995. We have saved these papers for the boys to this very day.

We ambled off in the direction of Redeemer Lutheran Church, sometimes called the "ice cream cone church" because its spire looks like an upside-down sugar cone. The name itself was interesting to us, because at home we lived only five blocks from Bethlehem Redeemer Lutheran Church (Missouri Synod). Now we were visiting Redeemer Lutheran Church in Bethlehem. It's a small thing, but sometimes these small matters catch our attention. The church has transepts and a dome over the altar where the transepts intersect with the nave. However, it's not large; more like a chapel than a cathedral. Not cathedral size at all.

Once again we were caught in shoulder-to-shoulder people traffic—there were more people here per square foot than at a Macy's Christmas sale. We made it to the church without losing children. When we walked in about 4:15 p.m., the sanctuary was empty. We sat down near the front and read the worship bulletin carefully. The service was to be in Arabic, German and English so we anticipated it taking quite a while. As it turned out, the pastor, an Arab, gave the message, a Lutheran bishop from Jordan delivered a message and the pastor of the Lutheran church in Jerusalem, an American, gave a message. Lots of messages on this important Night of Messages.

As the service was about to begin—the nave was now crammed with worshippers, many latecomers seeking a place to sit making embarrassed inquiries as to whether "this seat is taken?", "is anyone sitting there?"—we heard a commotion at the rear. I usually resolve not to be distracted by such things, but this time it was different. Suha Arafat, the blond, young, Christian wife of the Palestinian president was escorted to some reserved seats in the front where she and her small entourage—which included not only security people but a moustached member of the cabinet in the newly formed Palestinian National Authority government—encamped. This caused quite a stir as photographers, only a lens or two short of being *paparazzi*, determined to seize the moment. They circled like cawing vultures, lights flashing and shutters whirring, and she sat through it all near the Christmas tree looking neither here nor there, enduring it with the patience of one who has come to expect this sort of attention and finds it amusing in a patronizing way. Suha, today no longer a Christian, converting to Islam after the birth of their child, is tall, certainly taller than Yasser, and thin and long of face, with eyes that are warm but drooping and the whole effect suggests a muleish but not unpleasant appearance. Her hair, blond as I mentioned, is long and her hairdressers had taken considerable pains *to use her own hair* to fashion a bow atop her head in a school girl manner. It made her look a little ridiculous. This detail, about it being her own hair, had escaped my attention. But Jeanie noticed.

When the service began,[1] the paparazzi retreated, the choir began with the singing of "Once in Royal David's City" and we were then welcomed in three languages. The Micah reading was read in German, the reading from Isaiah 9 was in Arabic, the reading from Isaiah 11 was in English, and the Gospel reading from Luke 2 was in Arabic (vv. 1-7), English (vv. 8-14) and German (vv. 15-20). Prayers of Intercession were in all three languages. The Lord's Prayer was said in our individual languages, a holy babel of petition. We departed following the singing of "Silent Night, Holy Night."

Like any church service, an offering was taken. In this case the offering was designated for Palestinian prisoners in Israeli prisons.

As I suspected, the worship was long, sometimes tedious, but meaningful nonetheless on many levels, especially when the wife of the Palestinian pastor sang "O Little Town of Bethlehem."

O little town of Bethlehem, how still we see thee lie!
Above thy deep and dreamless sleep the silent stars go by.
Yet in thy dark streets shineth the everlasting Light;

283

The hopes and fears of all the years are met in thee tonight.

As she sang, every atom of air in the church was charged with emotional voltage. Her quavering voice was not particularly beautiful. She clearly was not a trained singer. So we sat very much conscious not of her voice and the beauty of the rendition itself but of the *words*, and their poignant meaning on this historic night. That—coupled with the innocence of a simple woman singing a hymn of faith—brought tears to just about everyone.

Our Christmas Eve observance, however, was not complete. Following the service, we caught two buses back to Tantur where we were able to get a quick bite to eat. Then, we were off on a rented Mercedes bus for the Fields of the Shepherds where we were to participate in a mass in one of the ancient grottos there.

We piled on the bus and drove out side the walls of the Tantur Ecumencial Institute but when we arrived at Gilo Junction just below us, we saw scores of the IDF with automatic weapons cocked and aimed. Two anti-riot tanks with water cannons had taken positions and were supported by mounted police, armored trucks, and other military paraphernalia. Orthodox Jews were staging a protest against the remanding of Bethlehem to the Palestinian National Authority and were now marching on the checkpoint where the IDF had set up a roadblock to ensure that Israeli citizens were unable to get into Bethlehem. At that time they were barred from entering any West Bank city. As we watched these developements, illuminated by the glow of amber intersection street lights, the IDF turned the water canons on the protesters sending them sprawling on their backs, their feet and hands all akimber.

Because of this problem, the bus driver was not able to take the route to the Fields of the Shepherds that he wanted and instead had to drive through Bethlehem itself which—on this the eve of the Savior's birth, or the celebration of it—was one huge traffic snarl. Traffic was worse than the Boston Dig at 5 p.m. It therefore took us two hours and 15 minutes to go seven miles.

We were to worship at 9 p.m.. It was now 10:30 p.m. The Fields are "managed" by the Franciscans, and organizations, churches, etc., can reserve certain grottos for a certain time. We were not sure that we would be able to worship as we planned. However, everyone else was having the same transportation problem and therefore we were able to worship as we had hoped.

To spend Christmas Eve in a grotto of the Shepherd's Fields was an indescribably sacred moment. We descended a stone stairway into one of the caves—ancient grottos used as shelters for shepherds tending their flocks, or as pens for the sheep and goats—to have our service. The cave was not cavernous. It could accommodate about thirty people, tops. We sat on small straight-back wooden chairs. The ceiling of the cave at its apex was not more than eight feet high. A stone floor had been installed. We dragged chairs, scrapping them across the granite floors until they were arranged to our liking, and quietly took our seats. Light was provided by candles placed in niches in the cave walls and by those on the cloth-draped altar. Incense caught our nostrils and reminded us of one of the ancient uses of incense: to sweeten the air in worship spaces that during the week were often used as barns and stalls for animals.

The service was led by Father Tom Sharansky, Director of the Tantur Ecumenical Institute. Shortly after it began, Martin read the Scripture:

In those days a decree went out from Emperor Augustus that all the world should be registered. This was the first registration and was taken while Quirinius was governor of Syria. All went to their own towns to be registered. Joseph also went from the town of Nazareth in Galilee to Judea, to the city of David called Bethlehem, because he was descended from the house and family of David. He went to be registered with Mary, to whom he was engaged and who was expecting a child. While they were there, the time came for her to deliver her child. And she gave birth to her firstborn son and wrapped him in bands of cloth, and laid him in a manger, because there was no place for them in the inn.

I confess my mind wandered as I sat there with my beautiful wife and two little boys. I squeezed her hand. I wondered how this trip would change our lives. The stitching in this little patchwork family had been tugged and pulled, but over a five month period, it had held fast. In fact, it was tighter now than ever. I looked down at Spenser on my left and Taylor on my right. Spense was playing with his fingers and looking around. Taylor was watching the priest intently. I glanced over to Jeanie. Her eyes were closed and head bowed. I wondered what she was thinking. Perhaps she wasn't thinking at all. Perhaps, unlike me, she was entirely focused on the reading of the Scripture, listening for the word of the Lord to her on this holiest of nights. But I was thinking about her, not about the birth of the baby Jesus. What a wonderful mother she was to these boys. And what a gift to me she was as a wife and friend. Her patience and steadiness was such a valuable contrast to my flammable nature. She was the oil of gladness, a balm for our tired spirits; I was usually a stream of petrol looking for a match. She'd endured much, loved me resolutely and with passion. She'd balanced her duties as a mother, her love as a wife and had managed to feed her own soul as well. She was remarkable! I was not worthy of such love and loyalty.

In that region there were shepherds living in the fields, keeping watch over their flock by night. Then an angel of the Lord stood before them, and the glory of the Lord shone around them, and they were terrified. But the angel said to them, 'Do not be afraid; for see—I am bringing you good news of great joy for all the people: to you is born this day in the city of David a Saviour, who is the Messiah, the Lord. This will be a sign for you: you will find a child wrapped in bands of cloth and lying in a manger.' And suddenly there was with the angel a multitude of the heavenly host, praising God and saying,

> *'Glory to God in the highest heaven,*
> *and on earth peace among those whom he favours!'*

Martin's reading jerked my thinking in another direction. Now I remembered the Christmas Eve services at a little country church in Colorado where I was the pastor. Every Christmas Eve, the Luke account of the Christmas Story was recited—not by a child from Sunday school, but by a pioneer resident of the Henderson community who was in her 80s. It was a tradition to invite Fredda Kallsen to tell the story again. Year after year, she would quote by memory the very text Martin was now reading. The Christmas Eve service was the most well-attended service of the year in that rural area. People from a ten-mile radius of the church came out to sit in the candlelight, hear the children recite, listen to Eldon Cooper sing "O Holy Night," and wait for the moment when Fredda would stand alone in front of the altar, flanked by two large candles, and tell us again the story of the baby wrapped in "swaddling" clothes and "lying in a manger." Her version was always the King James.

Perhaps this grotto was the very cave where the shepherd's that night had gathered to discuss what it was they'd seen and heard. It was possible, wasn't it?

> *When the angels had left them and gone into heaven, the shepherds said to one another, 'Let us go now to Bethlehem and see this thing that has taken place, which the Lord has made known to us.' So they went with haste and found Mary and Joseph, and the child lying in the manger. When they saw this, they made known what had been told them about this child; and all who heard it were amazed at what the shepherds told them. But Mary treasured all these words and pondered them in her heart. The shepherds returned, glorifying and praising God for all they had heard and seen, as it had been told them.*

Father Tom had a meditation and officiated of course at the mass itself. We're not Catholic, but Father Tom invited us to take Communion—it was an ecumenical institute after all—so we, too, including the boys, stood before the Father for the wafer and the cup.

After the singing of a carol, we returned to our temporary home on a hillock outside of Bethlehem. We went to the "Bethlehem Room" of the Institute, so-called because the balcony afforded a spacious view of this ancient and sleepy town. We stepped out on this veranda, and breathed deeply the midnight air, cool as promises kept and dreams fulfilled. Our long trip was now at a regretable close. We interlocked our arms and gazed upon the little town of Bethlehem bright with pale lights flickering, a town situated beneath a night sky spangled with spreading fireworks dropping like flaming bangles of blessing upon this oft-beleaguered village. The magi had but a single nova to guide them; we had an entire pyrotechnic display that left no doubt as to the site of Bethlehem or the great news that the Palestinians were celebrating on this night.

We watched in silence. Then—

"I love you," Jeanie whispered.

"I love you, too," I said.

---

[1]Participants in the service:

Bishop Naim Nasser, Evangelical Lutheran Church of Jordan

Rev.Mitri Raheb, Pastor, Lutheran Christmas Church, Bethlehem

Propst Karl-Heinz Ronecker, German Propst in Jerusalem, Lutheran Church of the Redeemer

Rev. John C. Melin, Pastor, English-Speaking Congregation, Lutheran Church of the Redeemer, Jerusalem.

Choir of the English-Speaking Congregation, Lutheran Church of the Redeemer, Jerusalem, Barbara Melin, Director

Viola Raheb, Vocal Soloist

Martin Boyadgian, French Horn Soloist

Gesa Luckhof, Organist

Epilogue

MARRIED OVER FIFTEEN YEARS NOW, JEANIE AND I ARE STILL crazy about each other. We've continued to travel, and in 2006, Jeanie even went to a remote area of India under the mountainous brow of Nepal in the Manapur province without me, traveling with some teaching colleagues to conduct workshops in Churachandpour for Indian teachers of English.

But the Adventure of 1995 will always top our list of favorite memories. They seemed shrouded now and when we revisit them, it's like peering through a silk screen at a sacred relic. The images are locked in time, and silent, although if we stop and close our eyes, we can hear distant echoes, perhaps of the boys yelling "Trick or treat," —but even then the voices have taken on a higher, tinnier pitch as though bouncing back to us through a long cylindrical pipe.

We departed Ben Gurion Airport in Tel Aviv on December 28 and returned to Istanbul. Jean Nilson had put out the Christmas presents we had pre-arranged with her to do so, and so we had our little Christmas a few days late. She and Paul also left some presents for Jeanie and me. She gave Jeanie a beautiful silk scarf since she figured Jeanie would need to dress in a civilized way—sometime. And a tie for me.

January 6, 1996, we were back in the United States where the inmates were running the asylum: The government had been shut down for almost three weeks. The lights were off and no one tending the store. On this very day, however, Congress agree to put 280,000 federal employees back to work, and to provide back pay to another 400,000 who were working without pay. A fine state of affairs. Headstones for veterans were on back order, loans were unprocessed, and Republicans were rattling sabers, threatening to shut down the governent again if more progress wasn't made to balance the budget.

We continued to home school the boys for the rest of the 1995-1996 school term. In the fall they returned to Dennison Elementary school in grades 3 and 5.

Today, Spenser is tall, still tending to blond hair which he keeps short. His features have sharpened as has his wit. His smile is broad and welcoming; his spirit, unrelentingly cheerful. He sports a shoulder tatoo at the base of his neck that reads VIRITUS, and he has a smaller one on the inside of his left arm which is the Chinese character for "Little Brother." He's a junior at Metropolitan State College in Denver working on a degree in Criminal Justice. He's also interested in screen-writing, and film work, and his musical talents turned in the direction of singing. A fine tenor voice, he was in several musicals in high school, including the lead role in *Footloose*.

The summer between seventh and eight grade, Taylor exploded out of the chubbiness to which he tended as a pre-adolescent. He shot up to six-foot-four over the next few years. Today's he's a big scuffy guy—longish hair and spotty beard—and sports some tat work as well. One simply reads: Romans 12:21. The text says, "Be not overcome with evil, but overcome evil with good." On the inside of his left arm is the Chinese character for "Big Brother." He's as gentle as a teddy bear and spends his time working primarily with youth in church settings. He was very active in high school, playing center on the basketball team, having the good fortune to go the state tournament with his team as underdogs and win it all in his senior year. He went on to Baylor University, in Waco, Texas, and graduated in 2008. He worked for three summers during college as a youth pastor for Rockland Community Church in the mountains above Denver. Now he's considering seminary, and is in youth ministry at a church in the Denver area. He's been team leader on several mission trips, including one to Romania. He's also developed a strong interest in photography, producing PowerPoint slides with Scripture verses, or black-and-white poster art with Christian themes.

Jeanie was back in college within a couple weeks of our arrival home and studied continuously from January, 1996, to August, 1997, including two summer semesters, taking full loads, to graduate after the summer session of 1997. The day after graduation, she began her teaching career as a third grade teacher in Jefferson County Schools, Colorado. A couple of years later, she added a Masters of Counseling to her résumé.

Within a year of our return, I took a position with Communication Resources, Inc., a publisher of resources for churches and church leaders. A couple years later I was the Executive Editor of *Homiletics*, a preaching journal. I also wrote a couple of books. In 2000, I returned on a part time basis to the church I had served from 1984 to 1990, Henderson Community Church, north of Denver, as their interim pastor, and stayed until 2007.

In August of 2007, the boys both in university, Jeanie and I moved to Shanghai, China, where Jeanie had accepted a position at the Shanghai American School (www.saschina.org). I continue to function as editor of *Homiletics*, and she teaches fourth grade. The school gave me a position in the Communications Office. For now, China is our home.

Mic and Sally returned to Istanbul, but a couple of years later, Sally passed away suddenly. We deeply mourned her death. Göksel married a Dutch girl who was working on a Ph.D. and studying in Istanbul and he now lives in Utretch, the Netherlands, and has two beautiful little girls. We learned that the noun fairy was none other than Norma Daly, who, along with her husband Keith, had loaned us the four red backpacks they themselves had used when they'd traveled around the world with their kids. Grandmother Barbara continues to reside in Denver, not far from the University of Denver where, over the years, she taught psychology at a number of colleges, including Regis University. She received her licensure as a chaplain, and today continues to maintain a full teaching schedule as well as a private practice as a family therapist. She's continued to travel, including a trip to Israel and Jordan.

I should interject a couple of events that happened in the days immediately following our Christmas Eve in the grotto. We visited the Church of the Nativity in Manger Square, first built by Helen, the mother of Constantine, in the fourth century. But the Christmas Day highlight was a dinner for all the staff and guests of Tantur at no charge!

We entered the banquet hall where folding tables were set up in a U-shape with another long table in the center parallel to the two arms of the U. On this latter table were all the goodies of an old-fashioned Christmas dinner: cranberry sauce, salads, rolls, yams, stuffing. All there, I say, except for the turkey. After we were seated, the chef came out bearing a large platter on which was a gorgeous roasted bird. He paraded in front of the tables with this turkey to our wild and enthusiastic applause and set the bird down on the head table as a centerpiece. He left and quickly returned with another platter of turkey meat. He had cooked two birds! One for show, one for chow.

December 29, 1995

Timothy did a service for us. I saw a Scripture Garden. It has a donkey, a lake and a quarry. I rode in a BIG airplane! I learned how people make olive oil. Having a service by Jesus' tomb made me feel warm. —Spenser, 8

At each table were bottles of wine, a red and white for our choosing. It was wonderful and delicious. Behind us, a Christmas tree was sparkling with festive ornaments and soft lights. It was a joyous occasion and we had more than we could eat, of course. Even Jeanie's appetite had returned.

But the best was yet to come. After we had had our fill, the lights were dimmed and the chef brought out a tray of the traditional Christmas pudding which he makes two years ahead of time. It was now produced for our eating pleasure, and as we watched in the dim candlelight, he poured rum atop the pudding and then lit it! Again, there was loud applause and a great clamoring that the pudding should be brought over to this table or that table. We all had our fill and then, when the eating was over we retired to the Bethlehem room for the singing of carols, drinking of coffee and conversation. It was wonderful, wonderful, if not very different, Christmas.

Finally, we also made it to the Garden Tomb. Vivi, the house matron at Tantur had given us a bottle of wine, about a third left. Our little family, had communion together by the empty tomb. I led the liturgy and the boys each read a passage of Scripture. We had a roll of bread and the wine was fine. Then we left.

January 6, 1996, we drove the Lumina into Colorado, and then rolled into Denver. As we turned down Bell Court, Taylor said, "We're almost home!"

"We've never left home, Taylor."

"Are we lost?" he said, joking.

"No Taylor, we're not lost."

We walked into the Bell Court house. I looked at him, tousled his hair, and then drew him close to me. Jeanie pulled in with Spenser. We gathered for a long hug in the sun room.

"We most certainly are found," I said.

Maybe Taylor was right.

We were home.

Appendix I

The Best and Worst Of

		SPENSER	TAYLOR	JEANIE	TFM
BEST CITY		VENICE	ISTANBUL		
BEST SUBWAY		PARIS			
HOTEL	BEST	FLORENCE	ROME	FARM	
	WORST	???	KOZANI	KOZANI	
BED	BEST	FLORENCE	FERRY	FARM	FARM
	WORST	THE FLOOR/ PARIS	THE FLOOR/ PARIS	ST. MALO	FERRY
BREAKFAST	BEST	PAIN DU CHOC.	CHAMBERY	ROME	
	WORST	CROISSANTS W/CHEESE	KONITSA	???	
ELEVATORS	BEST	THESSALONIKI		???	ROME
	WORST	WHEN WE DIDN'T HAVE ONE		IOANNIA	???
OUTDOOR VIEW		BRONZE DOORS	ST. PETER'S	MATTERHORN	
MOST EXCITING MOMENT		DISNEYLAND	TRAIN TO FLORENCE	PIETA/ DAVID	MATTER-HORN
BEST MUSEUM		SISTINE CHAPEL	SISTINE CHAPEL	D'ORSAY	LOUVRE
PIZZA	BEST	VENICE		???	
	WORST	VENICE		???	
BEST SHOWER		FARM	PARIS	FARM	
MARKETS	BEST	???		PARIS	
	WORST	FLORENCE		???	

		SPENSER	TAYLOR	JEANIE	TIMOTHY
TOILETS	BEST	KOZANI	FERRY	FARM	FARM
	WORST	KOZANI BUS STOP	REST STOP IN LOIRE VALLEY	REST STOP IN LOIRE VALLEY	BUS STATIONS
TRIP	BEST	FERRY		TRAIN TO ZERMATT	PLANE
	WORST	TRAIN TO FLORENCE		TRAIN TO FLORENCE	BUS TO KOZANI
WEATHER	BEST	FERRY	FERRY	PARIS	???
	WORST	???	FIRST NIGHT AT FARM	SECOND DAY VENICE	SECOND DAY VENICE
BEST CHURCH		THESSALONIKI		CHARTRES	SANTA CROCE
BEST PARK		BOIS DE BOULOGNE/ PARIS		LUXEM-BOURG	MONCEAU
BEST SQUARE		ARISTOTLE		"HEAD" PARK	ST. MARK'S
BEST PAINTING		LAST JUDGMENT			???
BEST SCULPTURE		THE DAVID			
MOST FUN THING		EURODISNEY		???	TRAM TO MATTER-HORN
BEST CEMETERY		PROTESTANT CEMETERY IN ROME		PERE LA CHAISE/PARIS	
BEST HOT CHOCOLATE		FARM		???	
BEST RESTAURANT		BURGHY		FLORENCE	
BEST MEAL		ROME	FERRY	ZERMATT	
BEST TV		LA SPEZIA		???	
BEST MOVIE		PARIS			
BEST BRIDGE		RIALTO			
BEST BOAT		FERRY		???	TRAGHETTO
BEST BOOK		POOH	SWISS FAMILY ROBINSON	AUSTEN/ PRIDE & PREDJUDICE	WILLA CATHER
BEST TV SHOW		FORT BOYARD IN PARIS		???	

Appendix II

The Church of the Holy Sepulchre

The Church of the Holy Sepulchre, known as the Church of the Resurrection (Anastasis) to Eastern Orthodox Christians, is a Christian church in the Old City of Jerusalem.

It stands on a site that encompasses both Golgotha, or Calvary, where Jesus was crucified, and the tomb (sepulchre) where he was buried.

The Church of the Holy Sepulchre has been an important pilgrimage destination since the 4th century, and it remains the holiest Christian site in the world.

Unlike many historical sacred sites, which often turn out to be based more on pious tradition than historical fact, most historians and archaeologists say the Church of the Holy Sepulchre is likely to be located over the actual tomb of Christ. The most important supporting evidence is as follows: [1]

In the early 1st century AD the site was a disused quarry outside the city walls. Tombs dated to the 1st centuries BC and AD had been cut into the vertical west wall left by the quarrymen.

The topographical elements of the church's site are compatible with the Gospel descriptions, which say that Jesus was crucified on rock that looked like a skull outside the city (John 19:17) and there was a grave nearby (John 19:41-2). Windblown earth and seeds watered by winter rains would have created the green covering on the rock that John calls a "garden."

The Christian community of Jerusalem held worship services at the site until 66 AD (according to historians Eusebius and Socrates Scholasticus).

Even when the area was brought within the city walls in 41-43 AD it was not built over by the local inhabitants.

The Roman Emperor Hadrian built a Temple of Venus over the site in 135 AD, which could be an indication that the site was regarded as holy by Christians and Hadrian wished to claim the site for traditional Roman religion.

The local tradition of the community would have been scrutinized carefully when Constantine set out to build his church in 326 AD, because the chosen site was inconvenient and expensive. Substantial buildings had to be torn down, most notably the temple built over the site by Hadrian. Just to the south was a spot that would have been otherwise perfect - the open space of Hadrian's forum.

The eyewitness historian Eusebius claimed that in the course of the excavations, the original memorial was discovered. (Life of Constantine 3:28)

Based on the above factors, the Oxford Archaeological Guide to the Holy Land concludes: "Is this the place where Christ died and was buried? Very probably, Yes."

Israeli scholar Dan Bahat, former City Archaeologist of Jerusalem, has said this of the Church: "We may not be absolutely certain that the site of the Holy Sepulchre Church is the site of Jesus' burial, but we have no other site that can lay a claim nearly as weighty, and we really have no reason to reject the authenticity of the site."[2]

The early Christian community of Jerusalem appears to have held liturgical celebrations at Christ's tomb from the time of the resurrection until the city was taken by the Romans in 66 AD. Less than a century later, in 135 AD, Emperor Hadrian filled in the quarry to provide a level foundation for a temple to Aphrodite.

The site remained buried beneath the pagan temple until Emperor Constantine the Great converted to Christianity in 312 AD. He soon showed an interest in the holy places associated with his new faith, and commissioned numerous churches to be built throughout the Holy Land. The most important of these, the Church of the Holy Sepulchre, was begun in 326 AD.

Constantine's builders dug away the hillside to leave the rock-hewn tomb of Christ isolated and with enough room to built a church around it. They also cleared away Hadrian's temple and the material with which an old quarry had been filled to provide the temple's foundations. In the process, according to contemporary Christian historians, the Rock of Golgotha was found. The Church was formally dedicated in 335 with an oration by Constantine's biographer, Eusebius of Caesarea.

In the course of the excavations, Constantine's mother St. Helena is believed to have discovered the True Cross near the tomb. She actually discovered three - those of the two thieves and that of Christ. To discern the one belonging to Christ, a sick man was brought to touch to each one, and he was miraculous healed by one of them. This is a relatively early legend, but one that Eusebius, the historian and contemporary of Constantine, did not know.

The Constantinian Church of the Holy Sepulchre was much larger than the one that stands today, but its layout was simple. It consisted of an atrium (which reused part of Hadrian's temenos wall), a covered basilica, an open courtyard with the stone of Golgotha in the southeast corner, and the tomb of Christ, enshrined in a small, circular edifice. The tomb of Christ was not completed at the dedication because of the immense labor involved in cutting away the rock cliff in order to isolate the tomb; it was completed around 384 AD.

This building was severely damaged by fire in 614 AD when the Persians invaded Jerusalem. They also captured the True Cross, but in 630, Emperor Heraclius marched triumphantly into Jerusalem and restored the True Cross to the rebuilt Church of the Holy Sepulchre. The church was reconstructed under the patriarch Modestus with no major changes to the original plan.

In 638, the Christians were forced to surrender Jerusalem to Muslim control under caliph Omar. In a remarkable gesture for the time, Omar refused to pray in the Church of the Holy Sepulchre, saying, "If I had prayed in the church it would have been lost to you, for the Believers [Muslims] would have taken it saying: Omar prayed here." This act of generosity would have unfortunate consequences, however.

The Church of the Holy Sepulchre continued to function as a Christian church under the protection of Omar and the early Muslim rulers, but this changed on October 18, 1009, when the "mad" Fatimid caliph Hakim brutally and systematically destroyed the great church.

Ironically, if Omar had turned the church into a mosque, Hakim would have left it alone. But instead, Hakim had wrecking crews knock over the walls and he attacked the tomb of Christ with pricks and hammers, stopping only when the debris covered the remains. The east and west walls were completely destroyed, but the north and south walls were likely protected by the rubble from further damage.

The poor Jerusalem community could not afford repairs, but in 1048 Emperor Constantine Monomachos provided money for reconstruction, subject to stringent conditions imposed by the caliphate. The funds were not adequate to completely repair the original church, however, and a large part of it had to be abandoned. The atrium and the basilica were completely lost; only the courtyard and the rotunda remained. The latter was made into a church by the insertion of a large apse into the facade.

This was the church to which the knights of the First Crusade arrived to sing their Te Deum after capturing Jerusalem on July 15, 1099. The Crusader chief Godfrey of Bouillon, who became the first king of Jerusalem, declared himself Advocatus Sancti Sepulchri, "Defender of the Holy Sepulchre."

The Crusaders were slow to renovate the church, only beginning to make modifications in the Romanesque style in 1112. They first built a monastery where the Constantinian basilica used to be, having first excavated the Crypt of St. Helena. In 1119 the shrine of Christ's tomb was replaced. The coronation of Fulk and Melisende at the church in 1131 necessitated more radical modifications. The Constantinian courtyard was covered with a Romanesque church (dedicated in 1149), which was connected to the rotunda by a great arched opening resulting from the demolition of the 11th-century apse. A bell tower was added in 1170.

The three primary custodians of the church, first appointed when Crusaders held Jerusalem, are the Greek Orthodox, the Armenian Apostolic and Roman Catholic churches. In the 19th century, the Coptic Orthodox, the Ethiopian Orthodox and the Syrian Orthodox acquired lesser responsibilities, which include shrines and other structures within and around the building. An agreement regulates times and places of worship for each Church.

Subsequent centuries were not altogether kind to the Church of the Holy Sepulchre. It suffered from damage, desecration, and neglect, and attempts at repair (a significant renovation was conducted by the Franciscans in 1555) often did more damage than good. In recent times, a fire (1808) and an earthquake (1927) did extensive damage.

Not until 1959 did the three major communities (Latins, Greeks, Armenians) agree on a major renovation plan. The guiding principle was that only elements incapable of fulfilling their structural function would be replaced. Local masons were trained to trim stone in the style of the 11th century for the rotunda, and in the 12th-century style for the church.

The church's chaotic history is evident in what visitors see today. Byzantine, medieval, Crusader, and modern elements mix in an odd mish-mash of styles, and each governing Christian community has decorated its shrines in its own distinctive way. In many ways, the Church of the Holy Sepulchre is not what one would imagine for the holiest site in all Christendom, and it can easily disappoint. But at the same time, its noble history and immense religious importance is such that a visit can also be very meaningful.

— *From www.sacred-destinations.com/israel/jerusalem-church-of-holy-sepulchre.htm. Retrieved May 17, 2008. Used by permission.*

Appendix III

Yad Vashem

Yad Vashem, the Holocaust Martyrs' and Heroes' Remembrance Authority, was established in 1953 by an act of the Israeli Knesset. Since its inception, Yad Vashem has been entrusted with documenting the history of the Jewish people during the Holocaust period, preserving the memory and story of each of the six million victims, and imparting the legacy of the Holocaust for generations to come through its archives, library, school, museums and recognition of the Righteous Among the Nations. Located on Har Hazikaron, the Mount of Remembrance, in Jerusalem, Yad Vashem is a vast, sprawling complex of tree-studded walkways leading to museums, exhibits, archives, monuments, sculptures, and memorials.

Yad Vashem's Information Repositories

The Archive collection, the largest and most comprehensive repository of material on the Holocaust in the world, comprises 68 million pages of documents, nearly 300,000 photographs along with thousands of films and videotaped testimonies of survivors. These may be accessed by the public and read and viewed in the appropriate rooms.

The Library houses some 112,000 titles in many languages, thousands of periodicals and a large number of rare and precious items, establishing itself as the most significant Holocaust library in the world. Holdings may be accessed by the public on site, and residents of Israel are entitled to limited borrowing privileges.

The Hall of Names is a tribute to the victims by remembering them not as anonymous numbers but as individual human beings. The "Pages of Testimony" are symbolic gravestones, which record names and biographical data of millions of martyrs, as submitted by family members and friends. To date Yad Vashem has computerized 3.2 million names of Holocaust victims, compiled from approximately two million Pages of Testimony and various other lists.

Education, Research and Publications

The International School for Holocaust Studies is the only school of its kind in the world. With 17 classrooms, a modern multimedia center, resource and pedagogical center, an auditorium and over 100 educators on its staff, the school caters annually to over 187,000 students from Israel, and thousands of educators from Israel and around the world. Courses for teachers are offered in numerous languages other than Hebrew, and the school also sends its professional staff around the world for the purpose of Holocaust education. The team of experts at the school is developing a variety of educational programmes and study aids on the Holocaust including advanced multimedia programs, maps, books, cassettes and other educational aids.

The International Institute for Holocaust Research coordinates and supports research on national and international levels, organizes conferences and colloquia and publishes a variety of important works on the Holocaust, including memoirs, diaries, historical studies, a scholarly annual and such like.

The Yad Vashem Studies is a series of 35 volumes to date, comprising conference proceedings and scholarly articles on every aspect of the Holocaust.

Yad Vashem Publications has a growing catalogue of Hebrew and English publications including history books, diaries and document collections. Yad Vashem has published over 200 books to date, which constitute the backbone of Holocaust literature in Israeli society. In recent years, 24 books have been published annually.

Museums

The new Holocaust History Museum occupies over 4,200 square meters, mainly underground. Both multidisciplinary and interdisciplinary, it presents the story of the Shoah from a unique Jewish perspective, emphasizing the experiences of the individual victims through original artifacts, survivor testimonies and personal possessions.

The Art Museum is a testimony to the strength of the human spirit and holds the world's largest and most important collection of Holocaust art. It includes works of art that were created under the inconceivably adverse conditions of the Holocaust and a selection of works done after the war by Holocaust survivors and by other artists.

Unique Memorial Sites

The Hall of Remembrance is a solemn tent-like structure which allows visitors to pay their respects to the memories of the martyred dead. On the floor are the names of the six death camps and some of the concentration camps and killing sites throughout Europe. In front of the memorial flame lies a crypt containing ashes of victims. Memorial ceremonies for official visitors are held here.

The Children's Memorial is hollowed out from an underground cavern, where memorial candles, a customary Jewish tradition to remember the dead, are reflected infinitely in a dark and somber space. This memorial is a tribute to the approximately one and a half million Jewish children who perished during the Holocaust.

The Valley of the Communities is a 2.5 acre monument that was dug out from the natural bedrock. Engraved on the massive stone walls of the memorial are the names of over five thousand Jewish communities that were destroyed and of the few that suffered but survived in the shadow of the Holocaust.

The Avenue and Garden of the Righteous Among the Nations honor the non-Jews who acted according to the most noble principles of humanity and risked their lives to help Jews during the Holocaust. 2000 trees, symbolic of the renewal of life, have been planted in and around the avenue. Plaques adjacent to each tree give the names of those being honored along with their country of residence during the war. A further 19,000 names of non-Jews recognized to date by Yad Vashem as Righteous Among the Nations, are engraved on walls according to country, in the Garden of the Righteous Among the Nations.

The Memorial to the Deportees is an original cattle-car which was used to transport thousands of Jews to the death camps. Perched on the edge of an abyss facing the Jerusalem forest, the monument symbolizes both the impending horror, and the rebirth which followed the Holocaust.
—*From www.yadvashem.org. Used by permission.*

Appendix IV

Torrance of Tiberius

I was very much moved by the grave I saw in Tiberias marking the site where David Torrance and some family members are buried. Many years later, I happened to run across a web site where I uncovered more information about the man. I also was able to be in contact with his grandson, David Byrne who gave me permission to reproduce here some material found on the web site.

A book was published in 1925 about Dr. Torrance. The book is out of print, but I found a rare copy of it and now have it in my possession. His life is an inspirational example of what it means to be faithful, not only to one's God, but also to one's fellow human beings. What follows now are not my words, but the words of others, reprinted with permission.

David Torrance was a Christian medical missionary born in 1862 in Airdrie, Lanarkshire, Scotland. He opened the first "modern" hospital in Tiberias, Palestine in 1894. For the next 30 years he dedicated his life to providing medical care and spiritual guidance to the inhabitants of one of the most remote regions of the middle east at that time. He lost two wives and several children to disease in this hostile environment and died himself in 1923 in Safed, Palestine. He is buried under a granite Iona cross in the garden of his beloved hospital on the shores of the Sea of Galilee.

Though scorned and spat upon when he first arrived in Tiberias, through his faith and kindness, he earned the admiration of all. At the time of his death he was "counted by the majority ... as a *Hassid* , or saintly one."

TORRANCE OF TIBERIAS

An Appreciation

By Rev. G.A. Frank Knight, D.D.

Convener of the Jewish Mission Committee of

the United Free Church of Scotland

The brief notice that appeared in "The Glasgow Herald" on Tuesday announcing the death of Dr. David W. Torrance of Tiberias must have brought a keen shock of sorrow to the hearts of thousands in this country. But even more throughout the East, where he was universally known and beloved, multitudes of all races and languages and faiths in Palestine, Syria, Arabia, and even further afield, must have experienced a keen pang of regret when the news spread through the bazaars that the great doctor, whose name was a household word, had passed away. It is a great thing to have so laid out one's life that, when death comes, one is sincerely mourned, and thousands feel that they are the poorer, and that earth is emptier, because of the loss sustained.

"Torrance of Tiberias" was such a one. He was one of the "big" missionaries, whose careers influence multitudes, and who bring honour to the Gospel. He has done a magnificent piece of work for the Kingdom of God. He gave his life for Palestine, and Galilee today is a place enormously changed for the better through the self-sacrificing labours of this hero who passed to his rest last Sunday.

David Watt Torrance was born in Airdrie in 1862, his paternal grandfather being the Rev. Robert Torrance, the first minister of the Auld Licht congregation in that town. His mother's father was a friend of Sir Walter Scott. His own father was a surgeon of eminence in Airdrie.

When the boy was sixteen his father died, and his mother removed with her family to Glasgow. Here in 1883 David graduated in medicine, and thus Glasgow University has the honour of having trained the medical apostle of Galilee. In 1884 he was sent out to Palestine by the then Free Church of Scotland, along with the Rev. Dr. Wells, of Pollokshields, and Dr. Laidlaw, of the Glasgow Medical Mission, on a mission of inquiry. The state of matters in the cities, towns, and villages of Galilee, from a medical point of view, was so appalling that, after overcoming the temptation to accept various lucrative offers of professional service in this country, Torrance decided to give his life to alleviate the awful conditions of suffering he had seen with his own eyes in the land where Christ had laboured as a medical missionary.

The difficulties, he had to contend with were tremendous. His ignorance of the languages of the country was a trifle compared with the unsettle condition of the country; the rapacity, venality, and malevolence of the Turkish officials; the antagonism of the Talmudic Jews; the bitterness of the Moslem Arabs; the fathomless superstition and bigotry of the peasantry; the insanitary state of every town and house; the dire poverty of the people; the general backwardness of the civilization; the tropical climate of Tiberias, where the temperature rises to 117 degrees in the shade. But Torrance had made a great discovery that patience and justice, fair dealing, and the exercise of the Christian love could work miracles, and with steady perseverance and invincible faith he overcame all difficulties. Gradually he saw his dreams of social betterment taking shape. With a noble ardour he rectified the terrible insanitary conditions which surrounded him on all hands; he helped to eradicate malarial fever and dysentery; he performed marvelous cures on patients who flocked to him from all neighbouring lands; he broke down hostility, and he established a reputation as a great Christian hakim. Arabs from Central Arabia, over 30 days journey distant, would arrive on camels, having heard in the midst of the sandy deserts of the wonderful skill of the Scottish doctor. Fellahen would show the most childlike faith in his ability to do anything. "Cut out my stomach, clean it , and put it in again" asked one sufferer from dyspepsia. So widespread was his celebrity that there was scarcely a tribe on the east of Jordan but revered his name, and in that "no man's land" where the lives of travelers hang by a thread Torrance could travel freely, even as a king among men.

One of his ambitions was realised in the erection of the noble hospital overlooking the lake, which is his monument. It is impossible to say how many tens of thousands of patients have been treated here, and have gone away cured to their distant homes to tell of the Christian kindness they have received. But can anyone estimate the strain of this incessant work of 39 years in a tropical climate? Torrance was a great traveler, and he was never happier than when he was acting as an itinerant medical missionary in the villages of Galilee. Frequently in his own case the experiences of his Divine Master would be repeated--"He went preaching the Gospel of the Kingdom and healing all manner of sickness and all manner of disease among the people, and his fame went throughout all Syria, and they brought unto him all sick people, and" — as far as human skill and modern medical and surgical science could go — "he healed them." I have sailed with him on the Lake of Galilee in his mission boat The Clyde, and I have heard from his lips tales of his adventures among the wild tribes of the east of Jordan, and how medical skill opened a door and brought a welcome. But is was even more wonderful to stand in his dispensary and see him at work as, with skillful hands, he passed from one patient to another, and always with good cheer brought hope and brightness to the daily crowds of miserable sick people.

He was a great lover of righteousness, and could not take wrongdoing with indifference. His manly life and character and outspoken words and deeds did much to create a new ideal of moral rectitude in a land where social equity was unknown, and much of the advance of Galilee in Western ideals of civilization is due to him. He was a great human, a masterful personality, one who did not suffer fools gladly; but the Oriental admires a man who is not afraid, and Torrance was singularly daring and courageous. Above all, he was a missionary of Christ. He loved the Jewish race and gave his life to serve them. "Strange," he said, "we take our Sacred Books from the Jews, we worship according to their system, we got our Saviour from them, our theology is largely based on the work of a Jew, yet Christendom turns on them, imprisons them in ghettos, and then condemns them for being what they are!" Among those who have laboured to befriend the Jews, to upraise their moral level, to heal their ancient woes, and to bring them the uplift of the Christian Gospel none have toiled more faithfully than the famous Scot, "Torrance of Tiberias."

Dr. Torrance's Epitaph
by David J. Byrne

When I visited my Grandfather's grave in Tiberias in 1996 I was struck by the simple epitaph on the granite cross that read "Bear ye one another's burdens." As soon as I could, I looked up "burdens" in a biblical concordance to find and read the full scripture surrounding the words . I anticipated a verse about caring for each other or perhaps a sermon about taking care of the less fortunate. Imagine my surprise upon reading Galatians 6, 1-5; the quotation is really a riddle! It is simply the key that unlocks a scripture of far deeper meaning and significance.

Caring for the sick and the poor was David Torrance's mission, his "work" you might say. Performing this work, his mission, was the most natural thing in the world for him. As a true Christian he would never "boast" to others about that work by placing it on his tombstone as a sermon or admonition. No, he is simply stating that to do the work he did was "fulfilling the law of Christ". It is the complete chapter that surrounds this 2nd verse that is the legacy of this true Christian Missionary: 1. Be gentle and humble when you correct others faults, and look to correct your own faults first. 2. Care for one another through love as Christ did. 3. Do not think too highly of yourself for fear you may be deluded. 4. Examine your own life's work and find satisfaction in that before you look to others for praise or to find fault. 5. Carry your own load, make your life a good one so that others can look to you as a true "missionary" of Christ.

How misguided to assume the simple explanation that "Bear ye one another's burdens" was the only meaning of his life. David Watt Torrance's life was much more than that. And of course any single line of words that you would apply to his life would have a much deeper meaning. Who ever selected those words must have known him well, and knew the scriptures, because the message they left was an instruction on how to lead your life. Grandfather would not have judged the people he cared for, he considered his mission of caring a means of keeping the commandments. I am certain that he died believing that he had not done enough, but knowing that he had done his best. He certainly carried his load while "bearing the burden" of others.

Printed in the United States
138288LV00004B/2/P

9 781440 114311